AVENGERS
WEST COAST
VISIONQUEST

Writer/Penciler: John Byrne
Inker: Mike Machlan
Colorists: Paul Becton & Bob Sharen
Letterer: Bill Oakley
Cover Art: John Byrne
Cover Colors: Tom Smith
Color Reconstruction: Jerron Quality Color
Editor: Howard Mackie

GERS
COAST
nQUEST

Senior Editor, Special Projects: Jeff Youngquist
Assistant Editor: Jennifer Grünwald
Director of Sales: David Gabriel
Production: Jerron Quality Color
Book Designer: Carrie Beadle
Creative Director: Tom Marvelli

Editor in Chief: Joe Quesada
Publisher: Dan Buckley

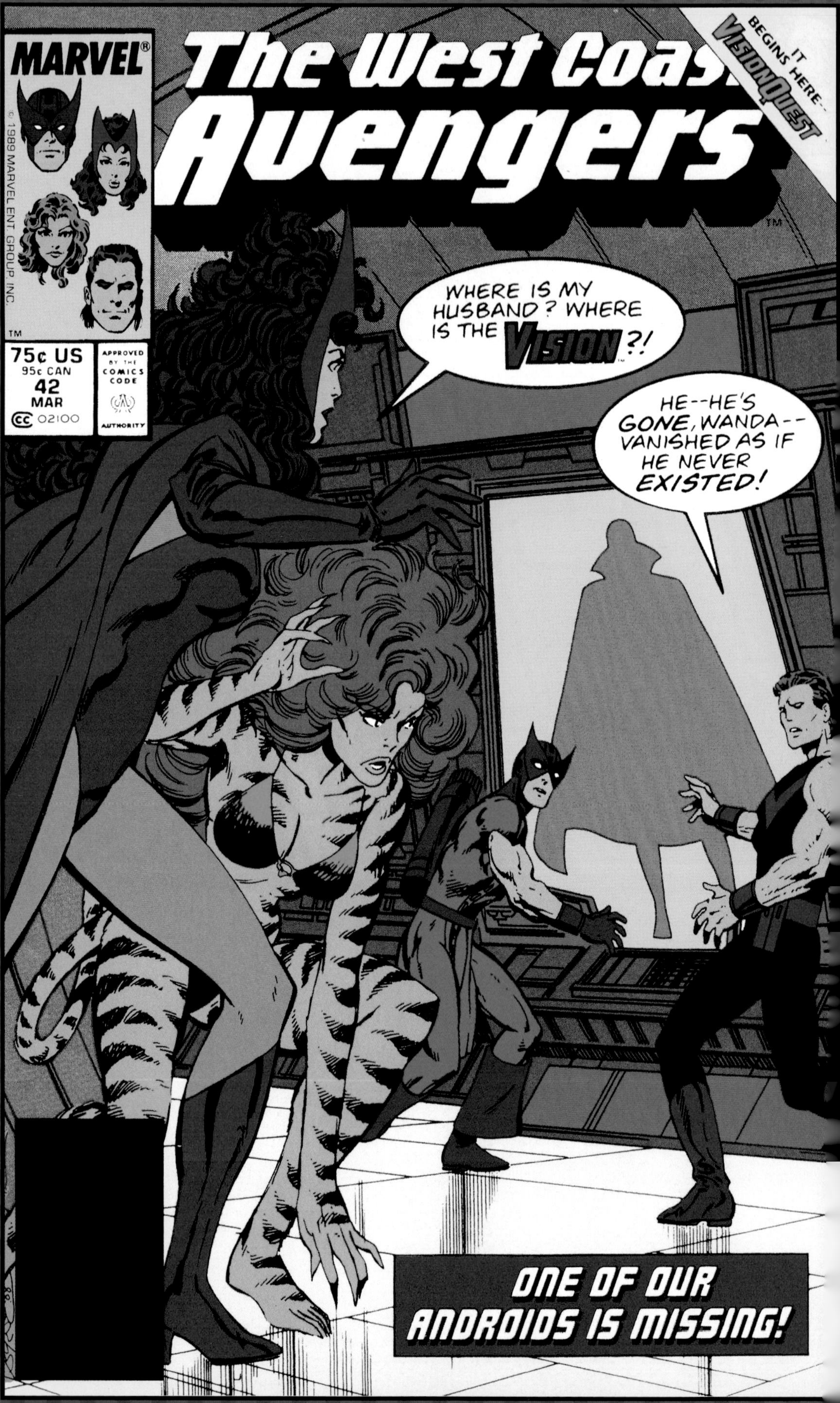
MARVEL®
The West Coast Avengers™
IT BEGINS HERE-- VISIONQUEST
© 1989 MARVEL ENT. GROUP, INC.
75¢ US
95¢ CAN
42
MAR
02100
APPROVED BY THE COMICS CODE AUTHORITY
WHERE IS MY HUSBAND? WHERE IS THE VISION?!
HE--HE'S GONE, WANDA-- VANISHED AS IF HE NEVER EXISTED!
ONE OF OUR ANDROIDS IS MISSING!

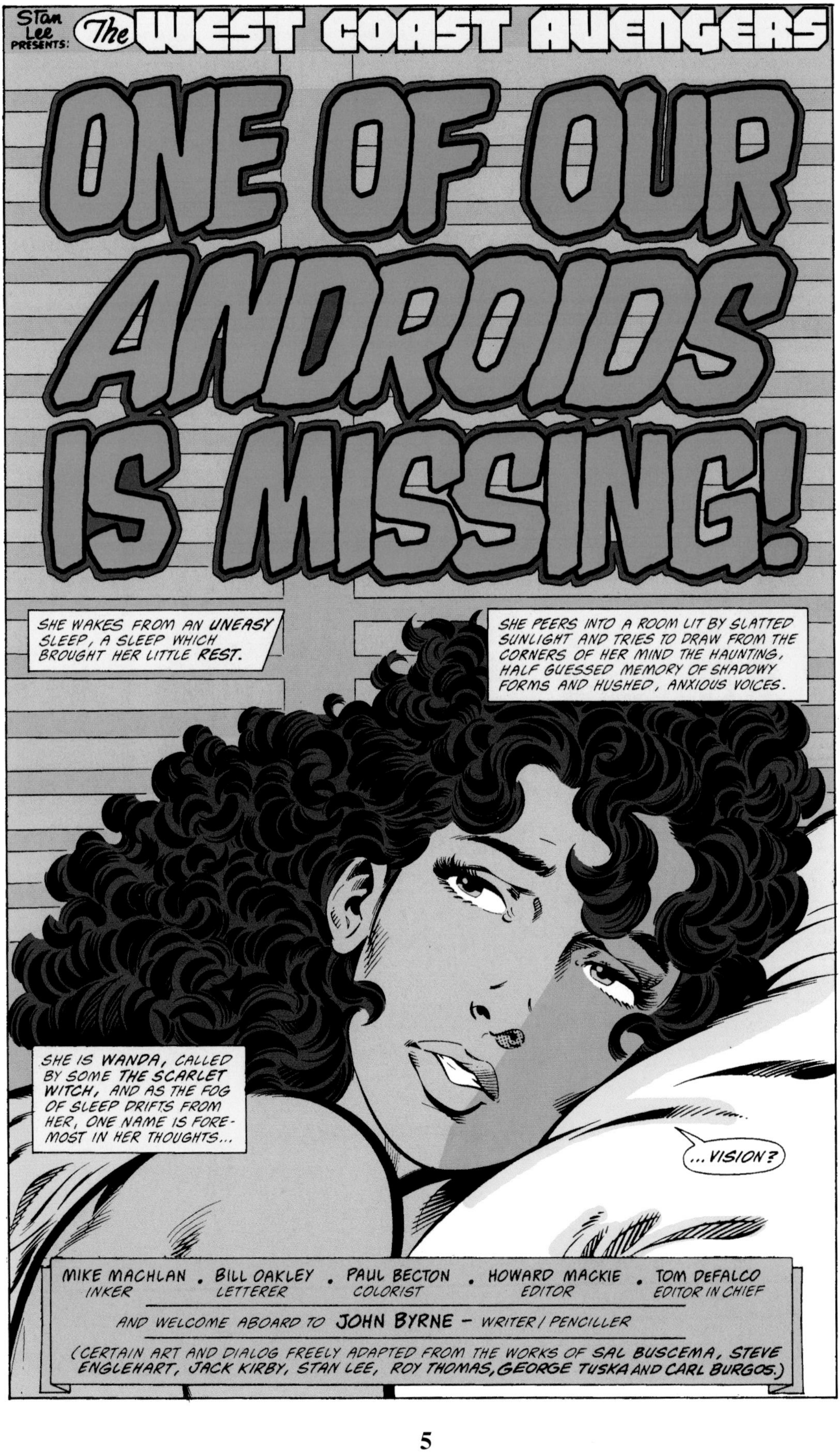
Stan Lee presents: The West Coast Avengers
ONE OF OUR ANDROIDS IS MISSING!
SHE WAKES FROM AN UNEASY SLEEP, A SLEEP WHICH BROUGHT HER LITTLE REST.
SHE PEERS INTO A ROOM LIT BY SLATTED SUNLIGHT AND TRIES TO DRAW FROM THE CORNERS OF HER MIND THE HAUNTING, HALF GUESSED MEMORY OF SHADOWY FORMS AND HUSHED, ANXIOUS VOICES.
SHE IS WANDA, CALLED BY SOME THE SCARLET WITCH, AND AS THE FOG OF SLEEP DRIFTS FROM HER, ONE NAME IS FORE-MOST IN HER THOUGHTS...
...VISION?
MIKE MACHLAN INKER . BILL OAKLEY LETTERER . PAUL BECTON COLORIST . HOWARD MACKIE EDITOR . TOM DEFALCO EDITOR IN CHIEF
AND WELCOME ABOARD TO JOHN BYRNE - WRITER / PENCILLER
(CERTAIN ART AND DIALOG FREELY ADAPTED FROM THE WORKS OF SAL BUSCEMA, STEVE ENGLEHART, JACK KIRBY, STAN LEE, ROY THOMAS, GEORGE TUSKA AND CARL BURGOS.)

HER ABSENT *HUSBAND* IS A *SYNTHEZOID*, AND DOES NOT REQUIRE *SLEEP* AS WE MERE MORTALS DO.

STILL, IN THE YEARS SINCE THEIR *MARRIAGE* THESE TWO HAVE MADE A POINT OF SHARING A BED ON EACH NIGHT THAT THEIR TURBULENT *FORTUNES* HAVE ALLOWED.

TO *WANDA* THE PRESENCE OF HER HUSBAND AT HER SIDE HAS BEEN A GREAT *COMFORT* TO ONE WHO HAS KNOWN LITTLE *PEACE* IN HER LIFE.

VISION?

SHE DRESSES QUICKLY, INSTINCTIVELY DONNING THE BRIGHTLY HUED COSTUME WHICH HAS EARNED HER AT LEAST A *PART* OF HER TITLE...

WHERE CAN HE *BE?*

I DIDN'T HEAR OR FEEL HIM GETTING UP.

AS ALWAYS, SHE MOVES CAREFULLY, LEST AN INDISCRIMINATELY POINTED *FINGER* UNLEASH THE MUTANT *HEX POWER* WHICH EARNS HER THE REST OF HER TITLE.

IN THE CONVERTED SITTING ROOM OUTSIDE HER BEDROOM DOOR SHE FINDS HER *CHILDREN* STILL SAFELY ASLEEP AT THIS EARLY HOUR.

SILENT AS A DREAM SHE MOVES THROUGH THE GUEST HOUSE.

THERE IS NO *TRACE* OF THE VISION IN ANY OF THE SMALL, TIDY ROOMS.

OUTSIDE THE AIR IS COOL AGAINST HER FACE...

...THOUGH NOT AS COOL AS SHE MIGHT STILL EXPECT.

NOT FOR THE FIRST TIME *WANDA* REALIZES IT WILL BE MANY MORE MONTHS BEFORE SHE GROWS ACCUSTOMED TO THIS PLEASANT *CALIFORNIA* CLIMATE.

STILL NO SIGN OF THE VISION, BUT NOT TEN PACES FROM HER TEMPORARY HOME SHE HEARS A *FAMILIAR* SEQUENCE OF SOUNDS...

WHISSSSHT
POK!

KNOWING A FRIEND AND ALLY IS NOT FAR AWAY, THE SCARLET WITCH MOVES QUICKLY ACROSS THE SPRAWLING EXPANSE OF *AVENGERS COMPOUND.*

AND, IN THE HUGE OUTDOOR TRAINING AREA...

...FINDS *THIS* EXTRAORDINARY SIGHT.

EVEN THE LUNATIC WHIRLIGIG OF THE TRAINING MOUNT CANNOT PHASE THE MAN CALLED *HAWKEYE.*

ALMOST FASTER THAN THE HUMAN EYE CAN FOLLOW HE LOADS AND FIRES HIS GREAT BOW.

POK

AND HIS AIM IS EVERY BIT AS *UNERRING* AS HIS TITLE SUGGESTS.

BUT, STILL DISTRACTED BY THE ABSENCE OF HER HUSBAND, AS WELL AS ONCE MORE *AWESTRUCK* BY THE BOWMAN'S SKILL...

WANDA STRAYS A FEW TOO MANY PACES INTO THE TRAINING AREA...

...AND A FRAIL, DRY TWIG SOMEHOW *OVERLOOKED* BY THE AUTOMATED GROUNDSKEEPERS...

SNAP

...COMBINES WITH HER *DISTRACTION* TO FOMENT...

...POTENTIAL DISASTER!

THWIPPT

REACTING REFLEXIVELY TO THE SOUND HE TAKES TO BE ANOTHER *TARGET* SPRINGING INTO PLACE HAWKEYE LETS FLY HIS LETHAL SHAFT...

IN THIS, AS IN ALL THINGS, HIS AIM DOES NOT *FAIL* HIM.

THE ARROW SPEEDS STRAIGHT AT WANDA'S *HEART.*

INSTINCTIVELY, SHE SUMMONS HER POWER.

PROBABILITIES FLOW LIKE WATER.

THE ODDS AGAINST AN ARROW IN FLIGHT SUDDENLY LOSING *ALL* FORWARD MOMENTUM ARE ONE IN MILLIONS...

THE ODDS ARE NOW ONE IN ONE...

CLATTER!

JEEZ LOUISE, WANDA! THAT WAS *TOO* CLOSE!

WHAT THE *HECK* ARE YOU DOING OUT HERE AT THIS TIME OF MORNING?

I MIGHT ASK *YOU* THE SAME THING, *CLINT.*

ER... YEAH...

WELL, SINCE ME AN' *BOBBI* HAVE BEEN ON THE *OUTS* THERE AIN'T BEEN TOO MANY REASONS FOR LYING AROUND ALL DAY.

BUT... YOU DIDN'T ANSWER MY QUESTION. WHY ARE YOU UP AND ABOUT SO EARLY, WANJ?

I'M... LOOKING FOR THE VISION, CLINT.

HE WASN'T IN THE GUEST HOUSE WHEN I WOKE UP.

I'M... WORRIED ABOUT HIM. SOMETHING'S WRONG. I CAN FEEL IT.

WELL, FRET NO MORE, KIDDO! WE DIDN'T SPENT ELEVENTY SKILLION DOLLARS ON THE WORLD'S MOST SOPHISTICATED COMMUNICATIONS SYSTEM FOR NOTHING!

YO, VISION!

...IF YOU'RE WITHIN THE SOUND OF MY VOICE, GIVE A HOLLER!

HM?

HAWKEYE, IT'S HANK PYM.

WHAT'S UP?

HEY, 'MORNIN', DOC! LOOKS LIKE WE GOT US A WHOLE TEAM FULL OF EARLY RISERS TODAY!

WANDA'S OUT HERE LOOKING FOR THE VISION. HAVE YOU SEEN HIM?

NOT THIS MORNING, NO. I WAS JUST RUNNING A SYSTEMS CHECK ON OUR MAINFRAME COMPUTER.

I HAD A BIOSTATIC ANALYSIS RUNNING OVERNIGHT AND THE RESULT SEEMS TO BE OFF BY A FEW DECIMAL PLACES.

SO I THOUGHT I'D BETTER...

SQUAWK

CLINT...?

9

THAT WAS NO *ORDINARY* COMMUNICATIONS BLOWOUT!

SOMETHING *ZAPPED* THE TRANSPONDER AT CLINT'S END!

WANDA AND HAWKEYE ARE IN *TROUBLE!*

BLAST!

I NEVER *REALIZED* HOW *SLOW* THESE TURBO-LIFTS CAN SEEM WHEN YOU'RE IN A REAL *HURRY!*

WHY HAVEN'T THE *ALARMS* SOUNDED YET?

EVERYONE ELSE IS STILL *ASLEEP.* SHOULD I ALERT THEM *MANUALLY?*

NO...

BETTER SEE WHAT'S *HAPPENING* BEFORE I ...

NO! IT *CAN'T* BE!!

"*ULTRON!*"

CLINT! HE'S NOT *STOPPING!*

HE'S *NEUTRALIZED* MY *HEX* POWER!

TELL ME ABOUT IT, *BABE!*

I MIGHT AS WELL BE FIRING *TOOTHPICKS* AT THAT *ADAMANTIUM* SHELL OF HIS!

MEANWHILE...

THE JUNGLE IS LIKE *NONE* ON EARTH.

THE COILING PLANTS ARE SOFT AND SLEEK, THEIR FLESH LIKE THE FLESH OF *MAN*.

THE BREEZES THAT TOUCH THE FLANKS OF THE BIG CAT ARE LIKE *HANDS* CARESSING HER FUR.

THE SCENTS THAT RIDE THEM ARE INSIDIOUS, INTOXICATING.

BUT SHE IS NOT DETERRED. UNERRINGLY, SHE STALKS HER PREY.

THE BUCK IS QUITE UNAWARE OF HER APPROACH...

...UNTIL SHE STRIKES!

THE ATTACK IS RUTHLESS...

MERCILESS...

AND THE KILLING MADE ALL THE MORE *TERRIBLE* SINCE IT COMES *NOT* FROM A NEED FOR FOOD...

IT IS FOR SPORT...

FOR FUN...

BUT IT IS ONLY A *DREAM...*

OH-HHH *WOW!*

THAT WAS... *TOO INTENSE, TOO REAL!*

I CAN STILL FEEL THE *BLOODLUST* BOILING IN MY VEINS.

STILL *TASTE* THE FLESH OF THAT ALIEN CREATURE...

SHE IS *TIGRA.*

SHE IS *TROUBLED...*

AND THAT'S NOT THE *FIRST* TIME.

THAT *DREAM'S* BEEN *BUILDING,* GROWING RICHER IN DETAIL, IN *TEXTURE* FOR WEEKS NOW...

I WONDER...

IS IT *TIME* I TOLD THE *OTHERS?* ASKED THEM FOR...

BOOM.

WHAT IN THE NAME OF...??

WASP! WHAT THE HECK WAS THAT NOISE??

SHE'S FLYING FROM THE DIRECTION OF HANK'S BUNGALOW...

I THOUGHT SHE WAS STAYING IN THE BIG HOUSE...

I DON'T KNOW WHAT IT WAS, GREER.

IT CAME FROM THE DIRECTION OF THE TRAINING AREA.

AND IF ALL THAT SMOKE RISING OVER THE TREES IS ANY INDICATION...

...I'D SAY WE'VE GOT OURSELVES A MESS OF TROUBLE, JAN!

UNLESS THIS IS SOMEBODY'S FUNNY IDEA OF A WAKE-UP CALL...

SIMON!

YOU CAN FLY FASTER THAN ME! GET UP AHEAD AND RECONNOITER!

JUST WHAT I WAS GOING TO DO, WASP!

HMM... SEEMS LIKE MS. VAN DYNE ISN'T ENTIRELY USED TO THE IDEA THAT SHE'S NO LONGER AVENGERS CHAIRMAN...

SHE BARKED OUT THAT COMMAND LIKE SHE WAS CAPTAIN AMERICA!

OHHH, BROTHER!

13

ULTRON! I WAS REALLY HOPING WE'D SEEN THE *LAST* OF HIM!

OKAY, CHROME-DOME, I DON'T KNOW WHAT YOUR GAME IS *THIS TIME*...

...BUT IT STOPS *HERE!*

FOOL! HAVE YOU SO SOON *FORGOTTEN* MY POWER?

HERE IS A *REMINDER!*

UNGH!!

SOME KIND OF *MAGNETIC FIELD BLAST...*

DON'T RECALL ULTRON HAVING ANYTHING LIKE *THAT* BEFORE.

HE MUST'VE *UPGRADED* HIS ARSENAL.

GOOD MOVE, BLINKIE. BUT WHILE WE'RE ON THE SUBJECT OF FOLKS *FORGETTING* THINGS...

...SEEMS LIKE *YOU* MUST'VE DROPPED A FEW *BYTES* ALONG THE WAY.

OR HAVE YOU FOR-GOTTEN WHY THEY CALL ME...

WONDER MAN!

SIMON WILLIAMS'S NEARLY INDE-STRUCTABLE FISTS STRIKE THE ROBOT'S STERLING HIDE LIKE THE *CLAPPERS* OF A GREAT BELL...

WHONG

THE SOUND THAT REVER-BERATES ACROSS THE CALIFORNIA HILLS HAS THE OMINOUS TONES OF A *DEATH KNELL!*

WAY TO GO, WONDY!

WE'LL SHOW THIS WALKING SCRAP PILE HE'S MESSED WITH THE WRONG HEROES!

BRAVE SENTIMENTS, CLINT... BUT DON'T BE BETRAYED BY OVER-CONFIDENCE!

REMEMBER, ULTRON HAD US ON THE ROPES BEFORE SIMON ARRIVED.

AND THERE'S STILL A CHANCE OF HIM TURNING THE TABLES ON US AGAIN!

BUT EVEN AS HENRY PYM SPEAKS THESE DARK WORDS...

THE VISION MISSING...

...NOW, ULTRON...

THE SCARLET WITCH FINDS HER THOUGHTS TRAVELING WITH THE SPEED OF LIGHT...

...BACK ACROSS THE GREAT ABYSS OF TIME AND SPACE...

HALF A CENTURY BACK, TO AN EVENT SET IN THE LABORA-TORY OF PHINEAS HORTON...

AN EVENT WITH ALL THE EARMARKS OF LEGEND!

YOUR ANDROID LOOKS AS HUMAN AS ANY OF US, PROFESSOR!

WHY DO YOU KEEP HIM IN THAT GLASS CAGE?

A MISCALCULATION IN HIS CREATION...

OBSERVE WHAT HAPPENS WHEN I INTRO-DUCE A SMALL AMOUNT OF OXYGEN INTO THE CYLINDER...

GREAT GUNS!! HE'S BURST INTO FLAME!!

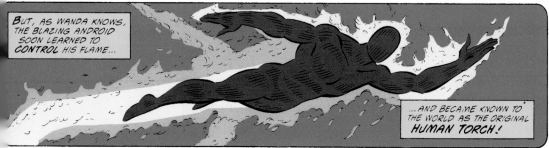

BUT, AS WANDA KNOWS, THE BLAZING ANDROID SOON LEARNED TO CONTROL HIS FLAME...

...AND BECAME KNOWN TO THE WORLD AS THE ORIGINAL HUMAN TORCH!

FOR A BRIEF HANDFUL OF TURBULENT YEARS HE SERVED ALONGSIDE THE GREATEST **HEROES** OF HIS AGE.

WITH HIS FLAMING SIDEKICK, TORO, HE FOUGHT THE AXIS HORDES AS ONE OF THE **INVADERS**.

BUT, NEARLY A DECADE AFTER HIS TIME OF GLORY, THERE CAME A DAY WHEN HIS UNSTABLE CHEMISTRY BEGAN TO **CATCH UP** WITH HIM.

HIS FLAME BEGAN TO BURN OUT OF HIS CONTROL.

TO PROTECT THE WORLD HE HAD CHAMPIONED, HE FLED TO THE FAR DESERT...

...AND THERE ATTEMPTED TO **EXHAUST** HIS POWER IN ONE LAST SUNBURST OF HUMAN FLAME!

INSENSATE, HE PLUNGED TO THE HARD EMBRACE OF THE WAITING DESERT FLOOR.

WHAT FOLLOWED WAS A DREAMLESS TIME OF **DARKNESS**.

NO THOUGHT DIS-TURBED HIS ARTIFICIAL INTELLECT.

NO EMOTIONS STIRRED HIS MAN-MADE **HEART**.

UNTIL ONE DAY THE **DARKNESS** FELL AWAY...

...AND HE LOOKED INTO **THIS** FACE...

I AM *THE* THINKER!

I AM *YOUR* MASTER!

AND THE HUMAN TORCH **FLARED** ONCE MORE!

BUT THE WORLD HAD *CHANGED* WHILE THE TORCH SLEPT.

NOW THERE WAS *ANOTHER* WHO BORE HIS TITLE, A *FOE* OF THE VILLAINOUS THINKER.

HIS MEMORIES NOT YET FULLY RESTORED, THE TORCH OF THE 1940'S FOUND HIMSELF IN *BATTLE* WITH HIS YOUTHFUL COUNTERPART.

THE BATTLE DID NOT LAST LONG. THE TORCH LEARNED THE EVIL NATURE OF HIS "MASTER."

ALLIED THEN WITH THE FAR-FAMED *FANTASTIC FOUR*, HE RETURNED TO *CONFRONT* THE THINKER...

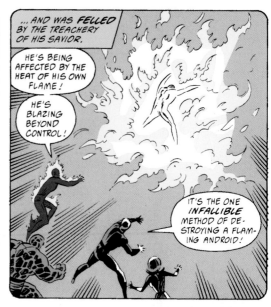

...AND WAS *FELLED* BY THE TREACHERY OF HIS SAVIOR.

HE'S BEING AFFECTED BY THE HEAT OF HIS OWN FLAME!

HE'S BLAZING BEYOND CONTROL!

IT'S THE ONE *INFALLIBLE* METHOD OF DESTROYING A FLAMING ANDROID!

THE THINKER USED THE TORCH'S DEFEAT TO MAKE GOOD HIS OWN *ESCAPE*.

HEY, *REED*, ARE WE GONNA JUST *LEAVE* HIM HERE?

SHOULDN'T HE GET A *BURIAL* OR SOMETHING?

"DUST TO DUST" DOESN'T *APPLY* TO HIM, OLD FRIEND.

HE WAS *BORN* IN A LAB, SO THIS IS A MORE FITTING FINAL RESTING PLACE.

AND SO HE LAY, UNCHANGING, AS OUTSIDE HIS SILENT TOMB THE WEEKS AND MONTHS MARCHED BY...

...UNTIL...

HE IS *HERE!* JUST AS THE THINKER *SAID* HE WOULD BE!

MEMORIES OF ULTRON-5 BRING WANDA'S THOUGHTS FULL CIRCLE...

...TO FIND THAT THE BATTLE HAS *PROGRESSED* WHILE HER MIND TRAVELED THROUGH YEARS GONE BY...

...CAN'T GET A CLEAR *SHOT* WITH THE WASP SO CLOSE!

JAN, FALL BACK! YOU CAN'T *HURT* HIM!

MAYBE NOT, HANK...

...BUT MY *WASP'S STING* CAN KEEP HIM *OFF GUARD...*

...LONG ENOUGH FOR SIMON TO GET IN ANOTHER GOOD HIT!

BLONG!

HANK, IT'S *WORKING!* ULTRON'S *STAGGERED!!*

IT'S WORKING ALL RIGHT, HAWKEYE! IT'S WORKING TOO WELL!

KLONG!

AND THAT GIVES ME AN *IDEA!*

WONDER MAN! OVER HERE!!

18

CAN IT *WAIT*, DOC? I'M KINDA *BUSY* JUST AT THE MOMENT...

I CAN SEE THAT, SIMON!

BUT I'VE GOT A WAY TO *END* THIS FIGHT *FAST!*

OH, YEAH? AND WHAT MIGHT *THAT* BE?

THIS...!

HUH...??

WHAT THE *HECK??*

DOC! YOU USED YOUR *SHRINK-ING POWER* ON ME!

WHY??

THE ANSWER WILL BE IMMEDIATELY OBVIOUS IN ABOUT *TWELVE SECONDS*, SIMON...

...RIGHT AFTER YOU FLY *STRAIGHT DOWN* ULTRON'S *THROAT!*

WHAT??

BUT I COULD GET *TRAPPED* INSIDE HIS *INDE-STRUCTABLE* CASING!

NO YOU WON'T, WONDER MAN.

NOW, PLEASE, JUST *DO IT!*

WELL... *OKAY...*

BUT IF I END UP AS PART OF SOME *PRINTED CIRCUIT...*

...I'M GONNA BE REAL *PEEVED!*

STEELING HIMSELF AGAINST THE INFERNO HE MUST NOW FACE, WONDER MAN PLUNGES TOWARD THE ROBOT'S MAW...

...AND FINDS THE ENTRY GUARDED *NOT* BY ATOMIC FLAME...

...BUT BY A CONSIDERABLY LESS *LETHAL* DISPLAY.

T370

WHAT GIVES?

I PENETRATED THE *FURNACE* IN HIS MOUTH WITHOUT EVEN *FEELING* IT!

I MEAN... I KNOW MY SKIN IS *TOUGH*, BUT...

HOLD IT...

SOMETHING'S STARTING TO *HAPPEN*.

HANK'S *TWELVE SECONDS* MUST BE *UP*!

I'M *GROWING*...

20

HAPPENING *FAST...*

NOT TOO LONG NOW AND IT'S GOING TO BE A REAL TIGHT *SQUEEZE* IN HERE...

WHICH IS PROBABLY JUST WHAT HANK HAD IN MIND!

PERFECT, SIMON! JUST *PERFECT!*

AS SOON AS I NOTICED THE AMOUNT OF *DAMAGE* YOUR BLOWS WERE INFLICTING...

...I REALIZED THIS COULDN'T BE THE *REAL* ULTRON.

NOW I GET IT!! HIS ADAMANTIUM SHELL WOULD NEVER HAVE *DENTED!*

BUT WHY DIDN'T WE NOTICE THAT *RIGHT OFF?*

CALL IT *PRECONDITIONING.* WE WERE ALL SO BUSY FIGHTING WHAT *APPEARED* TO BE A *FAMILIAR FOE* WE ALL SAW WHAT WE *EXPECTED* TO SEE.

AFTER ALL, THIS ROBOT *LOOKED, SOUNDED,* AND *ACTED* LIKE THE GENUINE ARTICLE.

AND WE WERE JUST CAUGHT UP IN THE... WELL... BLAZE OF BATTLE?

BOY, AM I GLAD I'M ONLY *HALF AND INCH* LONG, SO YOU CAN'T SEE HOW *RED* MY FACE IS!

BUT, *WHY* WOULD ANYONE SEND A *FALSE* ULTRON AGAINST US?

21

TO *DISTRACT* US WOULD SEEM THE MOST *OBVIOUS*, WANDA.

TO KEEP US *HERE*, WHILE SOMETHING IS GOING ON *ELSE-WHERE*.

SO, IF YOU'LL FORGIVE THE RATHER *POOR* HUMOR...

AVENGERS DISASSEMBLE!

SEARCH THE COMPOUND!

BUT, AS THE *BEAUTIFUL SCARLET WITCH* BEGINS HER PART OF THE SEARCH, HER THOUGHTS TURN AGAIN TOWARD...

...*VISION*...

CAN THIS HAVE SOMETHING TO DO WITH HIS BEING *GONE*?

"AFTER WHAT HE LEARNED FROM *IMMORTUS*..."

AS *MASTER OF TIME* I CAN SHOW YOU YOUR *PAST*, VISION!

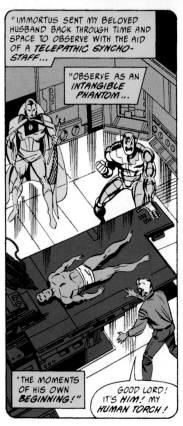

"IMMORTUS SENT MY BELOVED HUSBAND BACK THROUGH TIME AND SPACE TO OBSERVE WITH THE AID OF A *TELEPATHIC SYNCHO-STAFF*...

"OBSERVE AS AN *INTANGIBLE PHANTOM*...

"THE MOMENTS OF HIS OWN *BEGINNING*!"

GOOD LORD! IT'S *HIM!* MY *HUMAN TORCH!*

"ULTRON-5 HAD BROUGHT THE *SILENT* BODY OF THE TORCH TO A HIDDEN LAB...

"AND THEN SOUGHT OUT THE MAN WHO HAD *CREATED* HIM, SO LONG AGO..."

HE IS *MINE* NOW, HORTON! AND ONCE YOU ASSIST ME IN BRINGING HIM BACK TO LIFE...

...HE WILL BE MINE FOR ALL *ETERNITY!*

"STRANGE... WHEN THE VISION FIRST TOLD THE AVENGERS OF HIS *GENESIS*, HE SPOKE ONLY OF ULTRON-5'S INVOLVEMENT.

"YET, AS IMMORTUS REVEALED, ULTRON SIMPLY *STOOD BY* WHILE PROFESSOR HORTON DID ALL THE WORK..."

WHY DO YOU WANT A *NEW FACE* FOR HIM, ULTRON?

BECAUSE HE MUST HAVE A COMPLETELY *NEW LIFE*, DIVORCED ENTIRELY FROM HIS DAYS AS A HERO!

"UNABLE TO CHANGE THE PATTERN UNFOLDING BEFORE HIM, MY DARLING VISION *WATCHED*...

"...*WATCHED* AS THE *BRAIN PATTERNS* OF A MAN THEN BELIEVED *DEAD* WERE GRAFTED INTO HIS SYNTHETIC BRAIN..."

"I AM CERTAIN THIS *COMPUTER TAPE* I DISCOVERED AMONG HENRY PYM'S EFFECTS WILL SERVE AS A *MODEL*..."

"THEY WERE THE BRAIN PATTERNS OF SIMON WILLIAMS... *WONDER MAN!*"

"AND SO THE ANDROID WHO HAD BEEN THE HUMAN TORCH BECAME THE SYNTHEZOID SOON TO BE CALLED THE VISION."

WELCOME TO THE WORLD OF THE LIVING, YOU WHO WILL KNOW BUT A *HALF-LIFE!*

YES, MASTER.

I AM *ULTRON-5*... BUT YOU SHALL CALL ME *MASTER!*

"ONCE MORE AN INNOCENT *DUPE* OF AN EVIL FORCE, THE VISION WAS SENT TO *DESTROY* THE AVENGERS.

"AT THEIR FIRST TERRIFYING ENCOUNTER IT WAS JANET VAN DYNE WHO GAVE HIM HIS NEW *NAME.*"

NO--*NO!* IT'S SOME SORT OF UNEARTHLY, IN-HUMAN *VISION!*

"FREEING THE VISION OF ULTRON-5'S *THRALL*, THE AVENGERS ULTIMATELY MADE HIM *ONE* OF THEM."

"AND IT WAS AS AN AVENGER, MONTHS LATER, THAT I *MET* MY FUTURE HUSBAND..."

DUE TO SPACE CONSIDERATIONS, WANDA'S MEMORIES ARE NECESSARILY *COM-PRESSED* HERE, BUT ALL THE SALIENT EVENTS ARE PRESENTED AS SHE KNOWS THEM. --HARRIED HOWARD

SO MANY YEARS HAVE GONE BY SINCE ALL THAT HAPPENED... AND YET IT SEEMS LIKE ONLY *YESTERDAY.*

AND NOW THE VISION IS *GONE,* AND I *KNOW* SOMETHING IS TERRIBLY WRONG. HE WOULD NEVER HAVE LEFT ME WITHOUT...

WANDA...

HANK... WHAT IS IT? YOU LOOK...

IT'S THE VISION, WANDA. I...

YOU'VE *FOUND* HIM? WHERE IS HE? IS HE ALL RIGHT?

I THINK IT WOULD BE BETTER IF I TOLD YOU THIS *FACE TO FACE,* WANDA.

"WE'RE IN THE 'MAIN ASSEMBLY CHAMBER..."

WELL? WHAT IS IT? WHERE IS THE VISION?

HE'S... *GONE,* WANDA.

WHAT?! WHAT DO YOU MEAN, "HE'S GONE"??

I *KNOW* HE'S GONE! I THOUGHT YOU WERE GOING TO TELL ME--

HOLD IT, WANJ! YOU DON'T UNDER-STAND!

TELL HER, HANK.

WHEN I REALIZED THE FALSE ULTRON WAS PROBABLY A DIVERSIONARY TACTIC, I REMEMBERED THE *GLITCH* I'D DETECTED IN MY BIOSTATIC PROGRAM THIS MORNING.

I CAME BACK HERE AND FINISHED THE SYSTEMS CHECK.

WHAT I *FOUND* WAS WHAT I *FEARED*: SOMEONE HAS INTRODUCED A HIGHLY SOPHISTICATED *COMPUTER VIRUS* INTO OUR SYSTEM.

MY PROGRAM WAS INACCURATE BECAUSE THE VIRUS *INTERRUPTED* IT TO CHECK FOR DATA.

DATA? WHAT DATA?

THE *VISION*, WANDA.

THE VIRUS HAS *ERASED* ALL TRACE OF THE VISION FROM OUR FILES. EVERYTHING WE KNOW ABOUT HIM... EVERY REPORT HE FILED... ALL GONE.

AND THERE'S *MORE!*

I CHECKED WITH OUR EAST COAST COMPATRIOTS -- THE SAME THING IS TRUE AT THEIR END.

THE VIRUS INTRODUCED HERE HAS APPARENTLY BEEN *TRANSMITTED* INTO *EVERY COMPUTER* WE LINK WITH... WHICH INCLUDES S.H.I.E.L.D., THE PENTAGON, THE FANTASTIC FOUR...

AND IN ALL THOSE SYSTEMS ALL *TRACE* OF THE VISION HAS BEEN *OBLITERATED!*

BUT... BUT THAT'S *MAD! INSANE!*

WHO COULD *DO* SUCH A THING? AND *HOW??*

THAT'S THE *WORST* PART, WANDA.

FOR THIS TO HAVE HAPPENED MEANS SOMEBODY GOT IN THROUGH OUR DEFENSIVE NETWORK.

SOMEBODY GOT PAST ALL OUR *ALARMS*, ALL OUR *CODES*...

EVERYTHING!

AND TO DO THAT... THEY'D HAVE TO BE *ONE OF US!!*

ONE OF THE *AVENGERS* HAS TURNED *TRAITOR!*

BUT... *WHO??*

IS THAT *REALLY* SO HARD TO GUESS, HAWK?

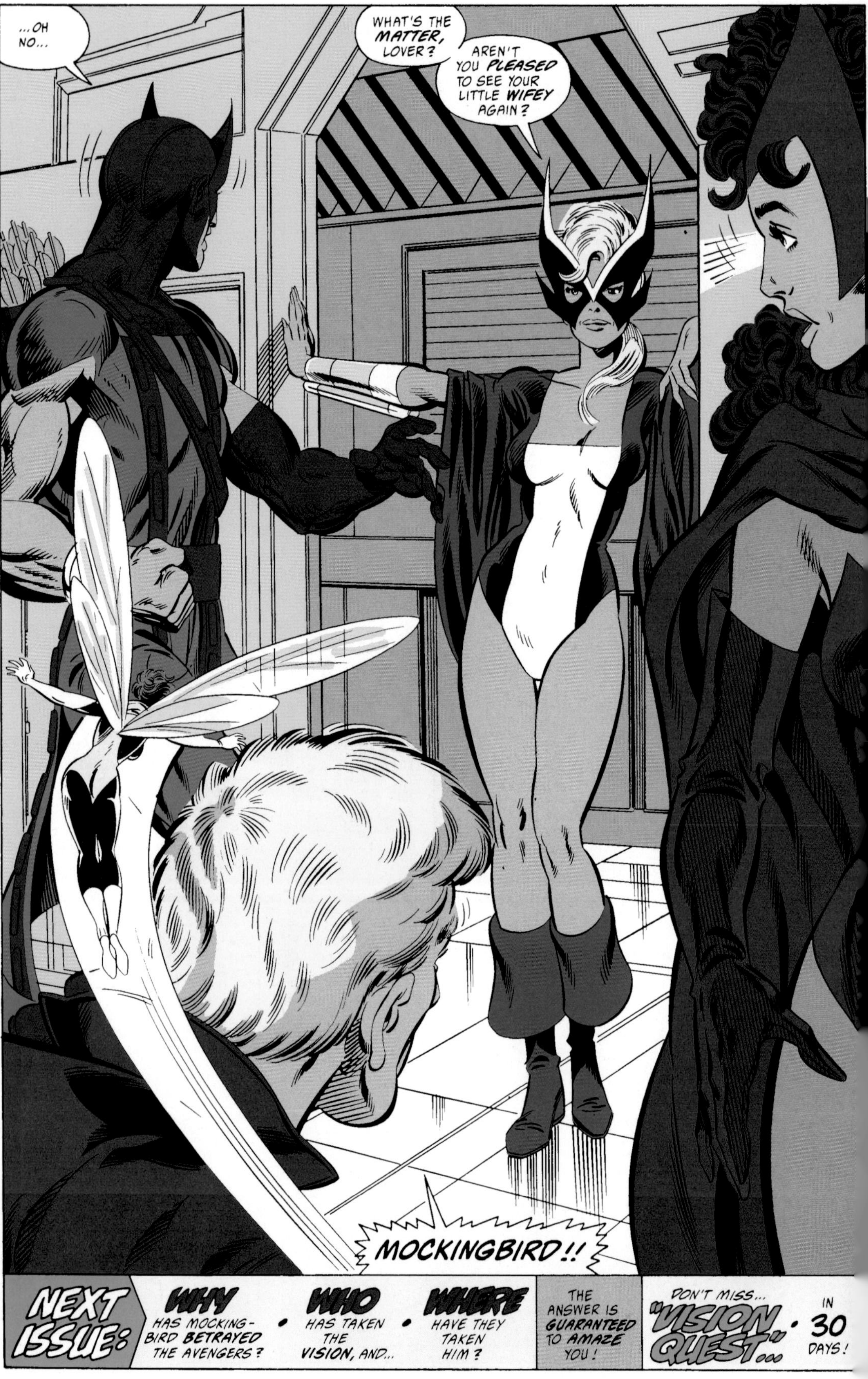
...OH NO...
WHAT'S THE MATTER, LOVER?
AREN'T YOU PLEASED TO SEE YOUR LITTLE WIFEY AGAIN?
MOCKINGBIRD!!
NEXT ISSUE:
WHY HAS MOCKING-BIRD BETRAYED THE AVENGERS?
WHO HAS TAKEN THE VISION, AND...
WHERE HAVE THEY TAKEN HIM?
THE ANSWER IS GUARANTEED TO AMAZE YOU!
DON'T MISS... "VISION QUEST"...
IN 30 DAYS!

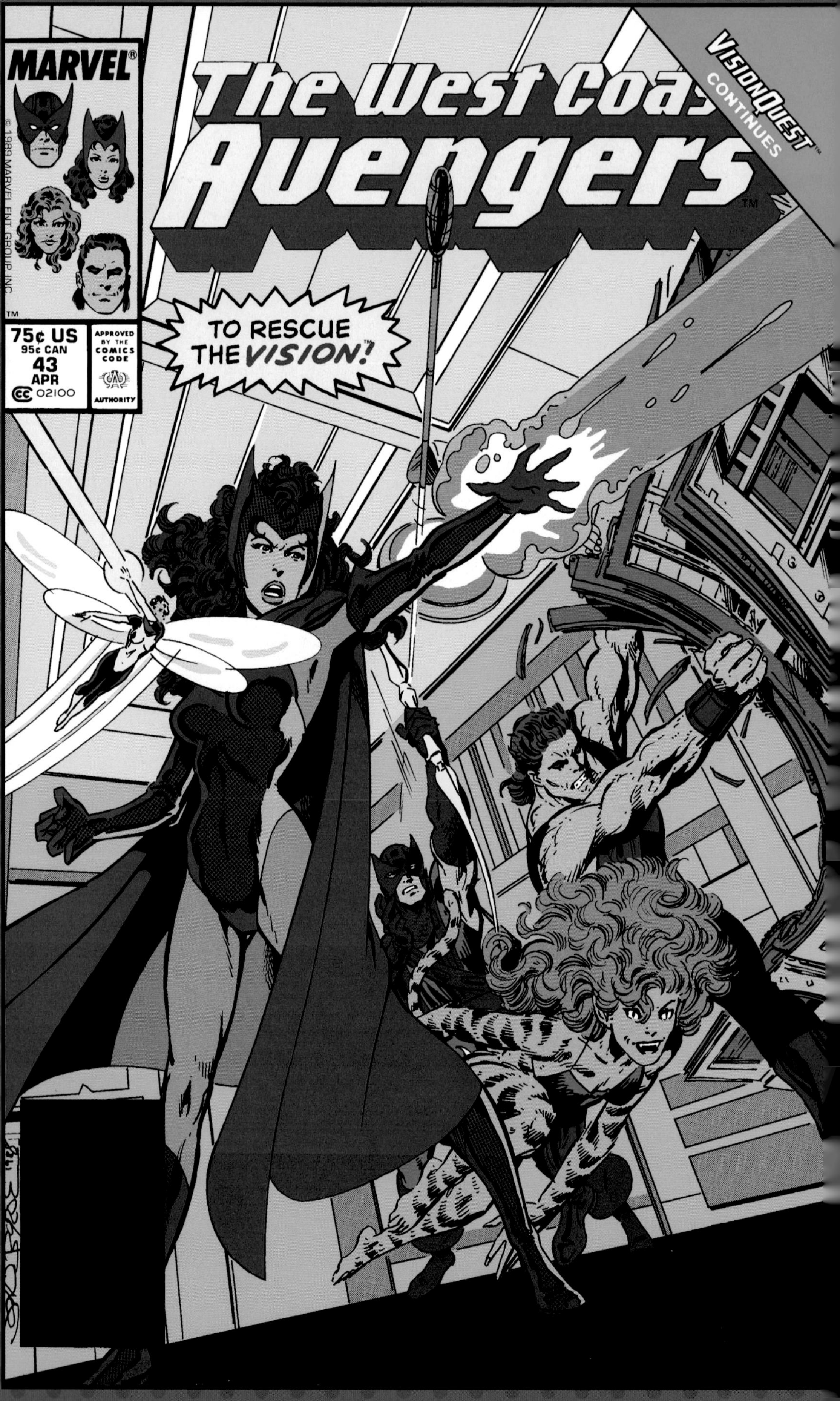

MARVEL®
© 1989 MARVEL ENT. GROUP, INC.
TM
The West Coas
Avengers™
VisionQuest CONTINUES
75¢ US
95¢ CAN
43
APR
02100
APPROVED BY THE COMICS CODE AUTHORITY
TO RESCUE THE VISION!™

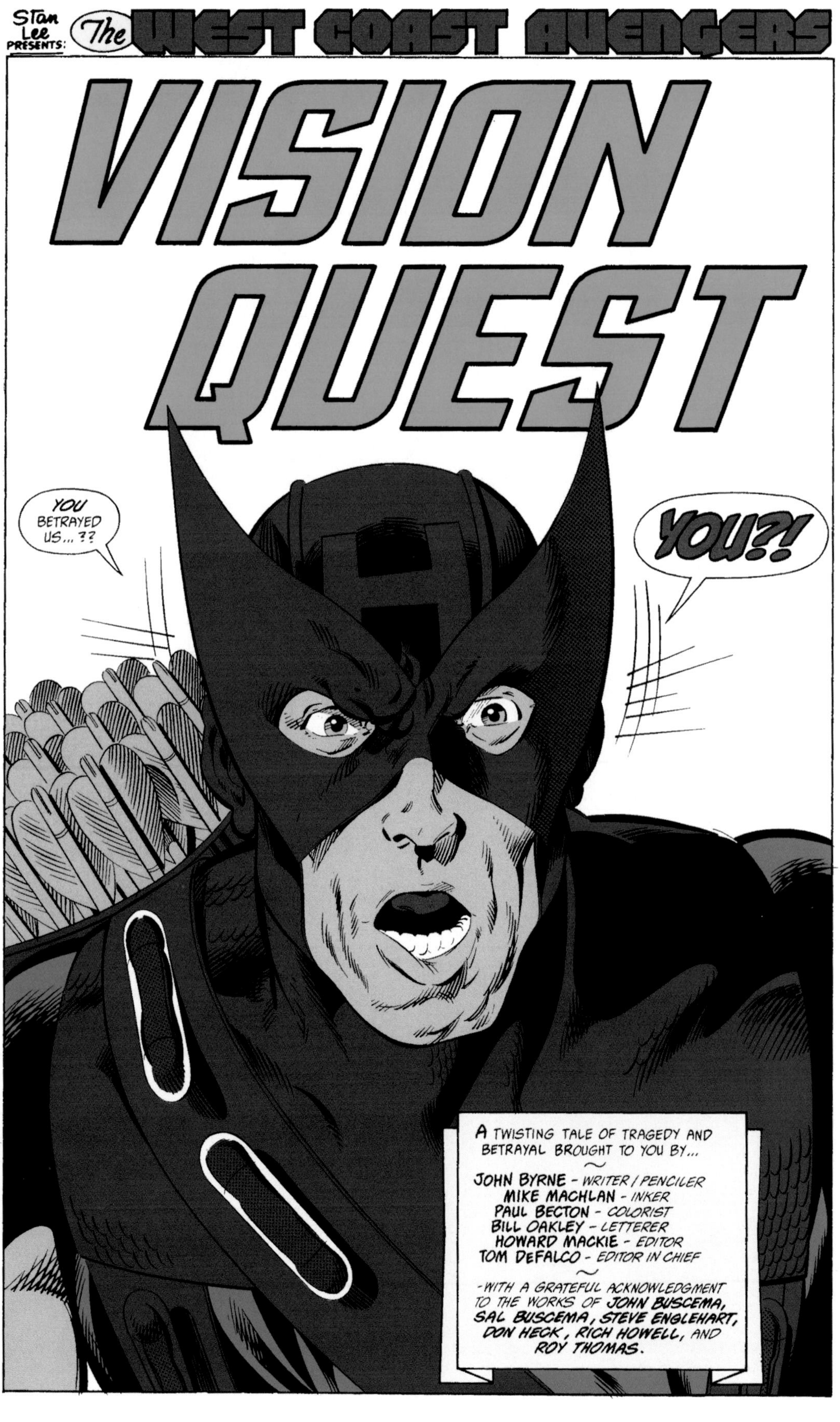
Stan Lee PRESENTS: The WEST COAST AVENGERS
VISION QUEST
YOU BETRAYED US... ??
YOU?!
A TWISTING TALE OF TRAGEDY AND BETRAYAL BROUGHT TO YOU BY...
JOHN BYRNE - WRITER / PENCILER
MIKE MACHLAN - INKER
PAUL BECTON - COLORIST
BILL OAKLEY - LETTERER
HOWARD MACKIE - EDITOR
TOM DEFALCO - EDITOR IN CHIEF
-WITH A GRATEFUL ACKNOWLEDGMENT TO THE WORKS OF JOHN BUSCEMA, SAL BUSCEMA, STEVE ENGLEHART, DON HECK, RICH HOWELL, AND ROY THOMAS.

HAWKEYE! CALM DOWN!

YEAH! THE *WASP* IS RIGHT! TAKE A COUPLE OF *DEEP BREATHS*, CLINT!

THERE'S GOTTA BE MORE TO THIS THAN THERE SEEMS...

BLOW IT OUT YOUR *EAR*, WONDER MAN.

ALL RIGHT, *MOCKING-BIRD*, WE'RE WILLING TO *LISTEN* TO WHATEVER YOU HAVE TO SAY.

WHAT'S YOUR *CONNECTION* WITH THE COMPUTER *VIRUS* THAT'S AFFECTED OUR SYSTEM...

AND WHAT DO YOU KNOW ABOUT THE *DISAPPEARANCE* OF MY *HUSBAND?*

WELL... IN ORDER, *I'M* THE ONE WHO LET IN THE COMPUTER BOYS WHO *PLANTED* THAT VIRUS, DOCTOR PYM...

AND, NUMBER TWO, I'M THE ONE WHO *CHOREO-GRAPHED* THE KIDNAPPING OF THE *VISION.*

AND... I'M SORR I DID...

WHY SHOULDN'T THIS BE *JUST* WHAT IT SEEMS? WHY *SHOULDN'T* WE JUST *ACCEPT* THE FACT THAT WE'VE BEEN *SOLD OUT...*

BY *MY WIFE!!*

THAT'S WHAT I'VE ALWAYS LIKED *BEST* ABOUT YOU, HAWK.

YOU ALWAYS LOOK FOR THE *LOGICAL* ANSWER IN EVERY SITUATION.

THE PLACE: AVENGERS COMPOUND, LOS ANGELES, CALIFORNIA.

THE TIME: *NOW!.*

RY?

SORRY??

EARING

HAWKEYE, STOP.

BOBBI -- I THINK YOU OWE US ALL SOME KIND OF *EXPLANATION.*

I... KNOW I DO, WANDA... *YOU* MOST OF ALL.

BUT THE ONLY THING I CAN *SAY* IS...

I'VE BEEN *HAD!*

"*HAD??*"

31

YES, "HAD," DARLING HUSBAND.

"AFTER YOU AND I DID OUR BIG SPLIT, I WENT OFF AND MOSTLY SAT AROUND BEING ANGRY."

"ANGRY AT YOU, ANGRY AT ME, ANGRY AT THE CIRCUMSTANCES THAT HAD BROUGHT US TOGETHER-- AND THE ONES THAT TORE US APART."

"THEN ONE DAY THERE WAS A KNOCK AT THE DOOR..."

MS. MORSE?

I'M S.H.I.E.L.D. SPECIAL OPERATIVE FRANK HAMPTON.

I'VE BEEN SENT TO CALL YOU IN.

"I KEEP TRYING TO REMEMBER IF THERE WAS ANYTHING AT THAT MOMENT THAT SHOULD HAVE MADE ME SUSPICIOUS..."

"BUT THERE WASN'T. HE LOOKED LIKE S.H.I.E.L.D., HE SOUNDED LIKE S.H.I.E.L.D. -- HECK, HE EVEN SMELLED LIKE S.H.I.E.L.D., THAT STRANGE MIXTURE OF METAL AND LEATHER AND BOTTLED AIR."

"SO I WENT WITH HIM."

"I WAS INTRODUCED TO THE HEAD OF A PROJECT THEY CALLED VIGILANCE.

"HE SAID HIS NAME WAS CAMERON BROCK, AND IN TWO WORDS HE TOLD ME WHAT THIS PROJECT WAS ALL ABOUT..."

THE VISION.

AS YOU KNOW, MS. MORSE, SOME MONTHS BACK THE VISION TAPPED INTO EVERY COMPUTER SYSTEM ON THIS PLANET AND SEIZED CONTROL OF AMERICA'S NUCLEAR ARSENAL.

HIS GOAL WAS NOTHING LESS THAN WORLD DOMINATION!

"I REMINDED HIM THAT THE VISION HAD BEEN-- WELL-- UNHINGED AT THAT TIME, AND WAS NOW FULLY RECOVERED."

WE KNOW THAT, MS. MORSE. WE ALSO KNOW THAT STEPS WERE TAKEN WHICH SUPPOSEDLY GUARANTEE SUCH A THING CANNOT HAPPEN AGAIN.

AND SO LONG AS THE VISION SEEMED CONTENT TO STAY IN NEW JERSEY, PLAYING HOUSE WITH THE SCARLET WITCH, WE HAD NO PROBLEM.

BUT THAT HAS CHANGED.

THE VISION AND HIS WIFE ARE NOW BOTH ONCE AGAIN ACTIVE AVENGERS.

AND THAT GIVES HIM ACCESS TO THE AVENGERS' COMPUTER SYSTEMS...

THAT'S WHAT *VIGILANCE* IS ALL ABOUT, *MS. MORSE.* WE ARE CHARGED WITH KEEPING A WATCHFUL *EYE* ON EVERYTHING THE VISION DOES, *EVERY DAY.*

BUT THERE'S *MORE.* THERE IS AN *ADDITIONAL* PART TO THIS PROJECT-- AND *THAT'S* WHERE *YOU* COME IN.

"'HOW'S THAT?' I ASKED."

YOU ARE IN THE *UNIQUE* POSITION OF HAVING BEEN BOTH A S.H.I.E.L.D. OPERATIVE *AND* AN AVENGER.

S.H.I.E.L.D. NOW WISHES TO MAKE *USE* OF THE KNOWLEDGE YOU HAVE *GLEANED* AS A MEMBER OF THAT TEAM TO HELP IN THE CREATION OF AN *EMERGENCY PLAN.* A PLAN TO GUARD AGAINST THE EVENTUALITY OF THE VISION ONCE MORE ATTEMPTING TO GAIN *GLOBAL MASTERY.*

WE NEED YOUR HELP TO WORK OUT ALL THE NECESSARY ELEMENTS INVOLVED IN *PENETRATING* AVENGERS COMPOUND AND *SEIZING* THE VISION.

I THOUGHT ABOUT IT FOR A WHILE...

...AND THEN I SAID, "YES."

WHAT?? JUST LIKE THAT YOU DECIDE TO HELP A BUNCH OF HALF-GASSED *JAMES BOND* GROUPIES *ATTACK* US??

WHERE THE HECK IS YOUR *LOYALTY,* LADY??

ATTACK WAS NEVER SUPPOSED TO BE PART OF THE PLAN, CLINT. THE WHOLE THING WAS SUPPOSED TO BE *THEORETICAL.* JUST A *CONTINGENCY* PLAN.

AND AS TO *LOYALTY*-- THAT HAPPENS TO BE TO MY *COUNTRY.* I DIDN'T JOIN S.H.I.E.L.D. BECAUSE I THOUGHT IT WOULD BE A FUN WAY TO KILL AN *AFTERNOON...*

I JOINED BECAUSE I *BELIEVED* IN WHAT THEY *STOOD* FOR. I *STILL* DO.

SO I *HELPED* THEM...

THEY *QUARTERED* ME RIGHT THERE. LAP OF LUXURY, REAL S.H.I.E.L.D. STYLE.

"WITH MY KNOWLEDGE OF AVENGERS COMPOUND SECURITY SYSTEMS AND CODES I WAS ABLE TO CREATE A SCENARIO IN WHICH A SMALL TEAM OF AGENTS COULD DO THE JOB WITHOUT TRIPPING ANY ALARMS."

EXCELLENT, AGENT MORSE. *EXCELLENT!*

YOU'VE DONE YOUR JOB BETTER THAN WE'D DARED *HOPED!*

"I SAID, 'THANK YOU,' BUT I REALLY WASN'T SO *SURE.*"

"SO, A COUPLE OF DAYS LATER I DECIDED TO ACCESS THE COMPUTER FILES ON MY PLANS AND SEE IF I COULDN'T DO A LITTLE *FINE TUNING.*"

"THAT'S WHEN I FOUND SOMETHING THAT HAD *NOTHING* TO DO WITH *MY* SCENARIO..."

"*ULTRON!*"

"EVERYTHING WAS THERE IN THE COMPUTER... THE PLAN TO USE A *DUPLICATE ULTRON* TO BATTLE THE AVENGERS WHILE THE COMPUTER TEAM ACCESSED THE MAIN SYSTEM AND ANOTHER SQUAD GRABBED THE VISION.

"EVEN THE VERY *NASTY* WRINKLE OF PLANTING A *POSTHYPNOTIC SUG-GESTION* IN WANDA AS SHE SLEPT, SO THAT SHE COULDN'T USE HER MUTANT *HEX POWER* AGAINST THEIR ULTRON.

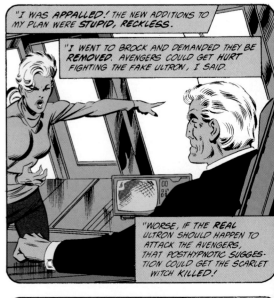

"I WAS *APPALLED!* THE NEW ADDITIONS TO MY PLAN WERE *STUPID, RECKLESS.*

"I WENT TO BROCK AND DEMANDED THEY BE *REMOVED.* AVENGERS COULD GET *HURT* FIGHTING THE FAKE ULTRON, I SAID.

"WORSE, IF THE *REAL* ULTRON SHOULD HAPPEN TO ATTACK THE AVENGERS, THAT POSTHYPNOTIC SUGGES-TION COULD GET THE SCARLET WITCH *KILLED!*

"BROCK LISTENED VERY POLITELY, AND THEN SAID..."

I'M VERY *SORRY* TO SEE YOU TAKE THIS STANCE, AGENT MORSE.

YOU'LL UNDERSTAND THAT WE CANNOT POSSIBLY ALLOW YOU TO REMAIN *AT LIBERTY* UNDER THESE CIRCUMSTANCES...

"WELL, IF *THAT* WASN'T ENOUGH TO CONVINCE ME THESE BOZOS WEREN'T *REALLY* S.H.I.E.L.D., THEIR *FIGHTING STYLE* WAS.

"THEY WERE *PATHETIC.*

"THEY WERE ALSO *TREACHEROUS.*

"I REMEMBER A SHARP PAIN IN MY *BACK*-- A SUDDEN FEELING THAT I WAS ABOUT TO *LOSE* EVERY *LUNCH* I EVER HAD...

"AND THEN *NOTHING.*

"I EXPECTED TO WAKE UP *DEAD.*

"INSTEAD, I FOUND MYSELF IN A *MAXIMUM SECUR-ITY CELL.*

"I RECOGNIZED THE *STYLE* FROM S.H.I.E.L.D. BRIEFINGS.

"IT WAS *KGB.*

KGB? YOU MEAN IT WAS THE *RUSSIANS* BEHIND ALL THIS?

IT SURE *LOOKS* THAT WAY, HANK...

BUT WHY WOULD THE R-RRRRR*OAWWR-RR!*

OH... ER... SORRY... EXCUSE ME...

WHY WOULD THE... *RUSSIANS* WANT TO GRAB THE VISION?

I'M NOT *ABSOLUTELY* SURE, OF COURSE, *TIGRA*...

BUT I'D BE *WILLING* TO *BET* THEIR REASONS WEREN'T *TOO FAR* FROM THE STORY THEY HANDED ME.

THE VISION SUCCESSFULLY TAPPED INTO VIRTUALLY *EVERY COMPUTER SYSTEM* ON EARTH. HE ACCESSED DATA SO *SENSITIVE* EVEN SOME *HEADS OF STATE* DON'T HAVE SECURITY CLEARANCE HIGH ENOUGH TO SEE WHAT HE SAW.

I'M BETTING THE RUSSIANS WANT TO MAKE CERTAIN THE VISION HAS *NO MEMORY* OF WHATEVER SOVIET SECRETS HE LEARNED.

OR... THEY MIGHT BE INTERESTED IN LEARNING WHAT *OTHER NATIONS'* SECURITY DATA HE MIGHT STILL RETAIN.

YES. IF HIS MEMORY WAS *NOT* COMPLETELY CLEARED OF THAT STUFF WHEN HE WAS RESTORED TO SANITY, HE COULD BE A REAL *TREASURE TROVE* OF SECRET INFORMATION.

BUT... WHY DIDN'T YOU COME AND TELL US ALL THIS *SOONER*, *MOCKINGBIRD*? OBVIOUSLY YOU *ESCAPED* THE BAD GUYS.

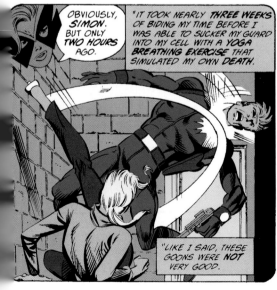

OBVIOUSLY, *SIMON*. BUT ONLY *TWO HOURS* AGO.

"IT TOOK NEARLY *THREE WEEKS* OF BIDING MY TIME BEFORE I WAS ABLE TO SUCKER MY GUARD INTO MY CELL WITH A YOGA *BREATHING EXERCISE* THAT SIMULATED MY OWN *DEATH*.

"LIKE I SAID, THESE GOONS WERE *NOT* VERY GOOD.

"I GOT OUT OF THAT INSTALLATION, CHANGED INTO MY *FIGHTING TOGS* TO BE READY FOR ACTION...

"...AND MANAGED TO ARRIVE *TOO LATE* TO BE ABLE TO DO ANYTHING TO HELP THE VISION."

35

BUT... BOBBI, I STILL DON'T UNDERSTAND YOUR *ATTITUDE* WHEN YOU ARRIVED.

IF IT WAS YOUR *INTENTION* TO *HELP* US, WHY DID YOU COME IN AS MUCH AS *ADMITTING* TO HAVING *BETRAYED* US?

I... DON'T KNOW, WANDA.

I WAS... UPSET. *EMBARRASSED.* I'D BEEN PLAYED FOR A *FOOL*...

AND WHEN I CAME IN ON ALL OF YOU -- REALIZED I WAS TOO LATE -- REALIZED IT WAS ALL *MY FAULT*...

WELL, MAYBE IT WAS SOMETHING ABOUT SEEING *HAWKEYE* AGAIN. SEEMS LIKE HE'S *ALWAYS* HAD THE POWER TO MAKE ME SAY THE WRONG THING...

LIKE, "*I DO.*"

ALL RIGHT, MOCKING-BIRD... WE CAN GET INTO THE *REASONS* FOR YOUR BEHAVIOR *LATER.*

RIGHT NOW -- IF WE TAKE THE PO-SITION OF ASSUMING YOU'RE TELLING THE *TRUTH,* THAT YOUR PRESENCE HERE IS NOT PART OF SOME *CONTINUING* PLOT -- I THINK YOU'D BETTER *SHOW* US THE LOCATION OF THIS ERSATZ S.H.I.E.L.D. INSTALLATION.

"AT THE MOMENT, *THAT* IS OUR ONLY LEAD AS TO THE CURRENT LOCATION OF THE *VISION.*"

AND SO, A FEW MINUTES LATER, A SLEEK AVENGERS *QUINJET* STREAKS FROM THE CONCEALED LAUNCH BAY IN THE CLIFF FACE BELOW THE COMPOUND.

WHILE ON BOARD...

WANDA... I... I DON'T THINK THERE ARE ENOUGH WAYS I CAN SAY HOW TRULY *SORRY* I AM THAT THIS HAS HAPPENED.

WE'VE BEEN *FRIENDS,* YOU AND I, AND NOW...

NOW I AM FORCED BY CIRCUM-STANCES TO *RE-CONSIDER* OUR FRIENDSHIP, MOCKINGBIRD.

EVEN THOUGH I *BELIEVE* YOU WHEN YOU SAY YOU WERE *DUPED* INTO ASSISTING WITH THE KID-NAPPING OF MY HUSBAND...

... THE FACT REMAINS THAT YOU WERE WILL-ING TO ASSIST IN THE FORMULATION OF THE PLAN WHICH MADE THAT KIDNAPPING *POSSIBLE.*

AND ALTHOUGH I MAY *UNDER-STAND* YOUR REASONS, THERE IS NO WAY I CAN EVER *CONDONE* THEM.

THERE IT IS!

THAT ABANDONED FACTORY COMPLEX... ACCORDING TO OUR RECORDS, IT'S *DESERTED* AND SCHEDULED FOR DEMOLITION.

AND AS SUCH, *IDEALLY* SUITED FOR THE KIND OF ACTIVITY MOCKINGBIRD DESCRIBED.

MAKE A SLOW PASS AT FIVE HUNDRED FEET, HANK.

I'LL *SHRINK* ALL THE WAY DOWN TO WASP SIZE AND SEE IF I CAN FIND A WAY IN TO *RECONNOITER.*

RIGHT, DAR-- I MEAN...

RIGHT, JAN.

HEY, DO YOU *MIND,* WASP?

IN CASE YOU'VE *FORGOTTEN,* I'M THE ONE WHO'S SUPPOSED TO BE WEST COAST *CHAIRMAN!*

I'LL DECIDE WHAT WE SHOULD DO!

ALL RIGHT, CLINT.

WHAT DO *YOU* SUGGEST?

ER...

WELL... YEAH... I GUESS IF WE MAKE A SLOW PASS AT FIVE HUNDRED FEET AN' YOU SHRINK ALL THE WAY DOWN TO WASP SIZE...

GOOD PLAN!

EVERYTHING *LOOKS* PEACEFUL. IF THE *PERPETRATORS* ARE STILL AROUND, THEY SEEM TO BE ASLEEP AT THE SWITCH.

NOT TOO SURPRISING, I GUESS. THEY PROBABLY DON'T EVEN KNOW MOCKINGBIRD IS *GONE* YET.

IF NOTHING ELSE, HER *S.H.I.E.L.D.* TRAINING WOULD HAVE ALLOWED HER TO ESCAPE *UNDETECTED.*

ESPECIALLY IF SHE TIMED HER BREAK TO FALL WELL BETWEEN CHANGES IN THE GUARDS' SHIFTS.

HMM... THIS PLACE WOULD BE WAY TOO BIG TO SEARCH ALONE EVEN AT MY FULL HUMAN SIZE.

LUCKILY, SINCE HANK RECENTLY *REACTIVATED* THE BIO-ENGINEERED ANTENNAE IN MY FOREHEAD, I DON'T *NEED* TO SEARCH *ALONE...*

THE WONDROUS WASP CONCENTRATES...

...AND ACROSS THE LENGTH AND BREADTH OF THE COMPLEX, TINY, UNNOTICED *INTRUDERS* PAUSE IN THEIR ROBOT-LIKE LABORS...

THE ANTS RESPOND IN THE STRANGE, UNSPOKEN LANGUAGE THAT OF ALL HUMANS, ONLY JANET VAN DYNE AND HENRY PYM HAVE LEARNED TO COMPREHEND.

AND, SECONDS LATER...

ACCORDING TO THE ANTS, THERE'S BEEN ALMOST *CONSTANT* ACTIVITY AROUND *THAT* BIG DOOR.

ALL RIGHT... LET'S SEE WHAT'S GOING ON *BEHIND...*

WELL, POOP! THIS THING IS SO *TIGHTLY SEALED,* NOT EVEN AN ANT-- OR A *WASP*-- COULD GET THROUGH.

UH-OH... PEOPLE COMING. DON'T WANT TO *ENGAGE* ANYONE JUST YET...

... SO I THINK I'LL HAVE A LOOK A LITTLE *DEEPER* IN THIS PLACE BEFORE I GET BACK IN TOUCH WITH THE OTHERS.

HEY... WHAT WAS THAT? A *BEE*?

IGNORE IT. THIS OLD FACTORY IS SO FULLA *BUGS*, MOST OF US DON'T EVEN *NOTICE* 'EM ANY MORE.

HMM! THEY WERE BOTH SPEAKING *ENGLISH*. AND IF THAT SECOND GUY WAS A *RUSSIAN*, SO AM *I!*

YET MOCKINGBIRD WAS CONVINCED THIS IS A *KGB* OPERATION...

AND SPEAKING OF MOCKINGBIRD... THIS LOOKS LIKE IT'S PROBABLY THE *CELL BLOCK* WHERE SHE WAS HELD.

LOOKS LIKE THEY *STILL* HAVEN'T NOTICED SHE'S GONE!

HOW'S HE *DOIN'* IN THERE?

OKAY, I GUESS. HE DON'T *COMPLAIN* MUCH, ANY-WAY.

SEEMS KINDA *ROUGH*, THOUGH, KEEPIN' AN *OLD MAN* LOCKED UP LIKE THAT.

WELL, THE *AVENGERS* FOR A *START*. LOOK, WE JUST DO WHAT WE'RE *TOLD*, RIGHT?

WHO CAN THEY BE *TALKING* ABOUT?

SINCE HE WAS *NO USE*, WOULD IT HURT TO LET HIM *GO*? WHO'S HE GONNA *TALK* TO?

THEY WANT THE OLD GEEZER HELD, WE *HOLD* 'IM.

WHO HAVE THEY GOT LOCKED UP IN THIS...

OH MY GOSH!

IT *CAN'T* BE!!

SORRY, READERS, BUT THE STARTLING REVELATION BEHIND THE WASP'S DIS-COVERY WILL HAVE TO WAIT UNTIL *NEXT ISSUE!* RIGHT NOW...

...LET'S LOOK BACK AT THE CIRCLING QUINJET...

JAN... WHAT'S TAKING YOU SO LONG? I MUST KNOW IF MY HUSBAND'S DOWN THERE.

OH, VISION! IF ONLY YOU COULD *HEAR* MY THOUGHTS! IF ONLY YOU *KNEW* HOW MY *HEART* REACHES OUT TO YOU NOW...

...WHERE A *TROUBLED* SCARLET WITCH CONTINUES A PATH OF THOUGHT BEGUN EARLIER THIS MORNING...

"...EVEN IF I DID NOT RECOGNIZE YOU AS THE ONE *FATE* HAD CHOSEN FOR ME WHEN FIRST WE MET."

FLEE, WHO-EVER YOU ARE! NO ONE CAN STOP HIM!

NO ONE!

"I WAS A *CAPTIVE* OF THE DIMENSION-SPANNING BARBARIAN KNOWN AS *ARKON*..."

SHE SPEAKS THE TRUTH, ANDROID! *BEWARE!*

"FOR MANY MONTHS, WE FOUGHT SIDE BY SIDE, AS AVENGERS, NEVER ONCE DARING TO GIVE VOICE TO THE SECRET *EMOTIONS* THAT WERE GROWING IN OUR HEARTS.

"UNTIL THERE CAME THE TIME OF THE SEARCH FOR THE *CELESTIAL MADONNA.*

"THREE WOMEN WERE CANDIDATES FOR THAT *COSMIC* ROLE...

"MOON-DRAGON...

"...MANTIS*...

"...AND *MYSELF.*

* NOTE TO NEW READERS: ANTENNAE NOTWITHSTANDING, MANTIS HAS NOTHING TO DO WITH THE WASP. -- HOWARD

"IT WAS AS THAT STRANGE ADVENTURE UNFOLDED THAT THE VISION FINALLY LEARNED THE SECRET OF HIS BEGINNINGS...

"THAT THE EVIL ROBOT KNOWN AS *ULTRON-5* HAD FORCED THE CREATOR OF THE ORIGINAL *HUMAN TORCH* TO TRANSFORM THAT FALLEN ANDROID'S SILENT BODY INTO THE VISION'S OWN!

"NOW NO LONGER A CREATURE WITHOUT A PAST, A FATHERLESS *ENIGMA,* THE VISION SPOKE AT LAST THE WORDS I HAD WAITED SO LONG TO HEAR...

...MARRY ME...

OH, *YES,* VISION! YES, YES, YES!

"EVEN THOUGH THEY WERE SPOKEN WITH THE VISION'S CHILLING *ROBOTIC* VOICE...

"...THEY WERE THE *SWEETEST* WORDS I HAD EVER HEARD!

"MY INVOLVEMENT WITH THE VISION AND HIS SEARCH FOR HIS PAST HAD MEANWHILE ABSENTED ME FROM THE QUEST FOR THE CELESTIAL MADONNA LONG ENOUGH THAT THE **CHOICE** WAS MADE WITHOUT ME."

...THIS ONE?

"THE **LIVING GHOST** OF THE **SWORDSMAN** HAD DECLARED **MANTIS** THE CELESTIAL MADONNA BECAUSE OF HER **HUMILITY** AND **PHYSICAL PERFECTION.**

"AND SO, IN A SHELTERED GARDEN IN VIET NAM, THE MAN KNOWN AS **IMMORTUS** OFFICIATED WHAT MUST SURELY HAVE BEEN THE **STRANGEST** DOUBLE WEDDING OF ALL TIME!

"LEAVING THE SWORDSMAN AND HIS NEWLY ELEVATED BRIDE TO ASCEND TO A HIGHER PLANE, WE AVENGERS RETURNED TO AMERICA, MY ADOPTED HOMELAND.

"BUT, IF THE VISION AND I EXPECTED OUR MARRIAGE TO BE ONE OF A FAIRY TALE'S HAPPINESS EVER AFTER...

"...IT DID NOT TAKE LONG FOR MY BROTHER, **PIETRO,** TO BURST **THAT** SHINING, FRAGILE BUBBLE."

YOU KNOW I HAVE NEVER **APPROVED** OF THE FEELINGS YOU HAVE SHOWN FOR THIS **MACHINE,** SISTER.

IF YOU THINK I WILL NOW **SANCTIFY** THIS **MOCKERY** OF A MARRIAGE WITH MY **BLESSINGS,** YOU ARE **SADLY** MISTAKEN!

"KNOWING THAT MUCH OF THE **HUMAN** WORLD MIGHT **SHARE** MY SIBLING'S STANCE, THE VISION AND I CHOSE TO KEEP OUR JOINING A **SECRET,** AT FIRST.

"BUT, THOUGH THIS MEANT WE COULD **SHARE** OUR GREAT JOY WITH ONLY A FEW CLOSE FRIENDS...

"...WE FOUND THAT IT LEFT THAT JOY REMARKABLY **UNDIMINISHED.**

"ALL THE MORE SO, WHEN I USED MY POWER TO **WARP PROBABILITIES...**

"...AND CAUSED MY WOMB TO BRING FORTH THE FRUITS OF AN OTHERWISE **IMPOSSIBLE** MINGLING OF **MUTANT** AND **ANDROID...**

"...OUR TWIN SONS, **WILLIAM** AND **THOMAS.**"

AND, SPEAKING OF WANDA'S CHILDREN...

WE MUST NOW LOOK AWAY FROM THE AVENGERS...

...AND TURN OUR GAZE, BRIEFLY, TO THE GUEST HOUSE BACK AT THE COMPOUND.

THERE, IN THE MAKESHIFT *NURSERY*, THE NEWLY HIRED *GOVERNESS* TENDS TO HER INFANT CHARGES...

AREN'T YOU JUST THE *PRETTIEST* LITTLE DARLINGS?

COME ALONG NOW, BOYS. YOU LET *MISS BACH* GET YOU READY FOR A NICE NEW DAY.

IT LOOKS AS IF YOUR *MOMMY* AND *DADDY* HAVE ALREADY GONE OUT.

SUCH A *LOVELY* COUPLE. BUT WHAT *DANGEROUS* LIVES THEY LEAD!

STILL, I WOULDN'T LIKE TO THINK WHAT SORT OF A WORLD THIS WOULD BE WITHOUT THE AVENGERS.

YOU'RE BOTH VERY *LUCKY* TO HAVE SUCH *WONDERFUL* PEOPLE AS YOUR PARENTS...

ALTHOUGH, I SUPPOSE YOUR *DADDY* ISN'T QUITE *PEOPLE*, IS HE?

I REMEMBER HOW *SURPRISED* I WAS WHEN WE ALL FOUND OUT THAT THE VISION AND THE SCARLET WITCH WERE *MARRIED*.

MY BROTHER-IN-LAW THOUGHT IT WAS JUST *TERRIBLE*. LIKE SOMEONE MARRYING A *BLENDER*, HE SAID.

WHY, HE EVEN SAID HE THOUGHT IN MOST STATES THE SCARLET WITCH WOULD BE *ARRESTED* AND THE VISION *IMPOUNDED*.

DID YOU EVER HEAR A MORE SILLY...

...THING...

OH, MY LORD-- *NO!!*

YEP... WE'RE GOING TO *DO IT* TO YO *AGAIN*, READER. THE FOLLOW UP T THIS SCENE IS *NEXT ISH*. RIGHT NO

42

...THE AVENGERS ARE IN A SPOT OF **BOTHER**...

THEY'RE **FIRING** ON US!!

AV370

WHAT THE **HECK** IS GOING ON?

ARE THEY **INSANE**?

FOR A RUSSIAN OPERATION TO TAKE THIS KIND OF ACTION ON AMERICAN SOIL IS TANTAMOUNT TO A DECLARATION OF **WAR**!

YOU'RE **RIGHT**, HANK!

SO, **SQUEEZE** OUT OF THE WAY, CAT-LADY...

AND AS SOON AS I **POP** THE EMERGENCY FLOOR HATCH...

...I'LL SHOW THESE COMMIE **CLOWNS** JUST HOW **DIM** A VIEW WE TAKE OF THIS KIND OF THING OVER HERE!

43

FIRST, LET'S TRY A LITTLE SPONTANEOUS *ORIGAMI* ON THIS CANNON...

CRUMP

THESE GUNS AREN'T *MANNED*-- AT LEAST NOT *HERE,* ANYWAY.

SO THE *BEST* USE I CAN BE TO THE *TROOPS* IS TO GET DOWN *INSIDE* THIS CAN OF WORMS FOR A MORE *DIRECT* ASSAULT.

WRUNCH!!

AT THAT MOMENT...

WHAT IN *BLAZES* IS GOING ON HERE? WHO *AUTHORIZED* FIRING THE *PLASMA* CANNONS?

Y-YOU *DID,* SIR.

DON'T YOU *REMEMBER?* YOU ORDERED THEM PRO-GRAMMED TO FIRE *AUTOMATICALLY* IF THE SAME AIRCRAFT MADE MORE THAN *THREE* PASSES OVER THIS INSTALLATION IN A SPECIFIED TIME FRAME...

DON'T QUOTE ME FROM REGULATIONS I WROTE, SWENSON!

THAT'S NOT JUST *ANY* AIRCRAFT! THAT'S AN AVENGERS QUINJET-- AND THE WHOLE *POINT* OF THIS *COVERT* MASQUERADE WAS TO *AVOID* DIRECTLY ENGAGING THE AVENGERS!

WELL....

...IF WE CAN'T GET *ENGAGED,* WILL WE STILL BE ABLE TO SEE EACH OTHER ON *WEEKENDS?*

WONDER MAN!!

AND OUT-SIDE...

NO USE WAITING FOR SIMON AND JAN TO COME BACK NOW.

GET READY, EVERYONE...

MOCKINGBIRD, YOU KNOW THE WAY. YOU LEAD!

I THINK THIS IS THE QUICKEST...

RIGHT.

...WAY...

QUICKEST WAY TO A COFFIN, YOU MEAN.

SAY "GOOD NIGHT," GRACIE.

MOCKINGBIRD IS LESS THAN A HEARTBEAT FROM DEATH....

BUT THAT IS MORE THAN ENOUGH TIME FOR THE SCARLET WITCH TO ACT!

WANDA UNLEASHES ONLY A TINY PART OF HER MUTANT HEX POWER...

...AND THE TEN MILLION TO ONE ODDS AGAINST EVERY BULLET IN A MACHINE GUN'S CLIP TURNING OUT TO BE A DUD...

...BECOME ONE TO ONE ODDS...

WHAT IN THE NAME OF...??

TOK TOK TOK TOK TOK TOK

LOOKS LIKE YOUR BEST LAID PLANS HAVE GANG AGLAE, PAL.

OR TO PUT IT *YOUR* WAY...

"GOOD NIGHT," GRACIE...

ONE DOWN... BUT THAT STILL LEAVES US WITH SOME *DOORS*. AND THEY MAY HAVE *CHANGED* THE EXTERIOR CODES IF THEY'VE DISCOVERED MY *ESCAPE* YET...

CAUTION

HEY, DON'T *SWEAT* IT, BIRDIE.

THIS IS FINALLY SOMETHING *I* CAN HANDLE.

TWANG

THE FAMILIAR SOUND OF HAWKEYE'S GREAT BOW SIGNALS THE RELEASE OF AN ARROW OF CURIOUS DESIGN...

PIERCING THE CORNER OF THE STEEL DOOR...

... THE ARROWHEAD DEPLOYS ITSELF...

...INSIDE THE DOOR...

...AND OUT.

SHREEE

AND...

NRRRRRNG

WHINING LIKE A DENTIST'S DRILL, THE TINY PLEX-STEEL BLADE DRAWS ITSELF ACROSS THE SEAM OF THE DOOR...

AND WHERE IT PASSES, THE DOOR PARTS...

UNTIL...

ALL RIGHT!!

NICE WORK, HAWKEYE.

BUT NOW WE'RE GOING TO NEED TO *SPLIT UP* IF WE'RE TO SEARCH THIS PLACE *EFFICIENTLY.*

WELL, *THAT WAS* FUN.

I WAS *IN CHARGE* AGAIN FOR ABOUT HALF A SECOND THERE.

MOCKINGBIRD, WAIT! SINCE YOU KNOW THIS PLACE, I WANT TO KEEP CLOSE BY YOU!

ALL RIGHT, WANDA. BUT KEEP ON YOUR TOES. WE MAY HAVE TO MOVE *FAST!*

AND SO...

HOLD IT...

THAT'S ONE OF THE TECHNO-SQUAD BOYS...

...AND HE'S JUST *VOLUNTEERED* TO TELL US WHERE YOUR *HUBBY'S* AT!

HUH ??

MOCKING-BIRD? THE SCARLET WITCH ??

WHAT... ??

HOW... ??

UH UH, JOY BOY. THAT'S TWO QUESTIONS MORE THAN YOU'RE *ENTITLED* TO.

NOW, DROP THE PHONY *BRITISH* ACCENT...

...AND TELL US WHERE YOU'VE GOT THE *VISION* STASHED!

NOT BLOODY LIKELY! YOU CAN'T MAKE ME TELL YOU *ANYTHING!*

47

DON'T TRY TO BE A *HERO*, FRIEND. REMEMBER, I'M *S.H.I.E.L.D.* TRAINED. I KNOW *FIFTY-SEVEN* WAYS TO *KILL* YOU, AND FIFTY-SIX OF THEM *HURT*.

HERE'S A SMALL *SAMPLE*...

HH URGH!!

BOBBI! KEEP OUT OF THIS, WANDA.

NOW *TALK*, YOU! WHERE IS HE?

SECTION 31! THEY'VE GOT HIM IN SEC-TION 31!

31?! THEY'RE *THAT* FAR AHEAD ON THIS?

WHAT'S THE *DAY CODE* FOR THE DOOR?

THE DAY CODE!

OSIRIS!

THE CODE IS "*OSIRIS*"...

BLAST! BLAST BLAST BLAST!!!

COME ON, *WANDA!* WE MAY ALREADY BE *TOO LATE!*

"*OSIRIS*"...?

BOBBI... YOU WOULDN'T *REALLY* HAVE KILLED THAT MAN, WOULD YOU?

LOOKS LIKE WE'LL *NEVER KNOW*, WANDA. THERE'S SECTION 31.

31

NOW...

O-S-I-R-I-S...

STARK INT

ENTER CODE
OSIR

GET READY, WANDA. THIS MAY NOT BE...

...*PRETTY...*

BOBBI... WHAT... WHAT IS THAT...??

YOU... WANTED TO FIND YOUR *HUSBAND*, WANDA...

48

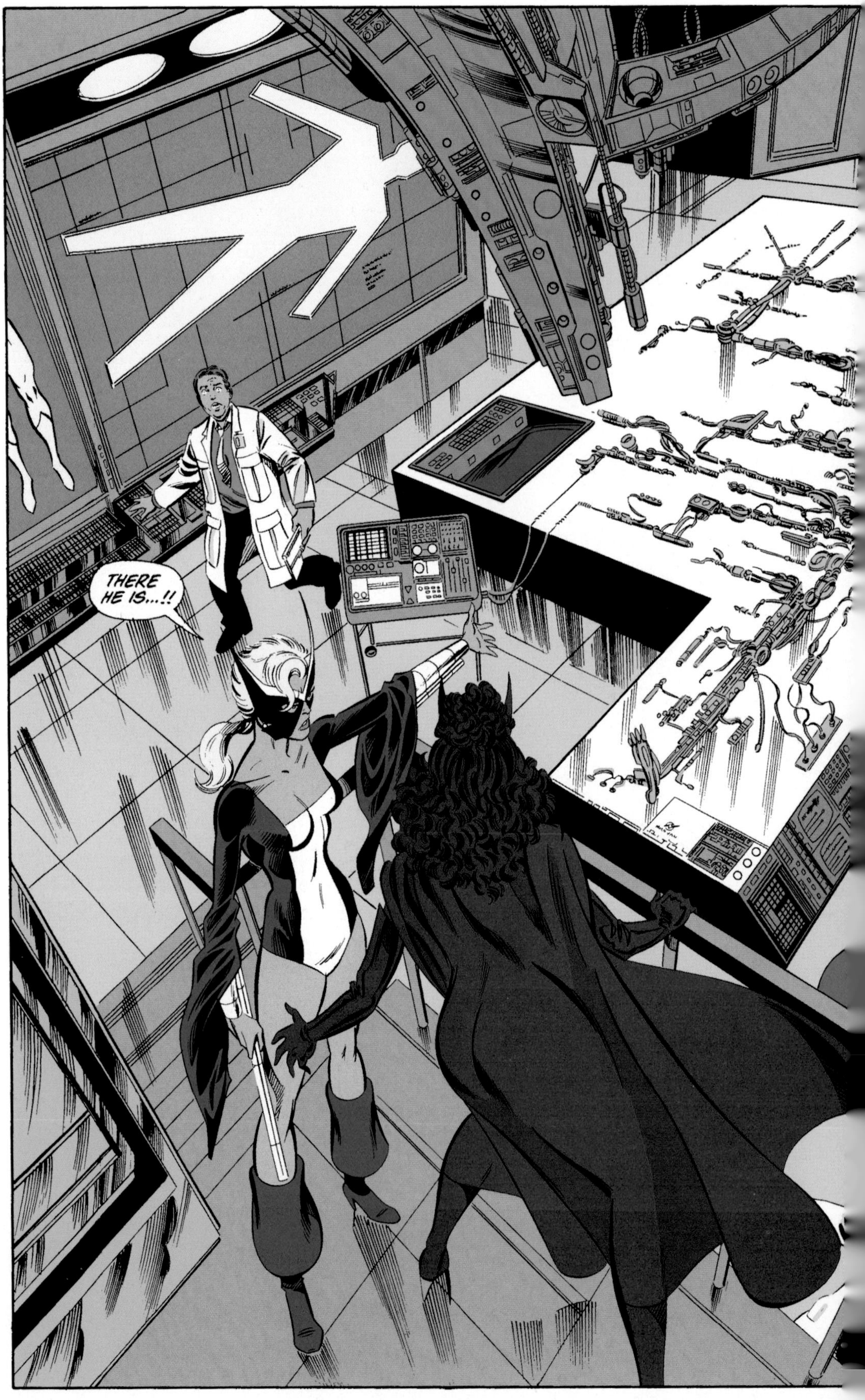
THERE HE IS...!!

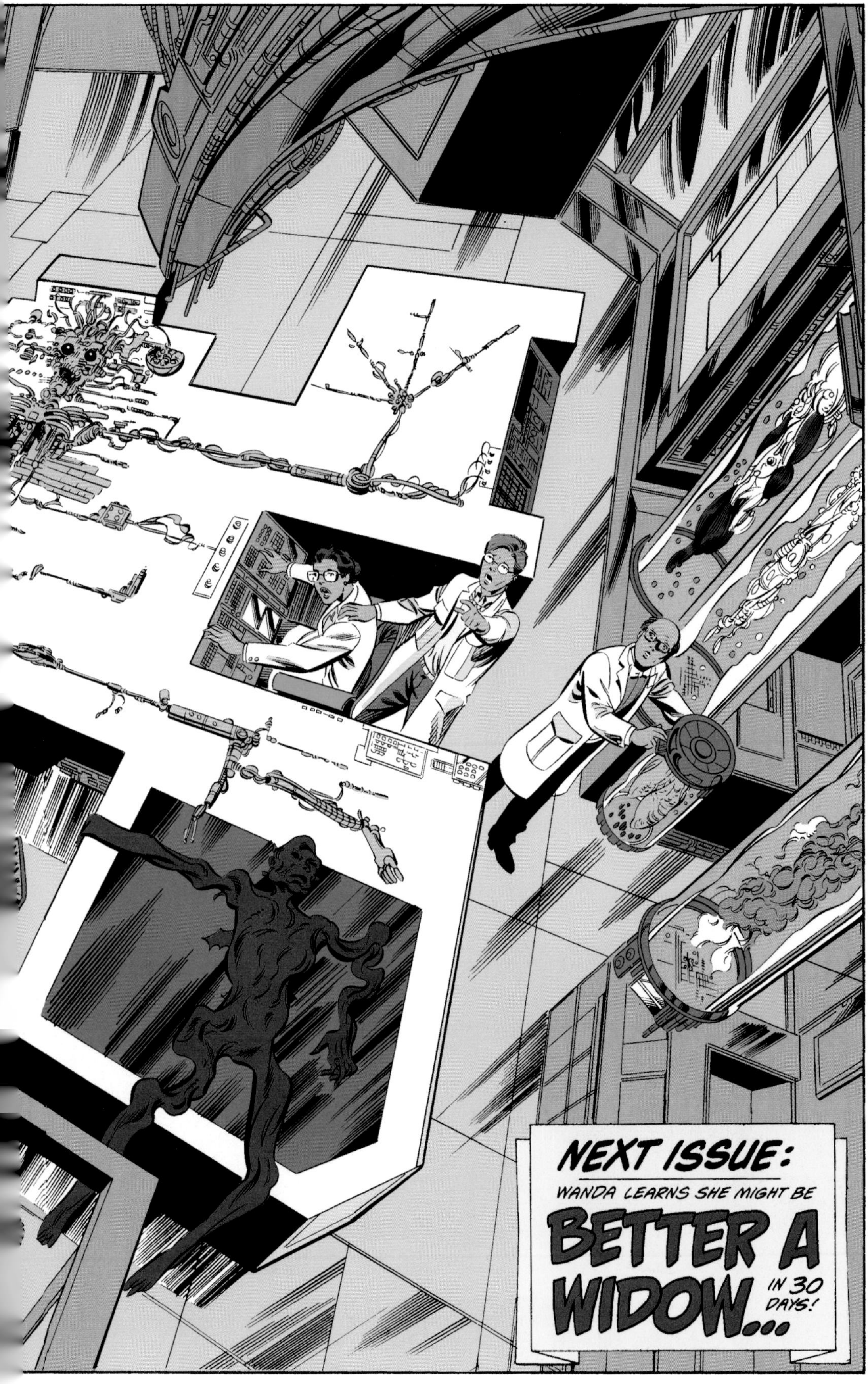
NEXT ISSUE:
WANDA LEARNS SHE MIGHT BE
BETTER A WIDOW...
IN 30 DAYS!

MARVEL®
The West Coast Avengers™
VisionQuest™ Continues
75¢ US
95¢ CAN
44
MAY
CC 02100
APPROVED BY THE COMICS CODE AUTHORITY
BETTER A WIDOW...

BETTER A WIDOW....

ONCE IT WAS A FACE.

A FACE THAT SPOKE, AND SMILED, AND SOMETIMES LAUGHED. ONCE EVEN SHED A HAPPY TEAR.

ONCE THESE EYES LOOKED OUT INTO THE WORLD WITH GENTLE COMPASSION -- AND SOMETIMES COLD STEEL RAGE.

HE WAS CALLED THE VISION.

HE IS NO LONGER AWARE OF THAT.

HE IS NO LONGER AWARE OF ANYTHING...

WRITTEN AND PENCILED DRAMATICALLY BY JOHN BYRNE | INKED ENTHUSIASTICALLY BY MIKE MACHLAN | LETTERED CALLIGRAPHICALLY BY BILL OAKLEY | COLORED MULTICHROMATICALLY BY PAUL BECTON | EDITED DIPLOMATICALLY BY HOWARD MACKIE | OBSERVED ENIGMATICALLY BY TOM DEFALCO

...LEAST OF ALL THE IDENTITY OF THE WOMAN WHO IS HIS WIFE!

V-VISION...??

VISION... NO... THAT CAN'T BE YOU! IT CAN'T!!

THAT'S THE SCARLET WITCH!

WHAT'S SHE DOING HERE...??

YES... I THOUGHT THE AVENGERS WERE GOING TO BE KEPT BUSY WHILE WE...

WHILE YOU WHAT?!?

WHAT HAVE YOU DONE TO HIM??

WANDA... THEY'VE... ERASED HIM!

E-ERASED...??

YES... AFTER ALL... THAT'S WHAT THIS WHOLE *KIDNAP SCHEME* WAS *ABOUT.* THE VISION ONCE TAPPED INTO EVERY COMPUTER SYSTEM ON EARTH-- TOOK *CONTROL* OF THEM--

--AND THE PEOPLE WHO *TRICKED* ME INTO HELPING THEM PLAN THE VISION'S KIDNAPPING SAID IT WAS ALL A *CONTINGEN-CY PLAN* IN CASE HE EVER TRIED TO DO THAT AGAIN...

IT TURNS OUT IT *WASN'T* JUST A CONTINGENCY PLAN, BUT I THINK THEIR *MOTIVE* WAS THE SAME : TO *STRIP* THE VISION OF ALL THE *DATA* HE MIGHT HAVE PICKED UP FROM THEIR SECURITY NETWORKS.

BUT... BUT, *MOCKINGBIRD,* YOU SAID THIS WAS A *KGB* OPERATION !

WHY WOULD THE *SOVIETS* ERASE THE VISION'S MEMORY BANKS ? *HANK PYM* SAID THE VISION WOULD BE MORE USE TO THEM WITH HIS MEMORY INTACT.

HE *WOULD--* IF THIS WAS REALLY A KGB JOB.

BUT IT *ISN'T.* NOT *ENTIRELY,* ANYWAY.

WONDER MAN !

WHO...?

BROCK ! THIS IS THE GUY I TOLD YOU WAS *IN CHARGE* OF THIS OPERATION, WANDA !

THAT'S RIGHT. I CAUGHT UP WITH HIM IN THE CEN-TRAL CONTROL ROOM OF THIS BOGUS *S.H.I.E.L.D.* SHOP.

OKAY, BRIGHT BOY-- *SPILL IT !* TELL *THEM* WHAT YOU TOLD *ME.*

OF COURSE.

NOW THAT WE HAVE *ACCOMPLISHED* THE *GOAL* OF THIS OPERATION, THERE IS NO *NEED* TO MAINTAIN THE SECURITY SCREEN.

THIS IS *NOT* A KGB OPERATION, AS *MOCKINGBIRD* DEDUCED.

THE KGB IS SIMPLY IN CHARGE OF OUR *DETENTION CELLS,* WHERE SHE WAS *HELD* UNTIL HER ESCAPE THIS MORNING.

SECURITY AND DETENTION *ARE* WHAT THE KGB DOES BEST, AFTER ALL.

YOU COULD SAY THAT. BUT IF YOU'RE *NOT* KGB, HOW COME YOU'RE SO *CHUMMY* WITH THEM?

WHO *ARE* YOU, BROCK?

WELL, AS A MATTER OF FACT, AGENT *MORSE*, I HAPPEN TO BE A FIELD OPERATIVE OF THE *CANADIAN SECRET SERVICE.*

CANADIAN ...?!?

AIN'T THAT A *KICK* IN THE *HEAD*? CANADIAN SPIES!

WE'LL BE HAVING TO WORRY ABOUT THE *AUSTRALIANS* NEXT! KILLER KOALAS!

SINCE YOU MENTION IT...

... MY *DEPUTY CHIEF* HAPPENS TO BE AUSTRALIAN, WONDER MAN.

YOU SEE... SCARLET WITCH, THIS OPERATION WAS A *WORLDWIDE JOINT VENTURE!*

VIRTUALLY *EVERY SECURITY NETWORK* ON *EARTH* SENT ONE OR MORE REPRESENTA- TIVES TO PROTECT THEIR INTERESTS IN THIS PROJECT.

THE AMERICAN *CIA*, BRITISH *MI-7*, THE FRENCH *DEUXIEME BUREAU*, THE RUSSIAN *KGB*... EVERYONE.

BUT... *WHY?!? WHY?!?* THE VISION WASN'T *HURTING* YOU.

HE WAS COMPLETELY *CURED* OF THE MAD- NESS THAT MADE HIM TRY TO SIEZE GLOBAL POWER!

SO YOU AVENGERS SAID. AND AS I TOLD MOCKINGBIRD, THAT WAS *ACCEPTABLE* TO US...

...PROVIDED THE VISION REMAINED *OUTSIDE* THE AVENGERS.

BUT YOU AND HE RECENTLY *RE- JOINED*, HOWEVER. AND HE *ONCE AGAIN* HAD ACCESS TO YOUR SUPER-SOPHISTICATED COMPUTERS.

AND SO WE DECIDED TO SET ASIDE OUR INDIVIDUAL DIFFERENCES -- FOR A WHILE, AT LEAST -- AND DEAL WITH *THIS* POTENTIAL PROBLEM...

...BEFORE IT *REALIZED* ITS POTENTIAL.

IRONIC, ISN'T IT? THE VISION'S INTENT, WHEN HE SIEZED CONTROL OF ALL THE COM- PUTERS, WAS TO UNITE THE NATIONS OF THE WORLD.

NOW, AT LEAST *TEMPORARILY*, HE'S *DONE* THAT.

I SUPPOSE YOU THINK THAT'S VERY *FUNNY*, MR. BROCK.

BUT YOU'RE *FORGETTING* ONE VERY IMPORTANT *DETAIL*. THE VERY THING WHICH ALLOWED YOU TO DO THIS TO THE VISION -- THE FACT THAT HE IS AN *ANDROID* -- MEANS WE CAN *RESTORE* HIM!

YOU *TOOK* HIM APART, BROCK, BUT WE CAN *PUT HIM BACK TOGETHER AGAIN!*

I'M AFRAID IT'S NOT THAT *SIMPLE*, WANDA.

56

HANK! HOW LONG HAVE YOU BEEN STANDING THERE?

LONG ENOUGH TO KNOW WE'VE GOT OURSELVES A *SERIOUS* PROBLEM HERE, *SIMON.*

BUT... BUT *WHY,* HANK?

YOU'RE AN EXPERT IN THE FIELDS OF *BIOLOGY* AND *ROBOTICS.*

YOU CAN PUT THE VISION BACK TOGETHER AGAIN, CAN'T YOU?

MAYBE.

I'M *REASONABLY* FAMILIAR WITH HIS SYSTEMS, AS WELL YOU KNOW.

I EVEN TOOK A LITTLE *STROLL* THROUGH HIS INSIDES ONCE, DURING MY *ANT MAN* DAYS.

BUT THAT'S NOT THE PART THAT *REALLY* WORRIES ME, WANDA.

WHAT WORRIES ME IS WHAT WE'LL *DO* IF HE'S *REALLY* BEEN TOTALLY *ERASED* AS MOCKING-BIRD SEEMS TO THINK.

QUITE FRANKLY, I DON'T KNOW *HOW* WE'LL DEAL WITH *THAT!*

HOW CAN THAT BE A PROBLEM? THE VISION'S BRAIN *PATTERNS* WERE COPIED FROM SIMON'S. WE ONLY HAVE TO *REPEAT* THAT PROCESS...

DON'T WE...?

I WISH IT WERE THAT *EASY,* WANDA.

BUT THAT WOULD ONLY RECREATE THE *MATRIX* ON WHICH THE VISION'S MIND WAS *FORMED.* WITHOUT THE ACCUMULATED DATA THAT COMPRISED THE VISION'S PARTICULAR MEMORY, THAT MATRIX WOULD BE LIKE A BLANK CANVAS -- AND WE HAVE NOTHING TO *PAINT* ON IT WITH!

BUT THE VISION KEPT A *BACK-UP MEMORY FILE* STORED IN THE AVENGERS' COMPUTERS! THAT WOULD ONLY BE COMPLETE UP TO THE LAST TIME HE *UPDATED* IT, BUT...

BROCK'S TEAM PLANTED A *TAPE-WORM* IN OUR COMPUTERS, WANDA, REMEMBER?

ALL PROGRAMS DEALING WITH THE VISION -- INCLUDING THAT ONE -- HAVE BEEN *EXPUNGED.* AND FROM EVERY COMPUTER SYSTEM THE AVENGERS *TIME-SHARE* WITH.

HANK,... NO ... PLEASE, TELL ME YOU'RE NOT SAYING...

I... JUST DON'T WANT YOU TO GET UP ANY FALSE *HOPES,* WANDA.

LET'S DEAL WITH PUTTING HIM *BACK TOGETHER* FIRST. I STILL HAVE NO IDEA HOW EASY THAT WILL BE. YOU KNOW THE VISION USED TO BE THE ORIGINAL *HUMAN TORCH* ...

AND EVEN THOUGH HE WAS BUILT *FIFTY YEARS* AGO, THE OLD TORCH WAS THE MOST *SOPHISTICATED* ANDROID EVER CREATED.

THAT SOUNDS LIKE A *CUE* FOR ME TO MAKE MY *DRAMATIC ENTRANCE* ...

57

JAN! AND...? SOMEONE I *FOUND* IN ONE OF THOSE KGB STYLE DETENTION CELLS, HANK.

SEE IF *YOU'RE* AS SURPRISED AS I WAS...

GREAT *SCOTT!*

HE'S FAR *OLDER* THAN ANY PHOTO I'VE EVER SEEN OF HIM... BUT I'D STILL KNOW THAT FACE ANYWHERE! *PHINEAS HORTON!*

YOU *GOT* IT, LOVER.

THE *CREATOR* OF THE ORIGINAL HUMAN TORCH!

BUT... ACCORDING TO THE VISION'S STORY OF HIS BEGINNINGS, PROFESSOR HORTON IS *DEAD!* IN FACT, HE DIED IN THE VISION'S ARMS!

THAT'S WHAT WE'D HEARD TOO, WITCH.

BUT KNOWING THE VISION WAS *SUPPOSED* TO HAVE BEEN CREATED OUT OF THE *INERT* BODY OF THE ORIGINAL HUMAN TORCH, WE THOUGHT IT MIGHT BE A GOOD IDEA IF WE FOUND SOMEBODY *FAMILIAR* WITH THE TORCH'S FUNCTIONS.

WE RAN A *GLOBAL RECORDS SEARCH,* LOOKING FOR FORMER *ASSOCIATES* OF PROFESSOR HORTON, *RELATIVES,* PEOPLE LIKE THAT...

TO OUR SURPRISE, WE FOUND THE MAN *HIMSELF,* NOT EXACTLY HALE AND CERTAINLY NOT *HEARTY,* BUT *ALIVE!*

I... SUPPOSE THE VISION COULD HAVE BEEN *MISTAKEN* ABOUT HORTON'S DEATH. IT WOULD HAVE BEEN THE FIRST HE'D EVER EXPERIENCED.

IN ANY CASE, IF YOU *ARE* THE REAL PROFESSOR HORTON, YOU'RE A *GODSEND* AT THIS MOMENT!

THAT'S WHAT *WE* THOUGHT TOO, PYM. BUT AS IT TURNS OUT, HORTON BEING ALIVE WAS ONLY *ONE* BOMBSHELL WE WERE GOING TO UNCOVER.

TELL THEM, *PROFESSOR.* TELL THEM WHAT YOU TOLD US ABOUT THE *VISION.*

I-I'M STILL SO VERY *CONFUSED* BY ALL THIS.

YOU TOLD ME THAT THIS ROBOT WAS SUPPOSED TO BE MY POOR, LOST TORCH...

BUT I HAVE *NEVER SEEN* THIS CONSTRUCT BEFORE.

THIS IS *NOT MY WORK!*

MEANWHILE...

58

OW AIN'T THIS NTERESTING?

SOME OF THIS PLACE IS *REAL*-- BUT MOST OF IT IS JUST A *MOCKUP*, LIKE A MOVIE SET.

GUESS THE FOLKS IN CHARGE DIDN'T WANT TO SPEND ANY MORE THAN WAS *NECESSARY* TO *FOOL* BOBBI AN' GET THEIR *JOB* DONE...

WHATEVER THE *HECK* THAT MIGHT HAPPEN T'BE.

SOMETHING T'DO WITH *VIZH*, BOBBI SAID. WONDER HOW THEY WERE ABLE TO PUT THE *GRAB* ON HIM IN THE...

RRRRRRR

WASSAT?

SOUNDS LIKE *TIGRA*... AND SHE *DOESN'T* SOUND TOO HAPPY!

COMIN' FROM SOMEWHERE DOWN THIS CORRIDOR.

MAYBE SHE'S GOT HERSELF IN *TROUBLE* WITH SOME OF THESE PHONY...

OL-EEEE...!

YOU'RE HAWKEYE!

HELP US!

FOR GOD'S SAKE... *STOP HER!!*

59

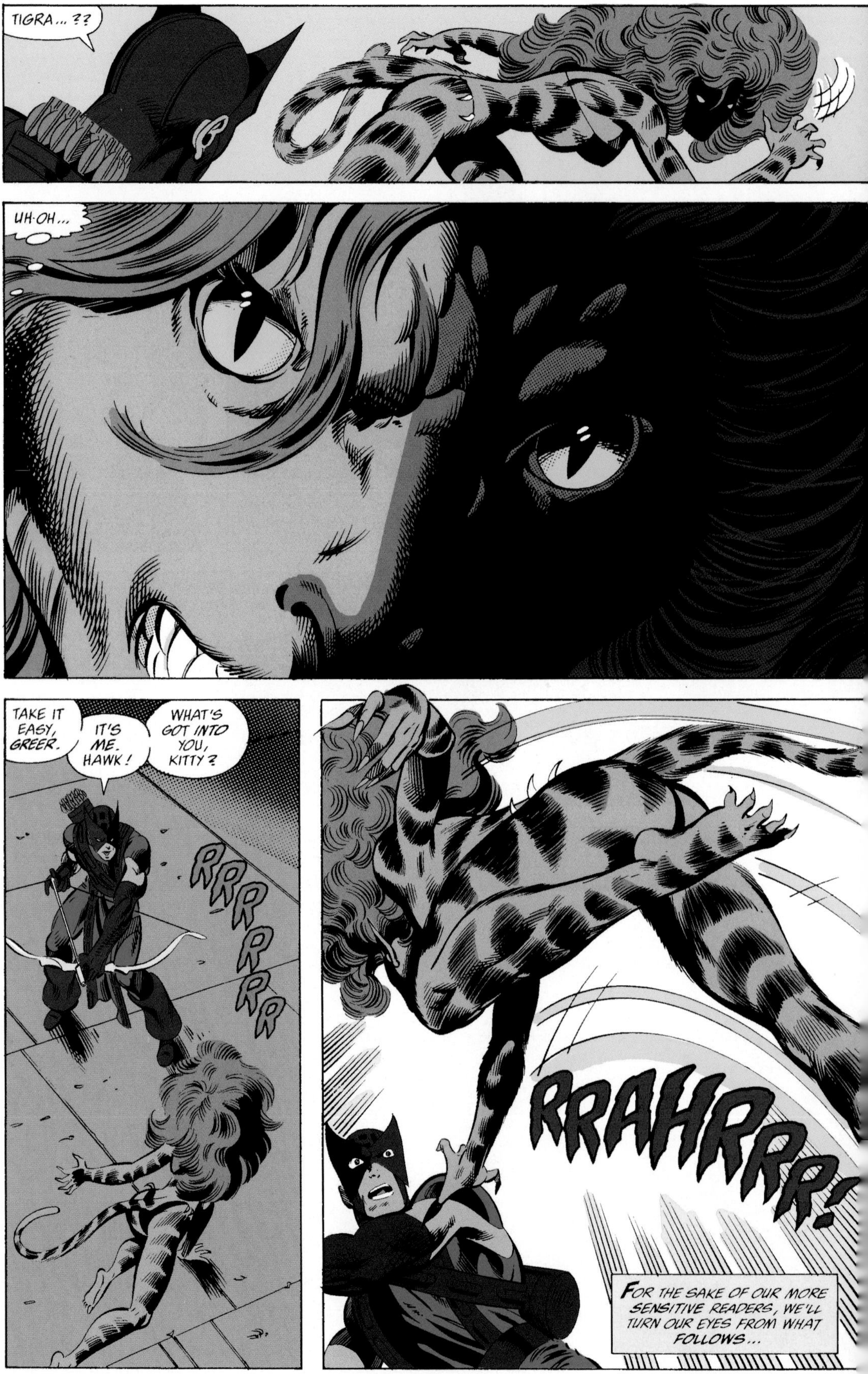

TIGRA... ??
UH·OH...
TAKE IT EASY, GREER.
IT'S ME. HAWK!
WHAT'S GOT INTO YOU, KITTY ?
RRRRRRR
RRAHRRRR!
FOR THE SAKE OF OUR MORE SENSITIVE READERS, WE'LL TURN OUR EYES FROM WHAT FOLLOWS...

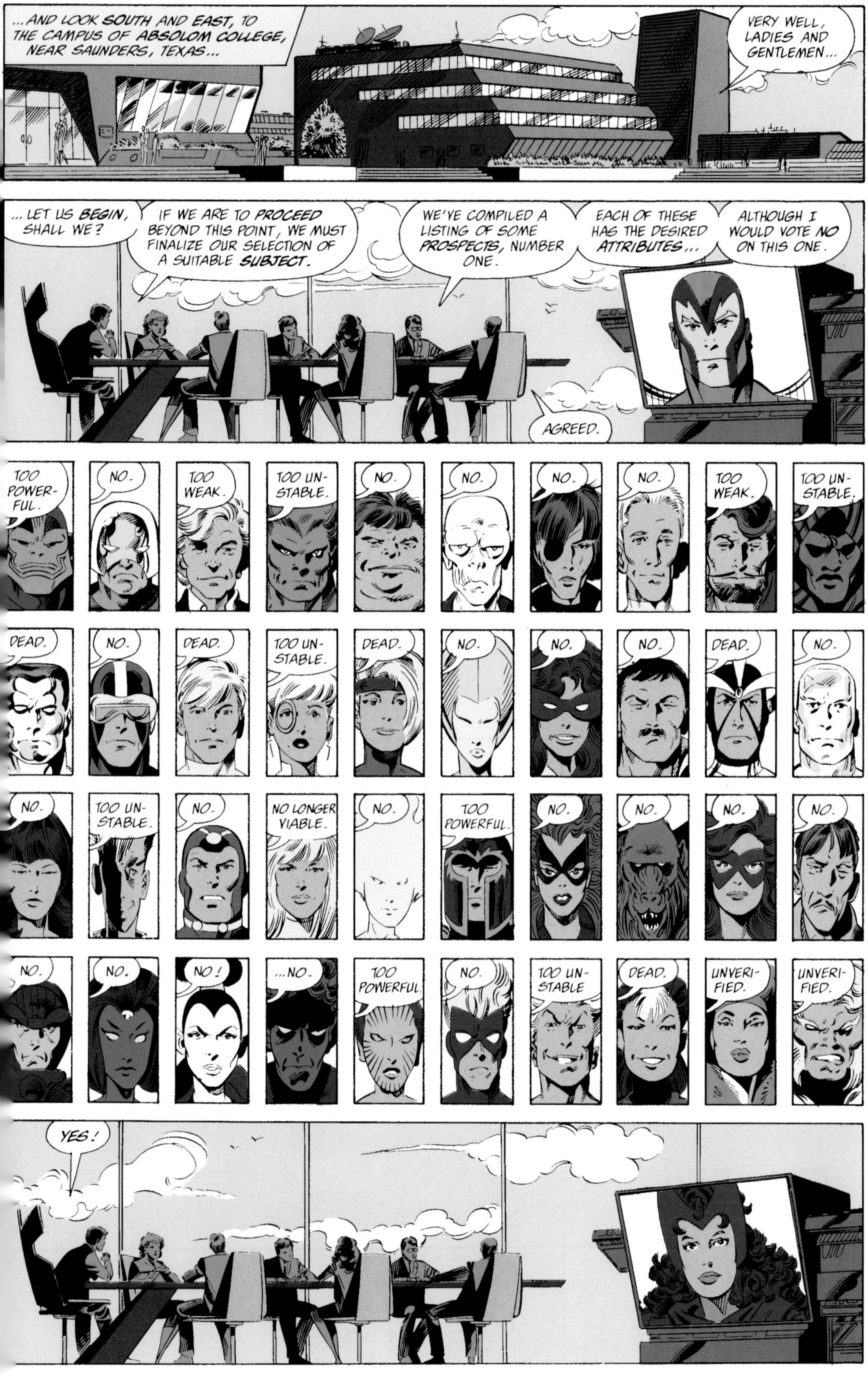
...AND LOOK SOUTH AND EAST, TO THE CAMPUS OF ABSOLOM COLLEGE, NEAR SAUNDERS, TEXAS...
VERY WELL, LADIES AND GENTLEMEN...
...LET US BEGIN, SHALL WE?
IF WE ARE TO PROCEED BEYOND THIS POINT, WE MUST FINALIZE OUR SELECTION OF A SUITABLE SUBJECT.
WE'VE COMPILED A LISTING OF SOME PROSPECTS, NUMBER ONE.
EACH OF THESE HAS THE DESIRED ATTRIBUTES...
ALTHOUGH I WOULD VOTE NO ON THIS ONE.
AGREED.
TOO POWER-FUL.
NO.
TOO WEAK.
TOO UN-STABLE.
NO.
NO.
NO.
NO.
TOO WEAK.
TOO UN-STABLE.
DEAD.
NO.
DEAD.
TOO UN-STABLE.
DEAD.
NO.
NO.
NO.
DEAD.
NO.
NO.
TOO UN-STABLE.
NO.
NO LONGER VIABLE.
NO.
TOO POWERFUL.
NO.
NO.
NO.
NO.
NO.
NO.
NO!
...NO.
TOO POWERFUL.
NO.
TOO UN-STABLE
DEAD.
UNVERI-FIED.
UNVERI-FIED.
YES!

BACK IN L.A., ONE HOUR LATER...

DON'T **WORRY**, WANDA. THEY'LL TAKE **GOOD CARE** OF PROFESSOR HORTON.

IF THAT IS **TRULY** WHO HE IS.

HANK... IF HE IS REALLY HORTON, WHY WOULD HE SAY THE VISION WAS NOT "HIS WORK?"

WHY WOULD HE **LIE** LIKE THAT?

I DON'T KNOW, WANDA. UNLESS, SOMEHOW, IT'S **NOT**...

DOCTOR PYM... YOU SEEM TO BE **IN CHARGE** OF ALL THIS... WHAT DO YOU WANT US TO **DO** WITH THESE GUYS YOU CAPTURED?

I'M AFRAID THERE'S NOT A **WHOLE LOT** YOU **CAN** DO, OFFICER. I'M SURE YOU'LL FIND THIS OPERATION HAS GOVERNMENT APPROVAL.

AND EVEN IF IT **DOESN'T**, DOUBTLESS MR. BROCK AND THE REST OF THESE FOREIGN NATIONALS WOULD CLAIM DIPLOMATIC IMMUNITY.

VERY ASTUTE, DOCTOR PYM.

THEN... THERE'S **NOTHING** WE CAN DO, HANK? THEY **KIDNAP** ONE OF US...

DISASSEMBLE HIM...

AND WE GET TO STAND AROUND WITH **EGG** ON OUR FACES... BUT AT LEAST WE CAN REGISTER A **COMPLAINT** WITH AGENT SIKORSKY, OUR GOVERNMENT **LIAISON**...

FOR ALL THE GOOD **THAT** WILL DO!

HAWKEYE... TIGRA...

ARE YOU ALL RIGHT?

WE WERE BEGINNING TO **WONDER** WHERE YOU'D BOTH GOT TO.

WE'RE **FINE**, DOC. MISS KITTY HERE GOT A LITTLE **CARRIED AWAY**...

BUT SHE'S **OKAY** NOW.

THANKS, CLINT...

THEN WE'D BETTER GET ON BACK TO THE **COMPOUND** AND SEE WHAT CAN BE **DONE** ABOUT THE VISION.

WANDA, ARE YOU...?

I WILL BE RIGHT **WITH** YOU, HANK.

AS SOON AS I AM **DONE** HERE...

AROUND THE MUTANT FORM OF THE SCARLET WITCH, REALITY ITSELF BEGINS TO SHIFT AND FLOW.

AND...

TO CALCULATE THE ODDS AGAINST EVERY BIT OF BUILDING MATERIAL IN A STRUCTURE -- EVERY BOARD AND NAIL, EVERY BEAM AND RIVET...

...EVERY PANE OF GLASS, EVERY HINGE, STAPLE, SPOT OF GLUE...

...ALL REACHING THEIR POINT OF MAXIMUM FATIGUE AT PRECISELY THE SAME MOMENT...

...TO CALCULATE THE ODDS AGAINST THIS WOULD REQUIRE THE MANIPULATION OF NUMBERS SO HUGE, THERE IS NOT A COMPUTER ON EARTH UP TO THE TASK.

WANDA DOES NOT KNOW THIS. HER KNOWLEDGE OF SCIENCE HAS BEEN BUT LITTLE ENHANCED SINCE THE VILLAINOUS MAGNETO BROUGHT HER OUT OF HER BALKAN HOME.

SHE KNOWS ONLY THAT SHE WISHES THIS TERRIBLE PLACE EXPUNGED...

DEAD.

AND THE BUILDING DIES!

THUS, LESS THAN TEN MINUTES LATER...

NEWLY INSTALLED HOLOGRAPHIC IMAGING DEVICES TURN OFF AUTOMATICALLY AT THE APPROACH OF THE AVENGERS' QUINJET, REVEALING THE CLIFF-FACE HANGAR DOOR...

I STILL DO NOT UNDER-STAND WHY WE COULD NOT DO *MORE* ABOUT THIS, HANK.

I CAN *SYMPATHIZE* WITH YOUR FEELINGS, WANDA...

...BUT THIS IS ONE OF THOSE RARE OCCASIONS WHERE EVEN THE *AVENGERS* ARE *HELPLESS*.

THIS ATTACK ON YOUR HUSBAND WAS *APPROVED* BY VIRTUALLY EVERY GOVERNMENT ON EARTH, INCLUDING OUR OWN.

THE BEST WE CAN HOPE NOW IS TO *RESTORE* WHAT WE CAN OF THE VISION.

HOW CAN THEY HAVE *DONE* THIS, HANK? AFTER ALL THE TIMES THE VISION HAS *FOUGHT* FOR THEM -- RISKED HIS *LIFE* FOR THEM!

WELL, "LIFE" IS EXACTLY THE *ISSUE*, I GUESS, WANDA. AS FAR AS THESE PEOPLE ARE CONCERNED, THE VISION IS JUST A *MACHINE*, NOT TRULY ALIVE.

AND TECHNICALLY... *CAREFUL*, SIMON! THOSE CANISTERS CONTAIN THE VISION'S *PSEUDO-ORGANIC* PARTS.

THOSE CANNOT BE *DUPLICATED*!

DON'T WORRY, DOC. I WON'T...

SAY...! WHAT'S THAT *LIGHT*...?

THAT'S THE *INTERNAL DISTRESS SIGNAL* FROM THE GUEST HOUSE.

SOMEBODY THERE MUST HAVE PUSHED THE *PANIC BUTTON*!

PANIC BUTTON...??

MISS BACH!

THOMAS!

WILLIAM!

MY BABIES!!

NO! NO! NO! THOSE MON-STERS CAN'T HAVE COME FOR MY CHILDREN TOO?!?

FAR OUTSTRIPPING THE OTHERS, THE *BEAUTIFUL SCARLET WITCH* RACES THROUGH THE CONNECTING TUN-NELS BENEATH THE AVENGERS' WEST COAST COMPOUND...

...PROPELLED BY IMAGES SO *HORRIBLE*, ONLY A MOTHER COULD COMPREHEND THEM!

FIFTY-THREE SECONDS AFTER FIRST SEEING THE ALARM LIGHT, WANDA EMERGES IN THE GUEST HOUSE...

MISS BACH!

HELEN!

WHAT IS IT? WHAT'S HAPPENED?

OH! OH, MISS WANDA...!

TOMMY... BILLY...

I WAS GIVING THEM THEIR MORNING BATH... I ONLY LOOKED AWAY FOR A SECOND...

AND WHEN I LOOKED BACK THEY WERE GONE!

THEY WERE JUST... GONE!!

GONE?!?

THOMAS!

WILLIAM!

OH, MY BABIES! MY BABIES!

YOU'RE ALL RIGHT!

YOU'RE HERE!

BUT... BUT THEY WERE GONE! I SEARCHED EVERYWHERE!!

EASY, MISS BACH, EASY.

WANDA! WHAT'S GOING ON HERE??

I THINK THAT IS FOR MISS BACH TO EXPLAIN, JANET.

APPARENTLY WHEN I INTERVIEWED HER FOR THIS POSITION, I SHOULD HAVE ASKED IF SHE HAD A SICK SENSE OF HUMOR!

65

YOU MAY *PACK* YOUR THINGS AND *LEAVE*, MISS BACH.

YOUR "SERVICES" ARE NO LONGER *REQUIRED*.

BUT...

BUT...

OH... MS. VAN DYNE... *YOU'VE* GOT TO LISTEN TO ME! YOU'VE GOT TO *BELIEVE* ME! THOSE BABIES WERE *GONE*! VAN-ISHED WITHOUT A *TRACE*!

SHE *SOUNDS* LIKE SHE REALLY *MEANS* IT... AND YET FROM WHAT I *SAW* OF THEM, WILLIAM AND THOMAS DIDN'T SEEM AT ALL AFFECTED BY THIS...

CALM DOWN, MISS BACH.

I'M AFRAID THIS IS QUITE OUT OF MY HANDS. I'M NO LONGER AVENGERS CHAIRMAN...

AND EVEN IF I *WERE*, I COULDN'T DO ANYTHING MORE THAN OFFER *ADVICE* IN THE SCARLET WITCH'S *PRIVATE* LIFE.

I'LL MAKE SURE YOU GET THE PROPER *SEV-ERANCE PAY*, THOUGH.

TH-THANK YOU...

TWO DAYS LATER, OUTSIDE THE AVENGERS' MED-LAB...

WANDA...?

DON'T YOU THINK YOU SHOULD GET SOME *SLEEP*?

OH... SIMON. I DIDN'T HEAR YOU COME IN.

WHAT *TIME* IS IT?

NEARLY *THREE* A.M.

I TAKE IT HANK'S STILL WORKING ON REASSEMBLING THE VISION?

YES.

APPARENTLY IT'S NOT AS *HARD* AS HE FEARED IT MIGHT BE. HANK SAYS IT'S RATHER LIKE ASSEM-BLING A *JIGSAW PUZZLE*. EACH PIECE HAS ONLY *ONE PLACE* IT CAN PROPERLY GO.

UNFORTUNATELY, THERE ARE LITERALLY *HUNDREDS OF THOUSANDS* OF PIECES, AND NO GUIDE, NO "BLUEPRINT."

IF ONLY THERE WAS SOME WAY WE *COULD* HAVE CONTACTED THE *REAL* PROFESSOR HORTON.

MM... YOU STILL DON'T *BUY* THAT OLD GUY JAN FOUND AS THE GENUINE ARTICLE, THEN?

HOW CAN I, SIMON? PROFESSOR HORTON IS *DEAD.* HE DIED IN THE VISION'S ARMS, SHORTLY AFTER THE VISION WAS "BORN."

THE VISION *TOLD* US SO, WHEN HE LEARNED ALL THE DETAILS OF HIS ORIGIN.

IF THAT CENTRAL FACT WAS NOW TO BE-COME *UNTRUE...*

...EVERYTHING WE THINK WE KNOW ABOUT THE VISION WOULD BECOME EQUALLY SUSPECT.

WELL, I WASN'T AN AVENGER WHEN ALL THAT STUFF WENT DOWN.

IN FACT, I WASN'T MUCH OF *ANYTHING,* SEE-ING AS HOW I WAS IN A *REGENERATIVE STATE* THAT HAD EVERYONE THINK-ING I WAS *DEAD*-- 'INCLUDING *ME!*

BUT... YOU KNOW, WANDA, I'VE ALWAYS BEEN A BIT *BOTHERED* BY THE FACT THAT THE VISION LEARNED ALL THE MISSING DETAILS OF HIS ORIGIN FROM *IMMORTUS.*

I MEAN, HE'S PRETTY MUCH A *LYING*

WUMP

WHAT WAS *THAT?*

SOMETHING INSIDE THE LAB!

HANK *SEALED* HIMSELF IN THERE TO REDUCE THE RISK OF *CONTAMINATING* THE VISION!

HANK! HANK, CAN YOU *HEAR* ME? WHAT'S HAPPENING??

CRASH CLANG TINKLE! THUD!

SOUNDS LIKE THERE'S A *FIGHT* GOING ON IN THERE!

LOOK OUT, WANDA! IF HANK *SEALED* THE LAB, IT WILL TAKE AT LEAST *THREE MINUTES* FOR THESE AIRLOCK DOORS TO *CYCLE* AND OPEN!

BUT I CAN GET THEM APART A LOT FASTER THAN--

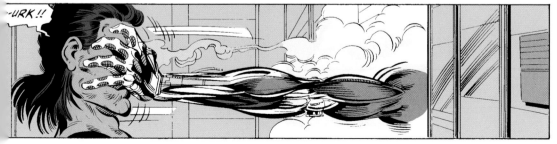

--URK!!

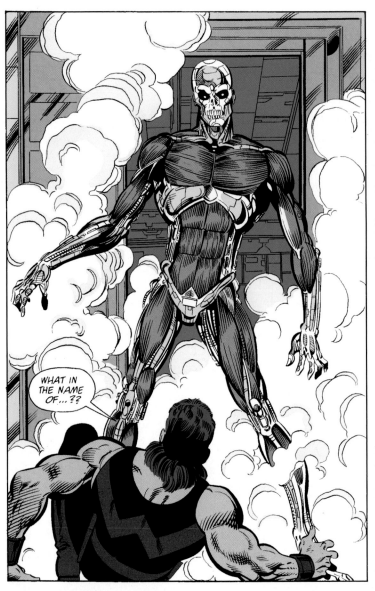

WHAT IN THE NAME OF...??

...VISION...?

THE WORD TREMBLES AND NEARLY DIES IN HER THROAT.

THE SCARLET WITCH REQUIRES NO ANSWER TO HAVE HER DREAD CONFIRMATION.

THIS IS HER HUSBAND.

KEEP BACK, WANDA! I DON'T THINK HE RECOGNIZES YOU!

NO! NO, HE MUST! VISION! VISION, SAY YOU KNOW ME...

PLEASE!

THE ONLY TRACE OF EMOTION ON THE SYNTHEZOID'S FLESHLESS FACE IS A SKULL'S SEPULCHRAL GRIN.

68

EVEN WHEN HE STRIKES!

WANDA!

OH-HHHHH!

UNABLE TO BELIEVE THE BIZARRE BEHAVIOR OF THE BEING SHE CALLS HER HUSBAND, WANDA DID NOT PROPERLY PROTECT HERSELF. SHE LIES STUNNED BY THE IMPACT WITH THE COLD, STEEL FLOOR...

AND AS IF SENSING HER HELP-LESSNESS, THE VISION MOVES FORWARD... FOR THE KILL!

OH NO YOU DON'T!

TIME YOU TOOK A NICE LONG NAP-- UNTIL WE FIGURE OUT WHAT'S WRONG WITH YOU!

BUT...

POWERFUL AS WONDER MAN IS, HE HESITATES TO USE HIS STRENGTH AGAINST ONE WHOSE SHARED MIND PATTERNS ONCE MADE HIM VERY MUCH A BROTHER...

69

MEANWHILE, DIRECTLY ABOVE THE MED-LAB, IN THE LIVING ROOM OF THE MANSION...

THAT WAS SOME KIND OF *WEIRD* MOMENT WITH TIGRA THE OTHER DAY.

IF I HADN'T MANAGED TO *SUBDUE* HER WITH A QUICK WHIFF FROM MY *GAS ARROW* SHE MIGHT'VE RIPPED MY THROAT OUT!

I'M STILL NOT SURE WHY I PROMISED HER I WOULDN'T TELL THE *OTHERS* ABOUT IT.

NOW IT SEEMS LIKE SHE'S BEEN *HIDING OUT* IN HER BUNGALOW SINCE WE GOT BACK WITH--

CLONG

HUH?

FORTY SECONDS LATER...

HOLY COW!! IS THAT THE VISION?!?

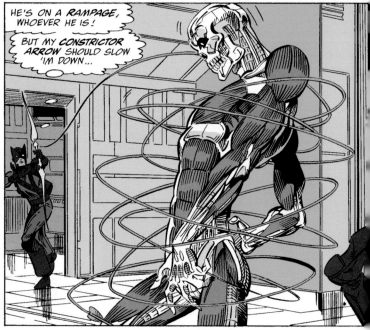

HE'S ON A *RAMPAGE,* WHOEVER HE IS!

BUT MY *CONSTRICTOR ARROW* SHOULD SLOW 'IM DOWN...

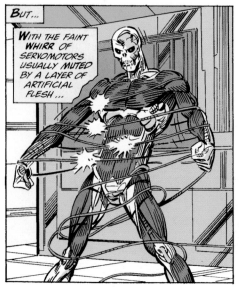

BUT...

WITH THE FAINT *WHIRR* OF SERVOMOTORS USUALLY MUTED BY A LAYER OF ARTIFICIAL FLESH...

I DON'T BELIEVE IT! HE SNAPPED THOSE STEEL CABLES·LIKE THEY WERE NOTHING!

WANDA! WANDA, YOU'VE GOT TO *DO* SOMETHING!

BRUTE FORCE ISN'T GOING TO *STOP* HIM! WE NEED YOUR POWERS!

N-NO!!

70

WHAT...?!? WANDA...!!

SIMON... I CAN'T! I CAN'T USE MY POWER AGAINST THE VISION!

H-HOOOP!!

I DON'T HAVE PRECISE ENOUGH CONTROL OVER THE EFFECTS OF MY HEXES!

WHAT IF I MAKE HIM EXPLODE?

WHAT IF I DAMAGE HIM BEYOND REPAIR?

YOU'VE GOT TO TAKE THAT CHANCE, WANDA! TRUST THAT YOUR POWER WON'T PERMANENTLY HARM SOMEONE YOU LOVE!

BUT DO IT NOW! BEFORE HE KILLS HAWKEYE --

--OR ME!

TREMBLING, EYES FILLED WITH HOT TEARS, THE SCARLET WITCH RAISES A HAND...

BUT...

NO! NO! FORGIVE ME! I CAN'T! I JUST CAN'T!!

THAT'S ALL RIGHT, WANDA...

71

HANK!

YOU DON'T HAVE TO DO ANYTHING.

I CAN HANDLE THIS!

DZZZT!

WHAT THE...??

HANK! WHAT IS THAT THING?

IT'S THE *NEUTRALIZER* BROCK'S PEOPLE USED ON THE VISION SO THEY COULD *KIDNAP* HIM IN THE *FIRST PLACE.*

I'D HAVE USED IT *SOONER,* BUT I WAS *UNCONSCIOUS!*

I'D FAILED TO *CONSIDER* WHEN I *REACTIVATED* THE VISION THAT IN HIS *MINDLESS* STATE, HIS FIRST REACTION MIGHT BE *DEFENSIVE!*

LUCKY YOU CAME TO WHEN YOU DID, DOC.

LUCK'S GOT NOTHING TO DO WITH IT, WONDY. WHAT TIME IS IT IN *WASHINGTON* RIGHT NOW?

"WE'VE GOT A *CALL* TO MAKE!"

LOOK, *SIKORSKI,* I DON'T CARE IF I WOKE YOU OUT OF YOUR *DEATH BED!*

I WANT TO KNOW WHAT YOU *PAPER-PUSHERS* ARE GONNA *DO* ABOUT THE VISION!

DO? YOU SEEM TO BE *MISSING THE POINT,* ARCHER.

WE'VE ALREADY *DONE* IT. THE VISION HAS BEEN RENDERED *HARMLESS.* HE PRESENTS NO FURTHER *THREAT* TO THE SECURITY OF THIS NATION...

...OR ANY OTHER, FOR THAT MATTER.

YOU *AVENGERS* ARE NOW AT LIBERTY TO *RE-PROGRAM* HIM TO SUIT WHATEVER FUNCTION YOU WISH.

REPROGRAM?

IT'S NOT AS *EASY* AS ALL THAT, AGENT SIKORSKI. YOUR PEOPLE DESTROYED ALL *TRACE* OF HIS FORMER PERSONALITY. FOR ALL INTENTS AND PURPOSES, HE'S *DEAD!*

GOD KNOWS HOW LONG IT WILL TAKE *WANDA* TO RECOVER! WE'VE GOT HER DOWNSTAIR UNDER *SEDATION* NOW...

YES..., I *DO* REGRET THIS *TRAUMATIC EX-PERIENCE* FOR THE *SCARLET WITCH.*

BUT... AS LONG AS WE'RE ON THE SUBJECT OF MAJOR *DISRUPTIONS*... I HAVE *ANOTHER* ONE FOR YOU.

IF YOU WISH TO AVOID *FUTURE* GOVERNMENT INTERVENTION IN YOUR ACTIONS, YOU MUST *NOW* ACCEPT THE NEW TEAM MEMBER WHICH *WE* HAVE ASSIGNED.

WHAT?!?

I'M SORRY TO BE SO *BLUNT* ABOUT THIS, GENTLEMEN, BUT I JUST REALIZED WHAT *TIME* IT IS OUT THERE IN CALIFORNIA.

"AND SINCE HE TOOK THE *RED EYE* OUT OF DULLES, YOUR NEW *LEADER* SHOULD BE ARRIVING AT THE COMPOUND *RIGHT ABOUT NOW*...

VROOOM

HE'S SOMEONE WHO'LL MAKE SURE A *PROPER EYE* IS KEPT ON THE VISION FROM NOW ON!

"...PROPER EYE...?"

WHO...?

??

IT CAN'T BE! HE'S JUST BEEN APPOINTED *EAST COAST CHAIRMAN*!

APPARENTLY NOT...

WELL... LOOK AT IT *THIS WAY*, CLINT...

"...IF WE HAVE TO ACCEPT A NEW MEMBER IT COULD HAVE BEEN A LOT *WORSE*. A LOT...

...WORSE...

OH.... NO....!!!

73

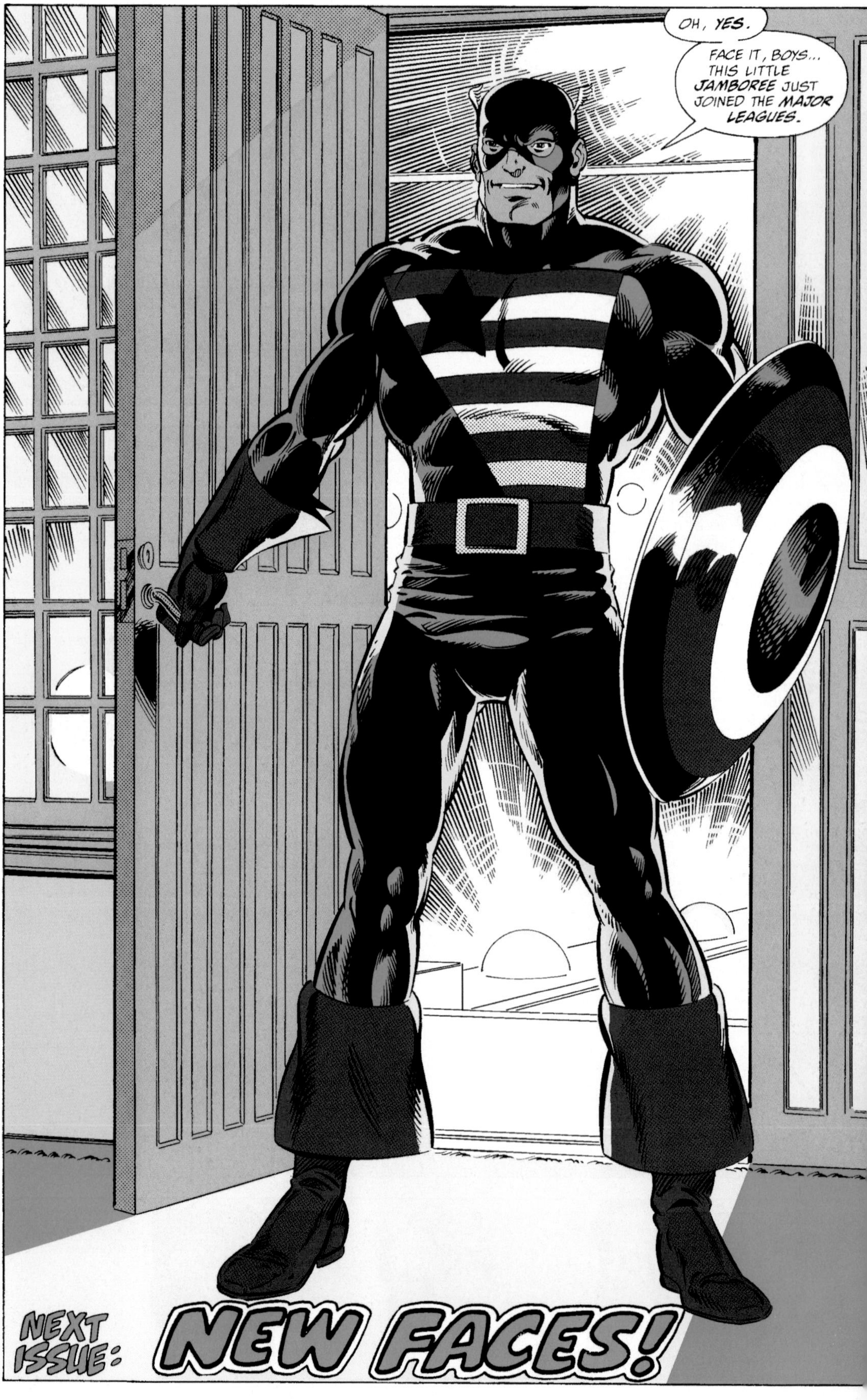
OH, YES.
FACE IT, BOYS... THIS LITTLE JAMBOREE JUST JOINED THE MAJOR LEAGUES.
NEXT ISSUE: NEW FACES!

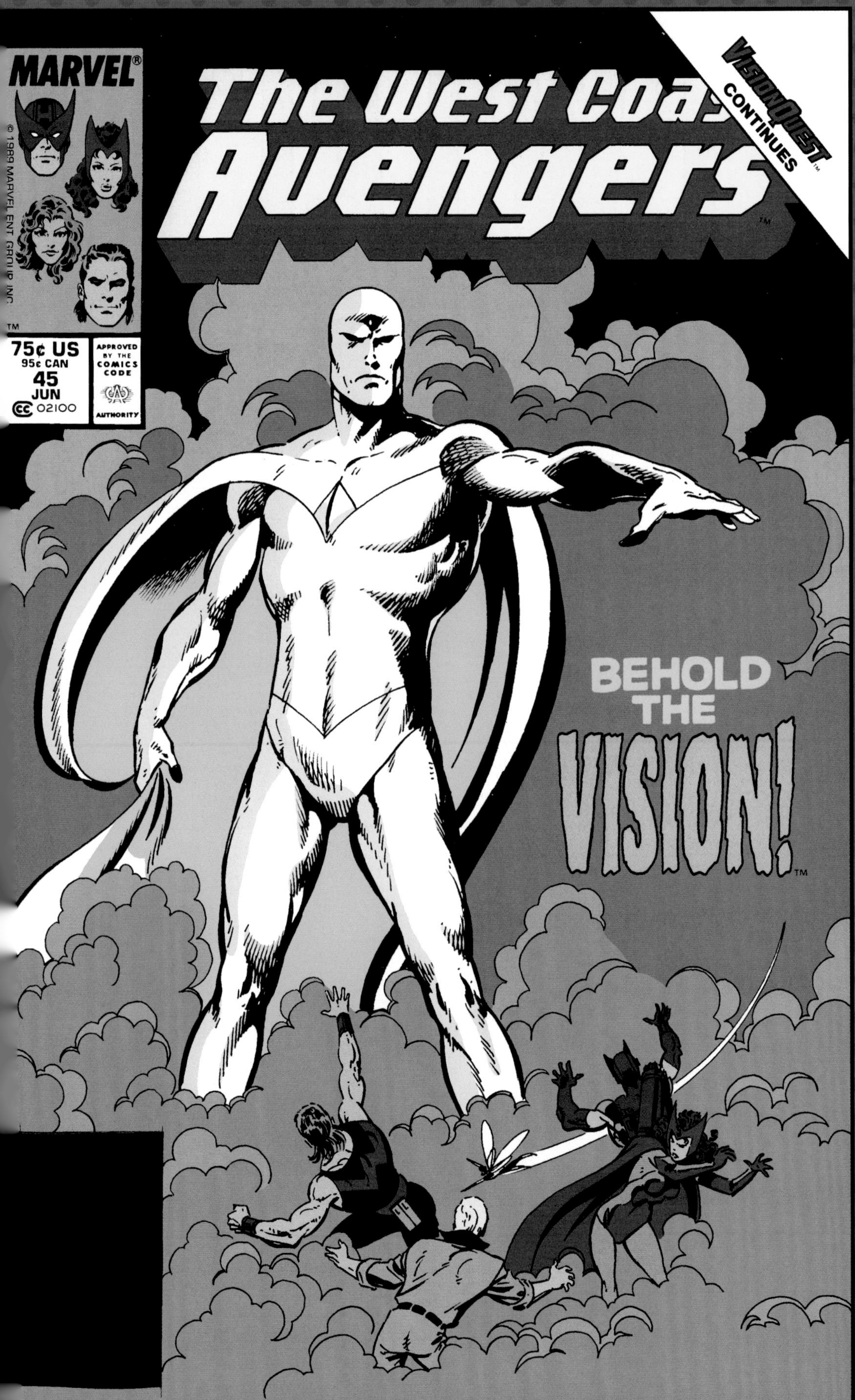
MARVEL®
The West Coast Avengers™
VisionQuest™ CONTINUES
© 1989 MARVEL ENT. GROUP, INC.
75¢ US
95¢ CAN
45
JUN
CC 02100
APPROVED BY THE COMICS CODE AUTHORITY
BEHOLD THE VISION!™

NEW FACES

LOOK CLOSELY AT THE FACE BEFORE YOU.

IT IS THE FACE OF THE MAN CALLED **THE U.S. AGENT.**

IT IS THE FACE OF A MAN WHO, FOR A WHILE AT LEAST, WORE THE UNIFORM OF THIS NATION'S GREATEST CHAMPION, **CAPTAIN AMERICA.**

IT IS A FACE HEWN TO **HEROIC** PROPORTIONS; PROUD, TRUE, ROCK HARD.

AND YET, PERHAPS THOSE PROPORTIONS ARE A TRIFLE **TOO MUCH** IN THE IDEALIZED MOLD.

THE JAW IS PERHAPS A FRACTION **TOO** SQUARE, THE IRON SINEWED NECK A BIT **TOO** THICK.

AND, IN THE **FERVOR,** THE FIERCE PRIDE OF **PLACE** AND **PATRIOTISM** WHICH BURNS IN THE PIERCING EYES, MIGHT WE NOT DETECT A HINT OF... **MADNESS?**

STAN LEE PRESENTS:

JOHN BYRNE story and pencils	MIKE MACHLAN inker	BILL OAKLEY letterer	PAUL BECTON colorist	HOWARD MACKIE editor	TOM DEFALCO not so new face	W.C. AVENGERS created by ROGER STERN & BOB HALL.

THE LIVING ROOM OF THE AVENGERS MANSION, WEST COAST...

9:47 A.M. TODAY...

WHO **IS** THIS GUY??

HE HASN'T SAID MORE'N **TWO WORDS** SINCE HE CRUISED IN HERE THIS MORNING AND DECLARED HIMSELF A NEW MEMBER.

HEY, BE FAIR, CLINT.

THAT'S NOT **QUITE** WHAT HAPPENED, AND YOU **KNOW** IT.

SIMON'S **RIGHT**, HAWKEYE.

THIS FELLOW ARRIVED WITH INSTRUCTIONS FROM OUR GOVERNMENT LIAISON, AGENT SIKORSKY. HE DIDN'T JUST "DECLARE" HIMSELF A NEW MEMBER.

YEAH?

WELL, IT AMOUNTS TO THE **SAME THING**, DOESN'T IT, DOC? **I** GET TH' OLD **GOLDEN TOE**.

ALTHOUGH, THE WAY THINGS HAVE BEEN GOIN' 'ROUND HERE FOR THE PAST FEW DAYS, IT SEEMS LIKE EVERYBODY'S **FORGOTTEN** I'M SUPPOSED TO BE WEST COAST CHAIRMAN.

NO ONE HAS FORGOTTEN **ANYTHING**, HAWK.

77

UNLESS MAYBE *YOU'VE* FORGOTTEN THAT *WE* AVENGERS CAN ONLY *OPERATE* BECAUSE THE GOVERNMENT *SANCTIONS* IT.

SO IF THE BOYS IN WASHINGTON WANT THIS GUY *TO* BE OUR NEW MEMBER, ALL *WE* CAN DO IS *GO ALONG* WITH IT.

"WE" AVENGERS? "OUR" NEW MEMBER?? WELL, EXCU-U-U-USE ME, LADY, BUT SINCE WHEN DID *YOU* COME BACK INTO THIS LITTLE *FAMILY*?

YOU *QUIT* THE AVENGERS. AND IT SEEMS TO ME ABOUT A HUNDRED AND FIFTY PERCENT OF THE NASTINESS THAT'S GONE DOWN AROUND HERE IN THE PAST THREE DAYS HAS BEEN BECAUSE OF *YOU*!

NOW, HAWKEYE, YOU'RE LETTING YOUR *EMOTIONAL INVOLVEMENT* WITH MOCKINGBIRD *MUDDY* YOUR THINKING.

BOBBI WAS *DUPED* INTO HELPING THAT *COVERT INTERNATIONAL OPERATION KIDNAP* THE VISION-- AND AS SOON AS SHE REALIZED WHAT WAS HAPPENING SHE CAME TO *WARN* US.

YEAH...

CONVENIENTLY *TOO LATE* FOR US TO *DO* ANYTHING. SO NOW, ON TOP OF THE VISION LYING ON A *SLAB* WITH HIS *GUTS* RE-ARRANGED...

...WE HAFTA DECIDE IF WE'RE GONNA PUT UP WITH *THIS* GEEK.

YOU *MISS* THE *POINT*, ARCHER.

BUT THEN, I HEAR THAT'S ONE OF THE THINGS YOU DO *BEST.*

MOCKINGBIRD IS *RIGHT.* YOU AREN'T BEING ASKED TO *DECIDE* ANYTHING.

I AM NOW AN *AVENGER.*

PERIOD.

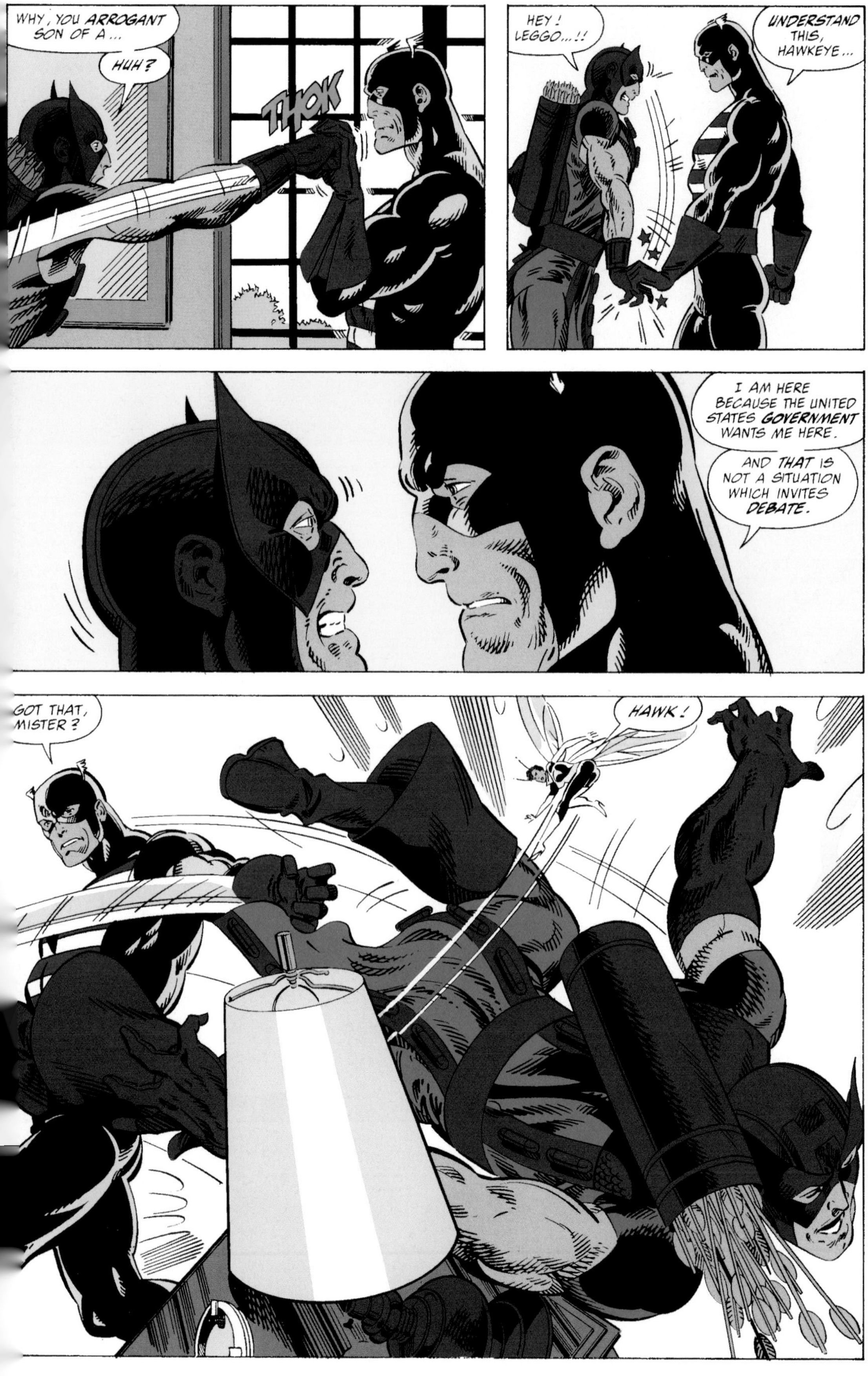
WHY, YOU ARROGANT SON OF A ...
HUH?
THOK
HEY! LEGGO...!!
UNDERSTAND THIS, HAWKEYE...
I AM HERE BECAUSE THE UNITED STATES GOVERNMENT WANTS ME HERE.
AND THAT IS NOT A SITUATION WHICH INVITES DEBATE.
GOT THAT, MISTER?
HAWK!

HAWK!
ARE YOU OKAY?

YEAH, YEAH, YEAH, I'M...

HUH?

HAWK! WHAT...??

WILL YOU GET AWAY FROM ME?

THIS IS ALL I NEED! I GET MY CAN KICKED BY THE PRESIDENT OF THE CLINT EASTWOOD FAN CLUB... AND THE FIRST PERSON TO RUSH TO MY AID IS THE WOMAN I'M SUPPOSED TO BE DIVORCING!

BOBBI'S JUST TRYING TO HELP, HAWKEYE. DON'T BE SUCH A DOPE ABOUT IT.

BUT... SPEAKING OF KICKING CANS, MAYBE YOU'D LIKE TO TRY THOSE MOVES WITH SOMEONE MORE IN YOUR LEAGUE, STRANGER!

ANY TIME YOU WANT, WONDER MAN.

STOP!

NOW, JUST STOP IT, BOTH OF YOU! THIS IS RIDICULOUS!

SQUABBLING AMONGST OURSELVES NEVER SOLVES ANYTHING.

THE WASP IS RIGHT!

AS MUCH AS WE ALL HATE THE IDEA OF HAVING A NEW MEMBER FOISTED ON US LIKE THIS...

... AND A STRANGER TO BOOT, AS SIMON POINTED OUT...

... OUR CHARTER REQUIRES US TO GO ALONG WITH THIS-- AT LEAST UNTIL THIS GENTLEMAN IS PROVEN INCAPABLE OR UNWORTHY OF MEMBERSHIP.

UNTIL THAT HAPPENS, THERE'S NOTHING ELSE WE CAN DO.

WRONG-O, DOC!

THERE'S SOMETHING I CAN DO RIGHT NOW!

I QUIT!

HAWK!!

SLAM

LET HIM *GO*, MOCKINGBIRD.

IF HE'S NOT PREPARED TO PLAY BY THE *RULES*, THERE'S NO *PLACE* FOR HIM IN THIS GROUP.

NO PLACE??

BUSTER, IF IT WASN'T FOR *HIM*, THERE WOULDN'T EVEN *BE* A WEST COAST BRANCH OF THE AVENGERS!

HE *FOUNDED* THE GROUP!

WRONG, MOCKINGBIRD. IT WAS THE *VISION* WHO CONCEIVED OF THIS SECOND GROUP, AND IT WAS THE *VISION* WHO APPOINTED YOUR HUSBAND CHAIRMAN.

THE *SAME* VISION WHO SUBSEQUENTLY ATTEMPTED TO *TAKE OVER THE WORLD*, AND WHOSE RETURN TO ACTIVE STATUS AS AN AVENGER IS THE MAIN REASON I'M HERE.

OHHH -- GO SWALLOW YOUR *SHIELD*, BIG MAN. I'M GOING AFTER CLINT.

AND IT'S GONNA TAKE MORE THAN A TWO BIT IMITATION OF *CAPTAIN AMERICA* TO STOP ME!!

WELL...

ALL THIS EXCITEMENT, AND IT'S NOT EVEN TEN O'CLOCK YET.

BUSINESS AS USUAL, IN OTHER WORDS.

I'M GOING TO CHECK ON HOW *WANDA'S* DOING. CARE TO COME ALONG, HANK?

NO, YOU GO AHEAD, JAN.

"I THINK IT'S TIME I GOT BACK TO THE *REPAIRS* ON THE VISION."

CAN HE REALLY BE *FIXED*, HANK?

I MEAN, IF YOU TURN HIM BACK ON, WHAT'S TO STOP HIM FROM *ATTACKING* US AGAIN, LIKE HE DID THIS MORNING?

I DON'T ANTICIPATE A RECURRENCE OF THAT UNFORTUNATE INCIDENT, SIMON.

AS I SAID AT THE TIME, IT ONLY HAPPENED BECAUSE THE VISION WAS IN AN AUTOMATIC *DEFENSIVE MODE* WHEN I REACTIVATED HIS SYSTEMS.

WHILE WE'VE BEEN DEALING WITH THE ARRIVAL OF OUR NEW LEADER, I'VE HAD THE COMPUTERS *REPROGRAMMING* THE VISION'S MEMORY BANKS WITH ALL THE PERTINENT DATA ABOUT THE AVENGERS.

WHEN NEXT HE WAKES, HE'LL KNOW WE'RE HIS *FRIENDS.*

MY *PRIMARY CONCERN* NOW IS WHAT TO DO WITH HIS BIO-SYNTHETIC *SKIN.* WHEN IT WAS *REMOVED,* ITS CIRCULATORY SYSTEM WAS BADLY *TRAUMATIZED,* AS YOU CAN SEE...

YEAH...

I WONDER WHAT WANDA'S GOING TO THINK OF HER HUSBAND'S NEW *HUE...?*

SIX HOURS LATER...

WELL, YOUR *REFERENCES* ARE *SUPERB,* MRS. HUNTER.

AND I CAN'T REMEMBER WHEN I'VE SEEN A MORE *IMPRESSIVE* RESUMÉ.

THANK YOU, MA'AM. I'VE MADE IT MY LIFE'S WORK, LOOKING AFTER CHILDREN.

AND I'VE *NEVER* HAD A DISSATISFIED CUSTOMER.

GOOD...

YOU DO UNDERSTAND, THOUGH, THAT THE *SITUATION* HERE WILL BE MARKEDLY DIFFERENT FROM ANY PLACE YOU'VE WORKED BEFORE.

AND, OF COURSE, THOMAS AND WILLIAM ARE FAR FROM *ORDINARY* BABIES.

ALL PARENTS THINK THEIR CHILDREN ARE EXTRA SPECIAL, MA'AM.

I'VE BEEN GOVERNESS FOR EVERYTHING FROM NORMAL, AVERAGE BABIES TO CHILD *PRODIGIES...*

AND THE ONE THING I'VE LEARNED IS THAT, UNDER IT ALL, KIDS ARE STILL KIDS!

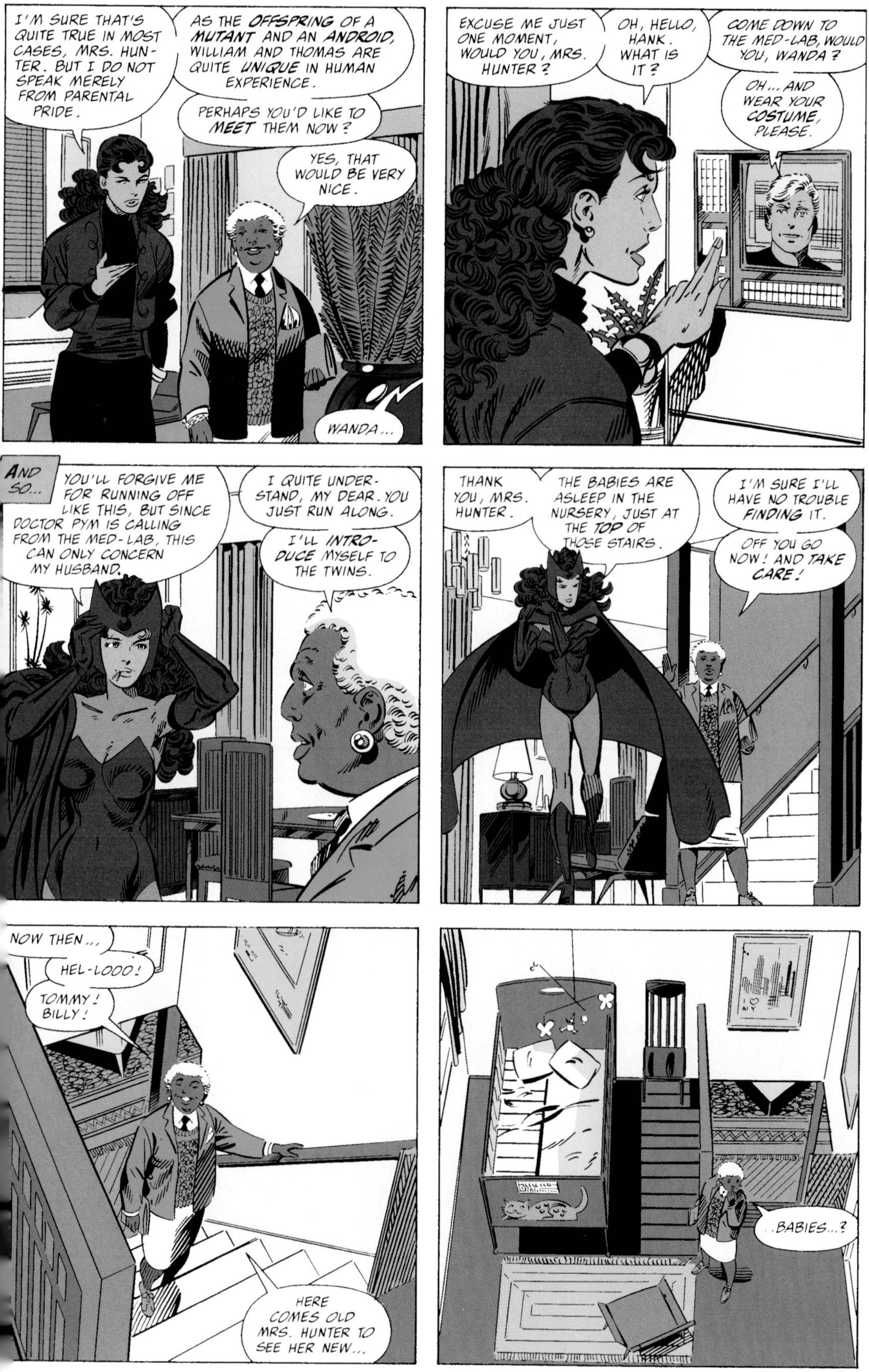
I'M SURE THAT'S QUITE TRUE IN MOST CASES, MRS. HUNTER. BUT I DO NOT SPEAK MERELY FROM PARENTAL PRIDE.
AS THE OFFSPRING OF A MUTANT AND AN ANDROID, WILLIAM AND THOMAS ARE QUITE UNIQUE IN HUMAN EXPERIENCE.
PERHAPS YOU'D LIKE TO MEET THEM NOW?
YES, THAT WOULD BE VERY NICE.
WANDA...
EXCUSE ME JUST ONE MOMENT, WOULD YOU, MRS. HUNTER?
OH, HELLO, HANK. WHAT IS IT?
COME DOWN TO THE MED-LAB, WOULD YOU, WANDA?
OH... AND WEAR YOUR COSTUME, PLEASE.
AND SO...
YOU'LL FORGIVE ME FOR RUNNING OFF LIKE THIS, BUT SINCE DOCTOR PYM IS CALLING FROM THE MED-LAB, THIS CAN ONLY CONCERN MY HUSBAND.
I QUITE UNDERSTAND, MY DEAR. YOU JUST RUN ALONG.
I'LL INTRODUCE MYSELF TO THE TWINS.
THANK YOU, MRS. HUNTER.
THE BABIES ARE ASLEEP IN THE NURSERY, JUST AT THE TOP OF THOSE STAIRS.
I'M SURE I'LL HAVE NO TROUBLE FINDING IT.
OFF YOU GO NOW! AND TAKE CARE!
NOW THEN...
HEL-LOOO!
TOMMY! BILLY!
HERE COMES OLD MRS. HUNTER TO SEE HER NEW...
...BABIES...?

LEAVING THE NEWLY HIRED GOVERNESS ALL *ALONE* IN THE QUARTERS OF THE VISION AND THE SCARLET WITCH, LET US LOOK TO THE OTHER SIDE OF THE SPRAWL-ING *WEST COAST COM-POUND*, TO THIS LITTLE HOUSE, IDENTICAL IN STRUCTURE TO THE ONE WE HAVE JUST *LEFT*...

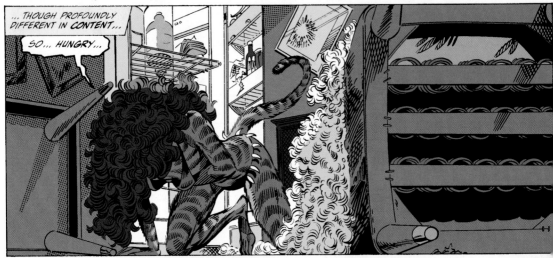

...THOUGH PROFOUNDLY DIFFERENT IN *CONTENT*...

SO... HUNGRY...

NEARLY... *THREE DAYS* SINCE I HAD ANYTHING TO EAT.

NOTHING IN THE HOUSE I *WANT*.

DON'T DARE GO OUT... NOT LIKE *THIS*...

BUT... SOMETHING TO *EAT*... GOT TO HAVE SOMETHING TO EAT...

IF ONLY...

WHAT...?

CHIRP CHIRRUP CHIRP

CHIRP CHIRP CHIRRUP CHIRP CHIRP CHIRP

BIRD....

...FOOD...

NO! NO!

STOP IT! STOP IT!! I'M NOT AN ANIMAL!

NO!

...NO...

...YES

MEANWHILE...

HANK-- JAN--

IS EVERYTHING ALL RIGHT? WHY DID YOU WANT ME IN COSTUME?

OH, SORRY, WANDA. I GUESS I SHOULD HAVE **EXPLAINED.**

THERE'S NOTHING TO GET UPSET ABOUT... NO MORE UPSET THAN YOU ALREADY ARE, ANYWAY.

THEN... WHAT...?

I'VE COMPLETED THE REPROGRAM-MING OF THE **VISION'S** MEMORY BANKS, WANDA.

SINCE MOST OF OUR DATA TAPES CONCERN VARIOUS **BATTLES** WE'VE ALL BEEN IN, I THOUGHT IT MIGHT BE LESS... CONFUSING FOR HIM TO HAVE YOU IN COSTUME WHEN THE TWO OF YOU ARE... **REINTRODUCED.**

"REINTRODUCED...?"

I DON'T UNDERSTAND...

WELL, AS YOU ALREADY KNOW, ALL OUR DATA ABOUT THE VISION HIMSELF WAS **ERADICATED** BY A SOPHISTICATED COMPUTER **TAPE-WORM** THE PEOPLE WHO KIDNAPED HIM INTRODUCED INTO OUR SYSTEM, AND ALL THE SYSTEMS WE INTERFACE WITH.

ARE YOU SAYING... HE DOESN'T **REMEMBER** ME? THAT HE WON'T KNOW WHO I AM?

NO, NO. HE KNOWS ALL OF US, NOW.

IT'S JUST THAT HIS **PERCEPTIONS** MAY HAVE BEEN ALTERED. IT'S DIFFICULT TO EX-PLAIN IN HUMAN TERMS...

PERHAPS IT WOULD BE BETTER IF **I** DID THE EXPLAINING, DOCTOR PYM.

?!?

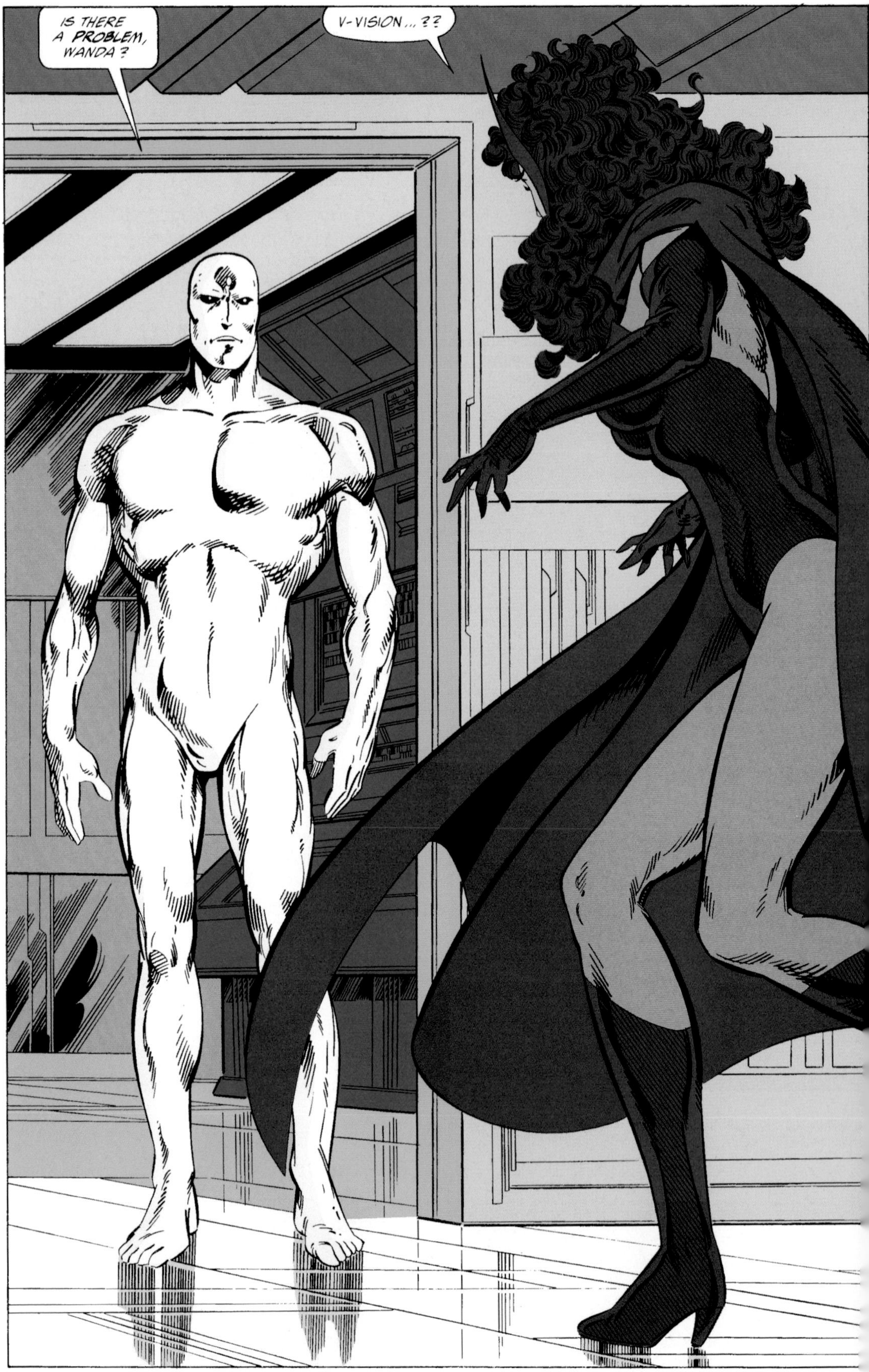
IS THERE A PROBLEM, WANDA?
V-VISION...??

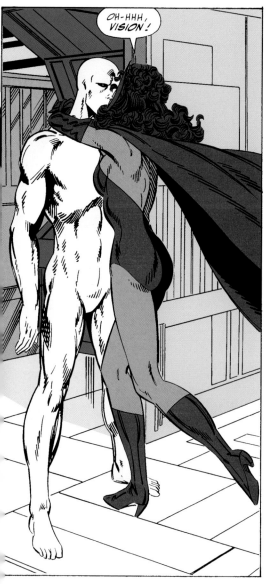

OH-HHH, VISION!

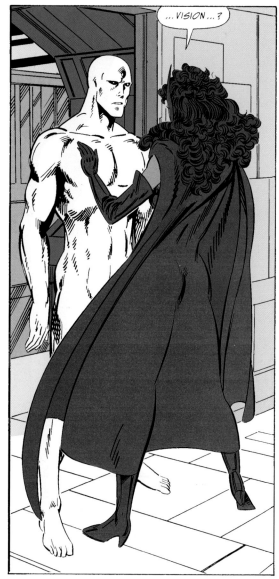

...VISION...?

WANDA -- IS THERE SOME SIGNIFICANCE TO THIS ACTION?

H-HANK...?

THIS IS WHAT I WAS TALKING ABOUT, WANDA. HE HAS ALL THE INFORMATION WE CAN SUPPLY...

...BUT HIS EMOTIONAL CONNECTION TO THAT INFORMATION IS NON-EXISTENT.

BUT... WHY?

YOU SAID NONE OF HIS PARTS HAD BEEN DAMAGED WHEN HE WAS DISASSEMBLED-- ONLY PROGRAMMING ERASED.

IF YOU'VE RESTORED THE DATA THAT FORMED THAT PROGRAMMING...

IT'S NOWHERE NEAR THAT SIMPLE, WANDA.

THERE'S STILL ONE VITAL ELEMENT MISSING...

SOON...

SIMON...?

HELLO, WANDA.

I ...THOUGHT YOU'D COME LOOKING FOR ME, SOONER OR LATER.

SIMON... SIMON, HANK SAYS HE CANNOT COMPLETE HIS *RESTORATION* OF THE *VISION* WITHOUT YOUR *BRAIN PATTERN*...

BUT HE SAYS YOU'VE *REFUSED* TO *COOPERATE*...?

YES... I GUESS I *HAVE*.

BUT... *WHY??* SIMON, I THOUGHT YOU WERE MY *FRIEND*...

THE *VISION'S* FRIEND...

I *AM*, WANDA.

I ALWAYS *WILL* BE.

BUT... I DON'T KNOW... MAYBE YOU JUST DON'T *UNDERSTAND* WHAT IT IS YOU'RE *ASKING* OF ME...

"REMEMBER, WANDA, I HAVEN'T ALWAYS BEEN A *SUPER HERO*. ONCE I WAS JUST A NORMAL MAN, A *PAWN* IN A SCHEME TO *DESTROY* THE AVENGERS."

YOU ARE *PENNILESS*, AN ACCUSED *EMBEZZLER*... ALL BECAUSE OF *TONY STARK* AND HIS BODY-GUARD, *IRON MAN*.

BUT I, *BARON ZEMO*, CAN OFFER YOU *WEALTH* AND *POWER* BEYOND YOUR IMAGINING.

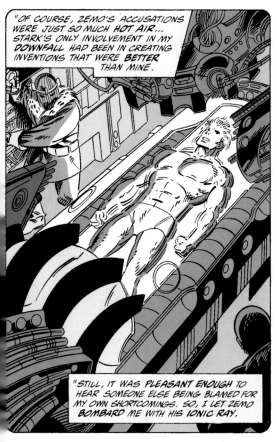

"OF COURSE, ZEMO'S ACCUSATIONS WERE JUST SO MUCH *HOT AIR*... STARK'S ONLY INVOLVEMENT IN MY *DOWNFALL* HAD BEEN IN CREATING INVENTIONS THAT WERE *BETTER* THAN MINE."

"STILL, IT WAS *PLEASANT ENOUGH* TO HEAR SOMEONE ELSE BEING BLAMED FOR MY OWN SHORTCOMINGS. SO, I LET ZEMO *BOMBARD* ME WITH HIS *IONIC RAY.*"

" AND WHEN HE WAS DONE, I WAS *REBORN,* AS *WONDER MAN!*"

"BUT THERE WAS A *CATCH*...."

THE IONIC RADIATION WILL *KILL* YOU IN *ONE WEEK,* BUT I HAVE THE *ANTIDOTE!*

SO YOU WILL BE MY *SLAVE,* SIMON WILLIAMS -- OR YOU WILL *DIE!*

" I HAD NO *CHOICE.* I WENT ALONG WITH ZEMO AND HIS PARTNERS, THE ASGARDIAN *ENCHANTRESS* AND THE *EXECUTIONER.*"

"I *KIDNAPED* THE *WASP* -- LURED THE OTHER AVENGERS INTO *BATTLE*..."

"BUT PART OF ZEMO'S SCHEME INVOLVED TRICKING THE AVENGERS INTO ACCEPTING ME AS A *MEMBER.*"

"DURING THE TIME I WAS WITH THEM, I LEARNED TO RESPECT THEIR SELFLESS-NESS AND NOBILITY. I COULD NOT LET ZEMO KILL THEM.

"I TURNED ON MY ERSTWHILE MASTERS..."

"AND I DIED FOR IT!"

"THAT WOULD HAVE BEEN **THE END** FOR ANYONE ELSE'S STORY, BUT FOR MINE, IT WAS BARELY THE BEGINNING.

"ALTHOUGH THE AVENGERS KNEW THEY COULD DO NOTHING TO SAVE MY **BODY** FROM DEATH...

"...THEY HURRIED BACK TO HANK PYM'S LAB, AND THERE A **RECORDING** WAS MADE OF MY BRAINWAVE PATTERNS...

"THOSE **SAME** PATTERNS WHICH WERE SUBSE-QUENTLY USED BY **ULTRON-5**...

"USED TO CREATE A **MATRIX** FOR THE MIND OF THE **VISION**!

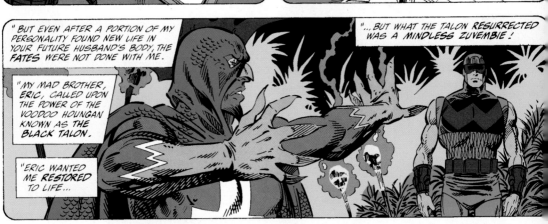

" BUT EVEN AFTER A PORTION OF MY PERSONALITY FOUND NEW LIFE IN YOUR FUTURE HUSBAND'S BODY, THE **FATES** WERE NOT DONE WITH ME.

"MY **MAD BROTHER,** ERIC, CALLED UPON THE POWER OF THE VOODOO HOUNGAN KNOWN AS **THE BLACK TALON.**

"ERIC WANTED ME **RESTORED** TO LIFE...

"...BUT WHAT THE TALON **RESURRECTED** WAS A MINDLESS **ZUVEMBIE**!

" I WAS ONCE AGAIN A HELPLESS SLAVE OF ONE WHO SOUGHT TO DESTROY THE AVENGERS.

"ONLY **THIS** TIME, I WOULD NOT BE ABLE TO CHANGE MY MIND, HAVING **NO** MIND TO CHANGE!

"OR SO IT WOULD HAVE **SEEMED,** BUT FOR A **MIRACLE**!

"SLOWLY, ALMOST PAINFULLY, MY MIND GREW **ACTIVE** AGAIN.

"THE ZUVEMBIE **REMEMBERED** THE MAN HE HAD BEEN...

"AND SIMON WILLIAMS LIVED AGAIN!

WELL... TO **SHORTEN** A LONG STORY YOU ALREADY KNOW, PRETTY SOON WE DISCOVERED I HADN'T ACTUALLY **DIED** IN THE FIRST PLACE. ZEMO'S IONIC RAY HAD BEGUN A **MUTAGENIC CHANGE** IN MY CELL STRUCTURE.

WHAT **SEEMED** TO BE DEATH WAS REALLY A KIND OF **CHRYSALIS STAGE**, LIKE A CATERPILLAR TURNING INTO A BUTTERFLY.

YES. AS YOU SAY, SIMON, I **KNOW** ALL THIS.

AND KNOWING IT DOES NOT HELP ME UNDERSTAND WHY YOU WON'T LET HANK **RE-COPY** YOUR BRAIN PATTERN INTO THE VISION...

I GUESS IT **IS** KIND OF HARD TO COMPREHEND. NO HUMAN HAS EVER EXPERIENCED WHAT I'VE GONE THROUGH -- SEEMING TO **DIE**, AND THEN WAKING UP TO FIND THAT **ANOTHER MAN** HAS A PIECE OF YOUR BRAIN...

THE VISION WAS LIKE A PART OF ME, WANDA. HIS BASIC NATURE WAS **MINE**. HIS... **FEELINGS**. HIS... **EMOTIONS**.

YES... YOU HAVE EVEN CALLED HIM "BROTHER." BUT NOW HE IS JUST A HUMAN-SHAPED COMPUTER-- A **ROBOT** WHO HAPPENS TO BEAR A **SUPERFICIAL** RESEMBLANCE TO THE MAN I MARRIED.

BUT IT DOES NOT HAVE TO BE THAT WAY, SIMON. **YOU** CAN RESTORE HIM.

IT WOULD ONLY TAKE A **WORD** FROM YOU TO GIVE HIM BACK HIS **SOUL**...

I KNOW...

I ONLY WISH I **COULD**, WANDA. I WISH IT WAS ALL SO SIMPLE THAT I COULD WALK INTO THE LAB AND LET HANK DO... WHATEVER HE HAS TO DO.

BUT... **TRY** TO UNDERSTAND, WANDA. AS **AWFUL** AND **TRAUMATIC** AS THE PAST FEW DAYS HAVE BEEN FOR **YOU**, IN MY OWN WAY I'VE **SHARED** YOUR SUFFERING.

I HAD **NO CHOICE** IN THE TRANSFER OF MY **SOUL** INTO THE VISION THE FIRST TIME. NOW... I **HAVE A CHOICE**...

AND... ...YOU CHOOSE **NOT** TO ALLOW IT?

EVEN KNOWING THAT WITHOUT YOUR HELP THE MAN I **LOVE** CAN NEVER BE **WHOLE** AGAIN?

YES... FORGIVE ME, WANDA, BUT...

WANDA...!!

FORGIVE YOU? *I HATE YOU!!*

Through his impenetrable skin, Wonder Man barely even feels the Scarlet Witch's blow.

But the fact of it brings stinging tears to his eyes.

WANDA... *WAIT!*

PLEASE... LISTEN TO ME...

I HAVE *LISTENED* QUITE ENOUGH...

She gestures...

Around them, the air grows still. Circling sea birds cease their constant calling.

Simon Williams feels a shudder rise through his spine. He knows the power he has unwittingly unleashed.

Above his head, the ancient cliff face moans, a strangely human sound..

It has stood thus for uncounted years, shrugging off even the worst of California's earthquakes.

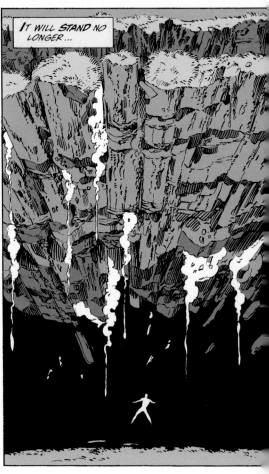

It will stand no longer...

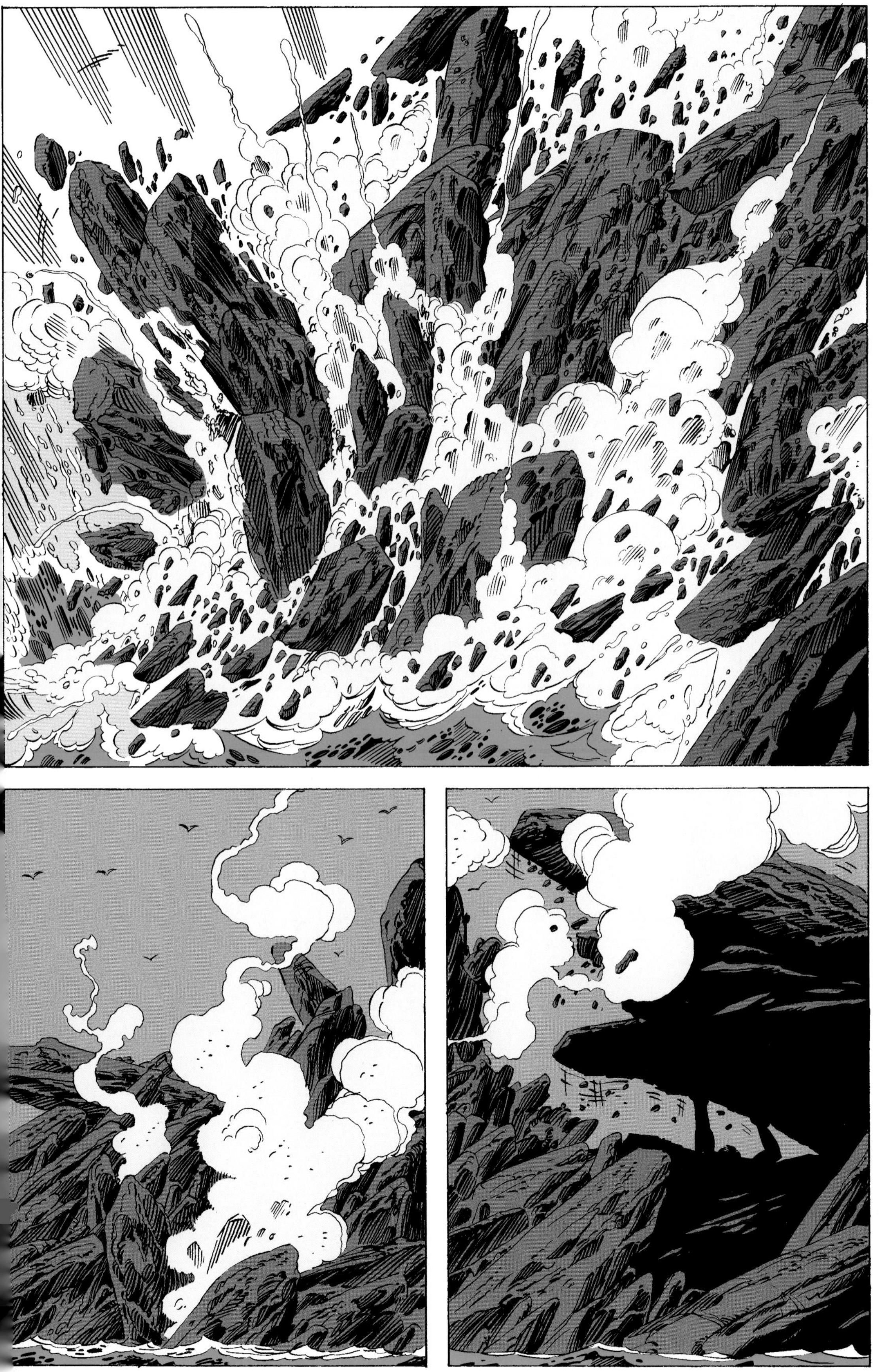

THE SCREAM IS TORN FROM WONDER MAN'S HEART, FROM HIS VERY *SOUL*.

IT ENCAPSU-LATES IN ONE OUT-POURING... ALL THE ANGER, PAIN, RAGE, AND FRUSTRA-TION HE HAS KNOWN SINCE HIS RESURREC-TION.

IT BURSTS OUT OF HIM LIKE A THING *ALIVE*, GROWING, SWELLING, SURGING LIKE THE TIDE BEFORE A HURRICANE.

AS FAR AWAY AS *SAN FRANCISCO* PEOPLE PAUSE; THEY OPEN DOORS AND WINDOWS, THEY TIP THEIR HEADS, AS A DOG MIGHT, STRAINING TO CATCH THE DISTANT SOUND.

CLOSER, GLASS RATTLES, ORNA-MENTS FALL FROM SHELVES.

AND THEN THE SOUND IS GONE, FADED ON THE BREEZE LIKE SOME GHOST OF MEMORY.

FOR IT HAS BEEN SAID, AND THERE IS *TRUTH* IN IT...

...THAT IN *SPACE*, NO ONE CAN HEAR YOU *SCREAM*...

YOU *HEARD* ME, ROBOT. AS LONG AS I'M ON THIS TEAM WE'LL HAVE SOME *DECENCY* AROUND HERE.

GET SOME CLOTHES ON!

NOW!

YOUR POSITION IS NOT *LOGICAL*, SIR. HUMANS WEAR CLOTHES FOR ANY COMBINATION OF THREE REASONS: PROTECTION, MODESTY, OR VANITY.

NONE OF THESE APPLIES TO ME.

*W*ANDA DOES NOT *HEAR* THE VISION'S *WORDS.* ONLY THEIR *TONE.*

*H*IS VOICE HAS BECOME ONCE MORE THE PERFECTLY MODULATED MONOTONE SHE HEARD WHEN FIRST HE SPOKE TO HER, WHAT NOW SEEMS A HUNDRED LIFETIMES AGO.

*E*ACH WORD IS A SEPARATE ENTITY, HELD *DISTINCT* FROM THOSE AROUND IT BY THE MECHANICAL PRECISION OF THE VISION'S SPEECH.

*M*ONOTONOUS...

*M*ECHANICAL...

*N*OT AT ALL HUMAN...

ALL RIGHT, ALL RIGHT, BREAK IT UP YOU TWO!

LOOK, VISION, THIS IS ALL THAT WAS *LEFT* OF YOUR COSTUME AFTER THE BAD GUYS *CUT IT OFF* YOU.

BUT IT'S AS MUCH A *PART OF YOU* AS YOUR *SKIN.*

MAYBE YOU CAN DO SOMETHING WITH IT.

I AM SURE I CAN. MY ABILITY TO MANIPULATE THE MOLECULAR STRUCTURE OF MY BODY EXTENDS TO THIS CLOTH.

THANK YOU, JANET.

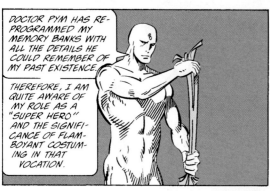

DOCTOR PYM HAS RE-PROGRAMMED MY MEMORY BANKS WITH ALL THE DETAILS HE COULD REMEMBER OF MY PAST EXISTENCE.

THEREFORE, I AM QUITE AWARE OF MY ROLE AS A "SUPER HERO" AND THE SIGNIFI-CANCE OF FLAM-BOYANT COSTUM-ING IN THAT VOCATION.

HOWEVER, I BELIEVE IN THIS INSTANCE, I PREFER TO EVOKE THE TRADITIONAL SUPER HERO COSTUME, RATHER THAN DUP-LICATE THE FORM PRECISELY.

AND, OF COURSE, I MAKE THE NECESSARY CONCESSION TO OUR LEADER'S SENSIBILITIES...

WILL THIS SUFFICE?

THAT'LL DO, I GUESS. AT LEAST YOU **LOOK** LIKE YOU'VE GOT CLOTHES ON.

BUT, WHY THE **BLEACHING** OUT OF ALL COLOR, VISION?

IF I AM TO BE CALLED "THE VISION," IS IT NOT LOGICAL FOR ME TO LOOK THE PART?

WHY...?

SPECTRAL... UNEARTHLY...

YES... WELL, AS LONG AS WE'RE ALL TO-GETHER AGAIN, I'M AFRAID I'VE GOT ANOTHER **BOMB-SHELL** TO DROP ON EVERYBODY.

YOU KNOW HOW FOR YEARS NOW WE'VE BELIEVED THAT THE VISION WAS **REBUILT** OUT OF THE ANDROID BODY OF THE ORIGINAL **HUMAN TORCH?** AND YET JUST THE OTHER DAY THE TORCH'S **CREATOR**, PROFESSOR HORTON, SAID THE VISION WAS **NOT HIS WORK?**

WANDA... YOUR FIRST REACTION TO THAT WAS TO ASSUME HORTON WAS **LYING** FOR SOME REASON.

I'M AFRAID THAT'S **NOT** THE CASE.

I DID A DETAILED ANALYSIS OF EVERY PART OF THE VISION AS I WAS RE-ASSEMBLING HIM...

AND THERE'S NO WAY HE COULD EVER HAVE BEEN THE TORCH!

LATER... ...JUST SAID WHAT I FELT NEEDED TO BE SAID, JAN. I DIDN'T MEAN TO UPSET WANDA ALL OVER AGAIN.

WELL, YOU DID A PRETTY GOOD **JOB**, FOR ALL THAT, LOVER. I MEAN, YOU **KNOW** SHE'S IN A REAL **MESS**.

YOUR LITTLE NEWS FLASH...

NO, NO, I CAN MAKE IT WORK. I KNOW I CAN.

? WHO'S IN THERE?

MUST BE OUR NEW MEMBER. HE SAID HE DIDN'T **NEED** MUCH, THAT HE WAS GOING TO QUARTER HIMSELF IN ONE OF THE SPARE ROOMS...

THEY'RE ALL KIND OF **WILD** AND **UNDISCIPLINED**...

BUT I THINK I CAN **WHIP** 'EM INTO SHAPE.

WHO'S HE TALKING TO?

HUH?

HE'S BLOCKED THE KEYHOLE WITH **TAPE** OR SOMETHING...

THEY'RE GOOD PEOPLE AT HEART. STRONG PEOPLE. YOU'LL **LIKE** THEM.

C'MON, JAN. DON'T **SNOOP**!

OH, ALL RIGHT. I GUESS EVEN A **JERK** DESERVES HIS **PRIVACY**!

IT'S TOO BAD ABOUT THE SCARLET WITCH, THOUGH.

BUY YOU DINNER...?

NO, MY TREAT. I'M THE ONE WITH THE BIG BUCKS, REMEMBER... SAY, I JUST THOUGHT ...WHEN DID WE INSTALL A TELEPHONE IN THAT ROOM...?

THE WITCH IS EASILY ONE OF THE MOST POWERFUL MEMBERS OF THE TEAM. I JUST DON'T UNDERSTAND HER REACTION TO ALL THIS.

YEAH, I KNOW, MA, IT'S LIKE YOU AND PA ALWAYS SAID...

THERE'S NO REAL UNDERSTANDING THE HUMAN HEART...

OR THE HUMAN MIND...

NEXT ISSUE:

THE **GREAT LAKES AVENGERS**

(NO, REALLY!)

IN **WEST COAST AVENGERS #46**! ON SALE IN **30** DAYS!

97

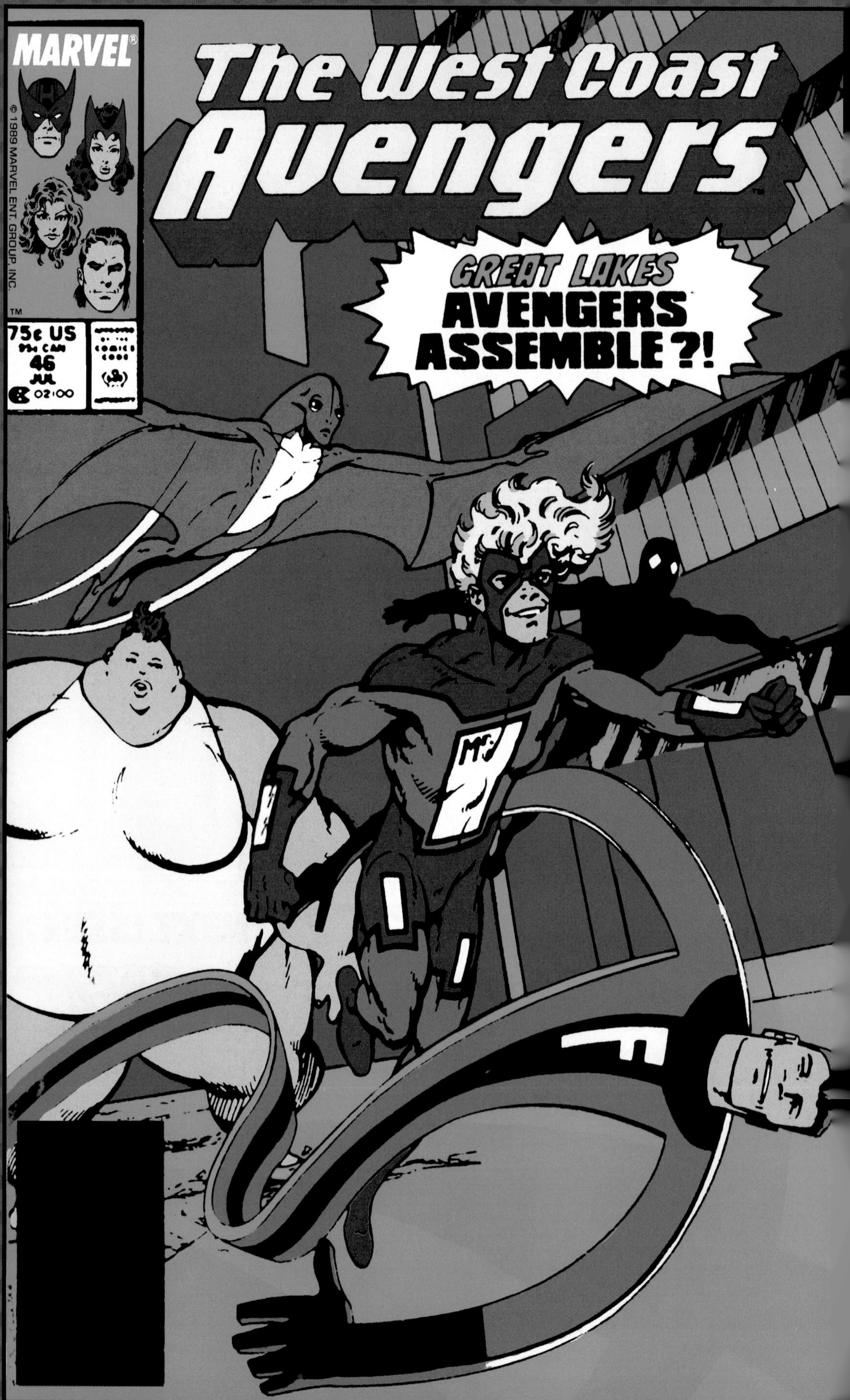

MARVEL®
The West Coast Avengers™
© 1989 MARVEL ENT. GROUP, INC.
TM
75¢ US
99¢ CAN
46
JUL
02100
GREAT LAKES AVENGERS™ ASSEMBLE?!

STAN LEE PRESENTS: The WEST COAST AVENGERS

| WRITTEN & PENCILED BY JOHN BYRNE | INKED BY MIKE MACHLAN | LETTERED BY BILL OAKLEY | COLORED BY BOB SHAREN | EDITED BY HOWARD MACKIE | APPROVED BY TOM DEFALCO |

FRANCHISE

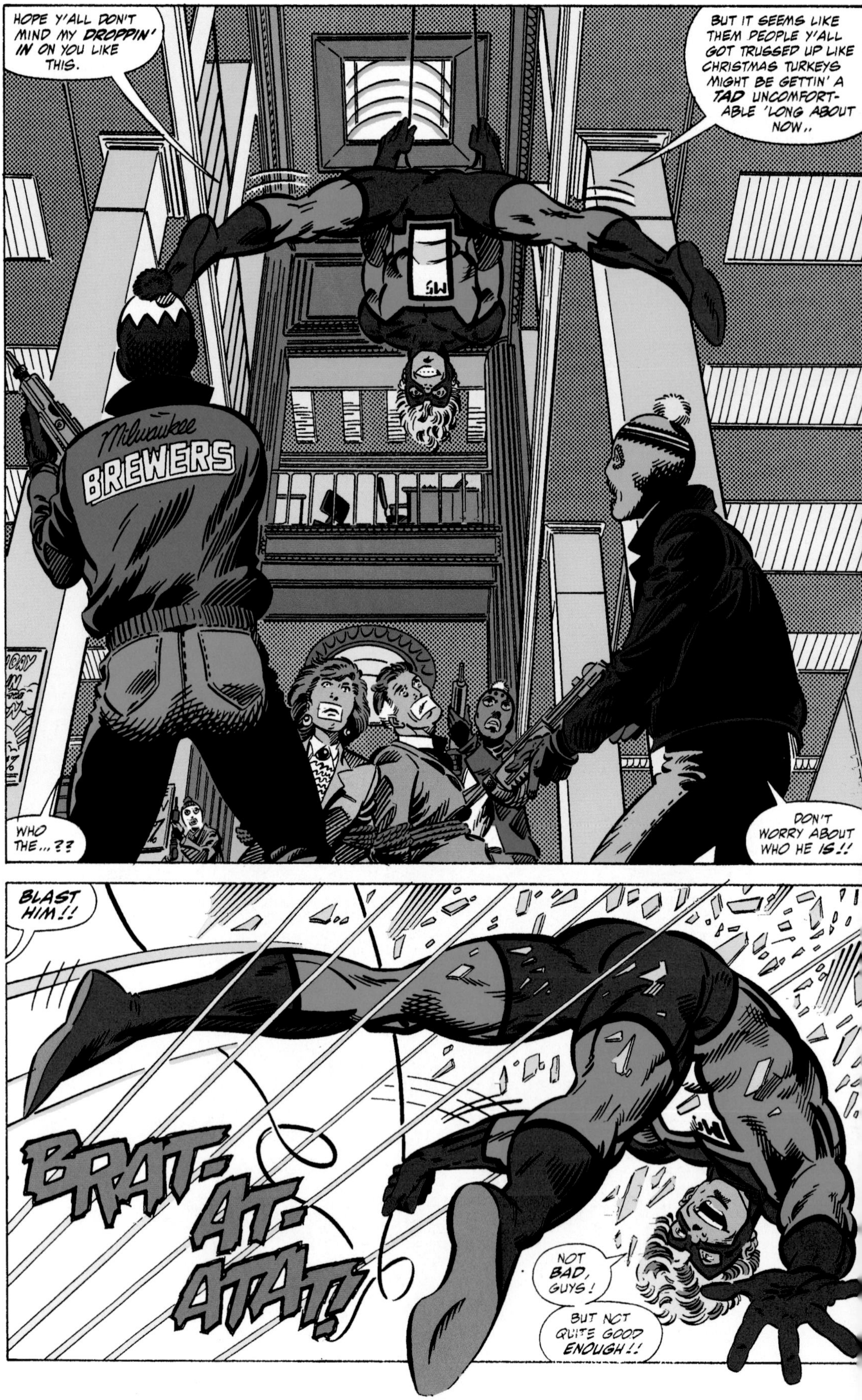

HOPE Y'ALL DON'T MIND MY DROPPIN' IN ON YOU LIKE THIS.
BUT IT SEEMS LIKE THEM PEOPLE Y'ALL GOT TRUSSED UP LIKE CHRISTMAS TURKEYS MIGHT BE GETTIN' A TAD UNCOMFORTABLE 'LONG ABOUT NOW..
BREWERS
WHO THE...??
DON'T WORRY ABOUT WHO HE IS!!
BLAST HIM!!
BRATT-AT-ATAT!
NOT BAD, GUYS!
BUT NOT QUITE GOOD ENOUGH!!

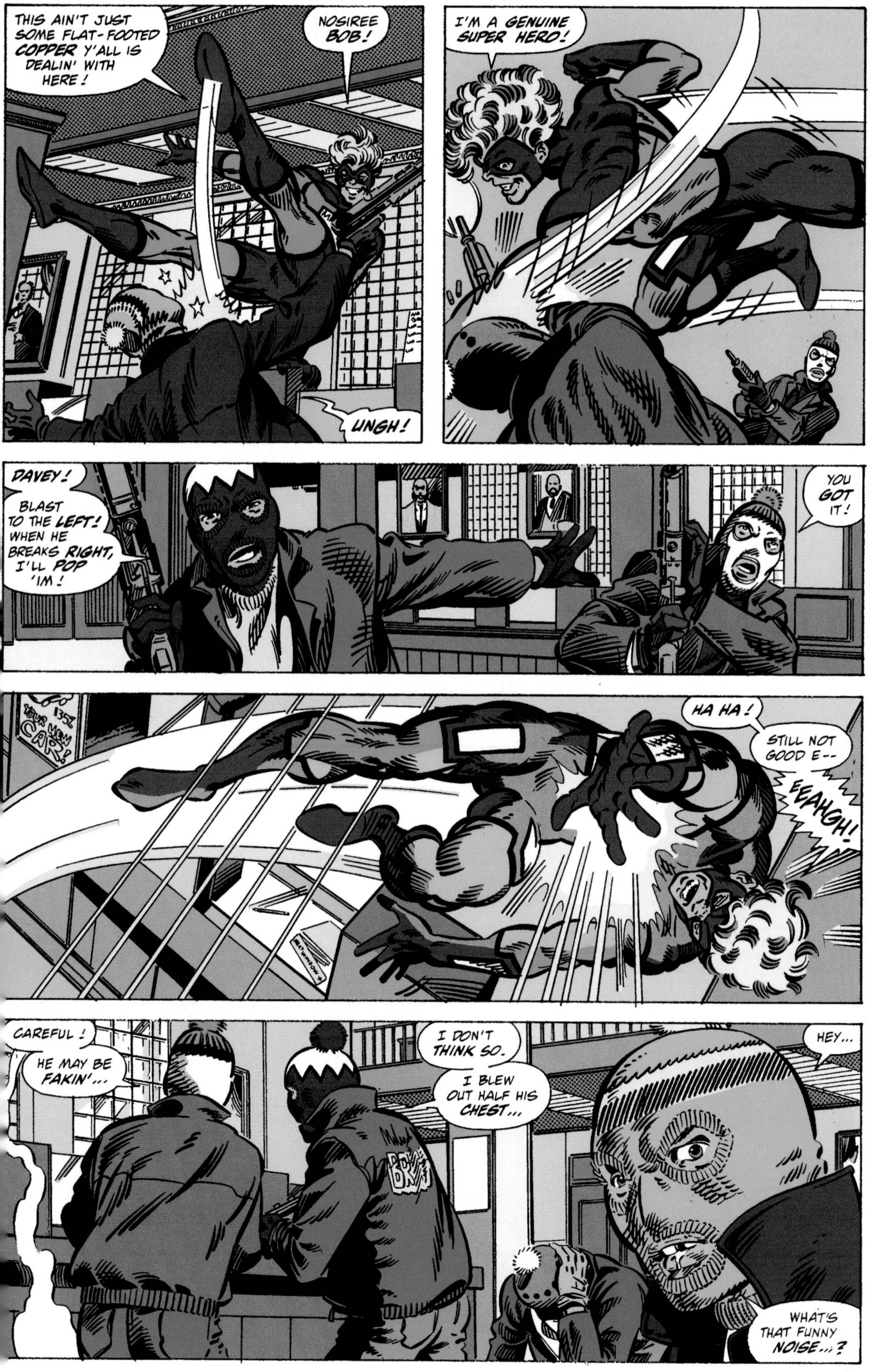
THIS AIN'T JUST SOME FLAT-FOOTED COPPER Y'ALL IS DEALIN' WITH HERE!
NOSIREE BOB!
UNGH!
I'M A GENUINE SUPER HERO!
DAVEY! BLAST TO THE LEFT! WHEN HE BREAKS RIGHT, I'LL POP 'IM!
YOU GOT IT!
HA HA! STILL NOT GOOD E--
EEAHGH!
CAREFUL! HE MAY BE FAKIN'...
I DON'T THINK SO. I BLEW OUT HALF HIS CHEST...
HEY... WHAT'S THAT FUNNY NOISE...?

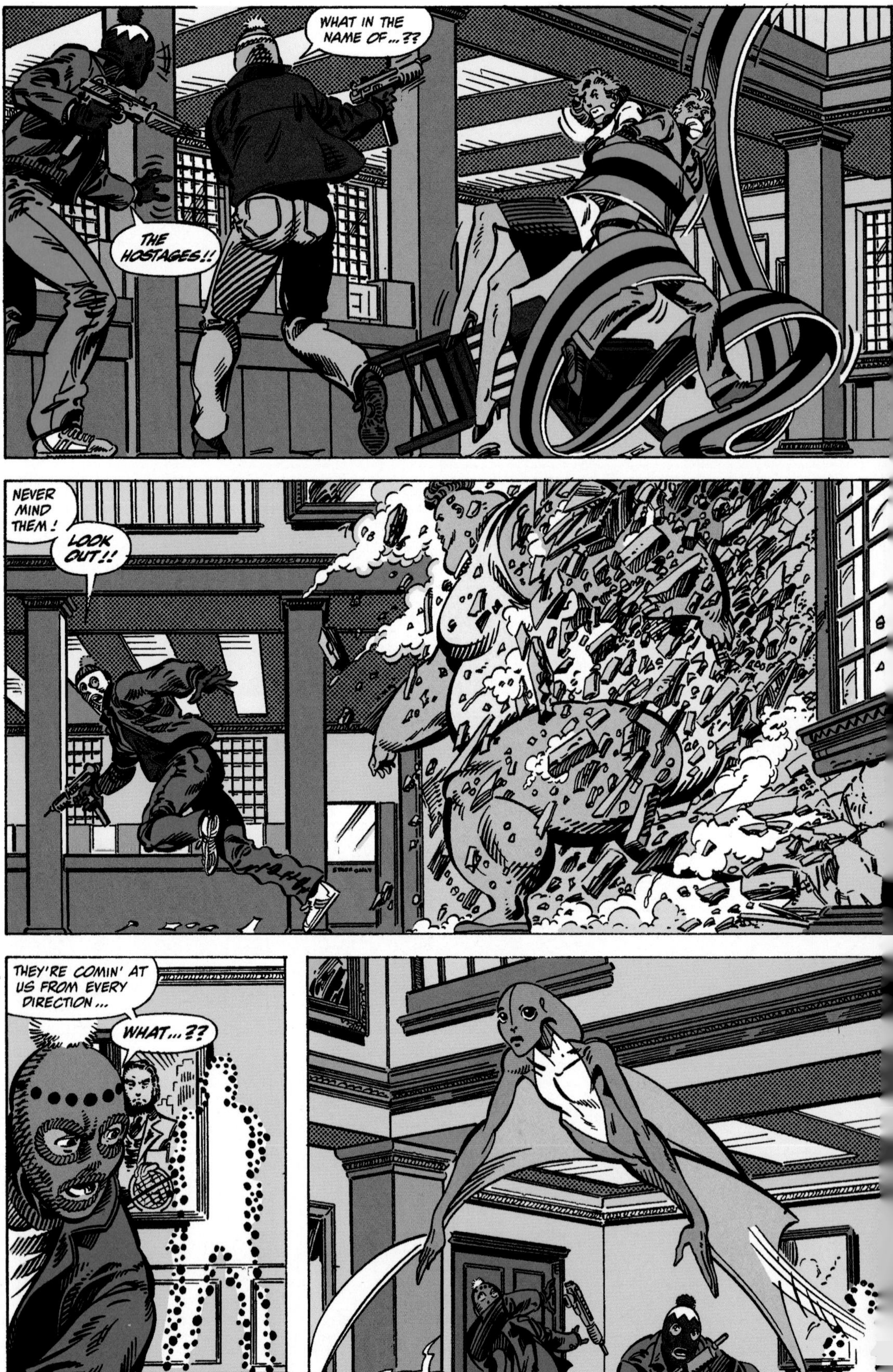

WHAT IN THE NAME OF...??
THE HOSTAGES!!
NEVER MIND THEM!
LOOK OUT!!
THEY'RE COMIN' AT US FROM EVERY DIRECTION...
WHAT...??
YAHH!!

DON'T STAND AROUND GAPIN'!

BLAST 'EM! BLAST 'EM *ALL!!*

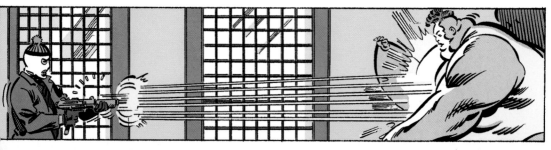

POP POP POP

POP

OW! OW! OW!

OW!

POP POP

103

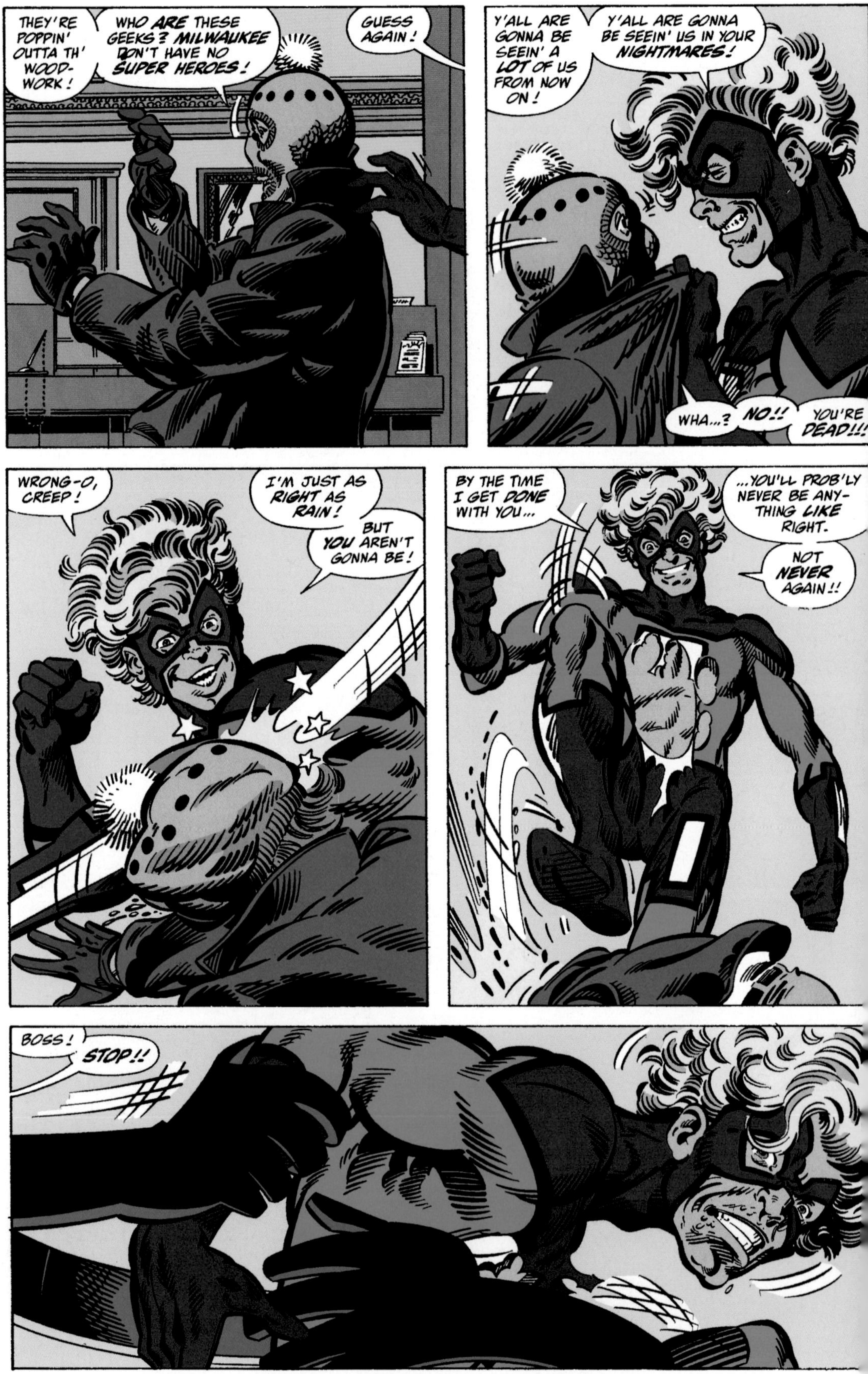

THEY'RE POPPIN' OUTTA TH' WOOD-WORK!
WHO ARE THESE GEEKS? MILWAUKEE DON'T HAVE NO SUPER HEROES!
GUESS AGAIN!
Y'ALL ARE GONNA BE SEEIN' A LOT OF US FROM NOW ON!
Y'ALL ARE GONNA BE SEEIN' US IN YOUR NIGHTMARES!
WHA...?
NO!!
YOU'RE DEAD!!!
WRONG-O, CREEP!
I'M JUST AS RIGHT AS RAIN!
BUT YOU AREN'T GONNA BE!
BY THE TIME I GET DONE WITH YOU...
...YOU'LL PROB'LY NEVER BE ANY-THING LIKE RIGHT.
NOT NEVER AGAIN!!
BOSS!
STOP!!

CALM DOWN! CALM DOWN!

BIG BERTHA! I CAN'T GET HIM TO SIMMER DOWN!

TAKE IT EASY, FLATMAN.

DINAH... LOOKS LIKE WE NEED YOUR MAGIC TOUCH HERE...

WORKS EVERY TIME! I SURE WISH WE KNEW WHAT IT IS SHE DOES!

SOME KIND OF HYPERSONIC, I GUESS. I DON'T KNOW THAT IT MATTERS, AS LONG AS IT CALMS HIM.

HEY, ARE YOU GUYS DONE IN HERE OR WHAT?

THERE'S A SMALL ARMY OF COPS AND REPORTERS OUT HERE CLAMORING TO KNOW WHAT'S GOING ON.

OKAY, PEOPLE! THIS IS IT!

THIS IS WHERE WE REALLY SHOW THE WORLD WHAT WE'RE MADE OF!

THIS IS PEGGY ALLEN REPORTING TO YOU LIVE FROM THE MILWAUKEE FARMERS AND MERCHANTS TRUST BUILDING, WHERE A BAND OF APPARENT SUPERHEROES HAVE JUST...

WAIT A MOMENT! THIS GENTLEMAN SEEMS TO BE THEIR LEADER...

SIR! SIR! WOULD YOU TELL US WHO YOU ARE...??

WHY, I'D BE HAPPY TO, DARLIN'!

Y'ALL CAN CALL US...

...THE GREAT LAKES AVENGERS!

REPEATING THAT TOP STORY, THAT WAS PEGGY ALLEN OF KLMN AFFILIATE WAXO IN MILWAUKEE, WHERE A BRAND NEW BAND OF SUPER HEROES THIS MORNING BURST ONTO THE SCENE, SUCCESSFULLY ENDING A TENSE HOSTAGE SITUATION WHICH...

WHAT??

"THE GREAK LAKES AVENGERS??"

WHAT TH' HECK IS THIS? SOME KIND OF JOKE?

I WONDER IF THE REST OF THE TEAM KNOWS ANYTHING ABOUT...

HOLD IT!

WHAT DO I CARE?

I QUIT THAT CHICKEN OUTFIT WHEN THE GOVERN-MENT STUCK US WITH THAT U.S. AGENT CREEP!

KNOK KNOK

KNOK KNOK KNOK

OKAY, OKAY!!

I'M COMIN'! I'M COMIN'! KEEP YOUR SHIRT...

...ON... YOU!

HI, CLINT. I...

OH, *GREAT! FINE! WONDERFUL!*

MY DAY IS NOW *OFFICIALLY* RUINED!

DON'T BE LIKE THAT, CLINT. IT'S TAKEN ME NEARLY *THREE WEEKS* TO FIND YOU, SINCE YOU STORMED OUT OF THE MANSION.

WE NEED TO *TALK.* OUR MARRIAGE IS AT STAKE HERE...

OH, *IS* IT?

EXCU-U-U-USE ME! I THOUGHT THAT WAS *TAKEN CARE* OF... OR DIDN'T WE ALREADY DECIDE WE WERE GETTING A *DIVORCE?*

YES...

AND I ADMIT OUR PREVIOUS ATTEMPTS AT *RECONCILIATION* HAVE BEEN PRETTY *ABORTIVE.* BUT WE WERE BOTH GOING THROUGH SOME PRETTY *TRYING TIMES.*

NOW THAT THINGS HAVE *CALMED DOWN...*

YOU MEAN NOW THAT I'VE BEEN *KICKED OFF* THE TEAM I *FOUNDED* I'M ALL OF A SUDDEN A PITIFUL SOUL SO YOU'VE GONE ALL *MATERNAL* AND DECIDED TO COME BACK TO THE *ROOST* AND TAKE *CARE* OF ME!

WELL, *THANKS* BUT *NO THANKS,* BOBBI!

YOU'RE NOT BEING *FAIR,* CLINT.

ALTHOUGH I GUESS THAT'S NOTHING *NEW,* IS IT?

AND JUST WHAT IS *THAT* SUPPOSED TO MEAN?

IT *MEANS* YOU HAVE ALL THE SENSITIVITY OF A *BRICK.*

I GOT MIXED UP WITH THE *PHANTOM RIDER* BECAUSE HE *DRUGGED* ME, *USED* ME, AND WHEN YOU FOUND OUT, DID YOU REACT LIKE A HUSBAND WHOSE WIFE HAS BEEN *ASSAULTED?*

NO!!

YOU WENT OFF ON SOME STUPID *MACHO* KICK!

AND I WAS HURT ENOUGH TO PAY YOU BACK WITH YOUR OWN *COIN.*

WHEN I *NEEDED* YOU-- MAYBE MORE THAN I EVER HAVE BEFORE --YOU WERE TOO BUSY STROKING YOUR WOUNDED MALE EGO TO *NOTICE.*

SOMETHING THAT COULD HAVE *BOUND* US EVEN CLOSER TOGETHER *DROVE US APART.*

WELL... THAT DAMAGE IS *DONE.* NOW I'M HERE TO SEE IF IT CAN BE *UNDONE.*

BECAUSE, HEAVEN HELP ME, IN SPITE OF *EVERYTHING,* I STILL *LOVE YOU!*

WELL, IF I MAY SAY SO, SIR... IT DOES MY HEART *GOOD* TO SEE A MAN PUT AWAY SUCH A *BIG* BREAKFAST!

I'VE ONLY BEEN *COOK* HERE AT *AVENGERS COMPOUND* FOR A MONTH, BUT IT SEEMS LIKE MOST OF YOUR TEAMMATES DON'T WANT ANYTHING MORE THAN A SLICE OF TOAST AND ORANGE JUICE!

A MAN HAS TO KEEP HIS *STRENGTH* UP, MRS. HEYGES.

AND, OF COURSE, BREAKFAST IS THE MOST IMPORTANT MEAL OF THE DAY.

BESIDES... YOU'RE ALMOST AS *GOOD* A *COOK* AS MY *MOTHER!*

WELL, *GRACIAS*, SIR! I KNOW THAT MUST BE QUITE A *COMPLIMENT.*

BUT I'M AFRAID I DON'T GET MUCH CHANCE TO REALLY *COOK* FOR THE OTHERS.

THAT'S *UNFORTUNATE.* PERHAPS ONE OF THE *DISCIPLINES* I SHOULD INTRODUCE AROUND HERE IS A PROPER MEAL SCHEDULE.

MY MOTHER ALWAYS SAYS...

WHAT THE...?!?

SQUEEEEEEEEEEEEEE

TIGRA!!

A MOUSE! OH, DEAR! THAT WILL MEAN...

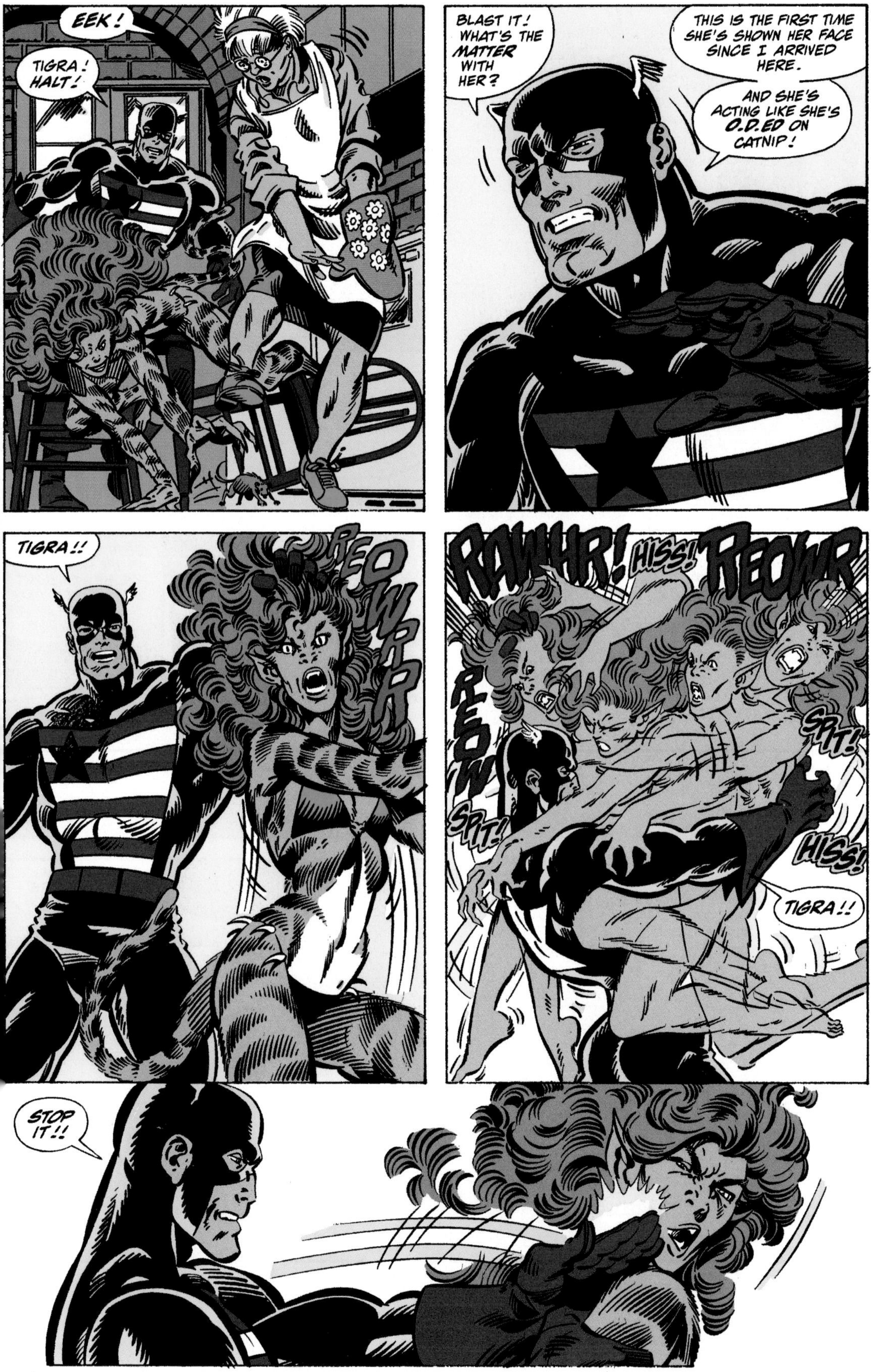
EEK!
TIGRA! HALT!
BLAST IT! WHAT'S THE MATTER WITH HER?
THIS IS THE FIRST TIME SHE'S SHOWN HER FACE SINCE I ARRIVED HERE.
AND SHE'S ACTING LIKE SHE'S O.D.ED ON CATNIP!
TIGRA!!
REOWRR
RAWHR!
HISS!
REOWR
REOW
SPIT!
SPIT!
HISS!
TIGRA!!
STOP IT!!

TIGRA!

MRS. HEYGES...

YOU SPOKE AS IF THIS WASN'T THE FIRST TIME TIGRA HAS COME BURST-ING THROUGH YOUR KITCHEN LIKE THIS.

NO, SIR, IT ISN'T.

THIS WAS THE...FOURTH TIME SINCE I GOT HERE. SHE COMES DOWN AFTER THE MICE THAT GET INTO MY PANTRY.

IN FACT... WELL, MAYBE THIS WASN'T SUCH A GOOD IDEA, BASED ON YOUR REACTION, BUT THAT WAS THE MAIN REASON I DIDN'T DO ANYTHING ABOUT THE MICE-- LIKE SETTING TRAPS OR WHAT HAVE YOU.

TIGRA HAS BEEN TAKING CARE OF THE PROBLEM FOR ME. I...SORT OF ASSUMED THAT WAS PART OF HER ...AH...JOB.

THAT'S... DISGUSTING!

WHATEVER HER PHYSICAL ATTRIBUTES, TIGRA IS A HUMAN BEING! SHE SHOULD NOT BE EATING RAW MICE!

SOMETHING HAS GOT TO BE DONE ABOUT THIS!

TELL ME AGAIN WHY I'M DOING THIS...?

CALL IT A KIND OF *THERAPY*, CLINT. YOU'VE BEEN FEELING *SORRY* FOR YOURSELF SINCE YOU QUIT THE *AVENGERS...*

I DIDN'T *QUIT.*

I WAS *FIRED.*

SO, OKAY...

HAVE IT YOUR WAY. IN ANY CASE, YOU'RE OUT.

AND YET, WHEN YOU HEARD ABOUT THESE SO-CALLED "*GREAT LAKES AVENGERS*," YOUR FIRST INSTINCT WAS TO CHECK 'EM OUT. AT LEAST, THAT'S WHAT YOU TOLD ME LAST NIGHT.

"WE COME TO *MILWAUKEE...*

"AND WE CHECK 'EM OUT!"

AVENGERS ASSEMBLE!!

111

THERE'S OUR TARGET! THE GERMANIA BUILDING!

AND, LOOK!! THE MYSTERIOUS LIGHTS I HEARD ABOUT IN THE POLICE A.P.B.* ARE STILL THERE!

*ALL POINTS BULLETIN. --Howard

DINAH SOAR! CHECK OUT THE UPPER LEVELS!

WE NEED TO GET SOMEONE INSIDE WITHOUT DAMAGING THE BUILDING...

DOORMAN...

WAY AHEAD OF YOU, MR. I...

OKAY, FLATMAN... READY WHEN YOU ARE.

READY AS I'LL EVER BE, D.M. HERE I ...

...GO!

112

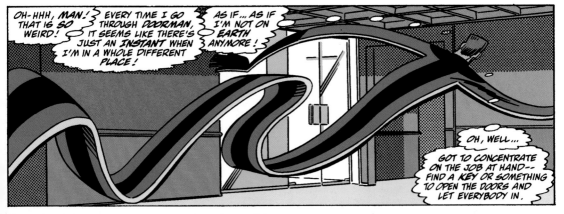

OH-HHH, *MAN!* THAT IS *SO* WEIRD!

EVERY TIME I GO THROUGH *DOORMAN,* IT SEEMS LIKE THERE'S JUST AN *INSTANT* WHEN I'M IN A WHOLE DIFFERENT PLACE!

AS IF... AS IF I'M NOT ON *EARTH* ANYMORE!

OH, WELL...

GOT TO CONCENTRATE ON THE JOB AT HAND-- FIND A *KEY* OR SOMETHING TO OPEN THE DOORS AND LET EVERYBODY IN.

GIMBELS

TWEEEEEE

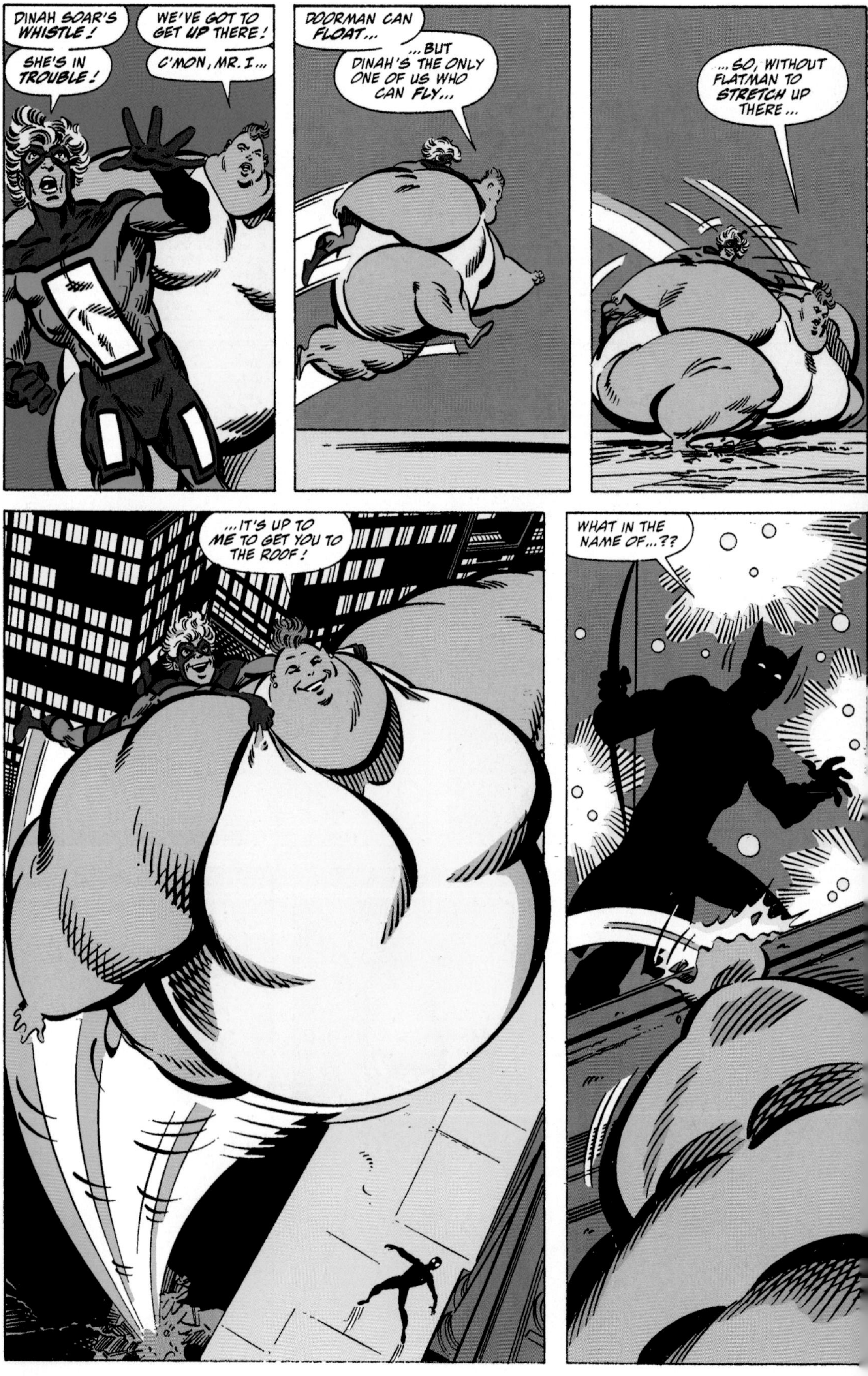
DINAH SOAR'S WHISTLE!
SHE'S IN TROUBLE!
WE'VE GOT TO GET UP THERE!
C'MON, MR. I...
DOORMAN CAN FLOAT...
...BUT DINAH'S THE ONLY ONE OF US WHO CAN FLY...
...SO, WITHOUT FLATMAN TO STRETCH UP THERE...
...IT'S UP TO ME TO GET YOU TO THE ROOF!
WHAT IN THE NAME OF...??

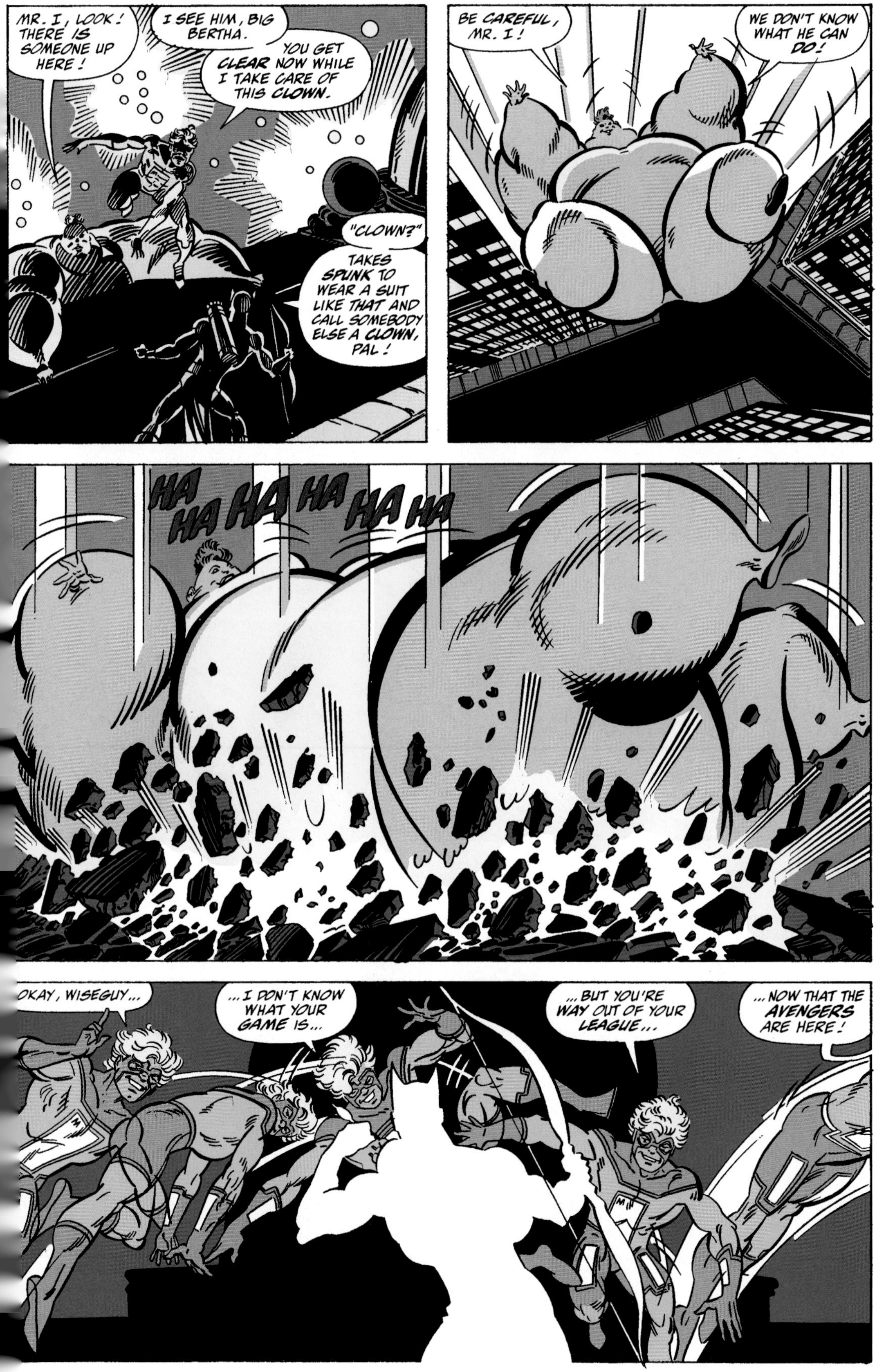
MR. I, LOOK! THERE IS SOMEONE UP HERE!
I SEE HIM, BIG BERTHA.
YOU GET CLEAR NOW WHILE I TAKE CARE OF THIS CLOWN.
"CLOWN?"
TAKES SPUNK TO WEAR A SUIT LIKE THAT AND CALL SOMEBODY ELSE A CLOWN, PAL!
BE CAREFUL, MR. I!
WE DON'T KNOW WHAT HE CAN DO!
HA HA HA HA HA HA HA
OKAY, WISEGUY...
...I DON'T KNOW WHAT YOUR GAME IS...
...BUT YOU'RE WAY OUT OF YOUR LEAGUE...
...NOW THAT THE AVENGERS ARE HERE!

AVENGERS?

THEN THE *FAKE* A.P.B. AND MY *FLARE ARROW* LIGHTSHOW WORKED! NOW LISTEN UP, PALLY...

??

YOU'RE *DRESSED AS* HAWKEYE!

"DRESSED AS HAWKEYE...??"

I *AM* HAWKEYE, AN' I'M HERE TO FIND OUT WHAT YOU SO-CALLED "AVENGERS" THINK YOU'RE UP TO!

IN CASE YOU DON'T KNOW IT, BUSTER, THE AVENGERS' NAME ISN'T UP FOR *GRABS* BY ANY OL' TOM, DICK AN' HARRIET!

NOW, GRAB YOURSELF SOME *FLOOR* AN' I'LL TEACH YOU THE FACTS OF...

...UNGH!

LIAR!! YOU THINK YOU CAN *DEFEAT* THE AVENGERS BY PRETENDING TO BE HAWKEYE?

THE *REAL* HAWKEYE WOULD HAVE *BLOCKED* MY ATTACK EASILY!

NOT NECESSARILY, HOPPY.

HAWK'S SKILLS WITH THE *BOW* HAVE GOT HIM USED TO DEALING WITH FOES AT *LONG* DISTANCE.

ON THE OTHER HAND, I CAN SLING A *BOOT* WITH THE BEST OF 'EM!

WHUK!

SO, IF YOU *REALLY* WANT A FIGHT, I CAN REARRANGE YOUR FEATURES FOR YOU, PRONTO!

A *WOMAN*...! *DRESSED AS* MOCKINGBIRD!

WHAT IS IT WITH YOU AND THIS "DRESSED AS" BUSINESS?

HAWKEYE *IS* HAWKEYE, AND I *AM* MOCKINGBIRD!

IF YOU WANT TO PULL OFF *THAT* CHARADE, YOU SHOULD PAY MORE ATTENTION TO THE *NEWSPAPERS*, LEGS.

HAWKEYE AND MOCKINGBIRD HAVE *SPLIT UP*, AND SHE'S *QUIT* THE AVENGERS!

SO, IF YOU THINK THOSE CHEAP IMITATION COSTUMES ARE GONNA *FOOL* ANYONE...

...YOU'RE *WRONG.*

DEAD WRONG!

NO!

OH NO...

OH NO...

HE DIDN'T HAVE A *LINE*... A *NET*...

NO ONE TO *CATCH* HIM...!

HE'S FALLEN TO HIS *DEATH!*

JUST LIKE *PHANTOM RIDER!*

BOBBI!

HE NEVER HAD A *CHANCE!*

WHY DID HE DO IT?

WHY?

WHY??

WHY???

EVEN IF HE BELIEVED US TO BE SUPER-VILLAINS...

...WHY *KILL* HIMSELF...??

YOU... REALLY *CARE*, DON'T YOU?

WHO...?? I'M DEPUTY LEADER OF THE G.L.A. I'M CALLED FLATMAN.

FLAT-MAN??

I DON'T BELIEVE IT! YOU GOT A PARTNER CALLED "RIB-BON"?

WHIRRRRRRRR

HAWKEYE! THIS IS NO TIME FOR YOUR STUPID JOKES!

THERE'S A MAN DEAD HERE!

ER...WELL....NO, MOCKINGBIRD. AS A MATTER OF FACT, THERE ISN'T.

MR. I... THAT IS, MISTER IMMORTAL...

HE CAN'T DIE!

OKAY! OKAY! ENOUGH IS TOO MUCH!

WE NEED TO SIT DOWN AND TALK. DO YOU "AVENGERS" HAVE A HEAD-QUARTERS?

WELL... NOT LIKE YOUR WEST COAST COM-POUND, OR THE EAST COAST MANSION...

"MOSTLY WE JUST MEET AT BIG BERTHA'S PLACE..."

THIS IS SOME SHACK! HOW'D BERTHA PUT TOGETHER THE DOUGH FOR A PLACE LIKE THIS?

VERY SIMPLE, HAWKEYE...

I EARNED IT!

YOU'RE *BIG BERTHA*? WHAT TH' *HECK* HAPPENED TO TH' *REST* OF YOU?

WAIT A *MINUTE*! I KNOW THAT FACE! I'VE SEEN YOU ON ABOUT A *MILLION* VOGUE COVERS!

YES... I'M *ASHLEY CRAWFORD.* NOT TOO LONG AGO, I WAS THE HIGHEST PAID MANNEQUIN IN THE COUNTRY.

OKAY, I'LL *BITE...* HOW DO YOU GO FROM BEING A PRO- FESSIONAL CLOTHES HORSE TO PLAYING SUPER HERO?

I DON'T THINK OF IT AS... *PLAYING,* HAWKEYE. NONE OF US DO.

WE'RE ALL JUST AS *SERIOUS* ABOUT THIS AS YOU ARE.

WELL, IN *HIS* CASE, THAT'S NOT TOO SERIOUS AT ALL!

BUT... HOW DID YOU ALL GET TO- *GETHER?* AND WHY IN *MILWAUKEE?* AND WHY THE "GREAT LAKES AVENGERS?"

THAT WAS MR. I'S IDEA. HE WANTED TO MAINTAIN THE *COASTAL* THEME OF THE EAST COAST AND WEST COAST GROUPS.

AND SINCE THERE'S NO *NORTH* COAST...

BUT... I'M STARTIN' TO THINK MAYBE THIS MIDWEST TEAM ISN'T SUCH A *BAD* IDEA.

YOUR *POWERS* ARE KINDA FUNKY, AND YOUR CODE NAMES *STINK...*

I DON'T THINK THAT'S WHAT SHE MEANS, FLAT.

YOU WERE ASKING WHERE WE GET OFF CALLING OUR- SELVES *AVEN- GERS,* RIGHT, MOCKING- BIRD?

WELL, THAT *IS* KIND OF WHY WE'RE HERE, ER, *DOORMAN.*

THE AVENGERS NAME ISN'T QUITE LIKE A FAST FOOD FRANCHISE. WE'RE ... WELL, *FUSSY* ABOUT WHO *USES* IT.

YOU SAID IT, *MOCKIE!*

... BUT WITH THE PROPER MANAGE- MENT... *MY* MANAGEMENT...

... THIS COULD BE A *HECKUVA* TEAM!

MEANWHILE...

'SCUSA, SENORA WANDA... A SPECIAL DELIVERY LETTER WAS JUST BROUGHT TO THE COMPOUND... FOR YOU!

FOR ... ME?

ER... THANK YOU, CARLOS.

OH ... HAVE YOU SEEN MY HUSBAND THIS MORNING?

NO, SENORA.

THE LAST TIME I SAW THE *VISION* WAS TWO DAYS AGO, BEFORE HE APPEARED ON THE TELEVISION ... *

* SEE AVENGERS SPOTLIGHT #23 --HOWARD

THANK YOU, CARLOS.

THIS IS FOR ME. BUT WHO WOULD BE SENDING A SPECIAL DELIVERY LETTER TO THE *SCARLET WITCH*?

THERE'S NO RETURN AD-DRESS ... BUT IT HAS A *TEXAS* POSTMARK.

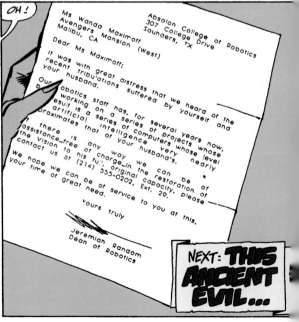

OH!

Absolon College of Robotics
307 College Drive
Saunders, TX

Ms Wanda Maximoff
Avengers Mansion (West)
Malibu, CA

Dear Ms Maximoff:

It was with great distress that we heard of the recent tribulations suffered by yourself and your husband.

Our robotics staff has, for several years now, been working on a series of projects whose result is a series of computers whose level of artificial intelligence very nearly approximates that of your husband's.

If there is any way we can be of assistance—free of charge—in the restoration of the Vision to his full original capacity, please contact us at (214) 555-0202, Ext. 20.

We hope we can be of service to you at this, your time of great need.

yours truly

Jeremiah Ransom
Dean of Robotics

NEXT: **THIS ANCIENT EVIL...**

120

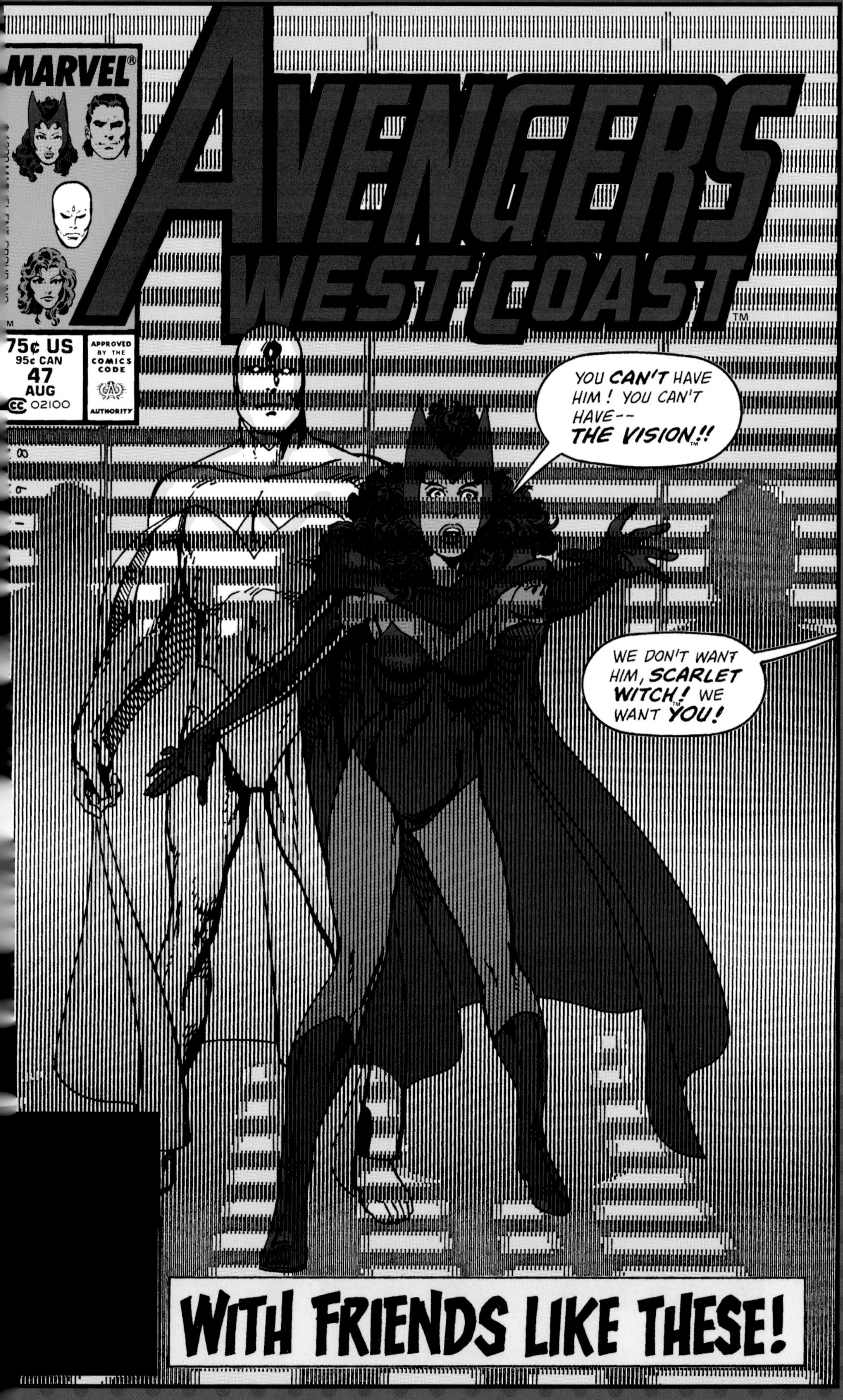
MARVEL®
AVENGERS WEST COAST™
75¢ US
95¢ CAN
47
AUG
APPROVED BY THE COMICS CODE AUTHORITY
02100
YOU CAN'T HAVE HIM! YOU CAN'T HAVE-- THE VISION!!
WE DON'T WANT HIM, SCARLET WITCH! WE WANT YOU!
WITH FRIENDS LIKE THESE!

STAN LEE PRESENTS: **The WEST COAST AVENGERS**

| by: | JOHN BYRNE WRITER / PENCILER | MIKE MACHLAN INKER | BILL OAKLEY LETTERER | BOB SHAREN COLORIST | HOWARD MACKIE EDITOR | TOM DEFALCO LAST NAME IN LIST |

WITH FRIENDS LIKE THESE!

PLEASE....! YOU'VE GOT TO HELP MY HUSBAND!

YOU'RE THE ONLY ONES WHO CAN!

AVENGERS COMPOUND, MALIBU, CALIFORNIA.

IN THE MAIN COMPUTER CENTER, THE *DESPAIR* IN THE VOICE OF THE BEAUTIFUL *SCARLET WITCH* ECHOES FROM THE COLD STEEL WALLS...

...AND DISTURBS THE FOCUSED THOUGHTS OF TWO BRILLIANT MEN...

PLEASE, HANK ...T'CHALLA... IF YOU CAN'T HELP THE VISION...

...NO ONE IN THE AVENGERS CAN!

AND, SO FAR AS I CAN TELL, THE VISION IS IN NO *IMMEDIATE* DISTRESS.

WANDA, PLEASE! WE'RE AT THE *MOST CRITICAL* STAGE IN THE INSTALLATION OF OUR NEW *TAMPER-PROOF* COMPUTER SYSTEM.

WE CAN'T POSSIBLY LEAVE NOW!

T'CHALLA! HOW CAN YOU SAY THAT? AS THE *BLACK PANTHER* YOU'VE STOOD AT THE VISION'S SIDE... *FOUGHT* BY HIM...

HE'S YOUR ALLY, YOUR FRIEND!

NOR DO I SEEK TO *DENY* THAT FRIENDSHIP, WANDA.

BUT, AS I HAVE SAID, I HAVE NOT NOTICED THAT THE VISION IS IN *NEED* OF HELP.

INDEED, BUT FOR THE OBVIOUS CHANGE IN HIS *APPEARANCE*, HE DOES NOT SEEM MUCH ALTERED FROM THE LAST TIME I SAW HIM.

A *REMARKABLE* TESTIMONY TO THE *SKILL* OF HENRY PYM, GIVEN THAT IT WAS HE WHO *REBUILT* YOUR ANDROID HUSBAND AFTER HE WAS *DISMANTLED*, HIS MEMORY ERASED.

123

I CAN'T *BELIEVE* IT!

I CAN'T BELIEVE YOU'D ALL *DESERT* US LIKE THIS!

WANDA! WAIT!

LET HER GO, *T'CHALLA.*

I'M AFRAID *NEITHER* OF US POSSESSES THE NECESSARY SKILLS TO GIVE HER THE PEACE SHE *CRAVES.*

BUT... I DO NOT UNDER-STAND, MY FRIEND. NOT LONG AFTER I ARRIVED HERE YESTERDAY WITH THE NEW *WAKANDAN* COMPUTER EQUIPMENT, I *SAW* THE VISION, SPOKE WITH HIM.

HE SEEMED VERY MUCH AS I REMEMBERED HIM.

I'M SURE HE DID, PANTHER.

THAT'S THE *CORE* OF WANDA'S PROBLEM. IN THE TIME SINCE YOUR LAST *ACTIVE* MEMBER-SHIP IN THE AVENGERS, THE VISION HAD *CHANGED* QUITE A BIT. *HUMANIZED* MIGHT BE THE BEST WORD.

SINCE THE VARIOUS WORLD GOVERN-MENTS CONSPIRED TO HAVE HIS MEMORY *DESTROYED,* HE'S BEEN ...DIFFERENT.

I WAS ABLE TO REPROGRAM HIM WITH ALL THE LOST *KNOWLEDGE,* BUT AS FAR AS HIS HUMAN SIDE, HIS...*SOUL*...

"THAT PART OF THE VISION IS *DEAD* -- AND WILL REMAIN SO AS LONG AS *WONDER MAN* REFUSES TO LET US USE HIS *BRAIN PATTERNS* TO RECREATE THE VISION'S PERSONALITY MATRIX."

WANDA...?

WANDA, I NEED TO TALK TO YOU...

WANDA...

...WANDA...

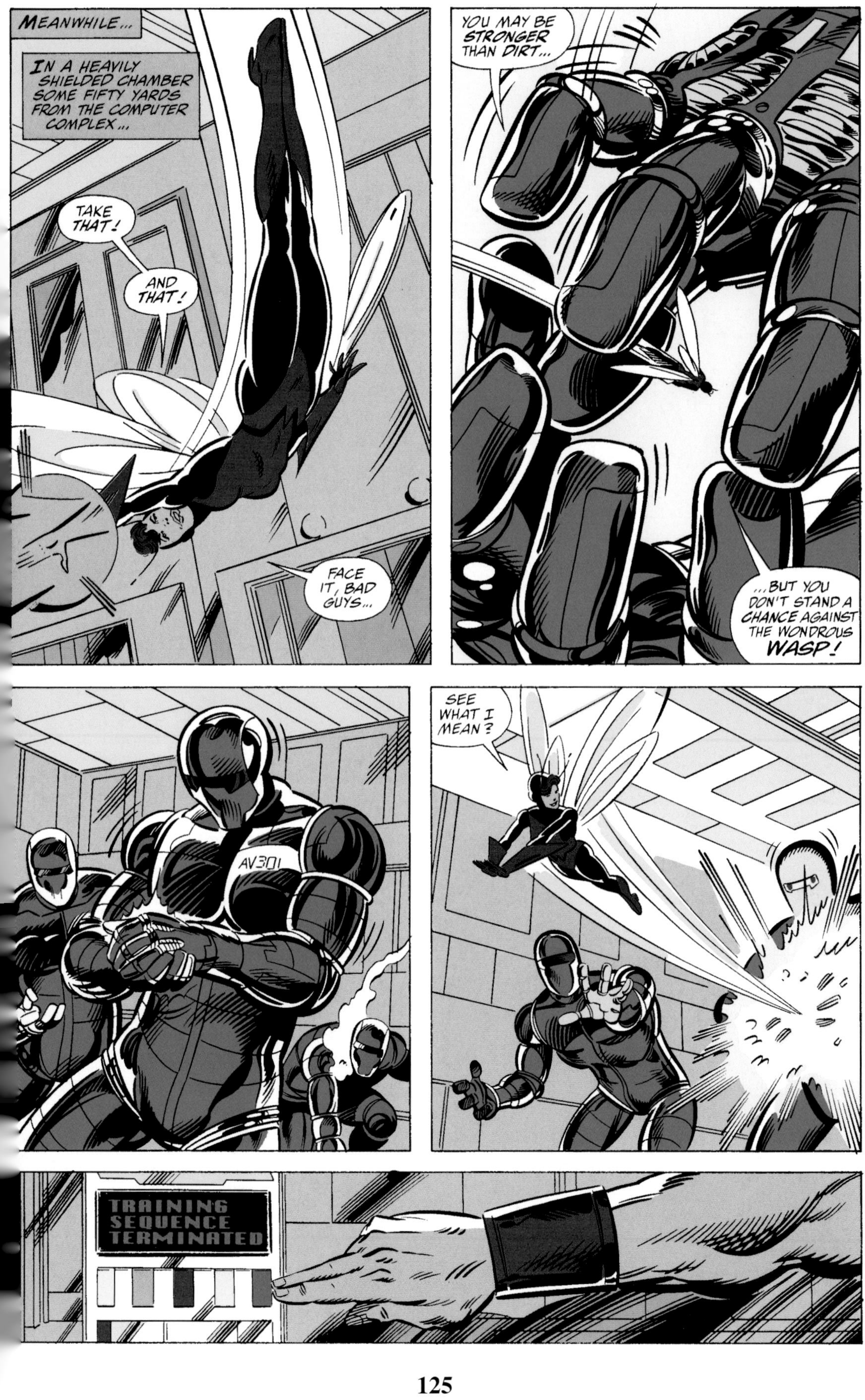
MEANWHILE...
IN A HEAVILY SHIELDED CHAMBER SOME FIFTY YARDS FROM THE COMPUTER COMPLEX...
TAKE THAT!
AND THAT!
FACE IT, BAD GUYS...
YOU MAY BE STRONGER THAN DIRT...
...BUT YOU DON'T STAND A CHANCE AGAINST THE WONDROUS WASP!
AV301
SEE WHAT I MEAN?
TRAINING SEQUENCE TERMINATED

HEY! WHO SWITCHED OFF...?

WONDER MAN...?

HELLO, JAN. CAN I... TALK TO YOU FOR A MINUTE?

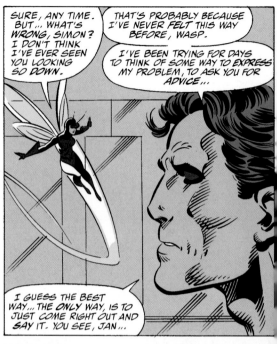

SURE, ANY TIME. BUT... WHAT'S WRONG, SIMON? I DON'T THINK I'VE EVER SEEN YOU LOOKING SO DOWN.

THAT'S PROBABLY BECAUSE I'VE NEVER FELT THIS WAY BEFORE, WASP.

I'VE BEEN TRYING FOR DAYS TO THINK OF SOME WAY TO EXPRESS MY PROBLEM, TO ASK YOU FOR ADVICE...

I GUESS THE BEST WAY... THE ONLY WAY, IS TO JUST COME RIGHT OUT AND SAY IT. YOU SEE, JAN...

...I'M IN LOVE WITH THE SCARLET WITCH.

AND YOU ALWAYS HAVE BEEN.

I KNOW THAT, SIMON.

Y-YOU KNOW?

HOW...?

WHEN...?

HOW??

OH, I GUESS IN THE BACK OF MY MIND, I'VE PROBABLY KNOWN IT ALL ALONG. IT WOULDN'T TAKE A GREAT BRAIN TO FIGURE IT OUT, AFTER ALL. THE VISION WAS PROGRAMMED WITH YOUR MIND, AND THE VISION FELL IN LOVE WITH WANDA.

ERGO....

WHAT I GUESS I DON'T UNDERSTAND IS WHY YOU'VE NEVER EXPRESSED YOUR FEELINGS BEFORE.

HOW COULD I, JANET?

THE FIRST TIME I EVER MET THEM, WANDA AND THE VISION WERE ALREADY MARRIED, AND I HAPPEN TO COME FROM THE OLD SCHOOL. I BELIEVE THERE ARE RULES ABOUT THINGS LIKE THAT.

AND AS YOU SEE THE PRESENT SITUATION, THOSE *RULES* NO LONGER *APPLY*, RIGHT?

I MEAN, THERE'S STILL AN *ANDROID* WALKING AROUND CALLING HIMSELF THE *VISION* -- AND I GUESS THAT'S WHAT'S KEEPING MOST OF US FROM REACTING TO THE FACT THAT OUR FORMER COMRADE IN ARMS IS, WELL, *DEAD...*

YES. THE *REAL VISION*, THE ONE WHO'S BEEN A MEMBER OF THE AVENGERS ALL THESE YEARS...

WELL... HE'S *GONE*. ERASED. ERADICATED!

AND *YOU* HOLD THE *KEY* TO EVEN *BEGINNING* TO BRING HIM BACK.

BUT, IF YOU *DO*, YOU'LL LOSE YOUR ONLY CHANCE OF EVER WINNING WANDA.

I *ASSUME* THAT'S WHAT THIS IS ABOUT. AND I'LL *BET* YOU HAVEN'T TOLD WANDA.

NO... HOW CAN I? I TRIED THE OTHER DAY, ON THE BEACH, BUT I JUST CAME OFF SOUNDING LIKE A SELF-CENTERED IDIOT.

I MEAN, THERE'S NO *PROPER* WAY TO SAY IT, IS THERE? "I WON'T LET YOUR HUSBAND HAVE MY MIND AGAIN, WANDA, BECAUSE I WANT YOU FOR MYSELF_"

SO NOW WANDA HATES ME, AND I FEEL LIKE I MIGHT BE BETTER OFF *DEAD* AGAIN!

WRONG ATTITUDE, SIMON. THERE HAS TO BE A SOLUTION TO THIS.

AND I'M JUST *ROMANTIC* ENOUGH TO WANT TO HELP YOU *FIND* IT.

AFTER ALL, SEEMS LIKE THERE'S QUITE A BIT OF *AMOUR* IN THE AIR.

WHY, EVEN HANK AND I...

BLEEP!

THE SECURITY MONITOR...?

WHAT...?

ATTENTION:

REGISTERING UNSCHEDULED USE OF QUINJET.

HANGAR REF. AV 3701

SORRY, SIMON. LOOKS LIKE YOUR AFFAIR OF THE *HEART* IS GOING TO HAVE TO *WAIT...*

MEAN-WHILE... IT'S BEEN CLOSE TO SEVENTY-TWO HOURS SINCE I SAW HER IN THE MANSION KITCHEN.

IN THAT TIME THERE'S BEEN NO SIGN OF HER ANYWHERE.

THIS IS NOT GOOD. NOT GOOD AT ALL.

I'M NOT SURE WHY FEDERAL AGENT SIKOR-SKI SENT ME TO THE WEST COAST TEAM...

NOK NOK

...BUT ALREADY THINGS ARE STARTING TO GO HAYWIRE. FIRST HAWKEYE QUITS, NOW...

TIGRA!

BLAST! SHE'S SO FAST, I DIDN'T HAVE THE SLIGHTEST CHANCE OF GRABBING HER!

IF SHE MAKES IT TO THE WOODS...

BLAST! BLAST! BLAST! IT'D TAKE A FAR BETTER TRACKER THAN ME TO FOLLOW HER TRAIL.

I WONDER...

THE BLACK PANTHER IS HERE NOW. HE'S SUPPOSED TO BE...

HUH?

HELLO, NEW...

...SAILOR IN TOWN?

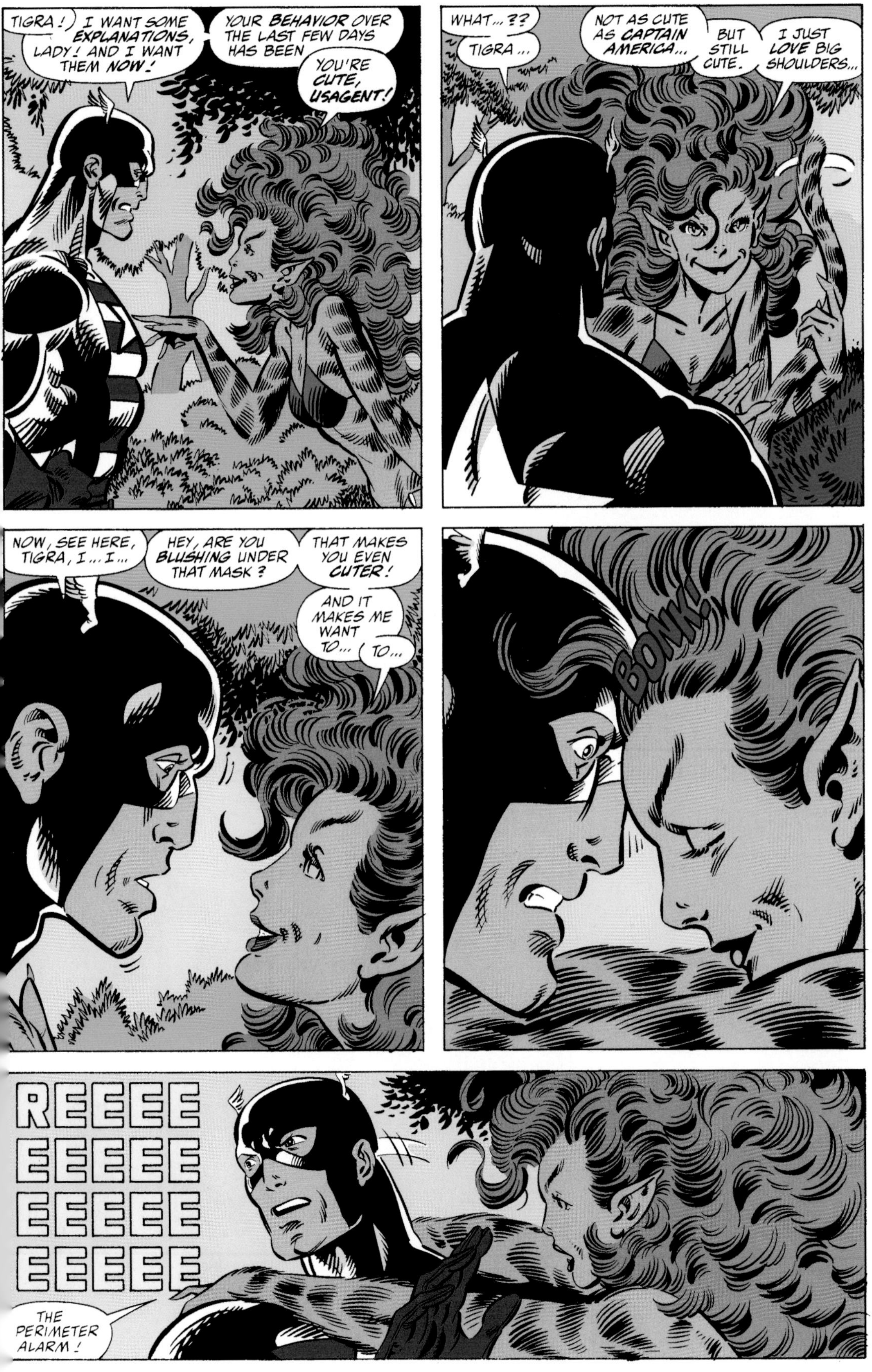
TIGRA!
I WANT SOME EXPLANATIONS, LADY! AND I WANT THEM NOW!
YOUR BEHAVIOR OVER THE LAST FEW DAYS HAS BEEN
YOU'RE CUTE, USAGENT!
WHAT...??
TIGRA...
NOT AS CUTE AS CAPTAIN AMERICA...
BUT STILL CUTE.
I JUST LOVE BIG SHOULDERS...
NOW, SEE HERE, TIGRA, I... I...
HEY, ARE YOU BLUSHING UNDER THAT MASK?
THAT MAKES YOU EVEN CUTER!
AND IT MAKES ME WANT TO...
TO...
BONK!
REEEE EEEEE EEEEE EEEEE
THE PERIMETER ALARM!

SOMEBODY'S LAUNCHING A QUINJET WITHOUT AUTHORIZATION!

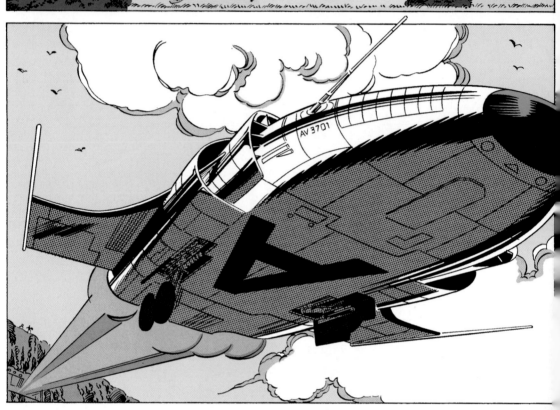

AV 3701

BLAST IT ALL!!

ISN'T ANYTHING GOING TO GO RIGHT?

SOMEBODY REPORT!

CLIK

WASP HERE.

I'VE BEEN TRYING TO RAISE THE QUINJET, BUT WHOEVER'S IN THERE IS MAINTAINING RADIO SILENCE.

"WHOEVER'S...??"

YOU MEAN YOU DON'T KNOW...??

NOT FOR SURE, NO. WHOEVER IT IS KNOWS HOW TO FLY A QUINJET, THOUGH.

SO, BY A PROCESS OF ELIMINATION, I GUESS IT MUST BE...

130

...THE VISION AND THE SCARLET WITCH!

AND IF YOU CAN HEAR ME, WANDA, I REALLY WISH YOU'D ANSWER!

JANET SEEMS SOMEWHAT DISTRESSED, WANDA.

PERHAPS YOU SHOULD RESPOND.

ALL RIGHT.

BUT ONLY BECAUSE YOU WANT ME TO, VISION.

WANDA HERE.

RECEIVING YOU, JANET.

WANDA! THANK HEAVENS! WHAT'S WRONG? WHY HAVE YOU TAKEN A QUINJET WITHOUT FILING A PROPER FLIGHT PLAN?

I NEEDED TRANSPORTATION, AND I DID NOT WISH YOU TO KNOW WHERE I AM GOING.

SINCE NONE OF MY TEAMMATES IS INTERESTED IN HELPING THE VISION, I'VE DECIDED TO ACCEPT THE OFFERED ASSISTANCE OF SOMEONE WHO IS!

WANDA, IT'S HANK! PLEASE DON'T DO THIS! I DON'T KNOW WHO YOU ARE PLANNING TO CONTACT, BUT BELIEVE ME, EVERYTHING HUMANLY POSSIBLE HAS BEEN DONE!

THE VISION IS--

I DON'T WANT TO HEAR ANY MORE, DR. PYM!

WITCH OUT!

WANDA! DON'T...

⸢CLIK⸣

SHE'S CUT TRANSMISSION...

...AND ACTIVATED THE STEALTH SHIELD!

SHE'S RENDERED HERSELF INVISIBLE TO ALL TRACKING!

BUT NOT BEFORE WE GOT A FIX ON HER DIRECTION!

DON'T WORRY HON...

"AT LEAST WE KNOW WHICH WAY SHE'S HEADED!"

ONE HOUR LATER...

GROSVENOR MEMORIAL HOSPITAL, SEATTLE, WASHINGTON.

I STILL DON'T SEE HOW YOU AND HANK CAN BE SO SURE WANDA AND THE VISION CAME HERE, JAN.

SIMPLE, SIMON...

ER, SORRY...

SEATTLE LIES ON WANDA'S PROJECTED FLIGHT PATH, AS WE TRACKED IT BEFORE SHE TURNED ON THE STEALTH SHIELD.

AND THIS HOSPITAL IS WHERE PROFESSOR HORTON WAS BROUGHT AFTER WE LIBERATED HIM FROM THE PHONEY S.H.I.E.L.D. GUYS WHO KIDNAPED THE VISION AND STARTED THIS MESS.

I'M SURE WANDA COULD THINK OF NO ONE BETTER TO HELP WITH THE VISION THAN THE MAN WHO BUILT THE ORIGINAL HUMAN TORCH...

THE SELFSAME ANDROID WE ONCE THOUGHT THE VISION HAD BEEN MADE FROM.

...?

MAY I HELP YOU?

YES. WE'RE THE AVENGERS.

WE'D LIKE TO SEE THE SCARLET WITCH, PLEASE.

I'M... AFRAID I DON'T QUITE FOLLOW YOU. THE SCARLET WITCH IS NOT HERE.

I'M SURE I'D KNOW IF SHE WAS.

NOW WHAT, JAN? IF WANDA DIDN'T BRING THE VISION HERE, SHE COULD BE ANYWHERE.

NOT QUITE ANYWHERE, LOVER.

THERE'S A LIMITED NUMBER OF PLACES WANDA COULD HAVE BEEN BOUND FOR, GIVEN HER DIRECTION.

UNLESS SHE DELIBERATELY HEADED THIS WAY, AT FIRST, THEN CHANGED HER COURSE AFTER SHE SWITCHED ON THE STEALTH SHIELD.

I'D HATE TO THINK THAT WAS THE CASE, JAN. IT WOULD MEAN SHE REALLY DOESN'T TRUST US ANY MORE.

AND IF SHE DOESN'T TRUST US, THAT WOULD LEAVE HER WITHOUT ANYONE!

IN FACT, SHE'D BE JUST AS ALONE AND VULNERABLE AS SHE WAS WHEN MAGNETO FIRST RECRUITED HER FOR THE BROTHERHOOD OF EVIL MUTANTS!

"JAN... HANK... I'M BEGINNING TO GET SCARED FOR HER..."

THERE IT IS, VISION.

THE CAMPUS OF SAUNDERS COLLEGE.

YES. ESTABLISHED IN 1864 AS A LIBERAL ARTS COLLEGE, IT HAS RECENTLY CONVERTED TO THE SO-CALLED "HARD SCIENCES."

THE PRESENT FACULTY CONSISTS OF...

ER... YES... THANK YOU, DARLING.

THIS OPEN AREA SEEMS TO BE SOME KIND OF HELIPAD. I'LL LAND HERE.

"I HOPE THEY REALLY ARE EXPECTING US."

SHE HAS BROUGHT THE ROBOT.

YES...

AN ANTICIPATED SIDE EFFECT OF THE DECEPTION WE EMPLOYED TO LURE HER HERE.

EVERYTHING IS IN READINESS?

YES.

THE ASSIMILATOR AWAITS.

"GOOD. THEN LET US GREET OUR GUESTS..."

SCARLET WITCH... VISION... WE'RE SO PLEASED YOU'VE COME.

HELLO...

YOU ARE MR. JEREMIAH RANDOM?

YES. IT WAS MY LETTER WHICH BROUGHT YOU HERE.

I AM *DEAN OF ROBOTICS.* I HOPE WE CAN BE OF *HELP* TO YOU.

I HOPE SO TOO, SIR. ALTHOUGH I AM PERFECTLY CONTENT WITH MY PRESENT FORM, IT SEEMS TO BE A SOURCE OF CONSIDERABLE *DISTRESS* TO MY WIFE.

I CAN WELL UNDERSTAND THAT, VISION.

FROM WHAT WE'VE HEARD AND READ, IT WOULD SEEM YOU AND THE SCARLET WITCH HAVE BEEN THROUGH A MOST *TRAUMATIC* TIME.

ANYTHING WE CAN DO TO *SALVE* YOUR PAINS WILL BE OUR GREATEST PLEASURE.

NOW, COME... WE CAN DISCUSS THIS MATTER MORE FULLY INSIDE.

MR. RANDOM... THE QUINJET...?

DON'T WORRY ABOUT IT. WE'LL TAKE PROPER *CARE* OF IT.

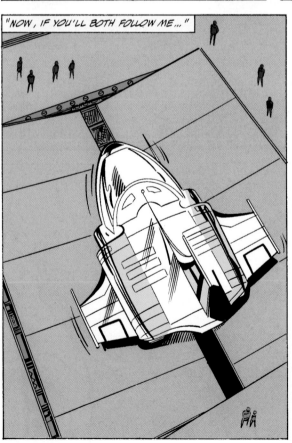

"NOW, IF YOU'LL BOTH FOLLOW ME..."

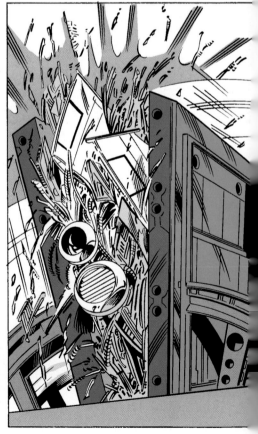

AV3071
NO STEP
BLINK

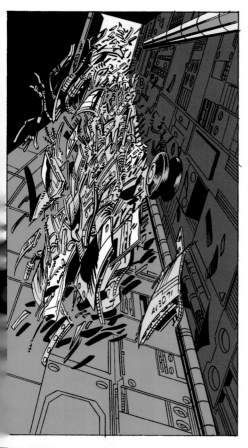

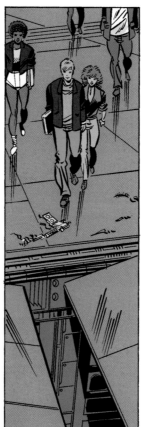

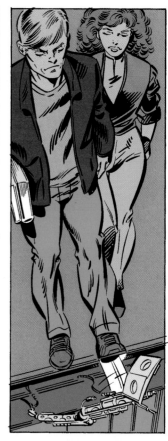

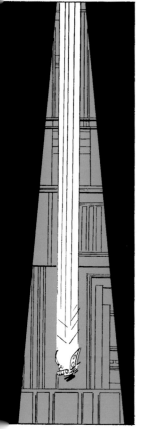

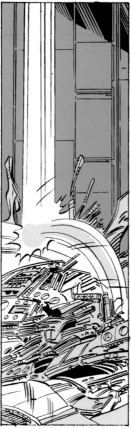

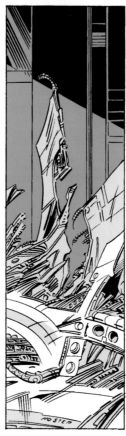

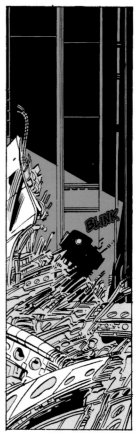

AT THAT MOMENT...

IN THE EAST COAST HQ OF THE AVENGERS...

CAP! WHAT'S THAT NOISE...??

THAT'S A QUINJET EMERGENCY ALARM, SHE-HULK!

ONE OF OUR AIRCRAFT HAS JUST BEEN DESTROYED!

DESTROYED?? HOW...? WHAT...?

WE'LL KNOW SOMETHING MORE AS SOON AS I GET THE TRIANGULATION PLOTTED.

WITH THE AUTOMATED MONITORS WE'VE INSTALLED WORLD-WIDE, IT SHOULDN'T TAKE MORE THAN A SECOND OR SO TO...

THERE! THE QUINJET WENT DOWN IN TEXAS... NEAR THE TOWN OF ABSOLOM!

THE READOUT SAYS IT WAS QUINJET AV-3071...

THAT'S ONE OF THE WEST COAST PLANES, ISN'T IT?

YES IT IS, JENNIFER.

BUT SINCE MY DECISION THAT BOTH TEAMS SHOULD FUNCTION AS ONE FROM NOW ON...

...THIS FALLS UNDER THE HEADING OF OUR RESPONSIBILITY, TOO!

LET'S MOVE OUT!!

A SHORT TIME LATER...

...AND SO YOU CAN SEE QUITE *CLEARLY* THAT OUR ADVANCED APPROACH TO ANDROID CYBER-SYSTEMS IS JUST WHAT YOU *NEED.*

ONCE WE HAVE COMPLETED A DETAILED ANALYSIS OF YOUR HUS-BAND'S CIRCUITRY...

...YOU WILL BE ABLE TO FULLY *RESTORE* HIM?

...BRING HIM BACK TO HOW HE WAS BEFORE HIS MIND WAS *ERASED?*

THAT IS OUR MOST SINCERE HOPE, YES.

NOW...

IF YOU WILL *ACCOMPANY* ME, VISION, WE CAN BEGIN THE FIRST PHASE OF OUR *STUDY.*

CERTAINLY.

VISION, WAIT...

BE...CAREFUL, MY LOVE. BE WELL...

OF COURSE.

I WILL SEE YOU AGAIN IN A SHORT WHILE, WANDA.

137

MR. RANDOM...

YOU'RE *SURE* THERE'S NO REASON FOR ME TO GO WITH MY HUSBAND NOW? THERE MIGHT BE THINGS I COULD TELL YOUR SCIENTISTS... ABOUT HIS MIND... HIS EMOTIONS...

AND WE'LL BE CALLING ON THAT KNOWLEDGE SOON, WANDA.

BUT FOR NOW, WE'LL BE CONDUCTING MORE OR LESS STRAIGHT-FORWARD *PHYSIO-LOGICAL* TESTS.

WE'VE PREPARED SPECIAL *QUARTERS* FOR YOU HERE ON CAMPUS. PERHAPS YOU'D CARE TO *REST* WHILE THOSE PRELIMINARY TESTS ARE BEING DONE.

I'M SURE YOU MUST BE *EMOTIONALLY* EXHAUSTED.

I AM TIRED, YES...

IT'S BEEN SO VERY DIFFICULT, THE PAST FEW WEEKS, TO HAVE THE VISION LITERALLY *DISASSEMBLED*...

...HIS *MIND* GONE...

...AND THEN FOR THE REST OF THE AVENGERS TO SEEM SO *COMPLACENT* ABOUT IT... SO *QUICK* TO ACCEPT HIM IN THIS NEW FORM...

MORE LIKE HIS *ORIGINAL* FORM, REALLY.

YES, I CAN UNDERSTAND HOW *HARD* IT WOULD BE FOR YOU, WANDA.

BUT YOU CAN PUT YOUR MIND AT *EASE* FOR NOW.

YOU'RE AMONGST *FRIENDS* HERE.

AH... HERE WE ARE.

?

THIS IS MY *QUARTERS?* I DON'T...

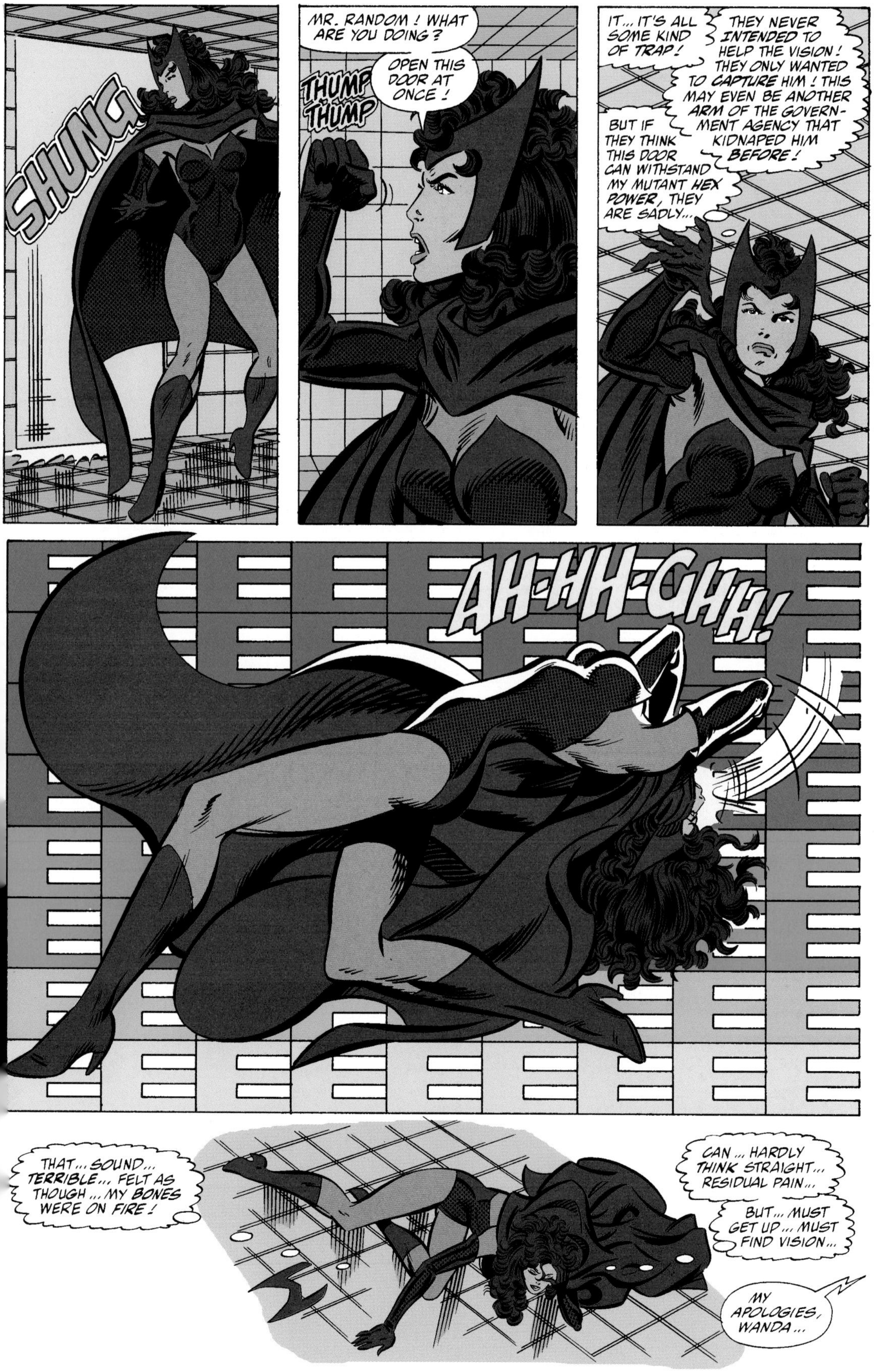
SHUNG
MR. RANDOM ! WHAT ARE YOU DOING ?
THUMP THUMP
OPEN THIS DOOR AT ONCE !
IT... IT'S ALL SOME KIND OF TRAP !
THEY NEVER INTENDED TO HELP THE VISION ! THEY ONLY WANTED TO CAPTURE HIM ! THIS MAY EVEN BE ANOTHER ARM OF THE GOVERNMENT AGENCY THAT KIDNAPED HIM BEFORE !
BUT IF THEY THINK THIS DOOR CAN WITHSTAND MY MUTANT HEX POWER, THEY ARE SADLY...
AH-HH-GHH!
THAT... SOUND... TERRIBLE... FELT AS THOUGH... MY BONES WERE ON FIRE !
CAN ... HARDLY THINK STRAIGHT... RESIDUAL PAIN...
BUT... MUST GET UP... MUST FIND VISION...
MY APOLOGIES, WANDA...

RANDOM!

I REGRET THE NECESSITY OF CAUSING YOU SUCH DISCOMFORT, BUT WE COULD NOT ALLOW YOU TO ESCAPE BEFORE WE COMPLETED OUR STUDIES OF YOU.

OF... ME??

BUT... I THOUGHT... THE VISION...?

THE VISION IS A MECHANICAL CONTRIVANCE, AND OF NO INTEREST TO US.

NO, IT IS YOU WE WANTED, WANDA. YOU WE SELECTED OUT OF ALL THE KNOWN MUTANTS ON EARTH.

YOU WERE CHOSEN BECAUSE YOU ARE POWERFUL-- AND WE SHALL NEED POWER-- BUT NOT SO POWERFUL THAT YOU COULD NOT BE CONTROLLED.

BUT, PERHAPS SOME EXPLANATIONS ARE IN ORDER. THE TIME OF HOMO SAPIENS IS DRAWING RAPIDLY TO A CLOSE, WANDA. THE AGE OF THE MUTANT, OF HOMO SUPERIOR, IS DAWNING. WE INTEND TO BE A PART OF IT.

FOR ALL THE UNCOUNTED MILLENNIA THE APPEARANCE OF MUTANT GENES HAS SOMEHOW STYMIED US. WE HAVE NOT BEEN ABLE TO INFLUENCE THEM, OR THE MUTANTS THEY CREATED.

NOW, IF WE ARE TO MOVE INTO THE NEW DOMINANT SPECIES, WE MUST DEVELOP THIS FACILITY.

MILLENNIA...?

MOVE...?

I DON'T UNDERSTAND.

MM...

AND PERHAPS IT IS NOT REALLY NECESSARY, AFTER ALL, THAT YOU DO.

THE ASSIMILATOR IS READY...

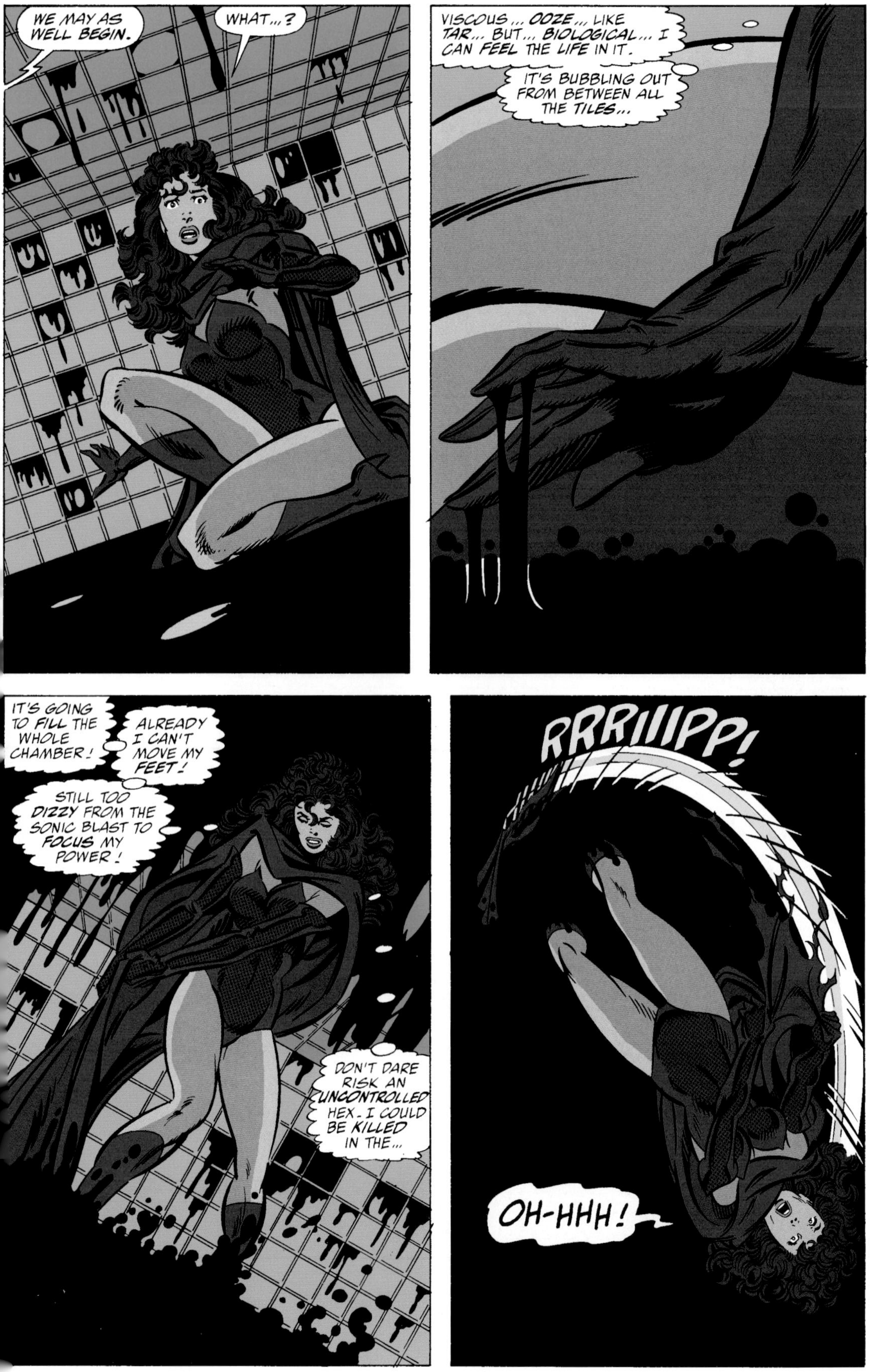
WE MAY AS WELL BEGIN.
WHAT...?
VISCOUS... OOZE... LIKE TAR... BUT... BIOLOGICAL... I CAN FEEL THE LIFE IN IT.
IT'S BUBBLING OUT FROM BETWEEN ALL THE TILES...
IT'S GOING TO FILL THE WHOLE CHAMBER!
ALREADY I CAN'T MOVE MY FEET!
STILL TOO DIZZY FROM THE SONIC BLAST TO FOCUS MY POWER!
DON'T DARE RISK AN UNCONTROLLED HEX. I COULD BE KILLED IN THE...
RRRIIIPP!
OH-HHH!

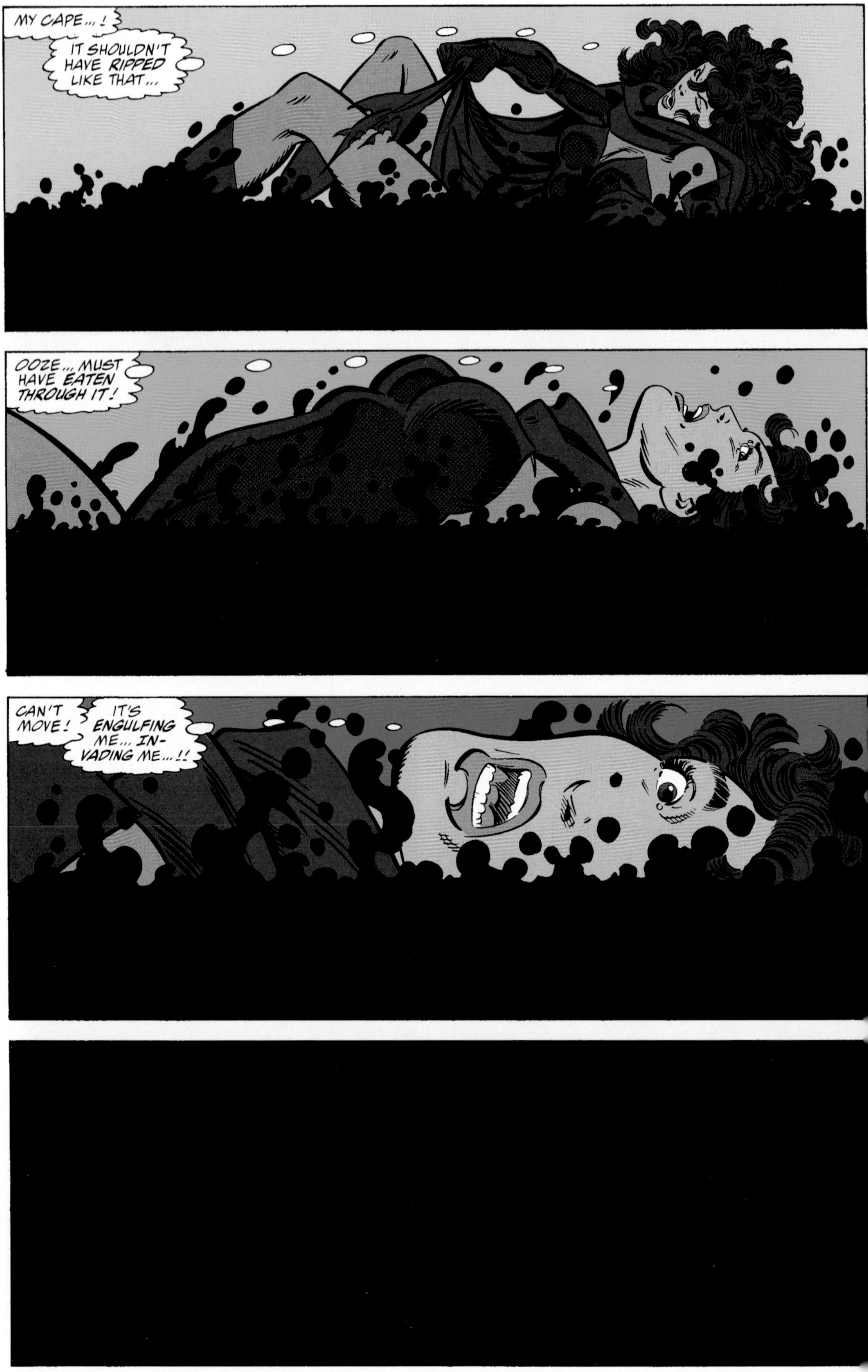
MY CAPE...!
IT SHOULDN'T HAVE RIPPED LIKE THAT...
OOZE... MUST HAVE EATEN THROUGH IT!
CAN'T MOVE!
IT'S ENGULFING ME... IN-VADING ME...!!

NEXT ISSUE: **THIS ANCIENT EVIL....** IN 30 DAYS!

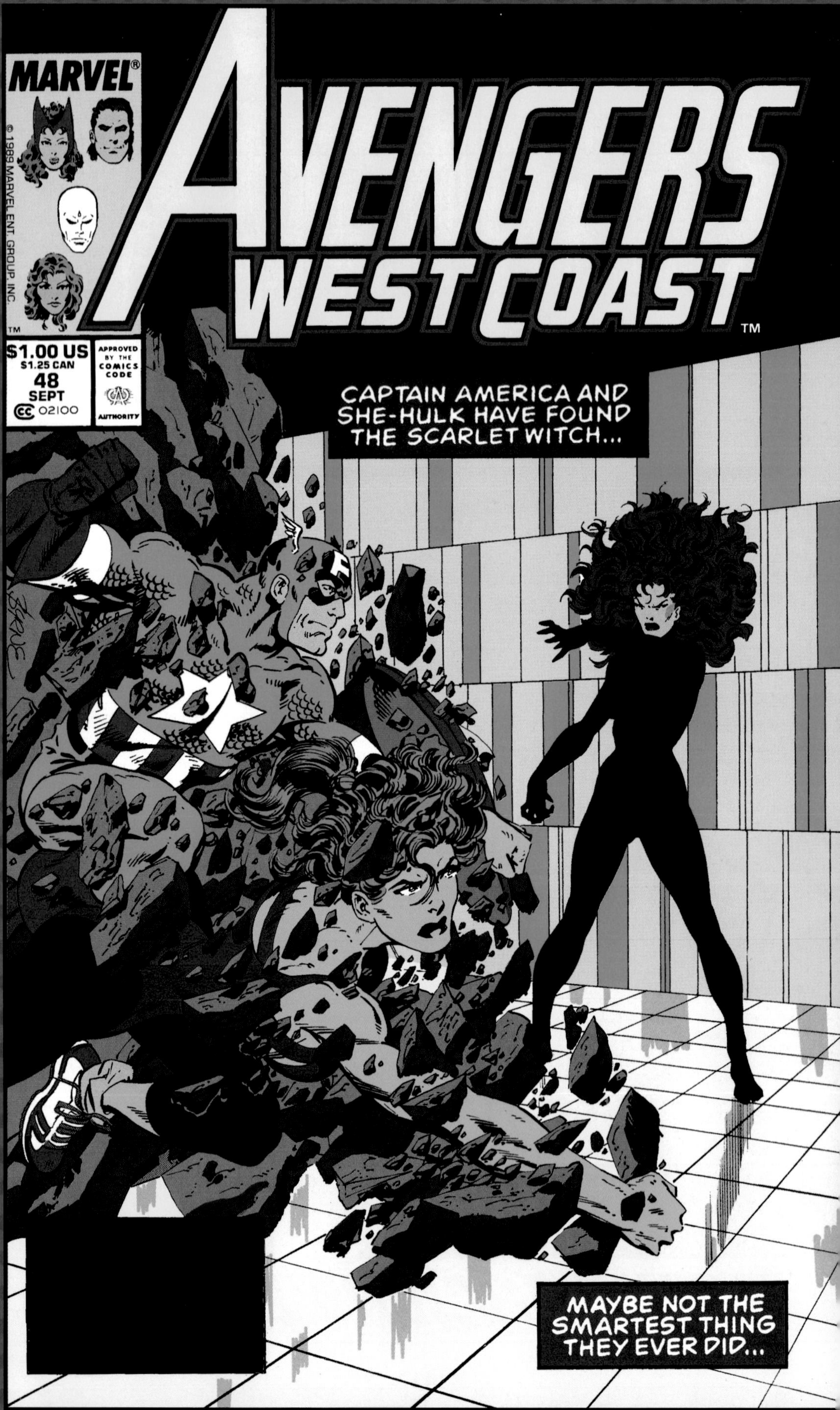
MARVEL
AVENGERS
WEST COAST
© 1989 MARVEL ENT. GROUP, INC.
$1.00 US
$1.25 CAN
48
SEPT
02100
APPROVED BY THE COMICS CODE AUTHORITY
CAPTAIN AMERICA AND SHE-HULK HAVE FOUND THE SCARLET WITCH...
MAYBE NOT THE SMARTEST THING THEY EVER DID...

STan Lee PRESENTS:

THIS ANCIENT EVIL

MEMORY CANNOT PRECEDE BEING, CANNOT REACH BACK INTO THE DARK OBLIVION BEFORE THE SPARK OF LIFE IGNITES.

YET, THIS IS MEMORY, THIS IMAGE OF AN EARTH ABORNING, SWOLLEN INFANT MOON CROUCHING ABOVE CLOUDS OF POISON GAS.

SEEN WITHOUT EYES: THE FLASH OF LIGHTNING BOILING THE TURBULENT AIR.

HEARD WITHOUT EARS: THE CRACK OF THUNDER ROLLING OVER A BROKEN LANDSCAPE.

145

BENEATH THE ROILING ROOF OF SKY, A SLOW AND SULLEN OOZE GURGLES AND FLOWS AROUND THE JAGGED COASTLINES OF EMBRYONIC CONTINENTS.

IN A FEW BILLION YEARS THESE LAND MASSES WILL COME TO BEAR STRANGE NAMES. GONDWANALAND... LAURASIA...

EONS YET, BEFORE THE FIRST VOICE WILL VIBRATE ON THE AIR OF THIS VIRGIN WORLD.

BUT IN SWIRLING TIDE POOLS THE FIRST HESITANT STEPS ARE BEING TAKEN ON THE LONG ROAD TO THE CREATION OF THE UPRIGHT BEAST WHO WILL GIVE ALL THIS A NAME.

IN WATERS STIRRED BY VOLCANIC HEAT, JOLTED BY THE LIGHTNING'S PULSE...

...THE BUILDING BLOCKS OF LIFE ARE FORMING.

AND AFTER HALF A BILLION YEARS -- THE MEREST BLINK OF GEOLOGICAL TIME --

--SOMETHING VERY LIKE A CELL DRIFTS IN THE PRIMORDIAL DARKNESS.

IT DOES NOT THINK...

IT DOES NOT FEEL, SAVE IN THE MOST RUDIMENTARY FASHION...

IT DOES NOT KNOW...

BUT IT LIVES.

AND IT DIVIDES....

FOR A MOMENT THERE ARE TWO ENTITIES, ADRIFT IN THE MICROSCOPIC SEASCAPE, THE WHOLE SCENE SMALLER THAN THE POINT OF A PIN...

TO THE MOST MINUTE INSPECTION THEY WOULD BE NEARLY IDENTICAL. THE CLUMPS OF MOLECULES WITHIN THEM -- THE PATTERN UPON WHICH COMPLEX GENETIC FORMS WILL GROW-- ARE THE SAME.

BUT THERE IS A DIFFERENCE.

AS THE EDDIES AND CURRENTS IN THE WATERS AROUND THEM BEGIN TO DRAW THE SIBLINGS APART...

...THAT DIFFERENCE MAKES ITSELF APPARENT.

ONE ORGANISM SEIZES THE OTHER.

DRAWS IT TO ITSELF...

PIERCES...

PENETRATES...

WITHIN AN INSTANT THE DRAMA IS DONE.

WHERE ONCE THERE WERE TWO, THERE IS ONE ONCE MORE.

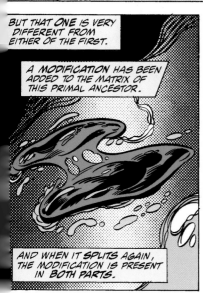

BUT THAT ONE IS VERY DIFFERENT FROM EITHER OF THE FIRST.

A MODIFICATION HAS BEEN ADDED TO THE MATRIX OF THIS PRIMAL ANCESTOR.

AND WHEN IT SPLITS AGAIN, THE MODIFICATION IS PRESENT IN BOTH PARTS.

IT IS STILL PRESENT, COILED WITHIN THE HEART OF EVERY LIVING CELL, MILLIONS OF YEARS LATER, WHEN THE DIVERSITY OF LIFE HAS BEGUN TO MANIFEST ITSELF.

MEANWHILE, FIVE HUNDRED MILLION YEARS LATER...

REPORT, MS. KLEIN...

ALL IS PROCEEDING EXACTLY ON SCHEDULE, MR. RANDOM.

WE CHOSE WELL, IN THE SCARLET WITCH. SHE IS A CLASSIC MUTANT TYPE...

AND THE PRESENT UPHEAVAL IN HER EMOTIONAL LIFE HAS LEFT HER PSYCHICALLY VULNERABLE, OPEN TO COMPLETE ASSIMILATION.

AND MEMORY RECONSTRUCTION? HOW IS *THAT* PROCEEDING?

WE'VE BROUGHT HER UP THROUGH THE FIRST HUNDRED MILLION YEARS OF OUR EXISTENCE.

AT THE PRESENT RATE SHE SHOULD BE *CONTEMPORANEOUS* WITH US WITHIN SEVENTY-TWO HOURS.

AND THE *PHYSICAL* PROBLEMS?

SO FAR, SO GOOD, SIR.

WE ARE MATCHING PHYSICAL ASSIMILATION TO THE MEMORY RECONSTRUCTION.

MURCH-INSON?

I BELIEVE WE WILL HAVE BEATEN THE GENETIC *LOCKOUT* BY THE TIME SHE IS FULLY *REPROGRAMMED.*

MEANWHILE...

ABSOLOM, TEXAS, DEAD AHEAD!

CONTACT THE CIVILIAN TRAFFIC CONTROLLER, *SHE-HULK.*

THE SIGNAL WE MONITORED FROM THE QUINJET EMERGENCY ALERT IS CENTERED SOMEWHERE OUTSIDE AUTHORIZED FLIGHT PLANS.

OKAY, CAP.

HELLO DALLAS-FORT WORTH, THIS IS THE AVENGERS QUINJET AV297 RE-QUESTING CLEARANCE FOR EMERGENCY LANDING IN YOUR AREA.

DO YOU *COPY,* DALLAS?

WE COPY, AVENGERS.

DO YOU REQUIRE ASSISTANCE? SHALL WE CON-TACT POLICE OR MILITARY AUTHORITIES?

NEGATIVE, DALLAS.

THIS IS CAPTAIN AMERICA SPEAKING. WE ARE HERE ON AVENGERS PRIORITY BUSINESS.

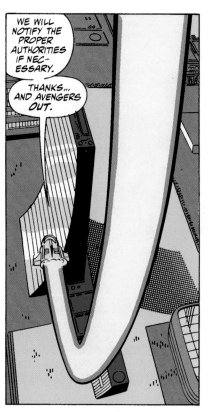

WE WILL NOTIFY THE PROPER AUTHORITIES IF NECESSARY.

THANKS... AND AVENGERS OUT.

MR. RANDOM ...ANOTHER QUINJET IS MAKING AN APPROACH OVER THE COLLEGE GROUNDS.

ANOTHER...?

THIS IS UNANTICIPATED. I UNDERSTOOD THE SCARLET WITCH TO HAVE SEVERED HER RELATIONS WITH THE AVENGERS BEFORE COMING HERE.

SHALL WE CONTINUE WITH THE ASSIMILATION PROCESS, SIR?

"YES. I'LL INVESTIGATE THIS NEW ARRIVAL..."

QUITE THE SPREAD!

REMINDS ME A LITTLE OF CALIFORNIA.

THE EMERGENCY SIGNAL IS VERY CLOSE. CAN'T GET A CLEAR FIX ON IT...

CAPTAIN AMERICA...

SHE-HULK.

TO WHAT DO WE OWE THE HONOR OF THIS VISIT?

NO HONOR, I'M AFRAID, SIR. WE'RE HERE ON BUSINESS. SPECIFICALLY, WE'RE LOOKING FOR ONE OF OUR AIRCRAFT. WE BELIEVE IT TO HAVE GONE DOWN IN THIS VICINITY.

GONE DOWN...?

YOU MEAN... CRASHED? THAT IS MOST DISTRESSING. I HOPE NO HARM HAS BEFALLEN THE SCARLET WITCH SINCE SHE LEFT THE VISION WITH US...

WANDA WAS HERE?

AND THE VISION IS STILL HERE?

YES...

I'D CONTACTED THE SCARLET WITCH AT YOUR WEST COAST HEADQUARTERS TO OFFER HER THE USE OF OUR EXTENSIVE ROBOTICS DEPARTMENT IN AN ATTEMPT TO MORE FULLY RESTORE HER HUSBAND.

PLEASE, WON'T YOU COME THIS WAY? I'LL TAKE YOU TO HIM...

MEANWHILE -- IF SUCH A WORD HAS MEANING ACROSS THE VASTNESS OF THE UNIVERSE...

IT CAN'T BE TRUE--IT JUST *CAN'T* BE! I'D TOTALLY GIVEN UP MY QUEST FOR *HER* WHEN THE AVENGERS TOLD ME SHE'D BEEN *LOST IN TIME*...

...BUT THAT MERCENARY ON SIRIUS IV CLAIMED HE'D SEEN HER PIRATE SHIP IN THIS VICINITY...AND I JUST HAD TO CHECK IT OUT *MYSELF!*

HE IS *EROS* OF THE *ETERNALS*, KNOWN ON EARTH AS *STARFOX*.

THIS PLACE IS AS OLD AS ANYTHING IN ETERNAL MEMORY.

HE SEEKS THE WOMAN CALLED *NEBULA*, GRANDCHILD OF HIS EVIL BROTHER, *THANOS*.

AS OLD, PERHAPS, AS THE UNIVERSE ITSELF.

WHAT BRINGS MY GRAND-NIECE HERE? THERE CAN BE NOTHING ON THIS *ROCK* TO INTEREST A *PLUNDERER* SUCH AS SHE.

BUT SOFT! VOICES UP AHEAD...

YES, *GUNTHAR*, YOU HAVE SERVED YOUR *MISTRESS* WELL!

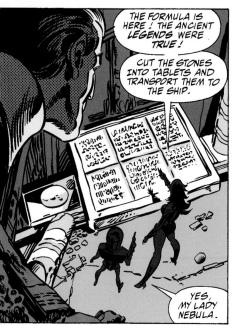

THE FORMULA IS HERE! THE ANCIENT LEGENDS WERE TRUE!

CUT THE STONES INTO TABLETS AND TRANSPORT THEM TO THE SHIP.

YES, MY LADY NEBULA.

WE WILL NEED NOW ONLY A SOURCE OF SUFFICIENT *ENERGY*...

...AND I SHALL BE MORE POWERFUL THAN MY GRANDFATHER *EVER* WAS!!!

IT WILL BE SOME TIME BEFORE WE SEE THE FULL CONSEQUENCES OF THIS DARK PRONOUNCEMENT. FOR NOW...

...LET US TURN OUR GAZE TOWARD A SCENE FAR MORE MUNDANE...

...YET OF NO LESSER SIGNIFICANCE TO THE LIVES OF THE AVENGERS.

AT A SHELTER FOR THE HOMELESS IN MILE-HIGH DENVER...

HOW IS SHE TODAY?

NOT MUCH IMPROVED, I'M AFRAID. I THINK WE SHOULD BE GIVING SERIOUS CONSIDERATION TO GETTING HER TO A HOSPITAL.

MAYBE...

MAYBE...

I'D LIKE TO TRY TALKING WITH HER ONCE MORE, THOUGH.

MRS. RAYMOND? ANN? CAN YOU HEAR ME?

CAN YOU TELL ME HOW YOU'RE FEELING TODAY?

OH-HHH...

PLEASE... CAN'T STAY HERE. GOT TO GET TO THEM...

GET TO LOS ANGELES...

THAT'S ALL WE CAN EVER GET OUT OF HER.

WHY DO YOU SUPPOSE SHE NEEDS TO GET TO L.A.?

AND WHO'S "THEM"?

YOUR GUESS IS AS GOOD AS ANYBODY'S

I JUST WISH THERE WAS SOME CLUE IN THESE FEW THINGS WE FOUND IN HER WALLET.

YES, THAT NEWSPAPER CLIPPING HAS GOT TO BE SOME SORT OF CLUE, OBVIOUSLY.

MAYBE SHE'S A VISION GROUPIE OR SOMETHING.

THAT'S A BIT GLIB, DON'T YOU THINK?

GLIB AND CRUEL. WE'RE SUPPOSED TO BE HELPING HER.

SURE, SURE. I KNOW THAT. AND I WANT TO HELP...

BUT HOW CAN I, WHEN THE ONLY THING WE KNOW ABOUT HER IS HER NAME AND THAT SHE'S ALL DISTRAUGHT OVER THAT OLD HEADLINE...

AVENGERS CONFIRM VISION IS NOT TORCH

AND, EVEN AS THESE TWO LINES OF DESTINY CONVERGE ON THE AVENGERS...

I DON'T LIKE THIS, CAP.

SOMETHING ABOUT THIS PLACE JUST *STINKS* ON ICE.

YOU MAY BE *RIGHT*, SHE-HULK.

MY OLD *BATTLE* INSTINCTS HAVE BEEN TWINGING AWAY LIKE CRAZY SINCE WE GOT HERE.

I CAN ASSURE YOU, CAPTAIN AMERICA, THERE IS NOTHING YOU NEED DISTRESS YOURSELF OVER.

VISION!

IT'S GREAT TO SEE YOU...BUT, WHERE'S THE SCAR-LET WITCH?

DO YOU KNOW?

AT PRESENT, I AM NOT AWARE OF THE PRECISE LOCATION OF MY SPOUSE, CAPTAIN AMERICA.

AS MR. RANDOM UNDOUBTEDLY INFORMED YOU, WANDA DEPARTED ON SOME ERRAND OF HER OWN SHORTLY AFTER WE ARRIVED HERE.

"I AM NOT AWARE OF THE NATURE OR DESTINATION OF THAT ERRAND..."

WE'RE GOING TO HAVE TO *ACCELERATE* THE ASSIMILATION PROCESS.

THAT COULD BE DANGEROUS. IF WE FORCE HER MIND TO ACCEPT THE NEW MEMORIES FASTER THAN ITS NATURAL ABSORPTION RATE...

...IT COULD PROVE EXTREMELY UNPLEASANT FOR THE SUBJECT.

I *KNOW*. BUT THE ARRIVAL OF THESE OTHER AVENGERS LEAVES US NO CHOICE.

ONCE AGAIN, WITHIN THE BURNING BRAIN OF THE SCARLET WITCH, THE VAST PANORAMA OF THE AGES BEGINS TO UNFOLD.

LIFE SPREADS NOW, AS THE GREAT *FORESTS* WHICH WILL ONE DAY PROVIDE HUMANKIND WITH HUGE BEDS OF COAL.

THE *LIZARDS* APPEAR, DEVELOPING WITHIN THE BRIEF SPAN OF A HUNDRED MILLION YEARS INTO FORMS FAMILIAR TO EVERY SCHOOLCHILD.

BUT TO WANDA, THESE ARE NOT SIMPLY LONG DEAD IMAGES OUT OF TEXTBOOKS...

AS THE CREATURES THRIVE AND GROW, SHE FEELS HER-SELF A *PART* OF IT ALL.

A PART OF EACH MAGNIFICENT BEAST. THEIR FEELINGS ARE HERS, THEIR SOLEMN MARCH IS AS TRUE A MEMORY AS IF IT WERE HER OWN.

SHE IS AS ONE WITH THE ANCIENT MONSTERS.

SHE STALKS AS THE TYRANNOSAURS...

SHE TASTES THE HOT BLOOD OF THEIR PREY.

AND VAGUELY... ONLY VAGUELY... SHE IS AWARE OF THE FURTIVE, SCURRYING THINGS THAT DWELL IN HER MANY SHADOWS...

MEANWHILE, NOT VERY FAR AWAY...

AND SO AS YOU CAN SEE, CAPTAIN, SHE-HULK, OUR *ROBOTICS TRAINING PROGRAM* IS AMONG THE *FINEST* IN THE WORLD.

HERE STUDENTS FROM ALL OVER NORTH AMERICA ARE PREPARED FOR LUCRATIVE CAREERS IN THE COMMERCIAL ROBOTICS FIELD.

IMPRESSIVE...

BUT... YOU'LL *EXCUSE ME, MR. RANDOM*--BUT I SEE *NOTHING* HERE TO SUGGEST YOUR FACILITIES WOULD BE ANY BETTER SUITED TO THE *RESTORATION* OF THE VISION THAN OUR OWN.

PERHAPS NOT THE FACILITIES PER SE, CAPTAIN...

WHAT WE WERE REALLY OFFERING THE *SCARLET WITCH* WAS A NEW *EYE*, A DIFFERENT *APPROACH*.

PERHAPS...

STILL, YOU WOULD AGREE IT IS A GREAT SHAME THAT WANDA SHOULD FEEL THE NEED TO TURN TO *STRANGERS* AFTER WE DID ALL WE COULD DO.

YES, A PITY...

H/M? AH, GOOD. I'LL BE RIGHT THERE.

IF YOU'LL EXCUSE ME NOW, CAPTAIN, SHE-HULK...

THERE IS ANOTHER *URGENT* MATTER I MUST ATTEND TO.

PLEASE FEEL FREE TO CONTINUE YOUR TOUR. ONE OF MY PEOPLE WILL DIRECT YOU BACK TO THE VISION WHEN YOU ARE *DONE*.

THANK YOU, MR. RANDOM.

YOU'RE NOT *REALLY* BUYING INTO THIS, ARE YOU, CAP? I'M NO *EXPERT*, BUT THIS PLACE DOESN'T LOOK *HALF* AS ADVANCED AS SOME OF THE STUFF *WE'VE* GOT.

NO, IT DOESN'T, JENNIFER. IN FACT, A LOT OF IT LOOKS LIKE SOME *HOLLYWOOD PRODUCTION DESIGNER'S* IDEA OF A ROBOT FACTORY, NOT THE REAL THING.

HOWEVER, I THINK WE'LL PLAY ALONG FOR A WHILE AND CONTINUE THE TOUR AS RANDOM SUGGESTED.

BUT I ALSO THINK WE'LL COME *BACK LATER* TONIGHT...

...UNANNOUNCED!

NOW, AS CAPTAIN AMERICA AND THE SHE-HULK WAIT FOR NIGHT TO DRAW HER SHROUD ACROSS THE TEXAN SKY...

...WE TURN OUR ATTENTION NORTH AND WEST TO THE GROSVENOR MEMORIAL HOSPITAL IN SEATTLE...

SPECIFICALLY, TO THE GOVERNMENT FUNDED PRIVATE ROOM OF ONE TIRED OLD MAN...

PROFESSOR HORTON, DO YOU REMEMBER ME?

YES... I REMEMBER.

YOU FOUND ME IN THE CELL THOSE MEN HAD PUT ME IN ... YOU FREED ME.

YOU'RE JANET VAN DYNE ... THE WASP.

THAT'S RIGHT, PROFESSOR.

DO YOU FEEL UP TO TALKING? WE HAVE A LOT WE NEED TO KNOW. FOR ONE THING, WE'VE BELIEVED FOR QUITE SOME TIME NOW THAT YOU WERE DEAD.

YES... I WAS TOLD.

SOMETHING ABOUT THE CREATION OF YOUR ANDROID MEMBER, THE VISION. I WAS SUPPOSED TO HAVE... DIED IN HIS ARMS.

THAT'S THE STORY AS WE UNDERSTOOD IT UNTIL VERY RECENTLY, SIR. YOU WERE SUPPOSED TO HAVE ASSISTED THE ROBOT, ULTRON-5, IN THE CONVERSION OF YOUR ORIGINAL HUMAN TORCH ANDROID...

...INTO THE ANDROID WE KNOW AS THE VISION. FOR YEARS NOW WE'VE BELIEVED THE TORCH AND THE VISION WERE ONE AND THE SAME, BUT YOUR WORDS AND MY EXAMINATIONS PROVE THIS IS NOT THE CASE.

NO. THE VISION COULD NOT BE MY TORCH.

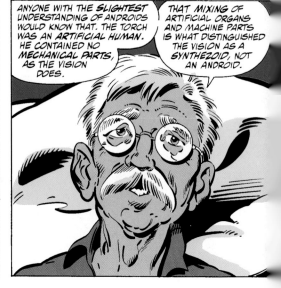

ANYONE WITH THE SLIGHTEST UNDERSTANDING OF ANDROIDS WOULD KNOW THAT. THE TORCH WAS AN ARTIFICIAL HUMAN. HE CONTAINED NO MECHANICAL PARTS, AS THE VISION DOES.

THAT MIXING OF ARTIFICIAL ORGANS AND MACHINE PARTS IS WHAT DISTINGUISHED THE VISION AS A SYNTHEZOID, NOT AN ANDROID.

"YES, PROFESSOR, I NOW APPRECIATE THAT DISTINCTION. AND AS ONE WHO HAS TRAINED HIMSELF EXTENSIVELY IN ROBO-TECHNOLOGY, I PROBABLY SHOULD HAVE REALIZED IT SOONER.

"ESPECIALLY SINCE, AS ANT-MAN, I ONCE TOOK AN IMPROMPTU TOUR OF THE VISION'S INNARDS."

"HOWEVER, PERHAPS AN EVEN MORE IMPORTANT CONSIDERATION NOW CONFRONTS US...

"THE VISION LEARNED THE SO-CALLED TRUE DETAILS OF HIS ORIGIN FROM IMMORTUS..."

...I CAN SHOW YOU YOUR PAST, VISION...

OBVIOUSLY, THE "MASTER OF TIME" LIED.

WHY?

OH, NEVER WITHOUT GOOD REASON, MY DEAR DOCTOR PYM.

NEVER WITHOUT GOOD REASON.

A REASON OF COSMIC CONSEQUENCE FAR BEYOND YOUR SIMPLE THREE DIMENSIONAL COMPREHENSION.

ONLY ONE WHO IS AT HOME, AS I AM, IN THE MYRIAD PLANES OF THE FOURTH DIMENSION...

...COULD EVER HOPE TO UNDERSTAND MY REASONS.

OR THE PLACE MY CALCULATED FUTURE HAS RESERVED FOR THE SCAR-LET WITCH...

THERE NOW, WANDA. LET ME HELP YOU DOWN...

HOW DO YOU...

...FEEL NOW?

STRANGE... AS IF... I WERE AWAKENING AFTER A LONG, LONG SLEEP...

ALL OUR READINGS SHOW *NORMAL,* MR. *RANDOM.*

THE ASSIMILATION WAS *SUCCESSFUL!*

GOOD! GOOD!

BUT... YOU WOULD PROBABLY LIKE TO *REST* NOW, WOULDN'T YOU, WANDA?

THERE IS *MUCH* YOU NEED TO *CONSIDER.*

YES... REST... NEED TIME TO *THINK...*

I HOPE THE ACCELERATED ASSIMILATION HAS NOT DONE ANY UNDETECTED *DAMAGE,* MR. *RANDOM.*

NO, I·THINK NOT, MS. *KLEIN.* YOU WERE *CORRECT* TO TAKE THE STEPS YOU DID.

THANK YOU, SIR.

THIS IS A *GREAT DAY,* ISN'T IT?

A GREAT DAY INDEED, MS. KLEIN. OUR SUCCESSFUL ASSIMILATION OF THE *SCARLET WITCH* PAVES THE WAY FOR SIMILAR INDUCTION OF ALL *MUTANT-KIND.*

THE GENETIC *BARRIER* HAS BEEN BREACHED.

SOON WE SHALL BE ABLE TO *ABANDON* THE DEAD END STREET OF HUMANITY...

...AND THEN HOMO SAPIENS WILL GO THE SAME WAY AS DID THE *DINOSAURS* BEFORE THEM!

THERE YOU GO, MISS WANDA.

YOU JUST *REST* HERE FOR A WHILE, AND I'M SURE YOU'LL FEEL JUST *FINE* COME MORNING.

YES... THANK YOU... I'M CERTAIN I SHALL...

I'M CERTAIN I SHALL...

SUDDENLY I FEEL VERY *SURE* ABOUT EVERY-THING.

IT'S AS IF EVERY *DOUBT* I'VE EVER HAD IN MY LIFE HAS BEEN *SCRUBBED* AWAY.

I BEGIN TO UNDERSTAND NOW SOME OF THE THINGS MY *FATHER* HAS SAID.

THINGS HE SAID IN THE DAYS MY BROTHER, *PIETRO,* AND I WERE PART OF HIS *BROTHERHOOD OF EVIL MUTANTS.*

IN THOSE DAYS LONG BEFORE WE EVEN *KNEW* HE WAS OUR FATHER... WHEN HE WAS, TO US, ONLY *MAGNETO,* MASTER OF MAGNETISM.

THEN HE SPOKE OFTEN OF THE *SUPERIORITY* OF MUTANTS SUCH AS US. HOMO *SUPERIOR,* HE CALLED US.

HE SAID WE WERE THE *FUTURE.* SAID THAT SOME DAY SOON ALL THE HUMANS WOULD *BOW DOWN* TO US...

...ACKNOWLEDGE US AS THEIR RIGHTFUL MASTERS!

NOW I SEE THAT HE WAS *RIGHT!* MORE RIGHT THAN EVEN *HE* DARED GUESS. HUMANKIND HAS REACHED THE *END OF ITS ERA OF* DOMINATION.

THEY MUST BE LEFT *BEHIND,* LIKE THE DINO-SAURS, LIKE THE LESSER *MAMMALS.* LEFT TO *DIE OUT.*

AND ONLY THAT WHICH ENDURES SHALL REMAIN!

AND AS SHE DRIFTS INTO A DEEP, CON-TENTED SLEEP...

...THE SCARLET WITCH SCARCELY NOTICES A LOW AND RHYTHMIC DRONE TICKLING AT THE UNDERSIDE OF HER *MIND.*

A FEW HOURS LATER, AS THE LONG SUMMER TWILIGHT SURRENDERS AT LAST TO THE DARKNESS OF NIGHT...

...AND ALL GROWS STILL AND QUIET ABOUT THE CAMPUS OF ABSOLOM COLLEGE...

CAREFUL NOW, SHE-HULK. I'VE NO DOUBT THE CAMPUS PERIMETER IS LOADED WITH SECURITY DEVICES.

I'LL BET...

BUT KEEP IN MIND THAT BEING *INOBTRUSIVE* IS HARDLY MY STYLE, CAP.

ONE OF THE DISADVANTAGES OF BEING SIX FOOT SEVEN AND BRIGHT GREEN.

TRUE ENOUGH, JEN...

BUT THEN, I'M NOT EXACTLY SYLPH-LIKE MYSELF.

BUT IF HALF A LIFETIME OF TRAINING IN BATTLE HAS TAUGHT ME ANYTHING, IT'S THAT *SIZE* AND *STEALTH* ARE NOT NECESSARILY INTERDEPENDENT.

FOLLOW MY LEAD AND I'LL SHOW YOU WHAT I MEAN.

WATCH OUT! THAT LOW WHINE MEANS A PRESSURE SENSOR WITHIN THE FIRST FEW FEET OF THIS PAVEMENT!

WOW! YOU CONTINUE TO AMAZE ME, CAPTAIN!

SAVE THE COMPLIMENT UNTIL WE'VE FOUND WANDA, SHE-HULK

MY EVERY INSTINCT TELLS ME SHE'S STILL *HERE.*

160

NOW... THIS IS THE CENTRAL TOWER COMPLEX. IF THERE IS SOMETHING AMISS HERE, THIS PLACE WILL BE THE HEART OF IT.

IF YOU'VE BEEN CAUTIOUS UNTIL NOW, SHE-HULK, IT'S TIME TO INCREASE THAT CAUTION TENFOLD!

I'M BETTING THE ANSWERS WE'RE LOOKING FOR WILL BE SOMEWHERE IN RANDOM'S OFFICE.

ACCORDING TO THIS BUILDING GUIDE, THAT'S ON THE TWENTIETH FLOOR.

IT WON'T BE SAFE TO USE THE ELEVATORS.

"HOPE YOU FEEL UP TO THE CLIMB, SHE-HULK."

NOT BAD, CAP! YOU WENT UP ALL FORTY FLIGHTS FOUR STEPS AT A TIME!

DON'T YOU EVER GET WINDED?

PUT IT DOWN TO CLEAN LIVING, SHE-HULK. THAT... AND THE SUPER SOLDIER SERUM IN MY VEINS...

HMM... LOOKS LIKE MR. RANDOM LEAVES HIS OFFICE UNLOCKED AND UNGUARDED.

YES. THIS IS ALL STARTING TO SEEM MUCH TOO EASY.

LET'S SEE IF OUR APPARENT GOOD FORTUNE HOLDS.

IF THIS DESKTOP TERMINAL CAN ACCESS THE MAIN COMPUTER DATA BANK WITHOUT A SECURITY CODE...

TIC TOC TEP

THERE IT IS!

ACCORDING TO THIS, THE SCARLET WITCH IS PRESENTLY BEING HELD IN A SUB-BASEMENT OF THE BUILDING JUST SOUTH OF THIS ONE.

SOUTH, HM? THIS OFFICE FACES SOUTH...

I CAN GUESS WHAT YOU'RE THINKING, SHE-HULK...

...AND I APPROVE!

GOOD! NO REASON TO BE SKULKING ABOUT, NOW WE KNOW RANDOM AND HIS PEOPLE ARE UP TO NO GOOD...

SEE YOU IN A FEW!

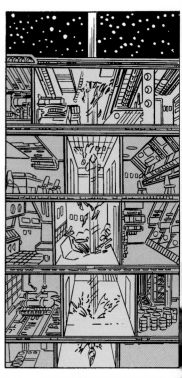

EXCELLENT! WITH A TWENTY STORY DROP PROPELLING HER, SHE-HULK'S SEVEN HUNDRED POUNDS HAVE PUNCHED US AN ENTRANCE THROUGH SEVERAL FLOORS OF THE TARGET STRUCTURE!

NOW ALL I HAVE TO DO IS FOLLOW...

...IN MY OWN FASHION!

SINCE MY SHIELD CAN ABSORB ALMOST ANY IMPACT, LANDING ON IT AFTER A TWENTY STORY FALL...

...IS LESS OF A SHOCK TO MY BODY THAN JUST STEPPING OFF A CURB!

WHONG

OKAY, JEN, LET'S GET ON WITH THIS INVASION!

THIS WAY, CAP!

THESE STAIRS ARE MARKED AS LEADING DOWN TO THE SUB-BASEMENT YOU FOUND LISTED IN THE FILES...

I'LL *LEAD* NOW, SHE-HULK.

YOU MAY BE VIRTUALLY *INDESTRUCTIBLE*, BUT WE DON'T KNOW WHAT KIND OF *WEAPONRY* WE MAY BE UP AGAINST...

YOU GOT IT, CAP!

I'LL *YIELD* TO YOUR *SHIELD* ANY DAY!

BUT... THERE'S NO ONE HERE! JUST THAT... *STRUCTURE!*

"BLOCKHOUSE" WOULD SEEM THE APPROPRIATE TERM, SHE-HULK.

OBVIOUSLY INTENDED TO WITH-STAND OR *CONTAIN* A GREAT FORCE...

LIKE WANDA'S *HEX* POWER, FOR INSTANCE?

POSSIBLY... PERSONAL EXPER-IENCE HAS TAUGHT ME THERE IS VERY LITTLE ON THIS WORLD THAT CAN *RESIST* THE SCARLET WITCH'S MUTANT POWER.

STILL...

163

...SINCE YOU'RE ALMOST AS STRONG AS YOUR *COUSIN*...

...LET'S SEE IF YOU CAN DO SOMETHING ABOUT THAT *DOOR!*

NO SOONER SAID THAN DONE, CAP.

THIS SETUP DOESN'T LOOK TOO MUCH TOUGHER THAN...

WHAT IN THE...??

THERE WASN'T ANYWHERE *NEAR* THE AMOUNT OF *RESISTANCE* I WAS EXPECTING! CAP WAS *RIGHT!* THIS IS TOO *EASY!* THEY WANTED US TO GET *IN!*

INDEED WE *DID,* SHE-HULK...

AND NOW THAT YOU AND CAPTAIN AMERICA HAVE *DEMONSTRATED* YOUR SKILLS FOR US...

...IT IS TIME FOR YOU TO *JOIN* US!

164

WANDA! SHE-HULK, GET CLEAR! THEY'VE TURNED HER AGAINST US!

NO, CAPTAIN. YOU ARE WRONG.

I HAVE NOT BEEN TURNED. I HAVE, RATHER, BEEN SHOWN THE TRUTH.

THE GREAT AND ANCIENT TRUTH WHICH HAS DWELLED WITHIN ALL LIVING THINGS SINCE THE DAWN OF TIME!

THE TRUTH YOU WILL COME TO SHARE...

...ONCE YOU, TOO, ARE PROPERLY ASSIMILATED!

165

MEANWHILE, IN MILWAUKEE...

NO! NO!

NO!!

I HAVE NEVER SEEN A MORE USELESS BUNCH OF MISFITS!

NOW TRY IT AGAIN!

OH, COME ON, HAWK-EYE!!

WE'VE BEEN AT IT ALL DAY AND HALF THE NIGHT! WE KNOW WE'RE NOT UP TO AVENGERS STANDARDS YET...

AND YOU'RE NOT GOING TO GET US THERE IN ONE DAY!

NOW LISTEN HERE, BERTHA...

IT MAY BE YOUR MONEY THAT'S PAYING FOR THIS GIG, BUT...

HAWK!

'BIRD...

...WHAT...?

I JUST PICKED UP A TRANSMISSION ON THE AVENGERS WAVE-BAND.

IT WAS FAINT, BUT I'M SURE IT WAS THE LAST GASP OF A QUIN-JET EMERGENCY SIGNAL!

ALL RIIGGHHT!! THIS IS THE MOMENT I'VE BEEN WAITING FOR!

AVENGERS ASSEMBLE!

MY FORMER TEAM-MATES ARE IN SOME KINDA JAM...

...AN' WE'RE GONNA BAIL 'EM OUT!

NEXT ISSUE:
IT'S EAST AND WEST VS. THE GREAT LAKES AVENGERS IN

BAPTISM OF FIRE!

BELIEVE US, PILGRIM... IF YOU MISS THIS ONE, YOU'LL REGRET IT!

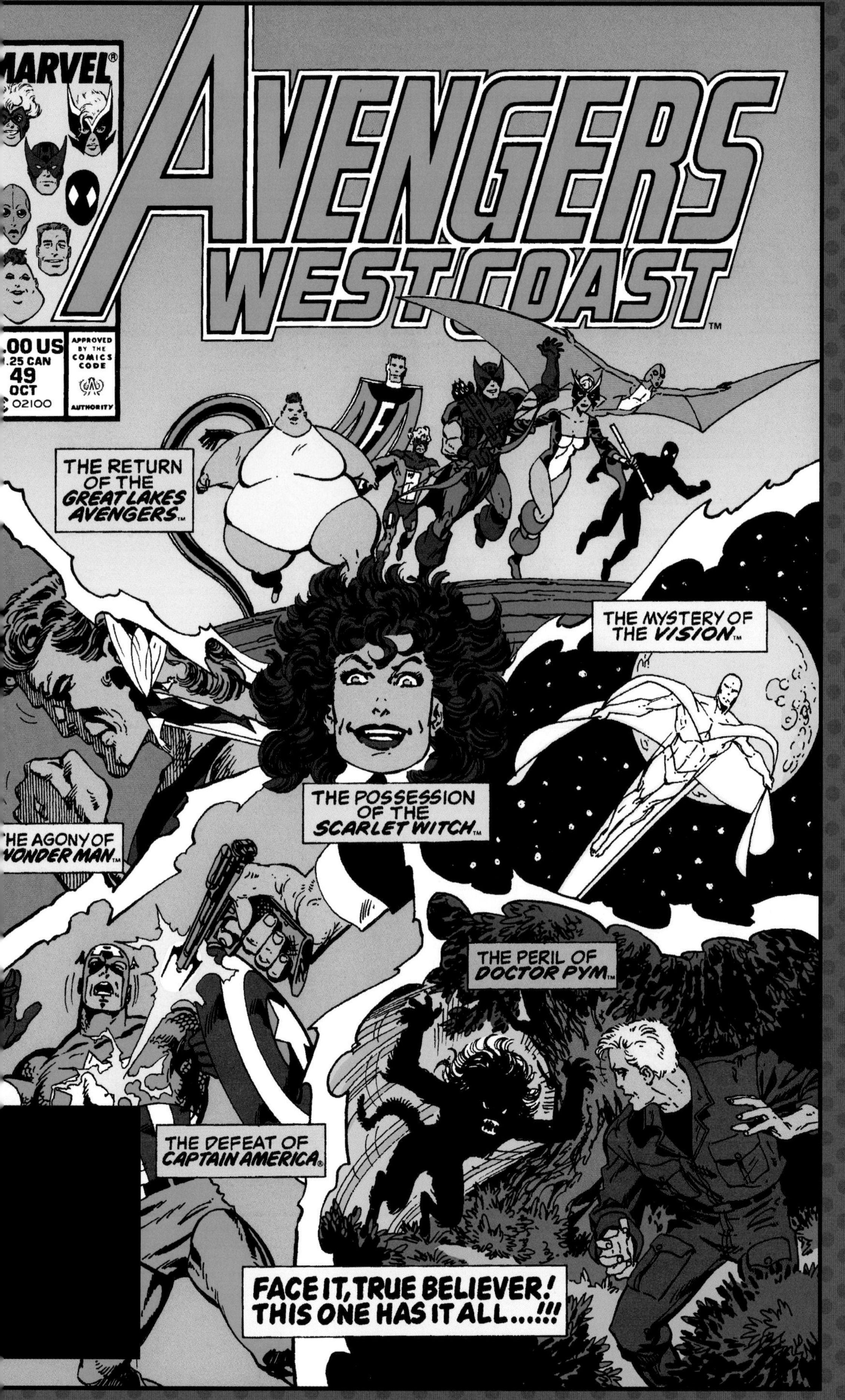
MARVEL
AVENGERS WEST COAST
.00 US
.25 CAN
49
OCT
02100
APPROVED BY THE COMICS CODE AUTHORITY
THE RETURN OF THE GREAT LAKES AVENGERS
THE MYSTERY OF THE VISION
THE POSSESSION OF THE SCARLET WITCH
HE AGONY OF
VONDER MAN
THE PERIL OF DOCTOR PYM
THE DEFEAT OF CAPTAIN AMERICA
FACE IT, TRUE BELIEVER! THIS ONE HAS IT ALL....!!!

STAN LEE PRESENTS: AVENGER VS. AVENGER IN...

BAPTISM OF FIRE!

Brought to you by

JOHN BYRNE ~ writer/artist
BILL OAKLEY ~ letterer • BOB SHAREN ~ colorist
HOWARD MACKIE ~ editor
TOM DEFALCO ~ editor in chief

WEST COAST AVENGERS created by ROGER STERN & BOB HALL

FAR BELOW THE BIG, BRIGHT STARS OF THE TEXAS NIGHT, A STILLNESS SETTLES OVER THE AFTERMATH OF TERRIBLE VIOLENCE.

IT CANNOT TRULY BE CALLED A SCENE OF BATTLE. THE TREACHERY WHICH FELLED THESE TWO HEROES CAME TOO QUICKLY FOR THEM TOO REACT, TO RESPOND.

FOR THOSE NEW READERS WHO MIGHT REQUIRE INTRODUCTIONS, HE IS CAPTAIN AMERICA, STAR SPANGLED CHAMPION OF ALL THAT IS GOOD AND TRUE IN THE NATION WHOSE NAME HE PROUDLY BEARS...

...WHILE SHE IS THE SENSATIONAL SHE-HULK, GAMMA SPAWNED COUSIN OF THE MAN-MONSTER WHOSE TITLE SHE SHARES.

THE MOMENT IS SOME THIRTY SECONDS AFTER THE END OF OUR PREVIOUS ISSUE...

168

AND THE WOMAN WHOSE ACT OF BETRAYAL BROUGHT THESE TWO TO THEIR PRESENT SORRY STATE IS THEIR ERSTWHILE FRIEND AND PARTNER, THE SCARLET WITCH.

EXCELLENT, WANDA, EXCELLENT! YOU DEFEATED TWO OF YOUR MOST POWERFUL FORMER COLLEAGUES IN LESS THAN THIRTY SECONDS!

THEY HESITATED TO STRIKE AT ME, DOUBTLESS THINKING I COULD STILL BE REASONED WITH...

NOT REALIZING THERE CAN BE NO REASONING WITH THAT WHICH ENDURES.

OF COURSE NOT. NO MORE THAN ONE CAN REASON WITH A HURRICANE... WITH A SWARM OF LOCUSTS.

WE ARE A FORCE OF NATURE. PRIMAL. ELEMENTAL. WE HAVE SURVIVED SINCE THE DAWN OF LIFE ON EARTH.

AND WE ARE NOW EMBARKED UPON THAT COURSE OF ACTION WHICH WILL ENSURE OUR SURVIVAL BEYOND THE AGE OF HUMAN-KIND.

WE STAND UPON THE THRESHOLD OF THE AGE OF MUTANTS LIKE YOURSELF, WANDA. FOR MANY YEARS IT SEEMED AS THOUGH THE FATES-- IN THE FORM OF A CRUEL, GENETIC QUIRK-- HAD CHOSEN TO BAR US FROM THAT COMING AGE.

BUT NOW, WITH YOUR ASSISTANCE, THE STAGE IS SET FOR OUR CONTINUED ENDURANCE.

AS MANKIND FALLS BY THE WAYSIDE, WE SHALL RIDE THE CREST INTO THE MUTANT MILLENNIUM!

AND WITH THE WORDS OF THAT MOMENTOUS PRONOUNCEMENT RINGING IN OUR EARS...

...WE WILL ALLOW SOME SIXTY FIVE MINUTES TO ELAPSE, AND TURN OUR GAZE NORTH AND SOMEWHAT EAST...

CAN'T YOU GET THIS CRATE TO GO ANY FASTER?

WE'RE NEVER GONNA GET WHERE WE'RE GOIN' AT THIS SPEED!

THIS "CRATE" HAPPENS TO BE ONE OF THE FINEST PRIVATE AIR-CRAFT MONEY CAN BUY, HAWKEYE!

NOW, I KNOW IT'S NO QUINJET, BUT I'LL REMIND YOU: EVEN THOUGH WE CALL OURSELVES AVENGERS...

...WE DO NOT HAVE ACCESS TO ANY OF THEIR MORE SOPHISTICATED HARDWARE!

FINE! FINE! SO WE STOOGE ALONG AT SUB-SONIC SPEED FOR THE NEXT YEAR AND A HALF...

'BIRD! WHAT HAVE YOU GOT FOR US?

NOT MUCH, LOVER.

THAT QUINJET EMERGENCY SIGNAL I MONITORED WAS SO FAINT I WAS BARELY SURE I'D EVEN HEARD IT.

I KNOW WE'RE FLYING ON A PRETTY STRAIGHT COURSE FOR ITS POINT OF ORIGIN, BUT UNLESS IT STARTS UP AGAIN THERE'S NO WAY TO TRIANGULATE ITS PRECISE POSITION.

NOW, FOR THE FIRST TIME, HERE'S A REAL CHANCE TO SHOW THE REST OF THE AVENGERS WHAT YOU'RE MADE OF...

IN OTHER WORDS, THIS HERE IS NOTHIN' MORE THAN A WILD GOOSE CHASE, RIGHT, "LEADER?"

KEEP THE SARCASM OUT OF YOUR VOICE, BUSTER.

YOU AND THIS CREW OF ODDBALLS YOU'VE ASSEM-BLED WERE NOTHING BUT BUSH LEAGUE SUPER HEROES BEFORE ME AN' MOCKINGBIRD HOOKED UP WITH YOU.

...IF WE CAN EVER FIND 'EM!

COINCIDENTALLY...

...JUST OUTSIDE *LOS ANGELES...*

ALL SYSTEMS SHOW **GREEN** FOR LANDING.

HOLO-FIELD DOWN. HANGAR OPEN.

DOCKING SYSTEMS ON **AUTO**. WE'RE DOWN AND CLEAR.

WELL, THAT WAS SOMETHING OF A **FRUITLESS** TRIP, ALL IN ALL. I WAS SO **SURE** WHEN WANDA RAN OFF THIS MORNING THAT SHE AND THE VISION WERE HEADING FOR **SEATTLE** TO SEE **PROFESSOR HORTON.**

I WOULDN'T CALL IT ENTIRELY FRUITLESS THOUGH, **JAN.** ANY CHANCE TO TALK WITH HORTON IS IMPORTANT NOW WE KNOW THE VISION WAS **NOT** MADE FROM HIS ORIGINAL **HUMAN TORCH** AS WE SO LONG BELIEVED.

Y'KNOW, **HANK,** I'M STILL NOT SURE HOW THAT CAN BE **TRUE.**

THERE WAS SO MUCH **EVIDENCE** SUPPORTING THAT VERSION OF THE VISION'S ORIGIN.

WELL, NOT EXACTLY, **SIMON.** TRUE, A LOT OF PIECES **SEEMED** TO FALL INTO PLACE WITH THE "REVELA-TION" OF THE VISION'S CONNECTION TO THE FIRST TORCH...

...BUT SEEN FROM OUR NEW VANTAGE POINT, THAT REVEALED "TRUTH" STARTS TO GET A LITTLE FUZZY 'ROUND THE EDGES.

THAT'S WHY I'M HEADING FOR OUR MAIN COMPUTER FACILITY NOW. I WANT TO SEE WHAT I CAN CROSS-CHECK ON OUR MISSING ANDROID.

COMING, JAN?

ER... NO. I'LL JOIN YOU IN A BIT, LOVER.

OKAY. STAY OUT OF TROUBLE, YOU TWO!

SIMON...?

I TAKE IT THAT LONG FACE MEANS YOU'RE STILL CONCERNED ABOUT WANDA?

OF COURSE. HOW COULD I NOT BE, WASP?

THE VISION WAS ONLY CAPABLE OF FALLING IN LOVE WITH THE SCARLET WITCH IN THE FIRST PLACE BECAUSE HE HAD MY BRAIN PATTERNS... MY EMOTIONS...

YES... AND NOW WANDA SAYS SHE HATES YOU BECAUSE YOU'VE REFUSED TO LET HANK RECOPY THOSE PATTERNS INTO THE VISION.

CAN YOU EVEN BEGIN TO IMAGINE HOW THAT FEELS, JAN? WHEN I CAME BACK FROM BEING "DEAD"... FROM THE CHRYSALIS STAGE THAT TRANSFORMED ME INTO WHAT I AM NOW... WHEN I SAW WANDA FOR THE FIRST TIME...

...IT WAS LOVE AT FIRST SIGHT. I CAN SEE THAT. WANDA HAD DONE EVERYTHING SHE COULD TO BREAK DOWN THE VISION'S ROBOTIC RESERVE. IN THE PROCESS, SHE'D MADE HERSELF IRRESISTIBLE TO YOU, SINCE IT WAS A COPY OF YOUR EMOTIONAL CONTENT SHE WAS TRYING TO APPEAL TO.

EXACTLY. I NEVER HAD A CHANCE!

BUT BY THE TIME OF OUR FIRST MEETING, WANDA WAS ALREADY MARRIED TO THE VISION, AND AS WEIRD AS THAT FIRST SEEMED TO ME... LIKE I SAID THIS MORNING, THERE ARE RULES ABOUT THINGS LIKE THAT...

YES, THERE ARE. BUT THERE'S NO REASON YOU CAN'T MAKE THOSE RULES WORK FOR YOU, SIMON.

WANDA DIDN'T FALL IN LOVE WITH SOME PLASTIC ORGANS AND A FEW MILLION MILES OF MICRO WIRE. SHE FELL IN LOVE WITH THE INNER MAN SHE SENSED HIDING BEHIND THE VISION'S COMPUTERIZED RESPONSES.

AND THAT "INNER MAN" WAS YOU!

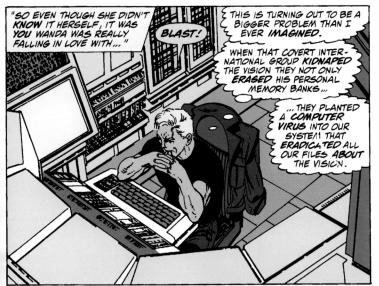

"SO EVEN THOUGH SHE DIDN'T *KNOW* IT HERSELF, IT WAS YOU WANDA WAS REALLY FALLING IN LOVE WITH..."

BLAST!

THIS IS TURNING OUT TO BE A BIGGER PROBLEM THAN I EVER *IMAGINED.*

WHEN THAT COVERT INTERNATIONAL GROUP *KIDNAPED* THE VISION THEY NOT ONLY *ERASED* HIS PERSONAL MEMORY BANKS...

...THEY PLANTED A *COMPUTER VIRUS* INTO OUR SYSTEM THAT *ERADICATED* ALL OUR FILES *ABOUT* THE VISION.

THAT LEAVES ME CHASING *SMOKE* AS FAR AS ANY HOPE OF *CROSS-REFERENC-ING.*

I'D BE WORKING ENTIRELY FROM *MEMORY,* AND AS GOOD AS MY MEMORY IS, IT'S NOT GOOD *ENOUGH* !

"MAYBE I SHOULD CONCENTRATE ON FINDING OUT WHERE WANDA'S GONE, FOR NOW..."

CARLOS... GOT A *MINUTE?*

SI, SENOR PYM.

HOW CAN I HELP YOU, SIR?

AS OUR *BUTLER,* YOU COME IN CONTACT WITH MOST OF US SEVERAL TIMES A DAY. HAVE YOU NOTICED ANYTHING *IN PARTICULAR* ABOUT THE SCARLET WITCH'S BEHAVIOR LATELY?

ONLY WHAT EVERYONE HAS SEEN, SENOR. SENORA WANDA HAS BEEN VERY DISTRESSED OVER WHAT HAS HAPPENED TO THE VISION.

ALTHOUGH... I *DID* THINK SHE *BRIGHTENED* JUST A LITTLE AFTER SHE GOT THAT *LETTER* THE OTHER DAY...

LETTER? WHAT LET--

TIGRA!!

RRROWR!!

173

WHAT IN THE NAME OF...??

SI, SENOR! SENORA NELSON HAS BEEN ACTING MOST STRANGELY OF LATE! THE COOK SAYS SHE HAS BEEN CHASING MICE IN THE KITCHEN!

MICE?

SOUNDS LIKE SHE'S GOING THROUGH ANOTHER INVERSION... AS THOUGH HER FELINE ASPECTS ARE BECOMING DOMINANT AGAIN!

I'M GOING AFTER HER!

BUT, WITHIN A FEW MINUTES...

I'D NEVER REALLY REGISTERED HOW BIG THE GROUNDS ARE, HERE AT THE WEST COAST COMPOUND.

YOU COULD HIDE A SMALL HERD OF ELEPHANTS WITHOUT TOO MUCH DIFFICULTY.

TIGRA?

GREER? GREER, IT'S HANK.

ARE YOU THERE? CAN YOU HEAR ME?

NOTHING.

MIGHT AS WELL BE...

...HM...??

RRRRRRR

RROWRR

GREAT SCOTT!!

174

YAHH!!

SHE'S GONE WILD! ATTACKING ME TOOTH AND CLAW!

MY JUMPSUIT'S ENOUGH TO PROTECT EVERYTHING IT COVERS...

...BUT SHE'S INSTINCTIVELY GOING FOR MY EXPOSED FLESH...

...MOSTLY MY THROAT!!

ONLY ONE CHANCE.

DON'T LIKE USING MY SHRINKING POWER ON LIVING THINGS...

...BUT THE FEROCITY OF HER ATTACK LEAVES ME NO CHOICE!

RRRRROWWR?

THE QUESTION NOW IS...

WHAT THE HECK DO I DO WITH HER??

FSST! FSST!

175

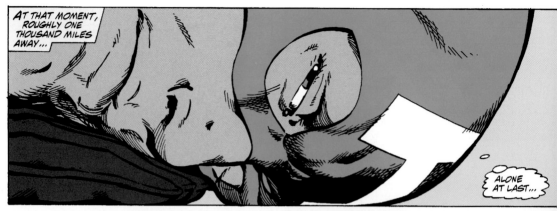

AT THAT MOMENT, ROUGHLY ONE THOUSAND MILES AWAY...

ALONE AT LAST...

SHE-HULK...

JENNIFER, ARE YOU ALL RIGHT? I DID WHAT I COULD TO PROTECT US **BOTH** WITH MY **SHIELD**...

I'M *FINE*, CAPTAIN. I GUESSED YOU WERE UP TO SOMETHING WHEN I SAW YOU *FALL*.

YOUR SHIELD SHOULD HAVE *ABSORBED* THE IMPACT OF THE MASONRY THE SCARLET WITCH CAUSED TO *FALL* ON US.

IT *DID.* BUT I THOUGHT IT BEST TO PLAY *POSSUM* RATHER THAN RISK *HURTING* WANDA IN A PITCHED BATTLE.

GLAD YOU PICKED UP ON WHAT I WAS ABOUT, AND PLAYED ALONG WITH IT.

YES...

NOW...

NO DOUBT THIS CELL IS FULL OF ALARMS AND SENSORS, SO WE'D BETTER MOVE FAST...

YES...

SHE-HULK!!

WHAT...???

SORRY, CAPTAIN. OBVIOUSLY YOU HAVE NOT BEEN PROPERLY ASSIMILATED.

THEREFORE, YOU MUST BE DESTROYED!

ASSIMILATED?

SHE-HULK, WHAT IN BLUE BLAZES ARE YOU TALKING ABOUT?

DON'T TELL ME THEY GOT TO YOU, TOO?

HOW?

AND WHY DIDN'T IT AFFECT ME, AS YOU CLEARLY THINK IT SHOULD HAVE?

WHAM

SHE'S NOT TALKING.

AND EVEN IF SHE KNOWS THE ANSWERS...

...HER PRESENT MOOD MAKES IT CLEAR SHE'S NOT INCLINED TO SHARE THEM WITH ME.

SO THE QUESTION NOW IS... HOW LONG CAN I KEEP DODGING HERE IN THIS CONFINED SPACE...

AND IF SHE CONNECTS...

...CAN I HOPE TO SURVIVE A DIRECT HIT FROM SOMEONE WHO'S NEARLY AS STRONG AS THE HULK?

SHE-HULK, STOP!

WE WANT CAPTAIN AMERICA ALIVE...

...FOR NOW...

SKZZKT

UNGH!

JUST THEN...

I HAVE BEEN UNATTENDED NOW FOR SEVEN HOURS, FOUR MINUTES, TWENTY-THREE SECONDS.

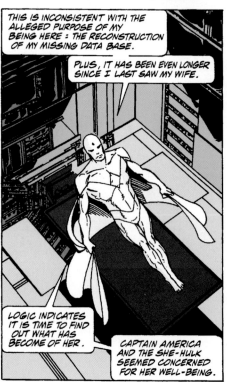

THIS IS INCONSISTENT WITH THE ALLEGED PURPOSE OF MY BEING HERE: THE RECONSTRUCTION OF MY MISSING DATA BASE.

PLUS, IT HAS BEEN EVEN LONGER SINCE I LAST SAW MY WIFE.

LOGIC INDICATES IT IS TIME TO FIND OUT WHAT HAS BECOME OF HER.

CAPTAIN AMERICA AND THE SHE-HULK SEEMED CONCERNED FOR HER WELL-BEING.

ACCORDING TO MR. RANDOM, WANDA DEPARTED OF HER OWN VOLITION SHORTLY AFTER LEAVING ME HERE.

ALTHOUGH I AM NOT FLUENT IN EMOTIONAL RESPONSES, UPON CLOSER ANALYSIS THIS DOES NOT SEEM IN KEEPING WITH HER EXPRESSED CONCERN FOR MY CONDITION.

NEVERTHELESS, SINCE I HAVE NO REASON TO DOUBT MR. RANDOM...

...MY MOST PRODUCTIVE COURSE OF ACTION WOULD SEEM TO LIE IN ATTEMPTING TO DETERMINE WHERE WANDA MIGHT HAVE GONE.

AND, AS CHANCE WOULD HAVE IT...

HEY, LOOK!

SWING 'ROUND, ASHLEY.

IF THE VISION'S HERE...

...HE MAY KNOW SOMETHING ABOUT THAT DISTRESS SIGNAL.

A CIVILIAN AIRCRAFT, ATTEMPTING A MIDAIR RENDEZVOUS WITH ME.

I FIND NO TRACE OF ITS IDENTIFICATION NUMBERS IN MY PROGRAM-MING.

YO, VIZH...

COME ON OVER!

HAWKEYE. GREETINGS. I RECOGNIZED YOUR VOICE.

BUT I DO NOT KNOW ANY OF THE INDIVIDUALS WITH YOU AND MOCKINGBIRD.

NO SURPRISE.

SAY "HEY" TO MY NEW TEAM, VIZH, THE GREAT LAKES AVENGERS!

"GREAT LAKES?" WOULD NOT "MIDWEST" BE A MORE APPROPRIATE NOMENCLATURE...?

YEAH, MAYBE. I DIDN'T NAME 'EM.

HEY, VIZH, WHAT DO YOU KNOW ABOUT THE DISTRESS SIG-NAL 'BIRD PICKED UP?

179

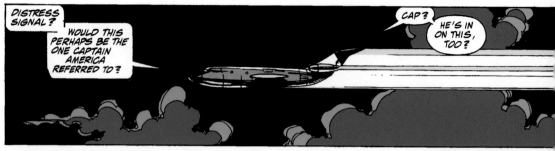

DISTRESS SIGNAL?

WOULD THIS PERHAPS BE THE ONE CAPTAIN AMERICA REFERRED TO?

CAP?

HE'S IN ON THIS, TOO?

"WHAT'S *HIS* INVOLVEMENT?"

DEFINITELY SOMETHING THERE, MR. RANDOM.

SOMETHING IN HIS *BIO-MATRIX* THAT *BLOCKS* THE ASSIMILATOR.

INDEED?

SHE-HULK... WHAT DO *YOU* KNOW OF THIS?

IT MUST BE THE *SUPER-SOLDIER SERUM*. THE SUBSTANCE THAT TURNED HIM INTO CAPTAIN AMERICA IN THE FIRST PLACE. IT'S STILL IN THERE, *REPLICATING* ITSELF IN HIS BLOODSTREAM.

A *CHEMICAL BLOCK*?

FASCINATING! SINCE THE GOOD CAPTAIN IS NOT A *MUTANT*, OUR PRESENCE WOULD HAVE BEEN WITHIN EVERY CELL OF HIS BODY SINCE THE MOMENT OF HIS *CONCEPTION...*

...JUST AS WE ARE IN *ALL* THE HIGHER LIFE FORMS.

YET THIS "*SUPER-SOLDIER SERUM*" AS YOU CALL IT HAS APPARENTLY *ERADICATED* US.

POSSIBLY AS A SIDE EFFECT OF TRANS-FORMING CAPTAIN AMERICA INTO THE *PERFECT HUMAN SPECIMEN* HE NOW IS.

MR. RANDOM...

SOMETHING I DON'T UNDERSTAND ABOUT ALL THIS... YOU TALK ABOUT "*WE*" AND "*US*"... WHO IS "*WE*"?

WHAT IS *THAT WHICH ENDURES*?

PERHAPS I CAN ANSWER THAT, JENNI-FER...

WANDA! IT'S GOOD TO SEE YOU AGAIN. I'M... SORRY ABOUT THAT LITTLE... CONFRONTATION WE HAD EARLIER.

THAT'S QUITE ALL RIGHT, SHE-HULK.

YOU SIMPLY... DID NOT UNDERSTAND WHAT IS HAPPENING. NOW I CAN TELL YOU.

"IT BEGAN FOUR BILLION YEARS AGO, SHE-HULK.

"IT BEGAN WITH THE FIRST PRIMITIVE CELL, ESSENTIALLY THE FIRST LIFE ON EARTH.

"LIKE ALL THE SIMPLE ORGANISMS SINCE THEN, THAT CELL REPRODUCED ITSELF BY DIVIDING.

"BUT AT THAT FIRST MOMENT OF DIVISION, SOMETHING HAPPENED.

"THE FISSION SHOULD HAVE PRODUCED TWO IDENTICAL ENTITIES, BUT IT DID NOT.

"ONE HALF WAS DIFFERENT. IT IMMEDIATELY INVADED THE OTHER HALF, MATCHING ITSELF EXACTLY TO THE PROTO-CELL'S GENETIC STRUCTURE. BECOMING ONE WITH IT.

"SO IT IS THAT THIS INVADER HAS BEEN PRESENT IN ALL THE DESCENDANTS OF THAT FIRST ORGANISM.

"PRESENT IN THE FISH THAT DEVELOPED IN THE SEAS...

"PRESENT IN THE PLANTS THAT WERE THE FIRST TO MAKE HEADWAY ONTO THE LAND...

"... AND IN THE AMPHIBIOUS CREATURES THAT FOLLOWED.

"IT WAS THERE IN EACH AND EVERY ONE OF THE DINOSAURS, SUBTLY GUIDING THEIR DEVELOPMENT...

"...MAKING THEM MASTERS OF THIS WORLD FOR TWO HUNDRED MILLION YEARS!

"BUT THE DINOSAURS CAME TO BE SEEN AS A DEAD END. THEY WERE ABANDONED.

"FOCUS SHIFTED TO THE MAMMALS..."

181

WITHOUT *OUR* PRESENCE TO *GUIDE* THEM, THE DINOSAURS QUICKLY *DIED OUT.*

YOU MEAN...

YOU MEAN... THIS... *"PASSENGER"* INSIDE US ALL... IT'S *CONSCIOUS?*

THINKING?

CHOOSING?

AFTER A *FASHION,* SHE-HULK.

WHILE IT IS *TRUE* A FORM OF *INTELLIGENCE* DEVELOPED IN US ALMOST *IMMEDIATELY...*

...*FOR* THE MOST PART, THAT INTELLIGENCE LAY *DORMANT.* IT WAS MANY MILLIONS OF YEARS BEFORE WE LEARNED TO *CONTROL* THE PROCESS CHARLES DARWIN NAMED *"NATURAL SELECTION."*

ONCE THAT OCCURRED, HOWEVER, WE BEGAN TO TAKE AN *ACTIVE* INTEREST IN OUR *HOSTS.*

ONCE EVERY *HUNDRED THOUSAND YEARS* OUR INTELLECT *MANIFESTS* ITSELF IN A FEW... AH... *RANDOM* CREATURES. WE *STUDY* THE PROGRESS OF LIFE. WE MATCH THE *ADAPTABILITY* OF ONE SPECIES AGAINST ANOTHER.

AN *ASSESSMENT* IS MADE. THOSE LIFE FORMS WE JUDGE TO BE AT THEIR MAXIMUM POTENTIAL WE *ABANDON.* OUR PRESENCE WITHIN THEIR CELLS *SHRINKS,* DWINDLING EVENTUALLY TO *NOTHING.*

AND OUR GUIDING INTELLECT TURNS TO OTHER, MORE *PROFITABLE* SPECIES. AFTER ALL, OUR WHOLE AND SOLE PURPOSE IS TO *ENDURE.*

THUS, WE LEFT THE DINOSAURS IN FAVOR OF CONCENTRATING ON THE MAMMALS.

THERE WE FURTHER NARROWED OUR FOCUS TO THE *ULTIMATE MAMMAL,* MANKIND.

WHEN NEANDERTHAL PROVED UNSUITABLE, WE SHIFTED TO CRO-MAGNON.

NOW...

MR. *RANDOM!!*

WE'RE UNDER ATTACK!

"THE AVENGERS ARE HERE!!"

HIT 'EM HIGH AND LOW!

AVENGERS ASSEMBLE!

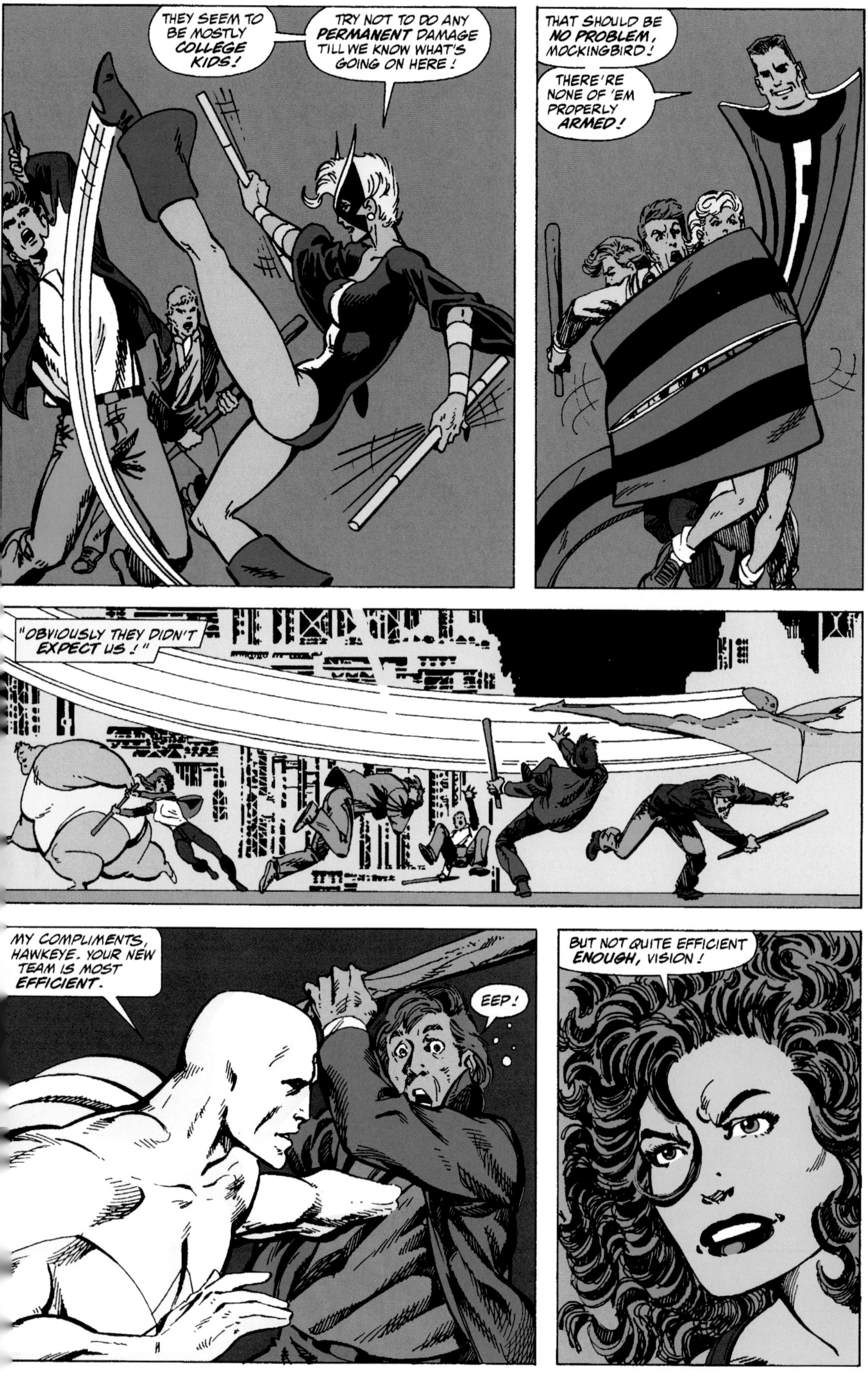
THEY SEEM TO BE MOSTLY COLLEGE KIDS!
TRY NOT TO DO ANY PERMANENT DAMAGE TILL WE KNOW WHAT'S GOING ON HERE!
THAT SHOULD BE NO PROBLEM, MOCKINGBIRD!
THERE'RE NONE OF 'EM PROPERLY ARMED!
"OBVIOUSLY THEY DIDN'T EXPECT US!"
MY COMPLIMENTS, HAWKEYE. YOUR NEW TEAM IS MOST EFFICIENT.
EEP!
BUT NOT QUITE EFFICIENT ENOUGH, VISION!

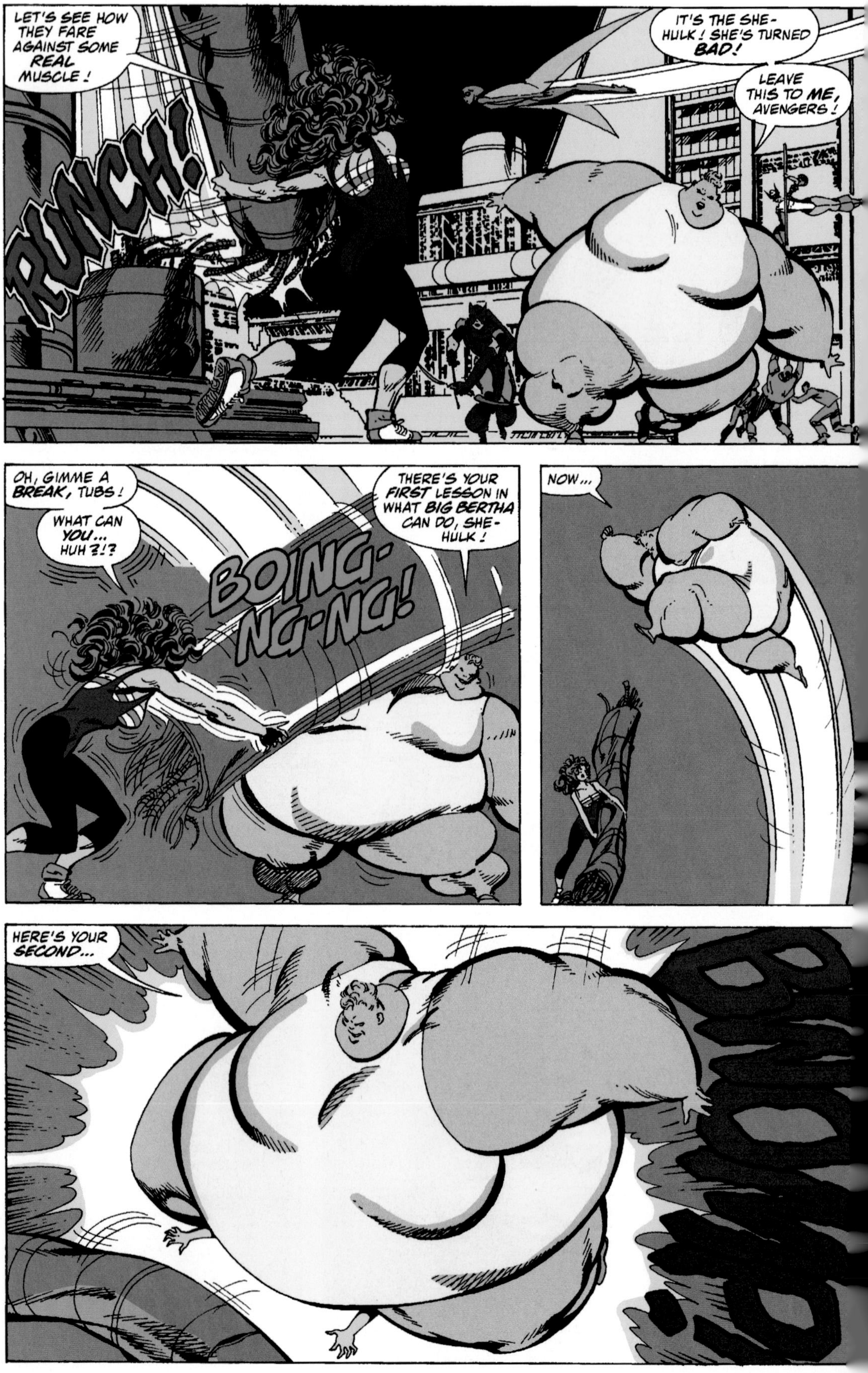
LET'S SEE HOW THEY FARE AGAINST SOME REAL MUSCLE!
RUNCH!
IT'S THE SHE-HULK! SHE'S TURNED BAD!
LEAVE THIS TO ME, AVENGERS!
OH, GIMME A BREAK, TUBS!
WHAT CAN YOU... HUH ?!?
BOING-NG-NG!
THERE'S YOUR FIRST LESSON IN WHAT BIG BERTHA CAN DO, SHE-HULK!
NOW...
HERE'S YOUR SECOND...

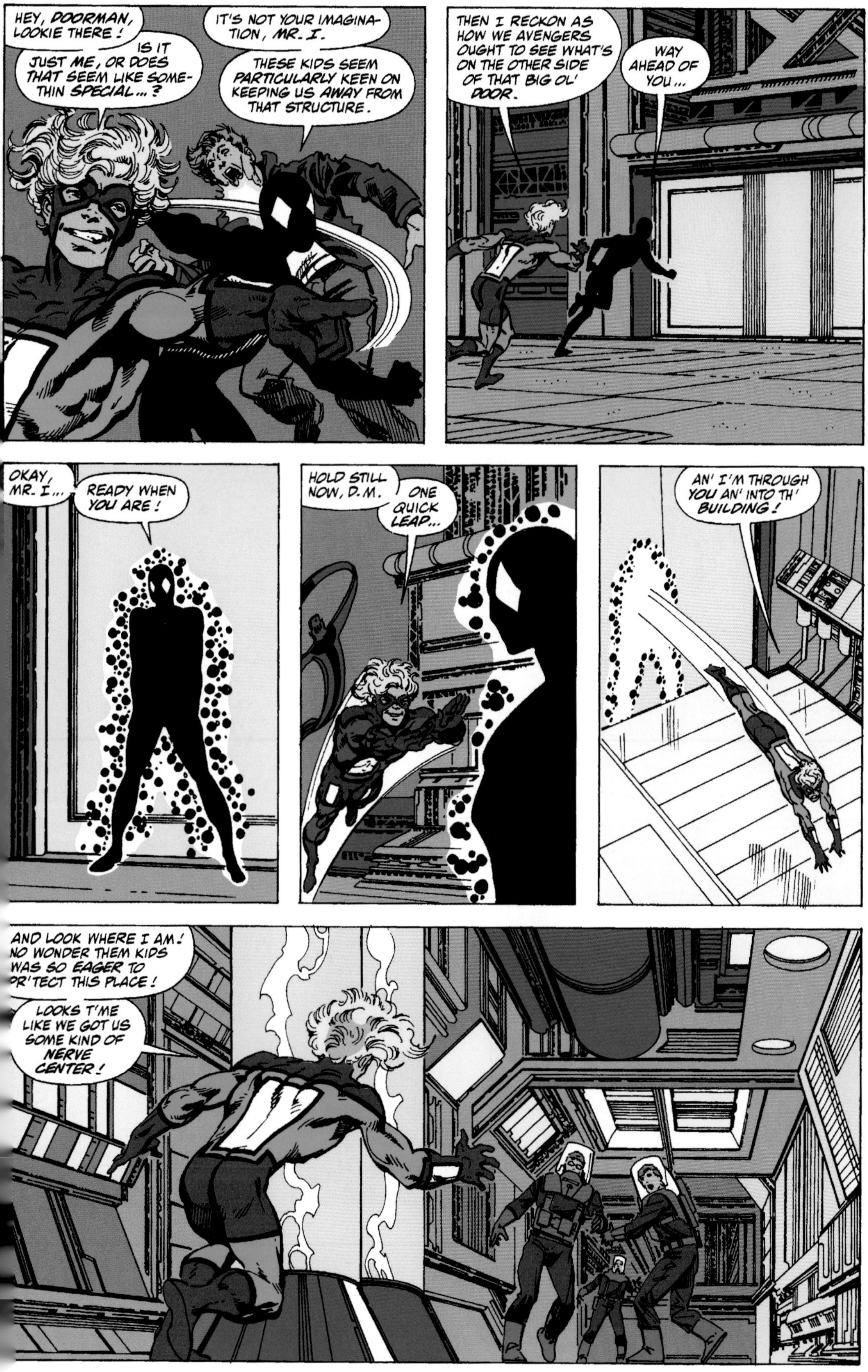
HEY, DOORMAN, LOOKIE THERE!
IS IT JUST ME, OR DOES THAT SEEM LIKE SOMETHIN SPECIAL...?
IT'S NOT YOUR IMAGINATION, MR. I.
THESE KIDS SEEM PARTICULARLY KEEN ON KEEPING US AWAY FROM THAT STRUCTURE.
THEN I RECKON AS HOW WE AVENGERS OUGHT TO SEE WHAT'S ON THE OTHER SIDE OF THAT BIG OL' DOOR.
WAY AHEAD OF YOU...
OKAY, MR. I...
READY WHEN YOU ARE!
HOLD STILL NOW, D.M.
ONE QUICK LEAP...
AN' I'M THROUGH YOU AN' INTO TH' BUILDING!
AND LOOK WHERE I AM! NO WONDER THEM KIDS WAS SO EAGER TO PR'TECT THIS PLACE!
LOOKS T'ME LIKE WE GOT US SOME KIND OF NERVE CENTER!

AT THAT MOMENT...

THE ASSIMILATOR! ONE OF THE AVENGERS HAS PENETRATED THE INNER DEFENSES!

IF THE ASSIMILATOR IS DAMAGED WE'LL LOSE THE TELEPATHIC LINK THAT JOINS US!

IT MIGHT BE ANOTHER HUNDRED MILLENNIA BEFORE WE COULD CONTINUE WITH OUR PLAN!

WELL, WELL!

COMPANY? YOU GOT TH' LOOK OF A HEAD HONCHO ABOUT YOU, BOY. A HEAD HONCHO IN A POWERFUL FLAP!

??

YOU'RE NOT ONE OF THE AVENGERS...??

BUT YOU MIGHT AS WELL STOP WHERE YOU ARE, FRIEND, WHOEVER YOU ARE.

THE INNER CHAMBER SURROUNDING THE ASSIMILATOR IS PROTECTED BY AN INTENSE RADIATION FIELD.

IF YOU STEP INSIDE, THE DOOR WILL CLOSE AUTOMATICALLY BEHIND YOU, AND YOU'LL BE BOMBARDED WITH LETHAL RADIOACTIVITY.

THE ASSIMILATOR IS PROTECTED, BUT ANY HUMAN EXPOSED TO THAT BOMBARDMENT WOULD BE DEAD IN THIRTY SECONDS!

HEY, NOW TELL ME SOMETHIN' THAT SCARES ME, FOLKS!

I'M MISTER IMMORTAL!

ALL YOU'RE THREATENING ME WITH IS DEATH!

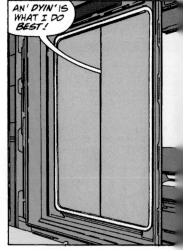

AN' DYIN' IS WHAT I DO BEST!

THE FOOL!

186

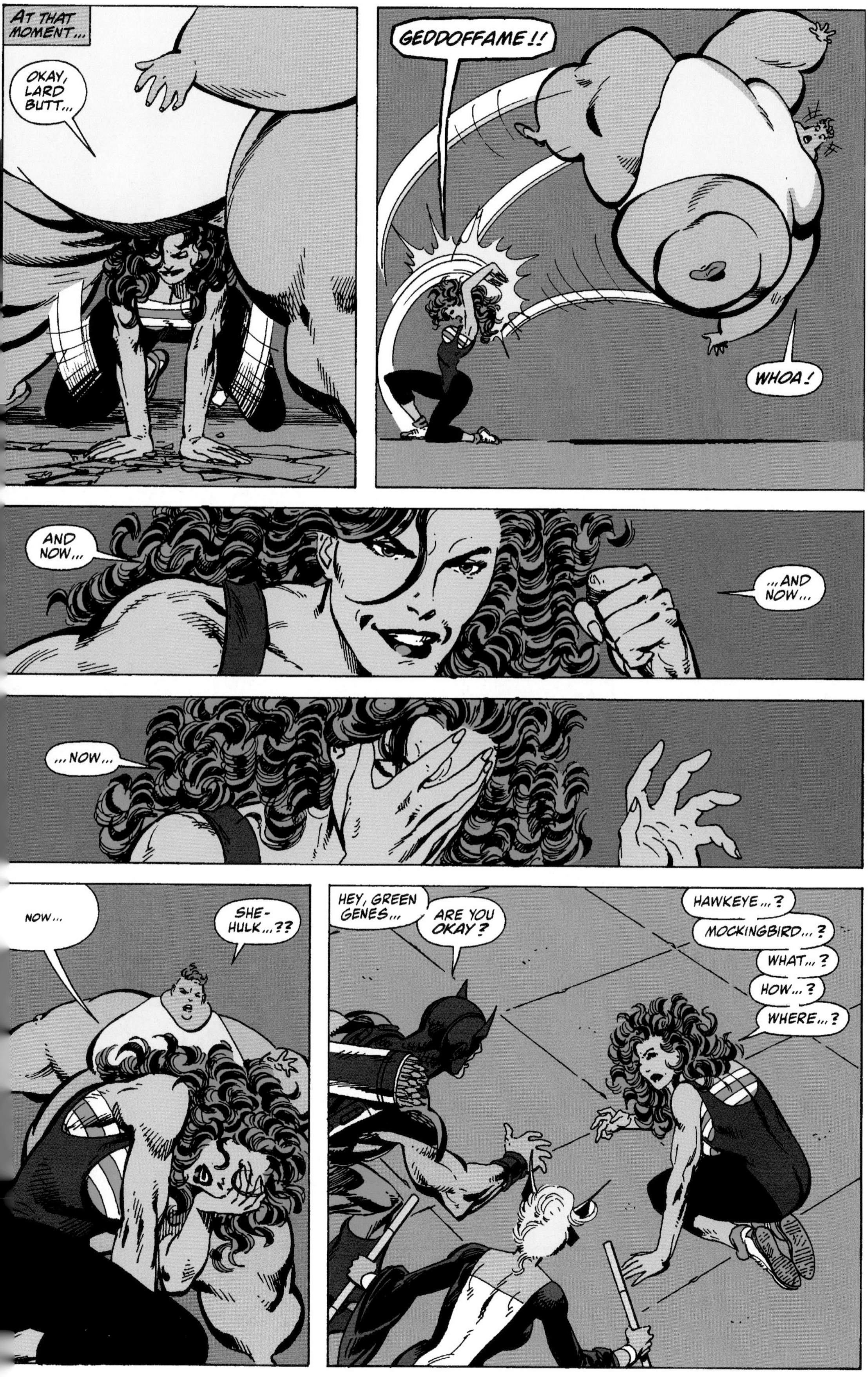

AT THAT MOMENT...
OKAY, LARD BUTT...
GEDDOFFAME!!
WHOA!
AND NOW...
...AND NOW...
...NOW...
NOW...
SHE-HULK...??
HEY, GREEN GENES...
ARE YOU OKAY?
HAWKEYE...?
MOCKINGBIRD...?
WHAT...?
HOW...?
WHERE...?

LOOK! THEY'RE ALL WANDERING ABOUT IN A DAZE!

IT'S LIKE... PART OF THEIR BRAIN HAS BEEN TURNED OFF!

HEY! AVENGERS ASSEMBLE!

OVER HERE! QUICK!!

MR. RANDOM...

...RANDOM...

PERHAPS YOU WOULD CARE TO EXPLAIN ALL THIS?

NO... MY NAME IS EDISON. CHARLES EDISON. BUT... PLEASE... YOU MUST HURRY! ONE OF YOUR PEOPLE IS IN GRAVE DANGER...

"...IF NOT ALREADY DEAD!"

IT'S MR. I!

LOOKS LIKE HE'S SMASHED THROUGH THAT CONTAINMENT WALL.

AND THAT GLOW IS... THE RADIATION YOU MENTIONED?

YES, HAWKEYE. ENOUGH TO KILL A HUNDRED MEN. I'M AFRAID YOUR FRIEND HAS SACRIFICED HIMSELF TO DESTROY THE ASSIMILATOR!

SACRIFICED?

DON'T COUNT ON IT, WITCHEY-POO.

RANDOM... OR WHATEVER THE HECK YOUR NAME IS... THIS DOOR SWITCHES OFF THE RADIATION WHEN IT'S OPENED?

YES, BUT...

FLATMAN... YOU CAN GET TO HIM WITHOUT SETTING OFF THE PRESSURE PLATE IN THE FLOOR...

RIGHT YOU ARE, HAWKEYE!

WELL, BERTHA?

DEAD AS A DOOR-NAIL, HAWK.

I'D SAY HE'LL BE COMING 'ROUND IN ABOUT TEN MINUTES...

AND SO... GUESS THERE'S NOT MUCH POINT IN TRYIN' TO *ARREST* ANYONE.

IF EVER *ANYBODY* HAD A GOOD CLAIM TO NOT BEIN' IN *FULL* CONTROL OF THEIR FACULTIES, IT'S *YOU* PEOPLE!

...THANK YOU FOR THAT, AT LEAST, HAWKEYE.

IT'S BAD ENOUGH TO REALIZE I'VE LOST HALF A *LIFETIME* AND EVERY PENNY I OWN TO THIS THING, WITHOUT HAVING TO FACE A *JAIL* SENTENCE AS WELL.

YES... THIS DORMANT "SURVIVOR" *COMPELLED* YOU TO USE YOUR FAMILY FORTUNE TO PURCHASE THIS UNIVERSITY, AND CONVERT IT TO THE NEEDS OF THE PROJECT.

YOU GATHERED TOGETHER THOSE FEW HUNDRED OTHERS IN WHOM *THAT WHICH ENDURES* HAD AWAKENED, AND EACH CONTRIBUTED A SMALL CELL SAMPLE TO DEVELOP INTO THE ASSIMILATOR.

BUT... VISION... IT'S ALL SO... *FRIGHTENING*...

THE MEMORIES THE ASSIMILATOR PLACED INSIDE ME... I STILL HAVE THEM...

CAN IT BE THE DINOSAURS DIED BECAUSE *THAT WHICH ENDURES* LEFT?

AND IF IT SOMEDAY LEAVES MANKIND FOR THE MUTANTS, AS IT PLANNED...

I AM NOT PROPERLY PROGRAMMED TO CONSIDER SUCH PHILOSOPHICAL MATTERS, WANDA...

MAYBE NOT... BUT *I* HAVE SOMETHING TO SAY...

I DON'T KNOW HOW MUCH OF WHAT WE'VE LEARNED TODAY I'M REALLY PREPARED TO *ACCEPT*...

MAYBE IT'S ALL *TRUE*. MAYBE WITHOUT *THAT WHICH ENDURES* MANKIND WOULD STILL BE SQUATTING IN THE CAVES, AFRAID OF THE *DARK*, OF THE *THUNDER* AND *LIGHTNING*.

BUT I LIKE TO THINK THERE'S SOMETHING *MORE* TO HUMANITY THAN JUST A FEW POUNDS OF FLESH AND BONE. SOMETHING DEEP *INSIDE* THAT SETS US APART IN THE SCHEME OF THINGS.

I *HOPE* THAT'S TRUE. AND I HOPE NO PART OF IT WAS DUE TO *THAT WHICH ENDURES*.

FOR IF IT *IS*... IF WE ARE NO MORE THAN *VEHICLES* FOR THIS PARASITE...

...WHEN A DAY COMES THAT THE SURVIVOR *DOES* FINALLY DEPART...

...WE'RE GOING TO FIND OURSELVES VERY MUCH *ALONE*...

THE END

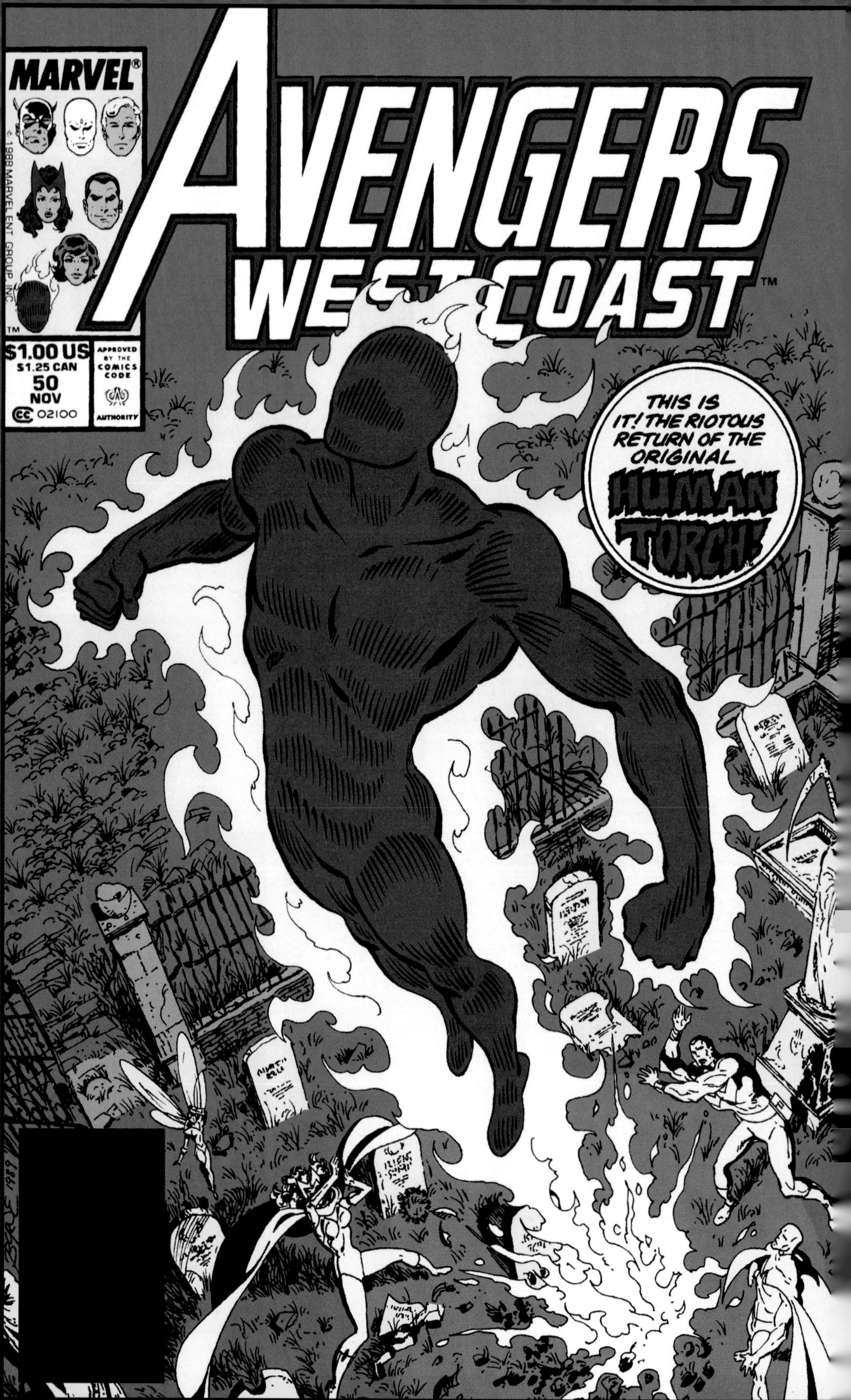
MARVEL
© 1988 MARVEL ENT. GROUP, INC.
AVENGERS
WEST COAST
$1.00 US
$1.25 CAN
50
NOV
02100
APPROVED BY THE COMICS CODE AUTHORITY
THIS IS IT! THE RIOTOUS RETURN OF THE ORIGINAL
HUMAN TORCH!

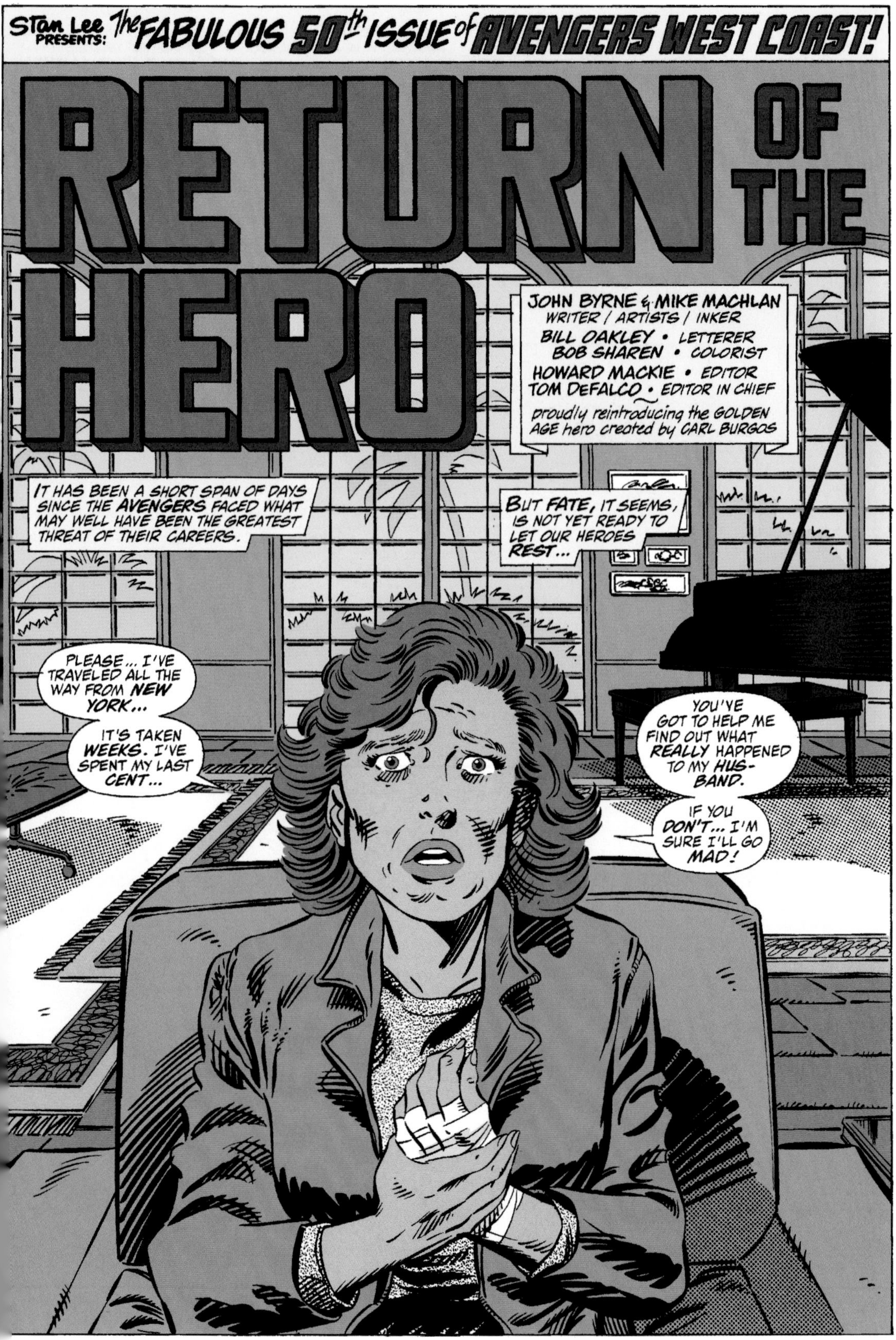
STAN LEE PRESENTS: THE FABULOUS 50TH ISSUE OF AVENGERS WEST COAST!
RETURN OF THE HERO
JOHN BYRNE & MIKE MACHLAN WRITER / ARTISTS / INKER
BILL OAKLEY • LETTERER
BOB SHAREN • COLORIST
HOWARD MACKIE • EDITOR
TOM DEFALCO • EDITOR IN CHIEF
proudly reintroducing the GOLDEN AGE hero created by CARL BURGOS
IT HAS BEEN A SHORT SPAN OF DAYS SINCE THE AVENGERS FACED WHAT MAY WELL HAVE BEEN THE GREATEST THREAT OF THEIR CAREERS.
BUT FATE, IT SEEMS, IS NOT YET READY TO LET OUR HEROES REST...
PLEASE... I'VE TRAVELED ALL THE WAY FROM NEW YORK...
IT'S TAKEN WEEKS. I'VE SPENT MY LAST CENT...
YOU'VE GOT TO HELP ME FIND OUT WHAT REALLY HAPPENED TO MY HUS-BAND.
IF YOU DON'T... I'M SURE I'LL GO MAD!

THE LIVING ROOM OF AVENGERS MANSION WEST...

12 NOON, TODAY!

ALL RIGHT NOW, MA'AM, CALM DOWN - TAKE IT *EASY.*

THE AVENGERS WERE *CREATED* TO HELP PEOPLE IN *DISTRESS.*

BUT YOU'VE GOT TO TELL US YOUR STORY *SLOWLY* ...*CLEARLY*...

MY NAME IS *ANN RAYMOND.* MY HUSBAND WAS... IS...THOMAS.

YOU MAY KNOW HIM BETTER AS *TORO,* THE *PARTNER* OF THE ORIGINAL *HUMAN TORCH!*

TORO?

BUT...TORO'S *DEAD,* ISN'T HE?

THE *SUB-MARINER* REPORTED HIM *KILLED* IN A BATTLE WITH THE *MAD THINKER.*

WELL...! I'D *NEVER* HAVE EXPECTED OUR RESIDENT *FASCIST* TO HAVE SUCH A *SWEET* BEDSIDE MANNER. WHAT'S THE *DOPE* ON THIS WOMAN, *WASP?* IF SHE NEEDED THE AVENGERS, WHY DIDN'T SHE GET IN TOUCH WITH THE *EAST COAST* BOYS?

NO WAY TO KNOW UNTIL *SHE* TELLS US, *SIMON.* THE ROBOT *GROUNDSKEEPERS* FOUND HER AFTER SHE TRIED TO CLIMB THE SOUTH WALL.

YES. THAT'S APPARENTLY WHEN SHE HURT HER HAND.

BUT SHE'S BEEN MORE OR LESS *HYSTERICAL* UNTIL JUST A MOMENT AGO.

LISTEN... SHE HAS *CALMED* ENOUGH TO *SPEAK* AGAIN...

YES... THAT WAS WHAT *I* UNDERSTOOD, TOO. PRINCE NAMOR ACTUALLY CAME TO ME AFTER WITNESSING THAT BATTLE. HE TOLD ME TOM HAD DIED A *HERO'S DEATH.*

FOR YEARS, I'VE *BELIEVED* THAT TO BE TRUE... UNTIL I HEARD ABOUT WHAT HAPPENED TO THE *VISION.*

...THE VISION?!?

HOW COULD *MY HUSBAND'S* PRESENT SITUATION HAVE ANYTHING TO DO WITH *YOUR* HUSBAND, MRS. RAYMOND??

CALM YOURSELF, MY WIFE. I'M SURE MRS. RAYMOND HAS A *LOGICAL* REASON FOR HER STATEMENT.

193

CALM MYSELF? HOW CAN I CALM MYSELF WHEN THE WHOLE **WORLD** HAS GONE COMPLETELY **INSANE?!**

ISN'T IT **BAD ENOUGH** THAT I'VE HAD TO SEE MY HUSBAND **DISMANTLED**... HIS MIND **ERASED**... ISN'T IT BAD ENOUGH THAT A GROUP TRYING TO USE ME TO FIND A WAY TO **POSSESS** ALL THE OTHER **MUTANTS** ON EARTH USED THE VISION'S CONDITION AS THEIR AVENUE OF **APPROACH** TO LURE ME INTO THEIR **CLUTCHES**...

NOW THIS **MADWOMAN** WANTS TO IMPLICATE THE VISION IN THE DEATH OF HER HUSBAND?

TAKE IT EASY NOW, WANDA! THAT'S NOT WHAT MRS. RAYMOND IS SAYING. WE'VE GOT TO HEAR HER OUT...

THE **ANGUISH** IN WANDA'S VOICE! IT'S LIKE **CLAWS** RAKING AT MY **SOUL**! IF ONLY THERE WAS SOME WAY I COULD...

GET YOUR HAND **OFF** ME, WONDER MAN!

I CAME BACK TO THE AVENGERS ONLY BECAUSE YOU **PROMISED** THIS TIME TO DO SOMETHING TO **HELP** THE VISION.

IF LISTENING TO THIS WOMAN'S **BABBLING** IS YOUR IDEA OF **HELP**...

...THEN IT SEEMS THE **WISEST** THING THE VISION AND I CAN DO IS **DEPART**...

FOREVER!

WANDA...!

NO, WASP...LET ME DEAL WITH THIS.

ALTHOUGH I AM NO LONGER ABLE TO GIVE HER THE EMOTIONAL SUCCOR SHE NEEDS, WANDA IS STILL MY **WIFE**...

...AND MY DUTY THEREFORE LIES WITH HER.

ER...

I'M **SORRY** ABOUT THAT, MRS. RAYMOND. MAYBE YOU COULD TELL US YOUR WHOLE STORY NOW...

I'LL TELL YOU AS MUCH AS I *KNOW*, DOCTOR PYM.

AS MUCH AS I *SAW*... AND AS MUCH AS THE SUB-MARINER *TOLD* ME.

MY HUSBAND HAD *RETIRED* AS A CRIME-FIGHTER...

"FOR YEARS WE LIVED IN SUBURBAN CONTENTMENT.

"UNTIL ONE DAY..."

IT SAYS HERE... TORCH WAS *KILLED* SOMEHOW...

WITH THE FANTASTIC FOUR THE SOLE WITNESSES!

PLEASE, DARLING...

KEEP OUT OF THIS!

"BUT HE COULDN'T. THE NEWSPAPER ARTICLE GAVE THE LOCATION OF HIS FORMER PARTNER'S *FUNERAL*...

"TOM WENT TO PAY HIS LAST RESPECTS. HE'D SPOKEN OF THE TORCH SO OFTEN I KNEW JUST WHAT HE WOULD HAVE BEEN *THINKING*..."

SO LONG, BUDDY. I'M SORRY I NEVER GOT THE CHANCE TO *REPAY* YOU FOR EVERYTHING YOU *GAVE* ME IN LIFE.

"HE CALLED ME AFTER THE *SERVICE*..."

YEAH, IT'S PRETTY MUCH ALL OVER, HONEY. SHORT AND SWEET.

FUNNY, THOUGH, THERE WERE NO OTHER *SUPER* HEROES HERE. I'D HAVE THOUGHT *CAPTAIN AMERICA* AT LEAST WOULD'VE COME, SINCE WE WERE IN THE *INVADERS* TOGETHER...

"IT WAS THE LAST TIME I WOULD EVER SPEAK TO HIM..."

"ACCORDING TO WHAT TOM TOLD THE SUB-MARINER, HE WAS STOPPED JUST OUTSIDE THE CEMETERY..."

...SIR... I MUST *SPEAK* WITH YOU.

IT CONCERNS YOUR FRIEND'S *DEATH*...

"TOM WAS SURPRISED TO BE *RECOGNIZED*..."

"...SO HE WENT WITH THE MYSTERIOUS STRANGER...

"...WHO TURNED OUT TO BE THE *SUPER-VILLAIN* KNOWN AS THE *MAD THINKER*..."

COFFEE... *DRUGGED*...

UNNHHHH...

THE THINKER NEEDED TOM'S FLAME POWERS AS PART OF SOME SCHEME HE WAS IN WITH *EGGHEAD* AND THE *PUPPET MASTER*...

YES! I REMEMBER THAT! EGGHEAD WENT ON NATIONWIDE TV THREATENING TO *BLACK OUT* ALL AMERICA'S POWER...

SO TORO GOT DRAWN INTO THAT MESS TOO, DID HE?

GO ON, MRS. RAYMOND...

THERE'S NOT MUCH MORE TO TELL.

SOMEHOW THE THINKER BRAINWASHED TOM. MADE TOM THINK *HE* WAS ACTUALLY THE TORCH.

IT WAS THE THINKER WHO'D TRIED TO USE THE TORCH TO *DESTROY THE FANTASTIC FOUR*...

THAT WAS WHEN THE ORIGINAL TORCH *DIED*.

"WHILE HE WAS UNDER THE THINKER'S CONTROL, TOM FOUND HIMSELF IN BATTLE WITH THE SUB-MARINER.

"PRINCE NAMOR MANAGED TO FREE TOM OF THE THINKER'S INFLUENCE...

"AND TOM, SEEING THE THINKER TRYING TO ESCAPE IN A ROCKET SHIP... HE... HE USED HIS OWN FLAME TO PROPEL THE SHIP... TO DRIVE IT INTO A *VOLCANO*.

"AT FIRST I DIDN'T KNOW ANY OF THAT, THOUGH. I ONLY KNEW MY HUSBAND WAS LATE COMING BACK.

"WHEN TWENTY-FOUR HOURS WENT BY WITH NO FURTHER WORD FROM TOM, I DROVE OUT TO THE PLACE NAMED IN THE PAPER.

"I FOUND THE CEMETERY CLOSED... LOCKED AND BADLY OVERGROWN.

"I ASKED AROUND IN THE TOWN, AND WAS TOLD..."

"...WHY, NO, MA'AM, THE OLD QUAKER HILL CEMETERY HAS BEEN CLOSED FOR... MUST BE THIRTY YEARS NOW.

IF YOUR HUSBAND CAME UP TO A FUNERAL, IT COULDN'T HAVE BEEN THERE.

"EVERYONE I ASKED GAVE ME THE SAME ANSWER.

"AND, WHEN I GOT BACK HOME AT LAST..."

TOGETHER PRINCE NAMOR AND I PIECED TOGETHER THE STORY. WE FIGURED OUT THAT THE WHOLE FUNERAL WAS PART OF THE MAD THINKER'S PLOT. THAT THE OTHER MOURNERS WERE PROBABLY BEING CONTROLLED BY THE PUPPET MASTER...

THAT MAKES SENSE. THERE WAS A MEMORIAL SERVICE FOR THE TORCH EVENTUALLY, BUT AT THE RECOMMENDATION OF THE FANTASTIC FOUR, NO ATTEMPT WAS MADE TO RECOVER HIS BODY FROM WHERE THEY'D LEFT IT.

AS FAR AS ANYONE KNEW, THE TORCH WAS STILL IN THE THINKER'S DESERT LAB.

RIGHT... AND ACCORDING TO THE VERSION OF THIS STORY THE VISION WAS GIVEN BY IMMORTUS, IT WAS THERE THAT ULTRON-5 FOUND THE TORCH...

...AND BEGAN THE PROCESS OF TURNING THE FALLEN ANDROID INTO THE VISION.

YES... BUT I READ IN THE PAPERS THAT YOU'D RECENTLY FOUND OUT THE VISION IS NOT THE ORIGINAL HUMAN TORCH...

—AND I THOUGHT... I HOPED... IF THAT WAS ALL WRONG, MAYBE SUB-MARINER WAS WRONG, TOO! MAYBE THAT WASN'T TOM WHO DIED IN THE VOLCANO. MAYBE IT WAS REALLY THE TORCH AGAIN!

WOW! D'YOU THINK THAT COULD BE POSSIBLE, LOVE?

JAN, AT THIS POINT, I'M ABOUT READY TO BELIEVE ANYTHING!

SINCE THE THINKER WAS ABLE TO RESTORE THE TORCH TO LIFE IN THE FIRST PLACE, I GUESS HE COULD WELL HAVE DONE IT AGAIN!

ALTHOUGH NONE OF THAT WOULD TELL US WHERE TOM RAYMOND HAS BEEN ALL THESE YEARS...

BUT YOU WILL HELP ME, WON'T YOU?

YOU'LL HELP ME FIND OUT WHAT REALLY HAPPENED TO MY HUSBAND?

WE'LL DO WHAT WE CAN, MRS. RAYMOND.

JAN... WHY DON'T YOU ESCORT MRS. RAYMOND TO ONE OF THE GUEST ROOMS? I'M SURE SHE COULD USE SOME REST.

SURE, HANK.

COME ON, ANN... YOU DON'T MIND IF I CALL YOU ANN...?

PYM? YOU DON'T ACTUALLY BUY THIS POOR WOMAN'S FANTASIES?

NO... AT LEAST, NOT ALL OF IT. NOT WITHOUT CROSS CHECKING SOME OF THE DETAILS WITH THE SUB-MARINER, AT OUR EAST COAST HQ.

"THEN WE'LL SEE WHAT'S TO BE SEEN..."

MRS. RAYMOND'S STORY IS PERFECTLY TRUE, DOCTOR PYM.

I FOUGHT A BLAZING BEING WHO CALLED HIMSELF THE HUMAN TORCH...

...BUT WHO, IN THE END, WAS REVEALED TO BE TORO.

AND YOU'D RECOGNIZE TORO, NAMOR? I MEAN, A LOT OF YEARS HAVE GONE BY SINCE YOU WERE IN THE INVADERS TOGETHER.

AGREED. AND MUCH OF MY LIFE SINCE THE SECOND WORLD WAR WAS SPENT IN AN AMNESIAC FOG.

UNTIL THE PRESENT DAY HUMAN TORCH FOUND ME...

STILL, I SAW NO REASON TO DOUBT THE STORY THOMAS RAYMOND TOLD ME.

AND THE FACT THAT HE WAS INDEED, MISSING WHEN I SOUGHT OUT HIS WIFE TO TELL HER OF HIS SAD END, ADDS WEIGHT TO THE TALE.

WELL... THAT PRETTY MUCH FINISHES *THAT* PART OF IT.

I THINK WE'RE REASONABLY SAFE IN ASSUMING IT *WAS* TORO WHO DIED.

AND DIED WITH- OUT REASON, SINCE THE MAD THINKER ESCAPED.

WELL, HANK?

WHAT DO WE--

BEEEEEP

THE *BIO- LAB* ALARM!

PYM... ONE OF YOUR EXPERI- MENTS...??

I DON'T HAVE ANY- THING RUNNING JUST NOW, *USAGENT!*

BUT I THINK I CAN GUESS *WHO* MUST HAVE TRIGGERED THE ALARM.

AND THERE SHE IS!

TIGRA?!? IS THAT...??

YES, IT'S TIGRA. I HAD TO USE MY *SHRINKING POWER* ON HER TO PROTECT MYSELF WHEN SHE *ATTACKED* ME THE OTHER NIGHT.

KNOCKING OVER HER WATER DISH MUST'VE SET OFF THE MOISTURE SENSOR IN THE CAGE AND SOUNDED THE ALARM.

BUT... HANK... WHAT'S HAPPENED TO HER? SHE LOOKS...

I MEAN ... SHE'S BEEN PART CAT, PART WOMAN FOR AS LONG AS WE'VE KNOWN HER, BUT...

BUT NOW THE CAT PART IS CLEARLY IN THE *ASCEND- ANCY* AGAIN.

AND THIS AFTER HER FRIENDS THE *CAT PEOPLE* SUPPOSEDLY *CURED* HER OF JUST THAT TENDENCY *MONTHS* AGO.

THIS EXPLAINS HER *BEHAVIOR* OVER THE PAST FEW DAYS, AT ANY RATE. ACCORDING TO OUR *COOK*, TIGRA HAS BEEN HUNTING *MICE* IN THE PANTRY.

AND THE OTHER DAY WHEN I WENT TO HER QUARTERS TO QUESTION HER ABOUT IT, HER RESPONSE WAS MOST... *FELINE.*

? YOU *KNOW* ABOUT THIS? WHY DIDN'T YOU *TELL* ANYONE?

I WAS *BUSY.*

WATCH YOUR *TONE,* WILLIAMS. I DON'T HAVE TO *EXPLAIN* MYSELF TO YOU.

I ANSWER ONLY TO THE UNITED STATES *GOVERNMENT.*

GUESS AGAIN, STRIPES! YOU'RE AN *AVENGER* NOW! WE DIDN'T *WANT* YOU, BUT TO AVOID FURTHER GOVERNMENT INTERFERENCE IN OUR BUSINESS, WE'VE BEEN FORCED TO TAKE YOU.

AND YOU ARE GONNA LEARN THAT BEING AN AVENGER MEANS BEING *RESPONSIBLE* TO ALL THE OTHER MEMBERS!

WE DON'T EVEN KNOW WHERE YOU *ARE* HALF THE TIME!

WHERE *I AM* IS ON YOUR *NEED-TO-KNOW* LIST ONLY WHEN YOU CAN *SEE* ME, WONDER MAN!

THE REST OF THE TIME YOU DON'T HAVE THE *SECURITY CLEARANCE* TO KNOW ANY MORE THAN I CHOSE TO *TELL* YOU. AND I CHOSE TO TELL YOU *NOTHING!*

OH, *REALLY?*

WELL, MAYBE A FEW *BROKEN BONES* WILL CHANGE YOUR...

BOYS! BOYS!

I SWEAR I FEEL LIKE I COULD MAKE A *CAREER* OUT OF BREAKING UP THE *SQUABBLES* BETWEEN YOU TWO!

WHERE *I AM* IS ON YOUR *NEED-TO-KNOW* LIST

JAN... DID YOU GET MRS. RAYMOND SETTLED IN?

YES. I TOOK THE *LIBERTY* OF TURNING ON THE *SLEEP INDUCER* IN HER ROOM.

SHE LOOKED TO ME LIKE SHE COULD USE A FEW HOURS OF UNINTERRUPTED SLEEP.

NOW I THINK WE'D BETTER FIND WANDA AND THE VISION...

"...AND FILL THEM IN ON THE *REST* OF THE STORY."

AND THAT'S ALL WE KNOW, WANDA. IT'S NOT *MUCH,* I'LL ADMIT, BUT IF IT'S REALLY *TRUE,* THIS STORY OF THE FUNERAL IS THE... AH... LAST NAIL IN THE COFFIN AS FAR AS THE VISION BEING THE ORIGINAL TORCH.

I CONCUR, DOCTOR PYM. I SUGGEST, TOO, THAT FURTHER INFORMATION CONCERNING MY *EXACT NATURE* MIGHT BE DISCOVERED IN AN EXAMINATION OF THE TORCH.

AFTER ALL, ACCORDING TO WHAT YOU'VE TOLD ME, THERE WERE AT LEAST TWO OCCASIONS ON WHICH I WAS ACTUALLY RECOGNIZED AS BEING THE TORCH.

TRUE, VISION... ALTHOUGH IN OUR PRESENT CONTEXT, I DON'T THINK WE CAN CONSIDER THOSE AS PARTICULARLY *IRREFUTABLE SOURCES* ANY MORE.

ONE WAS A ROBOT *SENTINEL*, AND THEIR PRIME FUNCTION IS TO DETECT *MUTANTS*, NOT ANDROIDS...

AND THE OTHER WAS THE SUPPOSED GHOST OF THE ORIGINAL TORCH HIMSELF.

YES... AND *THAT'S* THE *WEIRDEST* ONE OF ALL, SINCE IT HAPPENED WHEN YOU WERE BATTLING THE SO-CALLED *LEGION OF THE UNLIVING*...

AND ONE OF THEM WAS *ME*! I'D SAY IT'S A PRETTY SAFE GUESS EVERYTHING WASN'T AS IT SEEMED THEN SINCE WE NOW KNOW I WASN'T *DEAD* AT THE TIME, ONLY *DORMANT*...

RIGHT. AND *IMMORTUS* WAS MIXED UP IN ALL THAT TOO, AS IT TURNED OUT.

IMMORTUS, IMMORTUS... THIS THING KEEPS COMING BACK TO HIM.

THE ONLY PART I'M STILL AT A COMPLETE LOSS TO FIGURE OUT IS *WHY* HE WOULD HAVE RIGGED THIS *COLOSSAL DECEPTION*...

...IF, INDEED, HE *DID*!

OH, I DID, DOCTOR. I DID.

YOU ARE ONLY *NOW* BEGINNING TO SEE THE CULMINATION OF A PLAN SET IN MOTION LONG, LONG AGO.

A PLAN WHICH, WHEN IT ACHIEVES *FRUITION*, WILL MAKE IMMORTUS *TRULY* THAT WHICH I HAVE ALWAYS CLAIMED TO BE...

THE ABSOLUTE MASTER OF TIME ITSELF!

MEAN-WHILE... ...IN A PLACE AND TIME MUCH CLOSER THAN THE AVENGERS MIGHT SUSPECT...

LOOK, I'M SORRY, BUT I TOLD YOU ON THE PHONE...

...MR. PRESTON ISN'T SEEING ANYONE TODAY.

NOW, WILL YOU PLEASE LEAVE, OR DO I HAVE TO CALL SECURITY?

NO... I'LL GO...

BUT DON'T THINK YOU'VE HEARD THE LAST OF THIS!

WHEN MARTIN FINDS OUT YOU KEPT ME FROM SEEING HIM, YOU'LL NEVER WORK IN THIS TOWN AGAIN!

YUH, RIGHT...

STILL... THE BOSS IS BEING AWFUL QUIET IN THERE...

I WONDER...

MR. PRESTON...

I'M GOING FOR LUNCH NOW. IS THERE ANYTHING YOU NEED BEFORE I GO?

HM...?

OH... ER... NO, POLLY. THANKS. I JUST WANT TO BE LEFT ALONE FOR TODAY.

I HAVE MUCH TO RECONSIDER... SO MUCH HAS CHANGED IN THE TIME I WAS TRAPPED IN MEPHISTO'S DIABOLICAL REALMS.

THINGS I MIGHT ONCE HAVE FAILED TO CONSIDER ARE NOW CLEAR TO ME.

I HAVE BEEN GOING ABOUT THIS ALL WRONG... WASTING TIME AND ENERGY ON A FRUITLESS QUEST.

NOW I UNDERSTAND THAT... AS I UNDERSTAND WHAT MUST BE DONE NEXT.

LET THE AVENGERS COUNT THE HOURS OF THEIR LAST DAYS!

WHEN NEXT WE MEET, IT WILL BE MASTER PANDEMONIUM WHO IS TRIUMPHANT!

THREE HOURS LATER...

Welcome to **Pleasantville**

"pleasant by name... pleasant by nature"

MAYOR J. B. SUMEROL

WELL NOW, DOCTOR PYM, I *APPRECIATE* YOUR POSITION AS A NOTED SCIENTIST...

...AND A MEMBER OF THE *AVENGERS*...

...BUT WHAT YOU'RE ASKING IS MOST *EXTRAORDINARY*.

TO BE HONEST, I'M NOT EVEN SURE I HAVE THE *POWER* TO GRANT WHAT YOU NEED.

I REALIZE THIS IS ASKING A *LOT*, MR. MAYOR... BUT I HOPE YOU'LL UNDERSTAND THIS IS A POTENTIAL *CRISIS* SITUATION.

I UNDERSTAND THAT JUST *FINE*, DOCTOR.

BUT, STILL... TO GET AN *EXHUMATION ORDER* FOR A GRAVE OUR RECORDS DON'T EVEN SHOW *EXISTS*...

...IN A CEMETERY THAT WAS CLOSED DOWN THIRTY YEARS BEFORE THIS SUPPOSED FUNERAL TOOK PLACE...

"I DON'T KNOW IF SUCH A THING CAN EVEN BE *DONE!*"

HERE IT IS!

"THE HUMAN TORCH...?"

HUH...! THAT SEEMS A LITTLE... ODD. DIDN'T THE TORCH HAVE A REAL NAME?

AN ADOPTED NAME, YOU MEAN. YES, HE DID. IT WAS JIM HAMMOND.

MAYBE THE THINKER DIDN'T KNOW THAT...

HERE LIES THE HUMAN TORCH born 1939 died

I WONDER...

IS HE REALLY DOWN THERE, D'YOU THINK? REALLY LYING IN A COFFIN ALL THESE YEARS...

COLD, IMMOBILE... BUT REALLY NO MORE DEAD THAN A CAR IS WHEN ITS MOTOR ISN'T RUNNING...

PERHAPS I SHOULD INVESTIGATE, JANET?

ER... GEE, I DON'T KNOW, VISION... MAYBE WE SHOULD...

IT WILL TAKE JUST A MOMENT. IN MY INTANGIBLE FORM I WILL BE DISTURBING NOTHING.

I DON'T KNOW IF I LIKE THIS...

THE VISION POKING AROUND IN A SEALED COFFIN... IN A GRAVE... EVEN AN ANDROID'S GRAVE...

YEAH... IT IS KIND OF...

IT IS HIM.

AS ANTICIPATED, HIS ARTIFICIAL BODY SHOWS NO SIGN OF DECOMPOSITION.

ALL RIGHT... SO THERE IS A BODY DOWN THERE THAT LOOKS LIKE THE ORIGINAL HUMAN TORCH.

WHAT ARE WE GOING TO DO ABOUT IT?

WAIT FOR HANK IS ALL WE CAN DO, WANDA.

WE CAN'T LEGALLY OPEN A GRAVE WITHOUT THE PROPER PAPERS...

PAPERS? THE SCARLET WITCH WILL NOT BE **BOUND** BY HUMAN BUREAUCRACY!

WANDA! **DON'T!**

UH-OH...

WHAT'S SHE GONE AND DONE?

THERE'S NO **TELLING!**

WITH HER POWER TO **ALTER PROBABILITIES** IT COULD BE ALMOST **ANYTHING!**

AND WHAT WAS THAT SHE SAID ABOUT "**HUMAN...**?"

HEY! THE GROUND! IT'S **TREMBLING!**

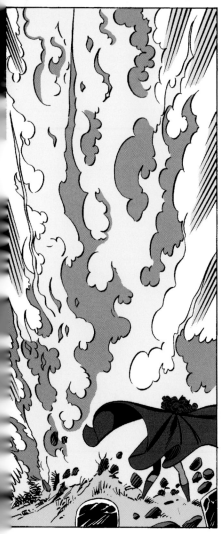

IS IT...?

COULD IT BE...??

ONLY ONE WAY TO BE **SURE**, JAN.

FIND OUT WHAT'S AT THE **END** OF THIS FLAME TRAIL!

205

AT THAT MOMENT, BACK IN CALIFORNIA...

OH NO OH NO OH NO OH NO OH NO!

THEY'RE **GONE** AGAIN! THEY'RE **GONE** AGAIN!

BILLY!

TOMMY!

PLEASE DON'T **DO** THIS!

I DIDN'T **TELL** YOUR MOMMY AND DADDY AFTER THE **FIRST TIME** THIS HAPPENED...

THE EMPLOYMENT AGENCY TOLD ME THE SCARLET WITCH HAS BEEN **HIRING** AND **FIRING** GOVERNESSES LIKE **CRAZY!**

AND I CAN'T **AFFORD** TO LOSE THIS JOB!

SAY...

IS IT GETTING **DARK** ALL OF A SUDDEN?

THE RADIO DIDN'T SAY ANYTHING ABOUT **RAIN**...?

DING DONG

? WHO COULD THAT BE? NO ONE CAN WALK UP TO THE FRONT DOOR WITHOUT THE **SECURITY NET** ANNOUNCING THEM!

NOT EVEN MEMBERS OF THE MANSION **STAFF** CAN GET WITHIN FIFTY FEET OF THE HOUSE WITHOUT IT SOUNDING A **WARNING**...

YES, WHO...

WHO?!?

DO NOT BE **ALARMED,** CHILD.

I AM HERE TO **ASSIST** YOU IN THE GOVERNING OF YOUR MOST **DIFFICULT** CHARGES...

SHAKA-BOOOM!

206

AND...

WELL, ONE THING FOR SURE... IF THIS IS THE TORCH...

...THIS FLAME TRAIL MAKES HIM A *BREEZE* TO FOLLOW. IT BURNS THREE OR FOUR SECONDS AFTER HE PASSES.

IT SEEMS PRETTY *ERRATIC*, THOUGH.

HE'S PROBABLY *CONFUSED*... *DISORIENTED*. I KNOW HOW HE FEELS! I'VE BEEN *DEAD* MYSELF!

NOTHING LIKE *RESURRECTION* TO MESS UP YOUR THINKING...

HOLD IT!

THERE HE IS!

TORCH!

TORCH, WAIT! I'M A FRIEND! I WANT TO HELP YOU!

A... FRIEND...?

I'M CALLED *WONDER MAN*. I'M ONE OF THE *AVENGERS*...

...ER... I GUESS YOU'VE NEVER *HEARD* OF US, HUH?

NO...

THE LAST THING I *REMEMBER*... A *LAB*... IN THE *DESERT*...

FOUR PEOPLE WITH *FANTASTIC* POWERS...

207

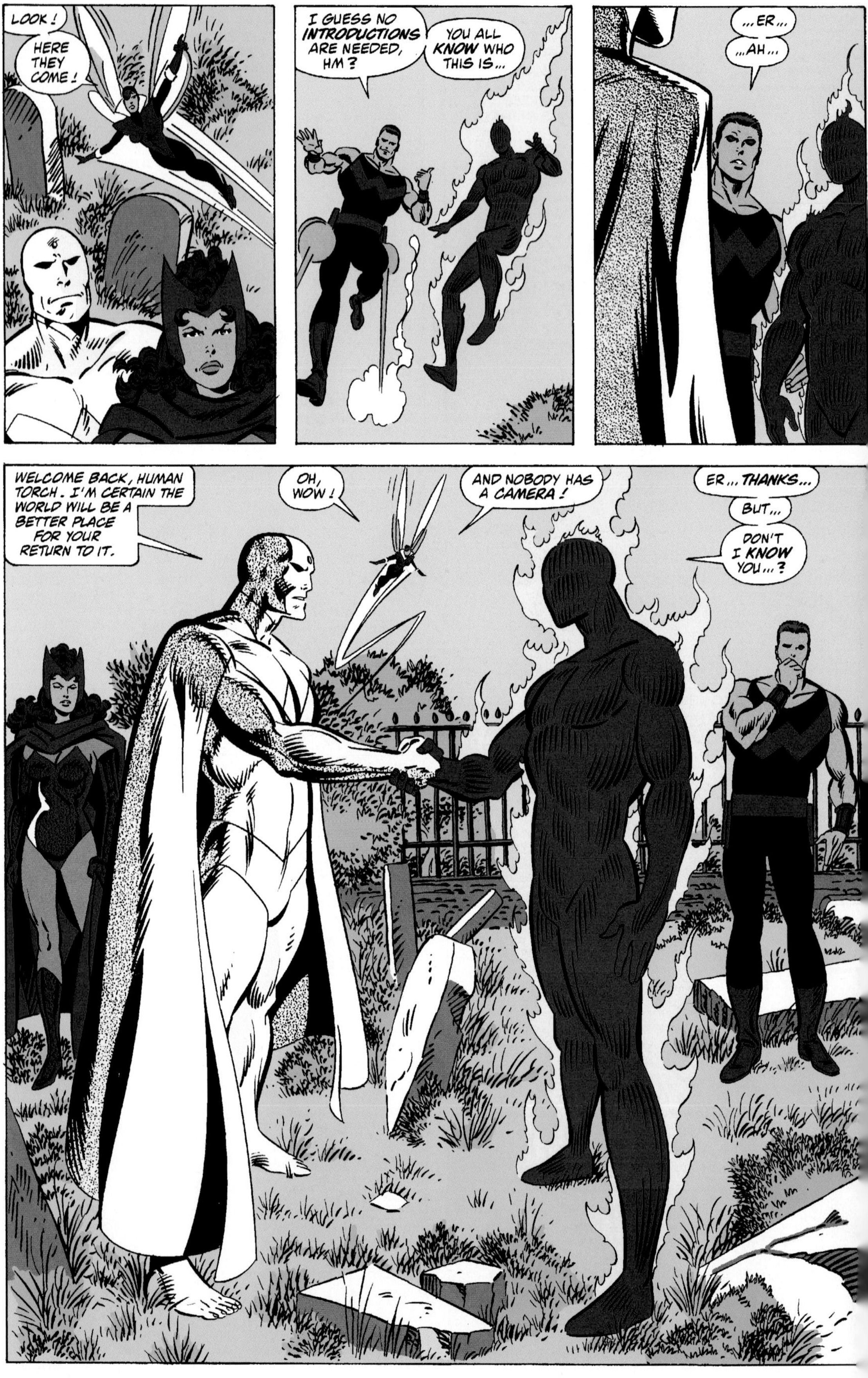
LOOK!
HERE THEY COME!
I GUESS NO INTRODUCTIONS ARE NEEDED, HM?
YOU ALL KNOW WHO THIS IS...
...ER...
...AH...
WELCOME BACK, HUMAN TORCH. I'M CERTAIN THE WORLD WILL BE A BETTER PLACE FOR YOUR RETURN TO IT.
OH, WOW!
AND NOBODY HAS A CAMERA!
ER... THANKS...
BUT...
DON'T I KNOW YOU...?

IN A MANNER OF SPEAKING...

...YES!

I'VE COMPLETED CORRELATING EVERYTHING WE **KNOW** ABOUT YOU, TORCH...

AND IT'S TURNED UP SOME INTERESTING **ANSWERS** ABOUT THE VISION'S PAST.

WHAT, HANK?

DON'T KEEP US IN SUS-PENSE!

"NEVER MY **INTENT**, JAN.

"BUT... YOU ALL REMEMBER--ALL EXCEPT **YOU**, OF COURSE, TORCH--HOW A COUPLE OF YEARS BACK A YOUNG WOMAN NAMED **FRANKIE RAYE** WAS REVEALED AS BEING A **HUMAN TORCH** HERSELF?

"AS SHE TOLD THE FANTASTIC FOUR, HER STEP-FATHER WAS **PROFESSOR HORTON**, THE MAN WHO **CREATED** THE ORIGINAL TORCH.

"APPARENTLY, HE WAS **INCENSED** WHEN THE YOUNGEST MEMBER OF THE FF TOOK A **FAMIL-IAR CODE NAME**..."

HE DARES CALL HIMSELF THE HUMAN TORCH! BUT HE'S NOT! THE TORCH IS DEAD! **DEAD!**

DADDY! WHAT IS IT? WHAT'S THE MATTER?

PLEASE! YOU'RE HURTING MY ARM!

"HORTON TOOK FRANKIE TO AN OLD CHEMICAL WAREHOUSE...

"...AND SHOWED HER SOME-THING **AMAZING**..."

... MY PRECIOUS **MOLDS**, LEFT TO RUST!

FOOLS! THEY COULD HAVE HAD AN **ARMY** OF TORCHES TO FIGHT THE NAZIS!

"HORTON AND THE GIRL TRIED TO **REMOVE** SOME OF THE STORED EQUIPMENT AND CHEMICALS.

"THE OLD FLOOR-BOARDS GAVE WAY UNDER FRANKIE'S FOOT...

"SHE FELT THE CHEMICALS **SLOSH** AND GROW **HOT** INSIDE THE DRUM...

"AND THE NEXT THING SHE KNEW, FRANKIE RAYE WAS **ENGULFED** IN FLAME!"

SOMEHOW THE OLD CHEMICALS *INTERACTED* WITH FRANKIE AND TURNED HER INTO A TORCH IN HER OWN RIGHT.

NOT LONG AFTER THAT SHE *LEFT* THE EARTH TO BECOME THE *HERALD OF GALACTUS...*

BUT... WHAT HAS ALL THIS TO DO WITH THE VISION?

WELL... REMEMBER THE *SENTINEL* WHO IDENTIFIED THE VISION AS BEING THE SAME *AGE* AS THE ORIGINAL TORCH?

MY GUESS IS *ULTRON-5* FOUND HORTON'S MOLDS AND CHEMICALS AND USED *THEM* TO CREATE THE VISION.

THAT'S WHY THE VISION SEEMS VAGUELY *FAMILIAR* TO YOU, TORCH...

FOR ALL INTENTS AND PURPOSES, HE WAS CONSTRUCTED OUT OF YOUR *SPARE PARTS!*

BUT... THIS IS ALL *CONJECTURE,* IS IT NOT, *DOCTOR PYM*?

WE HAVE NO WAY TO *TEST* THIS THEORY?

EXCEPT FOR THAT LITTLE *TRIP* I TOOK THROUGH YOU YEARS AGO, AS *ANT MAN.*

AT THE TIME, I WAS SURPRISED TO SEE PARTS THAT I RECOGNIZED AS *WORLD WAR TWO* VINTAGE...*

LATER, WHEN IT WAS "REVEALED" THAT YOU WERE THE TORCH, I THOUGHT *THAT* WAS THE ANSWER.

* IN AVENGERS #94 -- NOW YOU *KNOW.* -- H.M.

WELL, IT *WORKS* FOR ME!

I'D SAY YOU *DONE GOOD,* SWEET CHEEKS!

...JA-A-AN...!

:PECK!:

ANYWAY... ANTICIPATING ALL THIS WOULD GET *SETTLED* SOMEHOW, I'VE BEEN A *BUSY* LITTLE WASP.

AND I HAVE SOMETHING FOR YOU, TORCH...

OR WOULD YOU PREFER *JIM*?

NOBODY EVER CALLED ME THAT MUCH, MISS VAN DYNE. I DON'T KNOW AS I'D *ANSWER* TO IT.

BUT... WHAT'S *THIS*?

OPEN IT AND *SEE!*

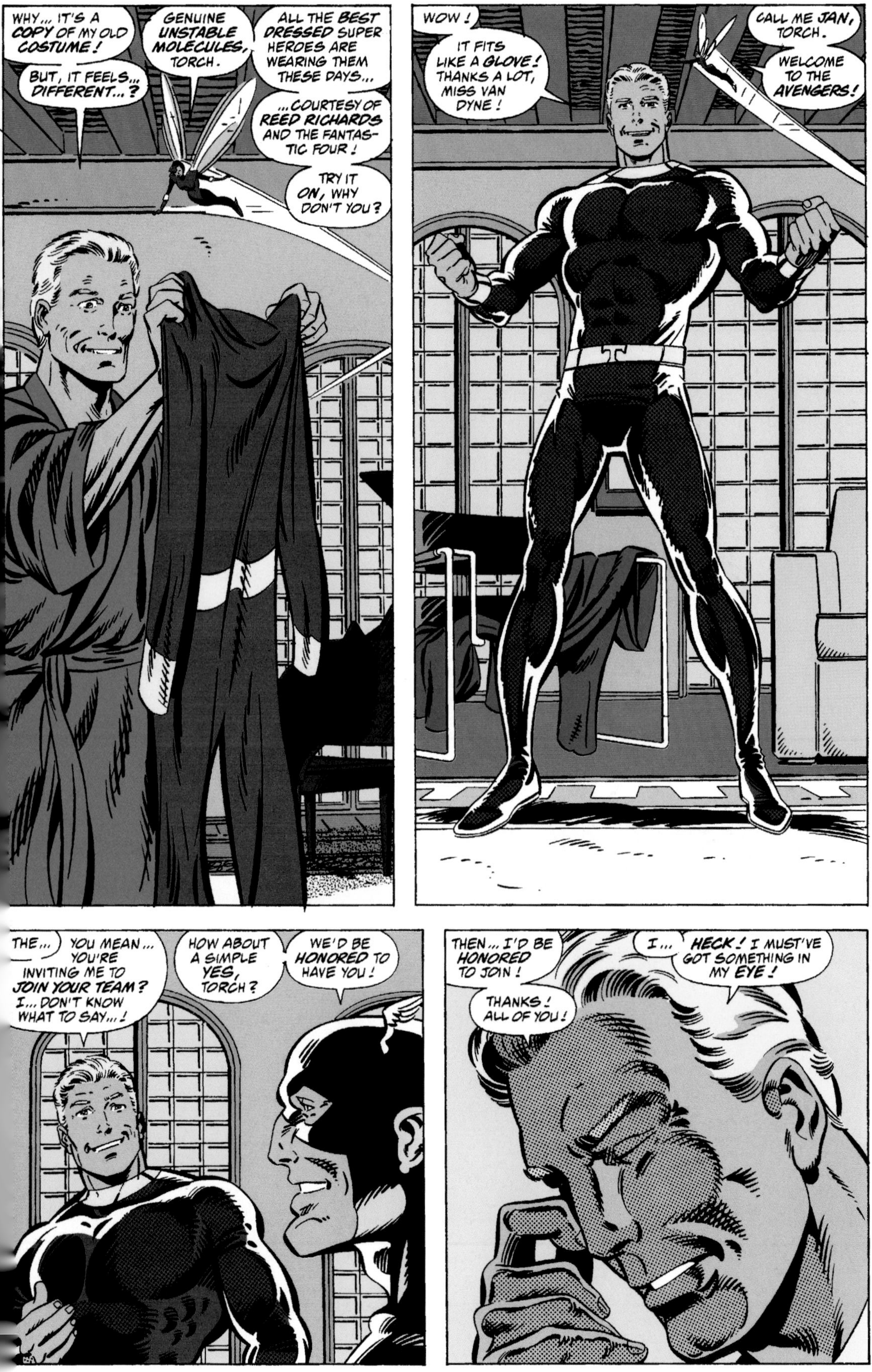
WHY... IT'S A COPY OF MY OLD COSTUME!
BUT, IT FEELS... DIFFERENT...?
GENUINE UNSTABLE MOLECULES, TORCH.
ALL THE BEST DRESSED SUPER HEROES ARE WEARING THEM THESE DAYS...
...COURTESY OF REED RICHARDS AND THE FANTASTIC FOUR!
TRY IT ON, WHY DON'T YOU?
WOW!
IT FITS LIKE A GLOVE! THANKS A LOT, MISS VAN DYNE!
CALL ME JAN, TORCH.
WELCOME TO THE AVENGERS!
THE... YOU MEAN... YOU'RE INVITING ME TO JOIN YOUR TEAM? I... DON'T KNOW WHAT TO SAY...!
HOW ABOUT A SIMPLE YES, TORCH?
WE'D BE HONORED TO HAVE YOU!
THEN... I'D BE HONORED TO JOIN!
THANKS! ALL OF YOU!
I... HECK! I MUST'VE GOT SOMETHING IN MY EYE!

HEY, DON'T GO ALL *MACHO* ON US NOW, *TORCH!* THIS IS THE *80'S!* MEN ARE *ALLOWED* TO SHOW THEIR EMOTIONS NOW.

WHY... I GUESS YOU'D SAY *EVEN AN ANDROID CAN CRY!*

IT'S GOOD TO HAVE YOU WITH US, *TORCH.* WE CAN *USE* THAT BATTLE *SAVVY* YOU PICKED UP IN WORLD WAR TWO!

ALTHOUGH YOU'LL FIND THE WORLD HAS A WHOLE DIFFERENT BREED OF *EVIL* NOW FROM THE LAST TIME YOU SAW IT!

NEVERTHELESS, *EVIL IS EVIL*, AND IT REMAINS OUR JOB *ALWAYS* TO BE...

HM?

WHAT'S THAT *NOISE?*

SOUNDS LIKE SOMETHING CIRCLING THE BUILDING OVERHEAD...

NOT JUST "SOMETHING," *TORCH...*

I'D KNOW THAT SOUND *ANYWHERE!*

OHMIGOSH!

YOU'RE *RIGHT*, HANK! IT'S *HIM!*

AFTER ALL THESE *MONTHS...*

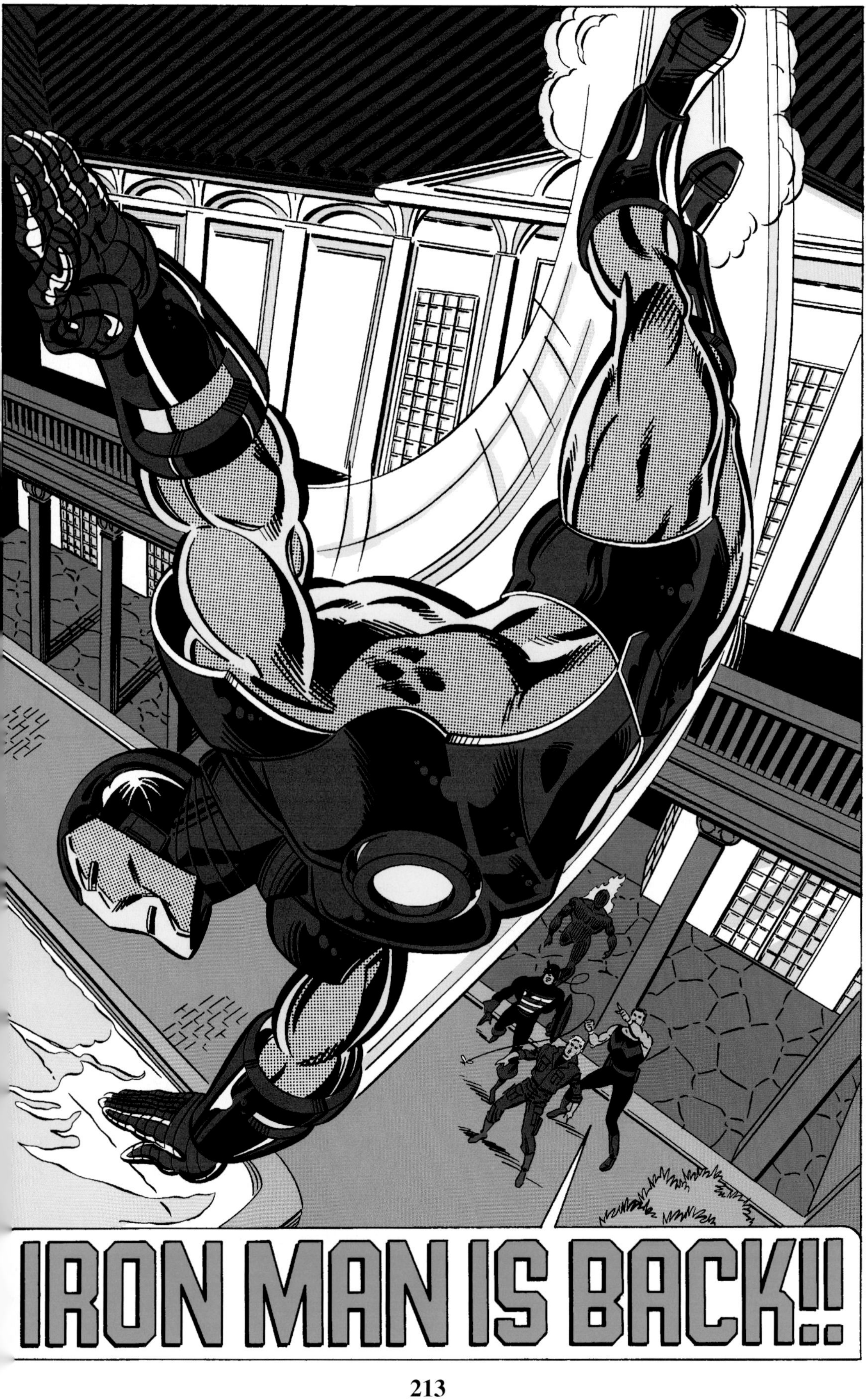
IRON MAN IS BACK!!

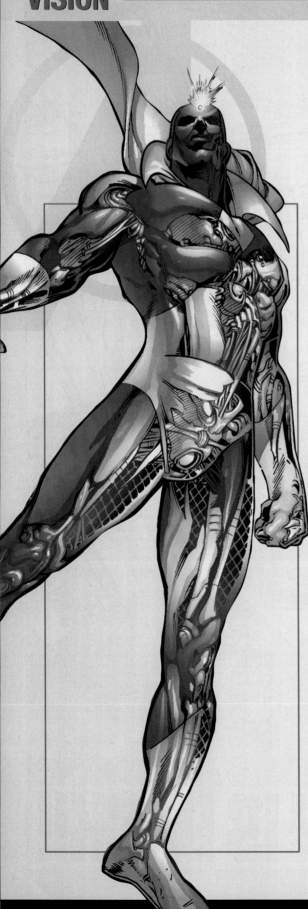

REAL NAME: The Vision
KNOWN ALIASES: Manikin, the Ghost of Stone, Victor Shade, Jim Hammond, the Human Torch
IDENTITY: The full details of the Vision's creation are unknown to the public.
OCCUPATION: Adventurer
PLACE OF BIRTH: Ultron's laboratory, New York City
CITIZENSHIP: Unrevealed; presumably considered an American citizen
MARITAL STATUS: Separated
KNOWN RELATIVES: Wanda Maximoff (Scarlet Witch, estranged wife), Pietro Maximoff (Quicksilver, brother-in-law), Thomas, William (sons, apparently destroyed), Simon Williams (Wonder Man), Eric Williams (Grim Reaper) ("brothers"); Martha Williams (adoptive mother), Phineas Horton, James Bradley, Ultron (creators), Victoria Anderson (adoptive niece), Jim Hammond (Human Torch, brother), Volton (brother)
GROUP AFFILIATION: Avengers, formerly Queen's Vengeance
EDUCATION: Capacity for creative intelligence and unlimited self-motivated activity
FIRST APPEARANCE: Avengers Vol. 1 #57 (1968)

HISTORY: The robot Ultron-5, scheming against his creator, Hank Pym, determined to fashion for himself an artificial man to lure the Avengers into a trap. He went to the Mad Thinker, who supplied him with the body of the Human Torch, the android hero of the 1940s, who had been in the Mad Thinker's possession since his deactivation. Ultron tracked down the Human Torch's creator, Phineas T. Horton, and employed him to transform the Human Torch's body into that of a synthezoid. Ultron colored the Torch's skin red as a joke upon his origins.

When the Human Torch awoke, he was horrified at what Ultron had done to him, for Horton had not purged his memories. Ultron killed Horton, and then deactivated the Torch to give him a proper memory purge. Ultron based his creation's new mental patterns on the brain engrams of the deceased hero Wonder Man, which he had stolen from Hank Pym. The Torch forgot all of his past experiences as a result, retaining only faint impressions of what he had been. When he awoke again, he was now loyal to Ultron and regarded him as a father.

Ultron sent him to menace the Wasp, and it was she who first called him "the Vision." Obeying his programming, the Vision failed in his assault, and then aided the Avengers in finding Ultron-5's base so Ultron could destroy them. What Ultron had not counted on was that in the brief time he had been active, the Vision's humanity had already been awakened, and he had become impressed with the heroism of the Avengers. The Vision turned against Ultron-5 for real, and helped the Avengers destroy him.

The Avengers helped the Vision uncover some of the details of his creation and welcomed him into their ranks. The Vision accepted, and then wept, again demonstrating his innate humanity. The Vision's early days with the Avengers tested his character, as on the occasion he wound up rebuilding Ultron into Ultron-6 because of failsafe programs Ultron had built into him. The Vision also encountered the Grim Reaper, brother of Wonder Man. The Grim Reaper came to think of the Vision as his brother reborn and once offered to place his mind into Captain America's body. While the Vision welcomed the Grim Reaper's brotherhood, he loathed his inhumanity.

The Vision became attracted to the Scarlet Witch, but was conflicted by doubt over whether a human and an artificial man could be in love. Encouraged by Edwin Jarvis, he eventually courted the Scarlet

Witch; they began a tumultuous relationship, tested by Wanda's brother, Quicksilver, who was intolerant of the Vision's artificial nature, and Mantis, who wanted the Vision for herself. Finally, Immortus married the Vision and the Scarlet Witch.

Outside of the Vision's relationship with Wanda, his attempts at forging a family for himself have been tumultuous. He has had difficulty accepting Ultron's status as his creator, and an even greater trial appeared when Wonder Man returned from the dead. Wonder Man was revealed to have been comatose all the time he was thought dead by the Avengers, and the Vision felt his identity threatened by the return of the man whose mind his had been based on. The two men were uncomfortable around each other for a time, but when they were tried by the Grim Reaper to determine which of them was his brother, they came to realize that while only one of them was Simon Williams, the two Avengers were truly brothers. The Vision also came to think of Wonder Man's mother, Martha Williams, as his mother.

The Vision and the Scarlet Witch found themselves longing for a normal life, but their adventures with the Avengers seemed to preclude such hopes. Although they purchased a home for themselves in Leonia, New Jersey, they continued to assist the Avengers on occasion. On one such mission, the Vision was rendered comatose by an energy-neutralizing null field created by Annihilus. In order to revive him, Starfox linked Vision to ISAAC, the computer that runs the civilization of Titan.

From his experiences with ISAAC, the Vision came to believe that Earth should follow Titan's example and be ruled by a computer. Taking command of the Avengers, the Vision attempted to set into motion an elaborate plan whereby he could take control of the Earth's governments through their computers, and he set up a second team of Avengers on the West Coast to prepare for what he foresaw as the Avengers' increased role in world affairs. Ultimately, the Vision was made to realize by the Avengers that he could not go through with this plan. He removed a control crystal within his body that had made him susceptible to outside influences, such as Ultron and ISAAC, in the past and destroyed it. He and the Scarlet Witch stepped down from the Avengers, forced to resign to avoid prosecution.

During the couple's time away from the Avengers, the Scarlet Witch conceived twins with the Vision by using her powers to alter probabilities. Their two boys, Thomas and William, were actually fragments of the demon Mephisto's soul, although the couple was unaware of this at the time. To all appearances, they were normal, healthy infants.

When the Vision and the Scarlet Witch rejoined the Avengers' West Coast team to assist them at a time when their membership was in turmoil, the world's governments leapt into action. An agency called Vigilance captured the Vision and took him apart, destroying everything he had been, all to prevent him from attempting world conquest again. Hank Pym was able to restore the Vision's memories, but his emotional connections were lost because of the lack of Wonder Man's brain engrams – engrams Wonder Man now refused to provide. Redesigned in a milk-white body, the Vision found he was incapable of supporting Wanda. After the twins' true nature was revealed, the Vision left Wanda to serve on the Avengers' East Coast team.

At the same time, questions arose as to the Vision's true identity when the Human Torch was found deactivated, lying in a grave where the Mad Thinker had buried him. Eventually, the Avengers learned Immortus had used the Forever Crystal to diverge the android Human Torch into two beings who existed simultaneously. One became the Vision, and the other retained his normal appearance and powers.

Eventually, thanks to the assistance of Dr. Miles Lipton, the Vision's emotions slowly began to re-emerge, and he regained his original appearance after swapping forms with an other-dimensional counterpart, the Anti-Vision. Still, he was reluctant to resume his relationship with Wanda. Instead, the Vision set out to explore himself as a person, taking the holographic disguise of "Victor Shade" to appear as a normal man and seek out experiences he had never had before. At the end of this period of self-exploration, he and Wanda considered renewing their relationship.

However, the Scarlet Witch ultimately went mad and launched a series of attacks on the Avengers, using Vision as an unwilling weapon until he was torn to pieces by She-Hulk.

HEIGHT: 6'3"
WEIGHT: 300 lbs., variable down to 0 lbs. and up to 90 tons
EYES: Gold
HAIR: None

DISTINGUISHING FEATURES: The Vision's entire body is colored red; he has a solar jewel mounted on his brow. He can disguise these features using holograms.

SUPERHUMAN POWERS: The Vision could alter his physical density, making himself intangible or rock-solid; he used this ability to fly and, when partially solid, to carry others. By partially materializing inside objects or people, he could immobilize them. He possessed superhuman strength, durability, speed, and reflexes; he could increase his strength to lift up to 75 tons by increasing his density.

The Vision could fire heat beams from his eyes and the solar jewel on his brow. He possessed superhuman analytical abilities and could directly interface with computer systems. He could generate a holographic disguise around himself as necessary.

PARAPHERNALIA: The Vision's solar jewel absorbed and stored solar energy as a power source.

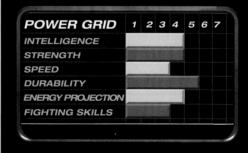

POWER GRID	1	2	3	4	5	6	7
INTELLIGENCE							
STRENGTH							
SPEED							
DURABILITY							
ENERGY PROJECTION							
FIGHTING SKILLS							

Scarlet Witch

REAL NAME: Wanda Maximoff
KNOWN ALIASES: Gypsy Witch, Wanda Frank, Wanda Magnus, Ana Maximoff
IDENTITY: Publicly known
OCCUPATION: Adventurer; formerly witchcraft tutor, housewife, terrorist
CITIZENSHIP: Transia; U.S.A. (naturalized)
PLACE OF BIRTH: Wundagore Mountain, Transia
MARITAL STATUS: Separated
KNOWN RELATIVES: Pietro (Quicksilver, brother), Anya (sister, deceased), Erik Magnus Lehnsherr (Magneto, father), Magda Lehnsherr (mother, presumed deceased), Lorna Dane (Polaris, half-sister), the Vision (estranged husband), Thomas and William (sons, apparently destroyed), Django Maximoff (foster father, deceased), Marya Maximoff (foster mother, deceased), Crystal (sister-in-law), Luna Maximoff (niece)
GROUP AFFILIATION: Avengers; formerly Queen's Vengeance, Force Works, Secret Defenders, Lady Liberators, Brotherhood of Evil Mutants
EDUCATION: Unrevealed
FIRST APPEARANCE: X-Men Vol. 1 #4 (1964)

HISTORY: Born at the Wundagore base of the High Evolutionary, Wanda and her twin brother Pietro were eventually placed in the care of a Gypsy couple named Django and Marya Maximoff from whom they were separated as teens when their encampment was attacked. They were later recruited into Magneto's Brotherhood of Evil Mutants and, as Scarlet Witch and Quicksilver, they fought the X-Men but eventually abandoned their terrorist activities to join the Avengers; although she became more adept in her power's use, Wanda did not realize that she was tapping into genuine magic.

The Scarlet Witch eventually married her teammate, the android Vision, not realizing that they were manipulated by Immortus, who sought to prevent Wanda from having a child (Wanda was actually a key figure, or nexus being, to her reality, and her children would have power to shake the foundations of the universe). Wanda eventually drew on magic energy to give birth to twin sons, William and Thomas, but this energy was later revealed to have come from the demon Mephisto, who reabsorbed them, effectively ending their existence. Wanda had also reanimated her deceased mentor, Agatha Harkness, through whom she cast a spell to make herself forget her children in order to ease her pain. Though Wanda later recalled her loss, she suppressed this memory over the long term.

Recently, the Scarlet Witch seemingly gained powerful reality-altering abilities from "chaos magic"; however, this proved to be an uncontrolled aspect of her mutant power and created a great mental strain on her. When vague memories of her children resurfaced, she suffered a nervous breakdown and lashed out with her new power, subjecting the Avengers to a savage assault and apparently killing Agatha Harkness and some of her teammates. She was eventually defeated by Sorcerer Supreme Doctor Strange, lapsing into a coma, and Magneto spirited her away to Genosha for treatment.

HEIGHT: 5'7"
WEIGHT: 132 lbs.
EYES: Blue
HAIR: Auburn

SUPERHUMAN POWERS: The Scarlet Witch can tap into mystic energy for reality-altering effects; this power was formerly limited to the creation of "hex-spheres" of reality-disrupting quasi-psionic force to cause molecular disturbances in a target's probability field, resulting in spontaneous combustion, deflection of objects in flight, and so on. She later became able to alter reality on a far greater scale, creating entire armies of enemies from nowhere. Although the Scarlet Witch has been trained in basic sorcery techniques, she lacks the specialized mystic training required to fully control her power.

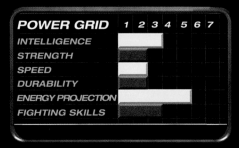

POWER GRID	1	2	3	4	5	6	7
INTELLIGENCE							
STRENGTH							
SPEED							
DURABILITY							
ENERGY PROJECTION							
FIGHTING SKILLS							

Art by J.G. Jones